David Anne was born in London in 1930. Following National Service in the RAF (Fighter Command 11 Group), he worked in advertising for several years. He now lives in Hampshire where he divides his time between writing and running his own furniture shop.

David Anne is author of the best-selling *Rabid* (*Day of The Mad Dogs*) and *The Folly*.

David Anne

Knight's Cross

A Futura Book
Macdonald Futura Publishers

A Futura Book

First published in Great Britain in 1980
by Macdonald Futura Publishers

ISBN 0 7088 1723 8

Photoset in Great Britain by
Rowland Phototypesetting Limited,
Bury St Edmunds, Suffolk
Printed and bound in Great Britain by
Collins, Glasgow

Macdonald Futura Publishers Limited
Paulton House, 8 Shepherdess Walk,
London N1

Some of the text of this story is based on well known and documented events and I am greatly indebted to many sources for such data. Among them are:

FIGHTER by Len Deighton
THE NARROW MARGIN by Derek Wood and Derek Dempster
THE RISE AND FALL OF THE LUFTWAFFE by David Irving
HITLER'S LUFTWAFFE by Tony Wood and Bill Gunston
CHARLTON by Air Commodore L. E. O. Charlton
DUAL OF EAGLES by Peter Townsend
THE FIRST AND THE LAST by Adolf Galland
STUKA PILOT by Hans-Ulrich Rudel
INSIDE THE THIRD REICH by Albert Speer
HISTORY OF THE GESTAPO by Jaques Delarue
THE RISE AND FALL OF THE THIRD REICH by William L. Shirer
NINE LIVES by Alan C. Deere
'HORRIDO!' FIGHTER ACES OF THE LUFTWAFFE and THE BLONDE KNIGHT OF GERMANY
by T. J. Constable and R. F. Tolliver
THE FIGHTERS by Colin Willock

I should also like to express my sincere gratitude to my good friend Air Marshal Sir Peter Horsley K.C.B., C.B.E., M.V.O., A.F.C., for his encouragement and invaluable technical advice.

Last, but far from least, my thanks are due to 'Nici' and Carol who, between them, somehow managed to type something in the way of a manuscript from my often mis-spelt and invariably illegible scribblings.

Dedication:
For my Mother

Author's Note

KNIGHT'S CROSS

The Knight's Cross, the *Ritterkreuz*, was the highest military decoration bestowed by the Third Reich. It was awarded in four grades. Starting with the basic Knight's Cross to the Iron Cross, there followed the addition of the Oakleaves, *Eichenlaub*, then the Swords, *Schwerten*, and finally the Diamonds, *Brillianten*. A fifth grade, the Golden Oakleaves, was specially created, and was awarded to only one man, the famed *Stuka* pilot on the Russian front, Colonel Hans–Ulrich Rudel.

Less than three hundred Luftwaffe personnel won the Oakleaves or better. One of their number, promoted to the rank of Flying Officer during the course of the Battle of Britain, was not in fact a member of the Luftwaffe at all. On the contrary, he flew for the Royal Air Force. For his exploits as a Spitfire pilot, one of the "immortal few", he was awarded the Distinguished Flying Cross. This same man was later to fly for the Luftwaffe under an assumed name by which all Germany would know and honour him. He was a nobleman from an old Bavarian family. For the purposes of this narrative he will be referred to as the Baron Johannes von Tahlmann, alias Peter Hutley.

PROLOGUE

The date: September 17th, 1940. Time: 15.30 hours. Weather: frequent heavy showers and some bright intervals.

Thunder crashed and rolled over the greyness of the sombre Sussex countryside. A sudden squall of rain lashed furiously at the buildings of R.A.F. Tangmere. Inside the control room the duty officer surveyed the local situation. Only two aircraft were aloft in the sector, a marked contrast to the conditions that had prevailed only two days earlier. On the 15th, the Battle of Britain had reached what has ever since been regarded as its climax, the day that the R.A.F. claimed to have destroyed 175 enemy aircraft.

Flying Officer Peter Hutley had missed the big show, grounded by the repeated malfunctioning of the two 20mm cannons fitted to his Spitfire Mk 1B, registration number E4-F. But now the frustrating wait at Boscombe Down was over and Peter was returning to the Special Fighter Interception unit at Tangmere. He hadn't reckoned on the weather closing in like this. Suddenly his R.T. crackled into life.

'Easy Fox, this is Dovecot . . . Hello, Easy Fox, do you read? Over.'

The Spitfire pilot hesitated for a moment before pressing the transmit switch.

'Dovecot, this is Easy Fox, reading your fives.'

The familiar voice of the controller of Tangmere, using his call sign of "Dovecot", had pre-empted a call from

Peter, who had himself been about to make contact for landing clearance.

'Easy Fox, you're approximately eleven miles from base but you're not alone. Customer for you – there's a single unidentified, presumed hostile, in your vicinity. Vector 165 and make angels eight.'

'Roger, Dovecot. *Damn*,' Peter acknowledged, uncertain whether he had added the mild expletive before or after he had released the transmit switch. Not that he cared. The visibility now was worse than ever and the last thing he wanted was a game of hide and seek with the Hun. His only wish was to get down on the ground as quickly as possible, out of the cloud and driving rain. The R.A.F. pilot peered through his cockpit perspex into the murk, but could see very little. The controller's voice, competing with the high level of static, crackled through his earphones once more.

'Easy Fox, your target, now confirmed hostile, is dead ahead of you. You should have visual contact any moment now.'

'Roger, Dovecot. Visual contact? You must be bloody joking. It's like pea soup up here—I can hardly see my own nose.'

On the ground, anxious eyes peered skyward as the sound of aero engines became clearly audible amidst the noise of the storm.

The controller could do no more. His skill had put friend and foe all but in the same bed. Ground personnel waited in silence. The R.T. came to life again.

'Tally – ho, Tally – ho. It's a 109. I'm going in now.'

The English fighter burst from the greyness of the storm clouds into brilliant sunshine. Momentarily dazzled, Peter blinked once or twice before spotting the hostile, unmistakeably a single 109, little more than 350 yards ahead, slightly below and to one side. A hint of left rudder. A gentle push on the stick. The duck was sitting. Peter had only to release the safety and depress the red firing button; with the range shortened to a dangerously close 150 yards it was impossible to miss. He muttered a short prayer that the fickle cannon wouldn't fail him, and pressed the tit. The airframe shuddered and shook reassuringly from the recoil of the big guns, but there was only time for a single short burst before pursuer and pursued plunged back once more into the cloud.

Peter banked his Spitfire and took it up to 500 feet, fearing the very real possibility of a collision. He pressed the transmit switch again.

'Dovecot, this is Easy Fox. Sorry, I've lost my bunny. But I'm pretty sure I hit the bastard.'

'Roger, Easy Fox. Vector 070, maintain your present angels but reduce speed. Bandit three miles ahead and losing height rapidly. Stand by.'

'Roger, Dovecot. Listening out.'

The Spitfire continued to stooge along on the course indicated for what seemed like an eternity. Impatient, Peter switched once more to transmit.

'Hello, Dovecot—I can't see a damn thing in this stuff. Where's the bloody target?'

'Roger, Easy Fox. Stand by, maintain your speed and angels. Orbit your present position.'

Tangmere controller's tone was terse. Feeling somewhat chastened, Peter didn't acknowledge. There was another short delay before the controller renewed contact. His voice was severely distorted by the electrical storm, but the message was clear enough.

'Easy Fox, well done. Your 109 has just gone in right on the edge of base. Come on to heading 285, reducing height. You are seven miles from touchdown. You are clear to land. Call Finals.'

'Roger, Dovecot. I still have no contact.'

'Easy Fox, visibility is reasonable below 500 feet. You should have nothing to worry about.'

'Roger, Dovecot. Listening out.'

The Bf 109 was Peter Hutley's fifth confirmed victory.

It may not have placed the young Flying Officer among the elite of the top-scoring R.A.F. aces, but at least he was now halfway to double figures. Peter also had special cause to feel pleased with himself: this was his first success against an enemy fighter. His other victories, two Ju 87s, an He 111 and a Dornier 17, had all been against bombers. The single-seater Messerschmitt should have been the most difficult. It hadn't turned out that way at all. In fact it had been the easiest. Thanks to the skill of the duty controller at Tangmere, the surprise had been complete. The ensuing battle had been brief and one-sided, but it had been final. By chance or by habit, the German pilot had glanced behind him in that instant before the Spitfire's guns had sealed his fate. The expression on his face, if Hutley had but seen it, had registered a mixture of astonishment and terror.

At last Easy Fox emerged from the clouds, with Tangmere immediately below the starboard wing. Peter executed a victory roll before making his approach and then, came in, turning tightly, threatening to overshoot; but with flaps right down and only one hop back into the air again, the Spitfire finally settled itself on all three wheels. The pilot taxied to dispersal and then cut the Merlin engine, undid the safety harness, pulled back the cockpit cover and climbed out. Only his L.A.C. fitter was there to greet him with a salute and a pat on the back. Everybody else seemed to have deserted the place in favour of a close inspection of the fallen 109.

Peter legged it back to the mess only to find that somebody had nicked his car. There was no means of transport available except a bicycle. He took that and set off for the Main Gate. An ambulance hurried by in the opposite direction, heading for the station sick-bay.

Peter had no difficulty in finding the crashed Messerschmitt. A livid scar of ploughed earth, gouged from the surface of the field by the belly of the plane, marked the point of impact clearly enough. Surrounding the smoking fuselage was an excited crowd of Peter's fellow pilots, deep in conversation and comment.

The throng turned to watch Hutley approach and raised a cheer. Flight Lieutenant Barney Walker had pinched Hutley's Austin 7 Swallow, and had been the first to get to the scene. He was also the first to notice the hero of the moment approaching, but now his gaze was concentrated firmly, and guiltily, on his own flying boots.

'You rotten swine, Barney', said Hutley as he strolled up to the group, slightly out of breath but smiling. Walker's face had broken into a grin. By way of answer he pointed a finger at the two rings on the shoulder of his uniform.

'OK, Barney, you may outrank me, but you're still a rotten swine. I've warned you before about pinching my car.' The next minute the pair of them were laughing uproariously, and the rest of the group came flocking round to slap Peter on the back and congratulate him.

Amid all the excitement Peter looked over towards the charred remnants of the enemy plane, his fifth victim, and felt a glow of pride. As a member of the experimental fighter unit he hadn't had the opportunities enjoyed by the regular squadrons for taking a crack at the enemy—so five victories in the air wasn't a bad score. But in the flood of congratulations Peter had not had time to notice the tail plane on the enemy machine. He saw it now, and stood in amazement and bewilderment as the full significance of the markings sank in. They denoted that his vanquished foe had been the victor of no less than fifteen previous aerial combats. As he felt himself being hoisted shoulder-high and carried back in triumph to the mess, the true scale of his victory that stormy afternoon was only just beginning to dawn on him: unbelievable as it seemed, he had succeeded in shooting down one of Germany's most renowned and feared flying aces.

Peter's success gave his comrades at R.A.F. Tangmere

the perfect excuse for a party. The first stage of the Battle of Britain was over. Everyone felt that the crisis had passed. The celebration would be their first chance to relax and let off steam after the gruelling weeks of tension.

By half-past eight the revels were well under way and the noise in the mess was deafening—so much so that at first nobody heard the bellowing voice of the adjutant calling Hutley's name from the doorway.

'*Hutley*!' The adjutant, a bull-necked First World War veteran, was forced to adopt a Drill Sergeant's roar to make himself heard above the din. Those nearest him fell silent at once, and as the jangling tones of the beer-soaked mess piano died away the adjutant's quarry emerged from beneath an impromptu rugger scrum in one corner of the room.

Squadron Leader Hill, the former ranker, assumed his more habitual speaking voice.

'Ah, Hutley, there you are. Filled in your 1151* yet?'

'No, Sir, I haven't had a chance.'

'You know the regulations, don't you?'

'Yes, Sir.'

'Well then, get on to it right away.'

'Yes, Sir,' replied Hutley disconsolately.

Miserable bugger, he thought, as he and Hill left the mess. Trust him to spoil the party. Couldn't he hear the barrage of raspberries that started the moment the door closed behind them?

Squadron Leader Hill had indeed heard the protests and winked at Hutley, quite used to the impertinence of his juniors in age and rank. 'Sorry to be a spoilsport, Peter, but we both have a job to do. Work now, play later, eh? Be a good chap and fill in the combat report. Then you're to report to the C.O.'

'But what about the thrash? I don't want to miss out on that.'

*R.A.F. Combat Report Form number.

'Oh, that'll be going for some hours yet. I'll be looking in myself later on, just to add my halfpennyworth. It's not every day a member of this unit shoots down an ace. Splendid show.'

Peter's disappointment at being dragged away from the party was replaced by a pleasantly warm feeling of satisfaction. The praise was sincere and it was flattering. Perhaps Hill was human after all.

'Thank you, Sir. I'll see you later then.' Peter saluted and the adjutant nonchalantly returned the courtesy.

After calling in at general admin for a 1151, Peter made his way to his room and sat down to fill in the form. Name, rank, serial number, unit, aircraft type, date, weather conditions—all had to go down. Peter swore. But thank God it hadn't been a bombing mission requiring lengthy de-briefing. He began to write.

'*At approximately 15.30 hours, ordered by Tangmere Controller to investigate and intercept single aircraft . . .*' Suddenly, his progress was interrupted by the tannoy.

'Flying Officer Hutley report to sick-bay immediately.'

There was a pause and then the message was repeated. There was no doubting it the second time. *What the hell could the medics want with him*? he wondered, setting off at a brisk walk.

On the way he passed men he hardly recognized who seemed to go out of their way to exchange salutes. But a growing sense of puzzlement kept him from enjoying their unspoken congratulations.

The tannoy blared again.

'This is urgent. Flying Officer Hutley report to . . .'

As the message was finishing he walked in through the door and reported to the reception desk. A white-coated orderly with Corporal's tapes on his sleeves was sitting there, deep in the throes of paperwork. He looked up as Peter approached.

'I'm Hutley. What's all the fuss about, Corporal?'

'Ah, Mr Hutley'. The orderly got to his feet and pointed down the passageway. 'Room 9A. Down the corridor and turn left, left again and it's third on the right.'

'What's it all about? Any idea?'

'Not really, Sir. That Kraut's in there, that's all I know.'

Hutley turned and followed the orderly's directions. Of course. The pilot of the 109 he had shot down was wounded and wanted to meet him. Perhaps he wanted to say there were no hard feelings. Nice to know there was still a place for chivalry in modern warfare, he thought. Then he found himself wondering what on earth he would say to the fellow. How would he react? An R.A.F. Station Police Corporal was on duty outside the door. He saluted as Hutley approached and then frowned uneasily. Hutley hesitated, about to speak. Then he changed his mind. The Corporal opened the door and Peter went inside, leaving him to close it behind him.

At first he didn't look at the face of the man on the bed. Pilots rarely had to meet their victims face to face, the men they sought to kill, and Peter suddenly realized how uncomfortable the scene was going to be. He looked instead at the doctor, Squadron Leader Crawford, then at the nurse. Both faces bore the same expression of bewilderment that he had noticed on the Police Corporal's face. For a moment nobody said a word. Peter's eyes travelled round the sparsely furnished room, taking in a mass of unsurprising and irrelevant details: the bed, a table, a chair, a regulation locker, a wardrobe, cream paint and brightly polished standard sludge-brown linoleum. Somehow he had to force himself to look at the man on the bed. He couldn't make himself, try as he might. Sometime soon somebody must say something. They all stood silent, as if held by the same mysterious spell.

'Hello, Peter. It's been a long time.'

In a flash Peter Hutley's eyes turned and focused on the face of his unfortunate victim. The muscles in his arms, his legs, turned to jelly and the marrow froze in his bones. He blinked, shocked to the point of incoherence. Feebly, hoarsely, he stammered, 'Y-yes. Yes, it has.'

The German pilot was obviously severely wounded. His flying overalls had been loosened to reveal the Iron Cross 1st Class pinned at the base of his left-hand breast pocket. The blue Luftwaffe uniform was darkly stained with blood, and the stain was spreading. But the face was unmarked. Peter would have recognized it anywhere—a cruel face, eyes a steely grey, the nose straight and aristocratic, the mouth hard and thin,—a model of Aryan good looks. It was a face that had haunted him through childhood and had returned to haunt him now.

Peter sank down into the nearest chair and looked up anxiously at Squadron Leader Crawford. Everything was clear now: the mysterious summons to sick-bay, that bewildered look on the face of the Police Corporal—the blank astonished silence which had greeted him the moment he stepped inside the room. Even now Crawford's eyes were travelling to and fro between Peter and the German, as if he simply couldn't believe the uncanny resemblance between the two men.

'My God, Hutley, it's extraordinary. You could be twins!'

Peter managed a feeble smile. 'We are.'

He stood up and walked falteringly to the edge of the bed, watched by the nurse and the baffled Squadron Leader.

'His name's Johannes von Tahlmann—you can put it in the records for what it's worth.'

Crawford stood scratching his head in amazement.

'But look here, it's impossible—the man's a German . . .'

'It's a long story, Crawford, so just take my word for it, will you? I'll explain it all some other time.'

Peter was staring at his brother now, at the bruised and bloodstained hands, the tattered blue uniform of the Luftwaffe, the gleaming Iron Cross. Johannes' eyes were closed now, but whether in sleep or unconsciousness Peter couldn't tell.

'How long do you reckon he's got?'

'An hour or two—three at the most. I doubt if he'll last the night.' The Squadron Leader laid a consoling hand on Peter's shoulder. 'Look here, old man, why don't you come away now—come and take a seat next door. There's no point in hanging about here.'

Peter angrily wrestled free. 'I'm staying here.'

'Come on, Hutley, don't stay and torture yourself like this. We can all see you're upset; now just—'

'For Christ's sake, shut up and leave me alone.'

Peter's words were harsher than he had intended, but there were tears in his eyes now, and he felt a raging anger inside that he knew he would have to give way to sooner or later.

'It must have been a million to one against, you know, but I always knew this would happen. It was only a matter of time. You begin to live with the fear—God knows, there are enough other things to worry about . . .' His voice tailed off into silence and for some time he sat by the bed, holding his head in his hands, saying nothing.

Crawford and the nurse slipped out, shutting the door softly behind them, leaving him alone by the bedside, with his thoughts. Some time later—it could have been midnight, it could have been after, Peter had lost all sense of time—the figure on the bed stirred briefly and the eyes flickered open. For a short while Johannes regained consciousness, murmuring a few words in German that Peter could not make out—delirious ramblings for the most part, without logic or meaning. Peter stumbled out into the corridor to seek help and within moments Crawford was with him. The pair of them hurried inside and Peter watched as the other man felt for a pulse and bent over the dying German's chest to listen for a heartbeat. A few more seconds and the nurse rejoined them. Crawford turned to Peter.

'Alright, Hutley, there's nothing you can do now. Go and wait in my office.'

Peter paused for a final look at his brother and did as he was told. Shortly after, Crawford entered the poky little consulting room, looking grave. Peter had no need to ask—he already knew the worst. He made a weary effort to get to his feet but Crawford gestured him back to his seat.

'I'm sorry, Peter. It's all over. There was nothing we could do for him.'

Whether from the exhausting strain of the previous weeks or the shock of the last few hours, or a combination of both, Peter felt an uncontrollable urge to cry, and fought it with all his might. But eventually the barriers to grief collapsed and he found himself sobbing like a child, grateful for the relief of tears. Crawford put an arm round him for a moment and then walked over to a cupboard in the corner, fetching out a small basin, cotton wool and a hypodermic.

'I'm going to give you a jab. It'll help you relax. Then you're going to bed. You're suffering from shock and nervous exhaustion.'

Peter muttered something inaudible but submitted his bared arm to the needle without protest. He felt a sharp prick and almost instantly the drug began to take effect. He was drifting back into the past, back to the years before he was born, to events he had learned of from his mother, his father, and his grandfather.

PART ONE

THE MARK OF CAIN

CHAPTER ONE

For more than three years during the 1914–18 war Isobel Hutley had served as a volunteer nursing auxiliary. For much of the time she had been posted from one Field Hospital to another and was therefore frequently near the front line.

In June of 1917 Isobel found herself charged with the care of a most handsome young German pilot. It was said that he was a member of the feared and famous von Richthofen's Flying Circus. Certainly, he boasted the Pour-le-Mérite, the Blue Max, Germany's highest decoration. But he was severely wounded; mortally, so the doctors thought.

The fact that he did survive was almost entirely due to the selfless devotion of Nurse Hutley. Even though their countries were engaged in bitter conflict, Isobel could not prevent herself from being attracted to the Hauptmann Baron Rudolf von Tahlmann. Perhaps the wounded German guessed this from a chance remark of Isobel's, a gesture, a touch of the hand—for before he was sent to another hospital, from which he would shortly be invalided home, the Baron wrote down the young nurse's address.

'When our countries are at peace again,' he announced, 'you must come and visit my family. My mother will be most anxious to meet the girl who saved my life.'

'We'll see,' replied Isobel, not believing for an instant that she would ever hear from him again.

'I owe you a great debt, Isobel. But I only have one thing that I can give you. That is my medal.'

'But you mustn't—it's yours—and besides, I—'

'Yes, Fraulein, it is very special for me. But that is why you must let me give it to you. Please accept it, with my thanks.'

Isobel was overwhelmed. The blue and white enamelled cross had no great intrinsic value, but to her it meant more than any bag of sovereigns or fistful of diamonds. It was a symbol to her of the peace and forgiveness that she knew could not be far away.

Nobody noticed that the Baron left without his cherished medal, and Isobel never mentioned that he had given it even to her closest friends. It was her secret, a treasured memento of a few moments of stolen happiness.

Shortly before Christmas 1918, Isobel Hutley left her wartime nursing job for good. For a while she intended to take it easy, to recover from the rigours of her work and forget the terrible sights she had had to endure and harden to. In due course she would seek civilian employment, but she swore that never again would she work as a nurse.

One morning, towards the end of February 1919, her father came into the breakfast room bearing the morning mail. A letter for Isobel from abroad was an exceptional event. Her father looked inquisitively at the envelope as he handed it to his daughter.

'I didn't know you had friends in Germany, my dear.'

Isobel could not believe her eyes as she studied the envelope. She didn't recognize the writing or the seal on the back, but the postmark of Schwandorf in Bavaria seemed distantly familiar. Although she didn't answer her father's question directly her facial expression told Ernest Hutley all he wanted to know.

The old man was proud of his only daughter, proud of her sweet nature and her good looks—not a classic English rose, perhaps, but fair-complexioned like her mother, with hair that went blond in the sun. Hutley gazed fondly at his daughter's trim figure, her blue eyes, her straight nose, neat mouth and the suspicion of a dimple in her chin. He had worried about her since she had come back from the war. His wife had died on the same day as Edward VII; his sons, both of them, had been killed in France, one in the R.F.C. and the other during the second battle of the Somme. Now she was all he had left, and her restlessness since her return from the front had given him much cause for concern. Now at least he knew the reason for it. There was no mistaking the signs: his daughter was in love. No doubt her young man would turn out to be a dashing young cavalry officer seconded to the duties of the Allied Army of Occupation. Perhaps it wouldn't be such a bad thing after all.

Isobel savoured the promise of the envelope and its contents for a full minute. When she could bear the anticipation no longer she put a knife inside the flap and slit it open. She took out a letter and some other papers. She read the letter first. Though formal, to Isobel it had an unmistakable underlying warmth.

'*Dear Isobel,*
I promised to ask you to come and stay with us in Bavaria, and I write now to fulfil that promise. It will be a very real pleasure to see you here and you may be assured that you will be made most welcome. Do not think me presumptuous in having already taken the liberty of making reservations for you by steamship and rail. If the dates I have selected are inconvenient, please change them and inform me of your plans as soon as possible. All being well, I will meet the train at Schwandorf on the 6th March at 13.27 hours. Do not forget to change at Nürnburg.'

Rudolf von Tahlmann

Besides the tickets there was also a money order for £100.

Isobel read the letter through a second and then a third time in a frenzy of excitement. Hutley had seen her eyes light up and gave her a kindly paternal smile.

'Good news, my dear?'

Isobel was so overjoyed that without a moment's thought she raced round to the other side of the table and flung her arms round her father's neck.

'German postmark, I see, Isobel,' Hutley remarked, somewhat overwhelmed. 'Some young gentleman friend of yours stationed out there?'

Hutley eyed her slyly. The moment he had set eyes on the letter his imagination had set to work, and by now he could picture her young gentleman friend almost as clearly as if he had been standing there in the kitchen in front of him: gallant, upright—all in all the perfect son-in-law.

Isobel hesitated. Much as she had longed to see Rudolf again, this was exactly the kind of scene she had been dreading.

'Well, father—it's all rather difficult to explain. You see—'

Hutley interrupted, giving her hand an affectionate pat.

'Come, come, Isobel. I've got eyes in my head, you know. I may be an old stick-in-the-mud, but I know true love when I see it.'

'Oh, father—' Isobel braved a smile, but her thoughts were in something of a tumult. Ever since she had returned from the front she had spent the winter nights thinking about nothing but Rudolf, but so many miles lay between them that it had seemed quite unthinkable they would ever meet again. She glanced at the letter: of course, it was marvellous news, *but* . . . Rudolf as an idle day dream was one thing; a flesh and blood Rudolf inviting—no, *ordering* her out to Germany was quite a different matter.

Hutley had returned to his toast and marmalade and

was pouring out a second cup of coffee.

'Come on then, Isobel, let your old father in on the secret.' He looked up at her with a twinkle in his eye. 'How did you meet the fellow?'

Isobel decided to play coy. 'Really, father. Don't be so inquisitive. And you've spilt coffee on the tablecloth—let me fetch a cloth.'

Isobel hopped up from the table, glad of a chance to escape her father's scrutinizing gaze and gather her thoughts in private. In a minute she returned and mopped at the dark-brown stain. Hutley grunted.

'Clumsy of me—bless you, Isobel, I don't know how I'd manage without you.'

'You managed before—remember? When I was away nursing?'

'Oh yes,—but I don't know, it's just not the same without you.'

There was a pause, and Isobel noticed her father's expression slowly alter. She followed the direction of his gaze and saw that while clearing away the breakfast things she had accidentally swept the envelope aside, scattering its contents. The £100 money order and the steamer ticket were now clearly visible on the table, and her father had spotted them.

Hutley cleared his throat. 'I say, Isobel.' His tone was suddenly serious; Isobel looked up slowly, and their eyes met. She had a faint premonition what was coming next.

'This young fellow of yours—he hasn't asked you out there to join him, has he?

She nodded. 'Don't worry, father—I've made up my mind. I'm not going. You said it yourself—you need me here.'

Hutley gave one of his indignant snorts.

'I said no such thing! I'll be damned if I'm going to stand in the way of your happiness.'

'Father, please don't make it any more difficult for me. My mind's made up and that's all there is to it. Now for goodness' sake finish your breakfast so I can clear away.'

Hutley pushed his chair back and stood up, waving an admonishing finger at her.

'You listen to me, Isobel. You're not my blasted wet-nurse, and I'm not one of your wretched patients. I'm an able-bodied fifty year old perfectly able to fend for himself—'

'Fifty-*five* year old.'

'—and I *will* not be used as an excuse to shackle yourself to hearth and home. My God, woman, do you want to die an old maid? Do you think I want that on my conscience?'

Isobel couldn't help smiling. She always found her father's tantrums irresistibly amusing. 'No, I suppose not.'

'So you'll go?'

Isobel went up to her father and gave him a kiss.

'If you say so.'

'That's more like it.' He gave her a broad, heart-warming smile, secretly deciding that she would catch that train to Germany if he had to drive her on board at pistol point. Fathers have to make sacrifices, after all.

The weather was bitterly cold even for late February, and Isobel guessed the German winter would be still colder, so she spent the few short days before her departure hurriedly knitting warm clothes for the trip. Part of the £100 that Rudolf had sent her she spent on new dresses and shoes—her old civilian clothes all looked horribly out of date after her years in the uniform of the nursing corps and she badly needed a new wardrobe. Her father was as kind and helpful as ever, insisting on buying her an expensive new coat out of his own pocket—she protested at first, but eventually had to give in. Hutley's kindness pained her rather; they had never spoken of the identity of her friend in Germany, and Hutley tactfully refrained from questioning her on the subject. Isobel told herself that all would be well in time, and that peace between England and Germany would put an end to the hatred and remove the need for concealment, but in her heart she knew that there was bound to be trouble when her father discovered the truth.

By the time March 5th arrived, Isobel was ready and packed, but was suffering agonies of nerves at the thought of the long journey ahead and the uncertain prospects at the end of it. At two in the afternoon she and her father arrived at Esher station to catch the train to Victoria.

Hutley saw her off at the station. He had insisted on being there to help her with her luggage, but Isobel guessed that his real reason was to delay the moment of parting for as long as possible. He seemed to be reconciled to the thought that she might be gone for some time, and did his best to appear cheerful. Isobel for her part did her best not to look nervous, but when the time came to kiss him goodbye there were tears in her eyes.

She stood at the carriage window, waving, as the train slowly gathered speed. As he watched his daughter disappear from view Ernest pulled out a handkerchief from his breastpocket and blew his nose, surreptitiously wiping his eyes before stuffing it back in his jacket. He stuck his chest out and strode back towards the barrier. Perhaps it wouldn't be too bad to be on his own again. Besides, Isobel had promised to write.

CHAPTER TWO

After an uneventful Channel crossing, Isobel continued by train through Belgium, stopping at Ghent, Brussels and Liège. From Cologne, where she had her first view of the Rhine, the train trundled on to Wiesbaden, Frankfurt, Wurzburg, and finally to Nürnburg.

Isobel's German was, to all intents and purposes, non-existent. So was the English of the official she sought to question on the matter of where to make the connection to Schwandorf. She was glad of her new coat and scarf. It was bitterly cold on the platform and more snow threatened. Now and then a discoloured flurry would stir itself, swept up by a gust of wind, or by the draught of a passing vehicle. Isobel stamped her feet in an effort to keep warm as she vainly sought to explain herself to the railwayman. So far her efforts had only been met with shrugs. She wasn't sure whether her surprise or relief was greater when another voice intervened.

'Bitte, Fräulein Hutley?'

'Yes, yes, I'm Isobel Hutley' she replied, turning.

She was confronted by a smart young man in his late twenties. He was on the short side, with a swarthy, clean-shaven face and a marked dimple in his chin, and he was wearing a peaked cap, grey tunic breeches and riding boots, the heels of which he clicked in the traditional manner. He bowed slightly, resumed the vertical, and spoke again.

'My name is Dietrich. I am Baron von Tahlmann's chauffeur. He has sent me down here to collect you. There has been an accident.'

'Not Rudolf . . . ?'

'No, Fräulein. A locomotive has left the rails and the trains cannot get through to Schwandorf for the time being. Rather than leave you here at the mercy of the Bundesbahn, the Baron sent me here to collect you. I hope you have had a good trip.'

'Fine, thank you.'

'The Baron will be pleased.'

'Is it far to the house, Dietrich?'

'About ninety kilometres, Fräulein.'

'How far is that in English miles?'

'About fifty.'

'Oh dear, then it is a long way.'

'Yes, Fräulein, I am afraid it will take some time, especially with the snow and ice on the roads. However, we shall be travelling in the new Benz. You will be perfectly comfortable.'

Dietrich conducted a brief exchange with the railwayman, who beamed at Isobel, clicking his heels and bowing; then the chauffeur led the way to the car. Two porters followed with her luggage.

The Benz was startlingly luxurious, though rather less so for the chauffeur, who was condemned to sit in the open air while Isobel reclined in comfort at the back with foot and hand warmers. The seats were of red leather, the roof lined in fawn felt and the floor was thickly carpeted. Clearly the war had left little mark on the von Tahlmann family fortunes—unlike those of many of their fellow countrymen.

To her surprise and pleasure, Isobel found a hamper on the back seat containing German sausage, cold pork, pheasant, bread, butter, cakes and a bottle of 1898 Moselle. With the help of the excellent food—Isobel found that travelling had given her quite an appetite—and a liberal slug of Schnapps that Dietrich had given her to help her thaw out, she felt able to sit back and enjoy the journey. Periodically she opened the glass panel separating driver and passenger, to enquire of this or that. The chauffeur spoke surprisingly good English, but the blast of icy air gave sufficient excuse to keep conversation to a minimum. Even though the pall of the dead winter hung over the countryside, the scenery passing outside was magnificent, and from the warmth and security of the car Isobel admired the elegance of the snow-clad conifers and the quiet dignity of the occasional houses.

The journey took rather longer than even Dietrich had expected. The roads had become slippery and treacherous since the return of the frost, and it was almost two hours later when Dietrich tapped on the glass, pointing to a wooded hillside on their right. Isobel peered out in the direction indicated.

There was no mistaking the Tahlmann family home. It was indeed imposing—even more so than Isobel had supposed. Partly obscured by trees, it was exactly as she had imagined it in everything but size—which she had hopelessly underestimated. Staggered at its vastness and strange wintry air, for a moment, she felt an insane urge to scramble out of the car and head back to dear, dull old Esher, but the car was speeding ahead regardless—there was no going back now. In an effort to keep calm and reassure herself, she thought back to her parting memory of Rudolf, lying helpless in the Flanders field hospital; to the Rudolf who had entrusted her with his most precious possession, the Blue Max. He had promised her they would meet again, and he had kept his word. But would he have changed? Looking out over the huge expanse of the Tahlmann family estate, Isobel feared the worst.

The memories evaporated as the car passed under an enormous archway and into a courtyard. Isobel was back in the present. The car drew up and Dietrich turned off the ignition, stepped out and opened the door for Isobel. As he did so the front entrance of the house opened too. Isobel had prayed that Rudolf would be there to meet her, and felt a pang of fear and disappointment when she saw that instead, three strangers formed the reception committee: the butler, a footman, and an old woman she took to be the housekeeper.

Isobel stood facing them in the courtyard, somewhat at a loss, not knowing quite what to say or how to behave. She looked towards Dietrich hoping for guidance and then looked again at the housekeeper. *Oh why wasn't Rudolf here to help her*? The housekeeper was a small woman, probably in her late sixties. Despite her years, she held her head proudly erect. Her eyes were small and dark, but still bright. Her straight grey hair was parted in the middle and plaited over either ear. The nose was straight and aristocratic, the mouth thinned by age. She wore a simple black dress and a brooch hung at her throat. This was no trinket, Isobel realized suddenly, seeing the Tahlmann Crest picked out in diamonds and gold. And she was no housekeeper. She had to be the old Baroness herself.

Isobel forced a smile and held out her hand to return the Baroness's greeting. She felt the boney fingers of the old woman close on hers.

'Welcome to Tahlmann, my dear. Do come inside quickly out of the cold. You must be tired after your journey.'

Isobel followed the black-clad figure as the Baroness led her up the steps, through the heavy oak-panelled front door and into the cavernous, marble-floored hall of the Tahlmann mansion, four servants following behind with her rather meagre luggage. Dietrich had taken his leave with a bow at the front door.

A huge fire was blazing as the party finally entered the room set aside for Isobel during her stay. A maid hurriedly finished her last-minute tidying, and stood stiffly to attention, blushing slightly. The Baroness motioned to the girl to approach.

'Come here, girl,' she said in German. Then addressing herself to Isobel, she continued in English.

'This is Elsa, my dear. She will look after you as your personal maid while you are here.'

The girl curtseyed. Isobel, unused to such pomp and ceremony, very nearly curtseyed back. Recovering, she put out her hand and greeted the girl formally.

'Elsa.'

'My dear, I expect you would like to have a rest before dinner so I will leave you with your maid.'

Isobel was about to ask after Rudolf, but before she could do so the old woman swept from the room with the four servants in tow. Isobel was left to look sheepishly at Elsa, who visibly gained in confidence the moment her mistress left the room. She motioned to Isobel to get undressed whilst she ran a bath. Isobel meekly obeyed. She very nearly fell asleep caressed by the warm water, but Elsa appeared with towel flapping from outstretched arms, signalling to her to get out.

When she was dry, Isobel sank down on the bed in her dressing gown. She felt drowsy, and closed her eyes. Elsa pottered about unpacking and when everything was done to her satisfaction, she crept from the room, leaving Isobel fast asleep on the bed.

After two hours the maid returned. Isobel did not awaken to the gentle but insistent knocking. Softly Elsa shook her, until her sleep-stiffened eyelids flickered open, and told her it was time to dress for dinner.

When Isobel was dressed a footman arrived and led her down to the drawing room. *Surely now she must see Rudolf at last*?

The footman opened the door and Isobel was ushered into a quietly furnished room, small by Tahlmann standards. The Baroness was seated in her chair, sewing table and needlework box beside her. The only other occupant of the room rose as she entered. The footman moved aside unobtrusively to make up the fire.

It was nearly three years since they had last set eyes on one another. For a moment both hesitated. Then Isobel smiled shyly as Rudolf came towards her with both arms extended. He was just as she remembered him, a little older-looking perhaps, but more marked by experience than lined by the passing of time. A stiff, formal veneer masked an inner hardness brought on by war and wounds and the bitterness of defeat.

Rudolf took both her hands in his and kissed them gently.

'Isobel, my dear, it is so very good to see you, and so very, very good of you to come all this way.'

The Baroness said nothing. Although she could not approve of her son's attachment to an English girl, who was the daughter and kin of erstwhile enemies and not of aristocratic birth, the old woman was making an effort to hide her misgivings. This was, after all, the girl who had saved Rudolf's life. And whatever her son might feel towards the young English girl, it was clearly more than just a passing fancy.

Rudolf motioned Isobel over to the sofa and sat down beside her. The Baroness was opposite them, strategically placed to watch their every move. Drinks were served immediately. Isobel chose sherry, secretly yearning for a large gin to drown the flutterings in her stomach.

The talk was of no great account. Rudolf apologized for not having been present to greet her, but thought she would rather be given her privacy until she had time to clean up and rest after the long journey. He had had to occupy himself with urgent estate business. They talked mostly of the journey and the weather.

Soon dinner was announced and Isobel was led into an enormous dining room. Rudolf sat at the head of the vast table. His mother was seated on his left hand and Isobel on the right. Both women wore full-length evening dresses, sombre in colour, whilst the Baron was attired in a formal dinner suit complete with waistcoat and a plain white shirt, topped with winged collar and black tie. Isobel had never seen him look quite so beautiful—and had never felt quite so awkward herself.

All through the meal she dreaded having to talk of the war, knowing the time must come sooner or later. She wondered how she would react, what she should say. Inevitably the conversation ran to conditions in their respective countries, and inexorably the dreaded subject loomed closer. There was no particular point at which it could be said that the moment had come, but quite suddenly, Isobel realized that the three of them were talking almost dispassionately about the past. It was the Baroness who brought matters to a head.

'My dear, I do hope that the English will see that the peace treaty is fair to all of us. The real enemy now lies to the east.'

CHAPTER THREE

In the days that followed, Isobel's love for Rudolf grew. His effect on her was near hypnotic. He took her everywhere. They were apart only at night. In the middle of the second week the Baron took his guest to the hunting lodge. It was a long ride and the weather was chilly, but spring was in the air. The shooting season was over but soon they would be able to fish for trout in the lakes. Isobel did fish, didn't she? No? Never mind, Rudi would teach her. At no point did it seem to cross his mind that sooner or later Isobel would have to return to England. The future was never discussed.

The hunting lodge was a log cabin deep in the heart of the pine woods, overlooking a large lake—a dangerously romantic setting. Rudolf dismounted first and then helped his companion down. They planned to have lunch by the fire in the lodge. Rudolf went off in search of brushwood whilst Isobel unpacked the hamper.

When he returned with his arms full of kindling, the two of them lit the fire and settled down to enjoy their picnic. In the few minutes she had been alone, Isobel had been thinking. It was only a couple of months since she had had his letter, and yet already she was a different person—it was as if Esher and her father belonged to an altogether different world.

Rudolf laughed when she told him. 'Tell me, what do

you write in your letters to your father?'

'Very little,' Isobel replied. 'I'm afraid he wouldn't understand. It worries me, though.'

Rudolf nodded. 'It must be difficult for you to deceive him.'

'I don't think of it as deception, quite. I tell myself it's because I don't want to hurt him. But I still can't justify it—I know it's wrong.'

Rudolf took her in his arms and kissed her gently.

'You must not upset yourself, Isobel. The war is over now and the peace treaty will soon be signed. Surely your father cannot object now that the hostilities have ended?'

'I wouldn't be so sure. He's very set in his ways. Do you know what he calls you?' She gave a little giggle. 'The Huns.'

Rudolf smiled and held her close to him again.

'I feel guilty too sometimes,' he said, stroking her hair.

'Guilty? Whatever for?'

'For uprooting you—taking you away from your home, your family, planting you among all these unfamiliar faces. I'm sorry if your reception hasn't been quite as warm as I hoped.'

'Your mother, you mean?'

Rudolf nodded. Isobel hesitated for a moment.

'Well, I must say she can be a bit . . .'

'Yes?'

Isobel had been about to call her a battleaxe, but managed to check herself. '. . . a bit alarming at times.'

Rudolf grinned. 'You choose your words carefully, Isobel. My mother is much feared and little loved, but she is a powerful and intelligent woman. Our family future means a great deal to her.'

'I'm sure. Goodness knows what she must think of me. She probably thinks I've got my eye on the Tahlmann family fortunes.'

Rudolf burst out laughing. 'And of course she's right!'

Isobel fell upon him, pretending to be furious, and the

pair of them mock-wrestled on the floor, both helpless with laughter. Finally Rudolf surrendered and Isobel generously allowed him to sit up straight and dust himself down.

By the glow of the wood fire they drank the last of their bottle of Burgundy and finished their picnic, sitting together hand in hand. Rudolf had turned pensive and sat staring into the embers for some minutes without speaking while Isobel nestled closer to him. She was used to his silences now and had learned not to question them. Finally he spoke.

'Isobel, I suppose you know why I invited you to Germany?'

Isobel looked up at him.

'I've an idea, yes.'

'All that business of saving my life—I'm grateful of course, but that wasn't the real reason.'

Isobel stayed silent, waiting for him to go on.

'I invited you here because I could see you were different—special, if you like. I was a sick man then, but I'm healthy now. I've changed—but you haven't. In fact you're even more special to me now.'

His words surprised her. The confession, so at variance with the formal, reserved mask he wore when the two of them were in the presence of others, revealed a new side to his nature—a new warmth and concern.

'But Rudolf, there must have been other girls, surely? German girls, I mean—girls of your own station in life. You're a nobleman, after all. What I don't understand is—why me?'

Rudolf gazed into her eyes searchingly.

'You don't believe I am serious?'

'I didn't say that—'

'I assure you I am, Isobel. I have never been more serious in my life. If you don't believe me, I'll prove it.'

Rudolf's solemn tone completely silenced her doubts.

'How?'

'By marrying you.'

The announcement momentarily left her lost for words and she sat in a daze, not sure whether to laugh or cry.

'Marrying me?'

'If you'll have me, of course.'

'Oh Rudolf, but it's impossible—what about our families?'

'Our families? I'm afraid they will just have to learn to live with it. They'll accept it—just give them time.'

'You really think so?'

'I know so.' Rudolf cradled her face in his hands and kissed her again. 'So what do you say? Will you be my wife?'

Too overcome to reply, Isobel flung her arms around his neck and pulled him closer to her; all her doubts and misgivings vanished in the emotion of the moment, and she felt her heartbeat quicken, excitement and fear mingling inside her, as Rudolf returned her embrace. His grip on her tightened, pressing her downwards to the bare wooden floor of the hunting lodge, the weight of his body forcing her to submit, and she felt his fingers searching for the buttons on her blouse. Suddenly alarmed, she wrestled in his grasp, vainly struggling to free herself, but a reckless impulse to bind herself to him, to make their union complete, was driving her irresistibly on, eroding her will. In moments Rudolf's probing hands had loosened her blouse and thick riding dress and were exploring her pale white body.

All thought of resistance cast aside now, Isobel abandoned herself to the rhythm of their lovemaking, eagerly responding to his caresses, drawing him down towards her, and gasping with the sudden stab of pain and pleasure as their two bodies became one. Almost immediately, unaware of anything but the intensity of her hunger for him, she felt a new, almost unbearably pleasurable sensation take hold of her and moaned as Rudolf's thrusts began to quicken in pace, forcing her to cry out and clasp him to her still closer, until both of them reached their climax simultaneously and sank exhausted in each other's arms.

It seemed like hours before Isobel's sense of time and place returned, and with it the full knowledge of what had passed between them. Words suddenly seemed unnecessary, so as the shadows lengthened and the last embers of the small wood fire died down, the couple merely sat in silence, gazing out through the door of the lodge over the peaceful Bavarian landscape beyond.

After returning to the mansion in the early evening, Isobel spent the time, as far as possible alone, desperately trying to come to terms with the sudden rush of events. She no longer had the slightest doubt that Rudolf had meant what he said, and her own love for him had grown immeasurably over the past days, but no matter how hard she tried she couldn't share his optimism about the future. From what she had seen of the Baroness, she was hardly likely to greet the news that her son intended to marry an English girl—and a commoner, at that—with unbridled joy. Nor would her father be likely to take kindly to the thought of a German son-in-law. Plainly Rudolf had little notion how jingoistic the British middle-classes could be. The way ahead seemed fraught with problems.

But now that she felt sure of Rudolf's good intentions, Isobel was in better heart. Sitting up in bed later that night she made her decision: she *would* marry him, come what may, and she would return to England as soon as possible to get her father's approval. If she was honest with him, and told him the full story as openly and frankly as she could, she knew she could win him over.

The next day brought no change in Rudolf's intentions. Before lunch, he once again declared his love for Isobel, and repeated his proposal. His mother had left the room shortly before the meal was due to be served and he seized his chance as they sat alone together.

'Isobel, I must have your answer. Do you agree to marry me?'

Isobel smiled. 'Did you ever doubt me?'

Unnoticed by either of them, the Baroness returned just in time to see Rudolf kissing Isobel on the lips, with something approaching reverence. The old woman looked sternly on. At first she had done her best to welcome this strange girl from England, a daughter of the enemy. She had donned a facade for her son's sake, but the mask of acceptance fell away now, to reveal obvious animosity. Isobel blushed. The Baroness's change in attitude made her deeply uncomfortable. A chill wind seemed suddenly to cut through the room's warmth.

Rudolf broke the uneasy silence.

'Mother, I have some marvellous news. Isobel has consented to become my wife.'

The Baron let go of Isobel's hand and went to his mother and kissed her on the cheek. A mechanical smile darted across her face, but in a trice she resumed her disapproving expression. The Baroness had already decided Isobel was quite unfitted for the sacred task of continuing the Tahlmann line. The fact that she was not German only made an unacceptable situation worse.

'Well, mother. Aren't you going to say something?'

Still the Baroness remained silent. Instead she went over to her son and kissed him on the cheek. Then she moved toward Isobel. Both women surveyed each other, and for the first time Isobel felt genuinely unwelcome. Then she felt the coldness of the thin lips on her cheek, as chilling as the touch of an iceberg.

'My dear,' said the Baroness, with acid insincerity, 'why don't we all go into lunch—I believe it is ready now.' The old woman led the way. Rudolf and Isobel exchanged nervous glances. He smiled, but she looked hurt.

'Never mind, my love,' he whispered in her ear as they

followed. 'Mother will come round in due course. Remember: give her time.'

Rudolf squeezed her hand reassuringly.

Rudolf and Isobel planned to be married as soon as possible, but Isobel had first to return to England and her father, and break the news to him. Around the middle of April 1919 she travelled home. Rudolf drove her to the main railway station in Nürnburg, there to entrain for the Channel coast. Their farewell was painful, made the more poignant for Isobel by the gift of a piece of the Tahlmann jewellery, a large diamond and ruby ring. Rudolf pressed it on her finger almost as an afterthought. Although it was too large, Isobel insisted it fitted perfectly. She promised she would return as soon as she could.

A whistle blew, the carriages jerked into motion and slowly began to gather speed. Rudolf relinquished his hold on Isobel's hand and was left standing alone on the platform as the train pulled away. A cloud of sulphurous smoke momentarily obscured Isobel's view, tugging at her lungs. One last glimpse of Rudolf, and then the curtain of vapour closed on the second act of the Tahlmann-Hutley story.

Isobel would always wish to remember Rudolf as she saw him then, a proud and upright figure gradually receding from view.

CHAPTER FOUR

'Why on earth you have to go and pick on a confounded Hun as a husband is quite beyond my comprehension. Aren't Englishmen good enough for you any more?'

Ernest Hutley's joy at the return of his daughter the previous day had soon been shattered by the news of the forthcoming nuptials. He had listened to Isobel's halting narrative with ill-concealed dismay and since then had nagged away at the contentious bone to the exclusion of virtually everything else. Now at breakfast, after a sleepless night, Ernest still wrestled to control his anger and disappointment.

'Well?' he enquired, looking up at Isobel as if expecting a fresh answer to a question he had already asked a dozen times last night. Isobel tried to smile at her father, but the hurtfulness of his remarks still stung her.

'You haven't answered my question,' he complained.

'Oh Father, I have, over and over again.'

'No, you haven't. You still haven't told me why you have to marry that infernal German.'

'Because I love him.'

'But how *can* you love one of your country's enemies?'

'Father, that is quite absurd. The war is over. We must forget and start again.' Isobel's emotions were being torn apart by her love for Rudolf and the loyalty and devotion she felt for her father. She had never seen him so angry and so deaf to reason.

Breakfast had become a total disaster. Ernest had relapsed into silence. He sat glumly surveying the congealing remains of his egg and the cold coffee.

'Let me get you some fresh coffee,' Isobel volunteered.

'No, thank you.'

Isobel tried again. She rose, and, collecting her father's cup, poured the contents into the slop bowl. She poured a fresh cup and placed it in front of her father, kissing him on his brow as she put it down. She felt she detected a slight relaxing, a softening in his features.

'Daddy darling, it may have escaped your notice, but our own dear King George is also a confounded Hun.'

Ernest Hutley's brief smile disappeared instantly.

'Don't be so damned impertinent, Isobel.'

'You'll change your mind when you meet Rudolf, I promise.'

'Oh no, I will not,' cried Ernest, enunciating each word with particular emphasis. 'Oh no, I damn well won't. I hope I never meet another German as long as I live. When the peace treaty is signed, I hope that the Allies have the gumption to extract every last pound of reparatory flesh, every last drop of blood out of the Huns.'

Despite the way his anger and emotion had built up, Isobel was surprised by her father's vehemence. Momentarily her own anger flared.

'Daddy, you ought to be ashamed of yourself. People with views like yours will only cause more bitterness, more strife, more war. You're a bigoted, spiteful old man.' Isobel bit her lip. She had gone too far now and she knew it. With a snort of fury, her father pushed his chair back and stood up so fast that he knocked his egg on to the floor, shattering it and spilling the contents on the carpet. Shaking with rage and scarcely coherent now, he thundered at his daughter.

'How dare you speak to me like that? Kindly leave my table this instant and go to your room.'

Isobel's only remaining defence was in tears. Without further comment she made her way to the door, sobbing as she went, her father's words echoing after her: 'God alone knows what your mother would say if she could see you now. She must be turning in her grave—God rest her soul.'

The tactless words merely accelerated Isobel's departure from the room. She ran upstairs and flung herself face downward on her bed.

In the days that followed it was difficult to discern who was the more miserable of the two. Father and daughter had each done their best to heal the rift between them. Each had apologized for the row. Ernest first, on the brink of tears himself, had gone to his daughter's room to ask her forgiveness after admitting to himself that his virulent hatred for the Germans was not the only reason for his anger. If he was honest, he had to admit that he wanted to keep his daughter with him.

For her part, Isobel was haunted by other, more immediate fears. One night, early in June, Ernest Hutley was reading a book after their evening meal. Isobel was staring at the empty fireplace. She now knew beyond all doubt that she was going to have a baby. She hadn't been to a doctor—she had told no one. She hadn't dared. But she knew. Her father no longer enquired when she proposed to leave for Germany again, simply hoping that the day would never come. Isobel was unusually on edge. She had felt sure that she must get a letter from Rudolf that Monday. Normally she had at least three letters a week, but now she had had no communication for a fortnight.

'It's not just the letters, is it, Isobel?' her father enquired, looking up from his book.

Isobel, startled, took a deep breath before answering.

'No, Daddy. No. It isn't just that.'

'Do you want to talk about it?'

Isobel hardly knew what to reply. But she had to tell somebody. If her own father didn't understand, then, she argued, his love for her would surely not be worth much. She nodded.

'Well, yes. I suppose I'll have to sooner or later.'

Ernest's show of patience and understanding, so completely at variance with his previous outbursts, surprised and moved her. As she took hold of his outstretched hand he said, quite calmly, 'Forgive me if I'm wrong, my dear, but I think I know. You are going to have a baby, aren't you?'

Her father's directness came as a complete shock.

'Oh Daddy, I don't know what to do. I love him so much—otherwise I'd never have been so foolish. But he'll never want to marry me now.'

Isobel started to cry. But through her tears she knew at

last that she had a true friend in her father, one who loved her despite all, one on whom she could rely absolutely. After the days of uncertainty and fear, the relief was intense, and the tears equally so.

Later that night she sat down and wrote the following letter to Rudolf.

'My very dearest Rudolf,
I am returning your ring with this letter, because I fear I can now no longer marry you. I am sure that you loved me truly, and I you. For that reason I feel I cannot bring the shame on you that my presence at your side would be bound to cause.

Since returning home I have discovered that I am bearing a child—our child. It seems that we both must pay the price for our one moment of indiscretion. Forgive me, please, for breaking our engagement, and believe me when I say how much pain it causes me to have to write this letter. Think of me fondly, as I shall always think of you, my love.

Isobel.'

The days passed, and still no word came from Rudolf until, three weeks after Isobel had last heard from him, an envelope dropped on to the mat, bearing the familiar Schwandorf postmark. Isobel was out at the time, and it was Ernest Hutley who picked it up and took it away to prop up on the mantle shelf in the sitting room. Gazing at it full of foreboding at the effect it would be likely to have on his daughter, he noticed something unusual. By now he was well acquainted with the young Tahlmann's handwriting—but this was in a different, stern and angular hand. Ernest was puzzled and curious. The postmark was the same as usual, but clearly the letter came from a different person altogether, a third party.

Hutley's only thought was to prevent Isobel from being

hurt further: if the letter contained bad news, news that might upset or injure his daughter, then she must be protected from it. Much as he disliked the idea, it would be by far the best thing under the circumstances if he were to read the letter first and break the news to her gently. His hands trembled slightly as he picked up the paper knife and slit the envelope open. Inside was a single sheet of crisp white writing paper. As he had suspected, the letter was not from Rudolf. Looking down at the foot of the page he saw the name Helga von Tahlmann. '*My dear Isobel*,' it began, warmly enough,

> '*You are no doubt wondering why you have not heard from Rudolf over the preceding weeks. Unfortunately he met with a slight accident recently, and his poor state of health has prevented him from writing to you. Pray do not be alarmed on his account: he is recovering fast and will shortly be restored to full health again.*
>
> '*I cannot pretend that the news contained in your last letter did not come as something of a shock to us, but both Rudolf and I remain adamant that the engagement must not be broken. I join him in insisting that you must return to Tahlmann as soon as possible and take your place among us as his wife.*
>
> '*We will make arrangements for you and your father to have special leave to come to Germany and the papers will be forwarded to you with all speed. Until we next meet, please be assured of my very best wishes. Rudolf asks me to add that he sends his love to you.*'

Hutley frowned. Bearing in mind its contents, the letter was brief and to the point, to say the very least. Strange, though, that Rudolf couldn't write in person. And even odder that the Baroness gave no details of his mysterious accident. As for the message—well, that seemed clear and genuine enough, and no doubt Isobel would be overjoyed. But in spite of his relief on that score, Hutley couldn't quite repress a feeling of misgiving.

When Isobel returned about an hour later, Erenest lost no time in explaining to her what had happened and was full of apologies for opening a letter addressed to her; but Isobel was far too excited to listen, and probably would not have minded if the whole of Esher had been privy to the news. Immediately she seized the letter from the mantlepiece and read it from beginning to end.

Hutley could hardly believe the transformation in his daughter. Even so, he noticed her gasp when she read of Rudolf's accident, and wonder aloud what could have happened to him. Hutley did his best to put her mind at rest—it could only have been a trivial matter, he assured her, otherwise the Baroness would surely have been more explicit.

The wedding was arranged for the 21st June 1919. Technically, Britain would still be at war with Germany for another seven days and despite much string-pulling, a travel permit could only be obtained for Isobel on compassionate grounds. In her father's case, the answer was a flat 'permission refused'. Sadly he would have to stay behind.

After another tearful farewell at Esher station, Isobel once more found herself en route by train and Channel steamer to Schwandorf.

CHAPTER FIVE

On the 14th June 1919, two weeks before the signing of the Treaty of Versailles and five days before the date set for her wedding, Isobel stepped down from the train at the Nürnburg Hauptbahnhof, familiar to her now after her last visit, and found the same chauffeur there to meet her. But this time Dietrich greeted his master's future wife very much more formally. Gone was the friendly, debonair manner of the dark-haired German who had collected her from the same station only a few months previously.

The reason for Dietrich's thinly veiled hostility was not hard to find. In a train not entirely unlike the one Isobel had just disembarked from, deep in the forests of Compiegne, a small town in the north-east of France, the last details of the peace treaty that would put a formal end to one of the worst and bitterest wars in human history—the war that many believed would end all wars—were still being argued out. The fierce debates that raged inside that cramped train compartment hidden in the seclusion of the Compiegne woods remained shrouded in secrecy. But already rumours had begun to leak out. They had reached Dietrich's ears, just as they had reached the ears of every German man, woman and child: rumours of crushing humiliation, of terms more cruelly punitive than any that had previously been inflicted by victor on victim. Germany seethed with discontent and hatred for her former enemies. English, French or American—it made no difference. All were equally hated and despised.

Dietrich's coldness towards her as they sat in the car gave Isobel her first taste of the country's bitter mood. She soon abandoned her efforts at polite conversation, and sank back on the leather seat and stared out of the window, drinking in the beauty of the Bavarian summer as the gleaming Benz sped on towards Schwandorf.

On arriving two hours later Isobel quickly stepped out of the car and searched around for a sign of Rudolf. He was nowhere to be seen. Nor was the Baroness there to greet her at the front door as she had been on Isobel's last visit. Mystified, she turned round to ask Dietrich where they might be, but the chauffeur had disappeared into the stables. She found herself standing quite alone in the deserted courtyard, apparently expected to carry her luggage upstairs on her own.

It was late in the afternoon before the Baroness put in an appearance at the door of Isobel's room. Once again she was dressed in black, but to Isobel's eyes it seemed that her face was more deeply lined, her expression even harder and sterner than she remembered. She extended a hand to Isobel, and offered her a wrinkled cheek to kiss.

'Isobel my dear, you must excuse me for not being there to welcome you.'

'Oh, that's quite alright—I was tired after the journey. I've been asleep up here since I arrived. Where's Rudolf?'

'I'm afraid Rudolf . . .' she paused, 'Rudolf will be with you shortly, my dear.'

'Is he well? It's just that you mentioned an accident, and I was so worried he might have . . .'.

'Rudolf is in perfect health.' The Baroness's tone was icy. 'The doctor has ordered him to relax, but apart from that he is fully recovered.'

'But the accident. Was it serious? How did it happen?'

The Baroness smiled, but there was steel in the look she gave Isobel.

'My dear, you really must not alarm yourself. Rudolf will be with you shortly. Then you will be able to see for yourself.'

Isobel found the answer anything but reassuring.

She felt a curious mixture of elation and fear as she dressed for dinner that evening: elation at the thought of seeing Rudolf again, of knowing that within a few days the two of them would be man and wife. And fear? Maybe it was wrong to call it fear. Perhaps it was only nervousness, brought on by weariness and the hours she had spent travelling. But the fluttering sensation in her stomach became worse as she descended the broad, carpeted staircase and made her way across the marbled hall to the drawing-room. She hesitated a moment before opening the huge oak double-doors, and shut her eyes, uttering a silent prayer that Rudolf would be as she remembered him. When she opened them again, the Baroness was standing before her, the doors had parted—and Rudolf could be seen seated at a chair by the fire, reading. He looked up as Isobel entered.

'My dear Rudolf—'

Isobel was about to rush forward and fling her arms around him, but something in his expression stopped her dead in her tracks. Instead of the joy she had expected to see, the joy she herself felt, Rudolf seemed to be peering at her with the terrified, panic-stricken look of a cornered animal, his features lined and distorted as if by some terrible inner sickness of spirit. There was some hideous change in him, and Isobel sensed it immediately. Her arms dropped to her side. Finally Rudolf found his voice.

'What the hell are you doing here, Isobel?'

Lost for words, Isobel stared at him in amazement.

'But Rudolf, I came here to—'

'Never mind your reasons. I gave you clear instructions never—*ever*—to come here again, and you have deliberately disobeyed my orders.'

'Rudolf—what on earth are you talking about?' Isobel felt her voice trembling with bewilderment and pain, tears welling up and beginning to cloud her vision. For a moment she was almost convinced that this was not Rudolf speaking, but some imposter. She had a sudden impulse to run from the room, but Rudolf's voice, a hoarse, thick voice quite unlike the voice she had known and loved, checked her.

'It's no use pretending to me, Isobel. I informed you of my wishes. I never want to set eyes on you again—now go.'

'But the wedding—'

'—There will be no wedding.'

The crushing finality of his words stunned Isobel into silence. But gazing at Rudolf she felt she detected the first signs of a crack in the bitter mask; it was as if, underneath the sickness and fatigue, he too was struggling to contain his emotions. He sank wearily back into his chair before speaking again.

'I am dead, Isobel,—dead as far as you are concerned. Go away and forget me. You read my letter—you know the worst. Now go home, go back to England.'

Isobel was unable to restrain herself any longer.

'*Letter*? What Letter? I haven't had a letter from you in three weeks. If it hadn't been for your mother I would never have known. . . .'

Her voice tailed off into silence. A fearful look of sudden realisation, and fury, had crossed Rudolf's face. In the moments that followed Isobel became aware of the third presence with them in the room, a stern black figure standing silently by the door, looking on. The Baroness came across to them.

'Really, Rudolf. A fine way to greet your bride-to-be. Especially after poor Isobel has travelled such a long way to see you.'

The Baroness's boney fingers were clutching Isobel's arm so tightly she almost cried out. Rudolf was staring at his mother with undisguised hatred and disgust.

'Mother, if this is some insane scheme of yours—'

'Hush Rudolf, you mustn't excite yourself so—remember the doctor's orders. You must have a little trust in me.'

Rudolf let out a bitter snort of derision.

'*Trust you*? I trust you to ruin my life and Isobel's. How dare you invite her here behind my back? If you seriously think I have the slightest intention of marrying her after what happened—'

The Baronesses's voice sank to a whisper.

'Your intentions, Rudolf, do not interest me in the slightest. I have other things to consider. The future of our family, for one. The Tahlmann line *must* be continued; Isobel is carrying your child—the only honourable thing to do under the circumstances is for you to marry the girl and legitimise her brat. Perhaps you see now why it was necessary for me to invite her here.'

'Honourable?' Rudolf's anger had reached boiling point. 'What do you know or care about honour? Where is the honour in wrecking two lives for the sake of the family name? An heir at any price—is that all you care about?'

The Baroness rounded on him with equal fury.

'Yes, Rudolf—I do care. I do care that centuries of tradition could be wiped out without trace. I do care that your spineless sentimental feelings towards this . . . this girl could threaten our family with extinction.' Isobel listened in horror and amazement, feeling the grip on her arm tighten. There was a pause, and the Baroness's voice altered in tone, becoming calmer, almost pleasant. 'But I see Isobel is looking confused. Perhaps we should explain. You see, my dear, we are in a most unfortunate position here. Perhaps Rudolf had better put you in the picture.'

But Rudolf had slumped forward exhausted in his chair, clasping his head in his hands.

'In that case I see I shall have to continue. Unfortunately, Isobel, the child you are carrying in your womb is the only one Rudolf is ever likely to father. You enquired about his accident. It is time you were told the truth. While attending a political meeting in an inn at Nuremberg—held, Rudolf tells me, to protest against the savage terms of the peace about to be signed between our two countries—he was injured by a bomb thrown from the street. Naturally the attack was the work of Bolshevik saboteurs, although I don't suppose the details will concern you. Rudolf was fortunate to escape relatively lightly—others were not so lucky; but he sustained several injuries to his legs and groin, which have left him—' Isobel let out a gasp of horror and wrestled free of the old woman's iron grip. The Baroness continued, '—which have left him permanently scarred, and unable to perform the duties normally expected of a husband or lover. I very much fear that there will be no more romantic excursions to the hunting lodge for Rudolf in future.'

Sobbing, Isobal sank down beside him and attempted to comfort him, but the Baroness continued regardless:

'Rudolf was in hospital for many days while his wounds healed. As soon as he was well enough to return home his first act was to write to you and break off the engagement. Unfortunately he made the mistake of giving me the letter to post. By this time of course we had heard of your pregnancy. Naturally, in his shock and distress, Rudolf felt unable to continue with the relationship. But I took a more practical view. I'm afraid I could not let the chance of a son and heir slip through my grasp.'

Rudolf had listened in silence to his mother's monologue, his head buried in his hands. Now he looked up, eyes red-rimmed, sick at heart.

'A son and heir, mother? What if it's a girl—how will that fit into your little scheme?'

'Come, come Rudolf. You know as well as I do, Isobel will give birth to a boy. The Tahlmanns always do.'

CHAPTER SIX

The Baroness's wishes prevailed. The wedding ceremony took place on the 21st June, just as she had planned, but the congregation was small. Apart from the local cleric, the bride and groom and the Baroness herself, there were only two other relatives and two witnesses present—all of them quite unaware of the tragic circumstances behind the marriage. During the previous few days, Isobel had watched Rudolf's resistance slowly crumble, bowing in the face of his mother's indomitable will. He had remained distant and aloof, inwardly tortured and deep in gloomy thoughts which he did not trouble to confide to her; the accident, as Isobel continued to think of it, had done more than purely physical damage to him. It had broken his spirit. Today, beside her at the altar, he looked more drawn and haggard than ever. There would be no honeymoon, not even a reception after the wedding service. Isobel accepted this bravely, but secretly dreaded the prospect of their new life together.

The Treaty of Versailles was signed by the representatives of the powers concerned—English, German, American and French—a week after the wedding. In the interim Isobel had barely seen her husband, let alone spoken to him, except for one occasion in which he came to her room at night to ask tenderly after her health and about her developing pregnancy. For a moment she had a glimpse of the old Rudolf, loving and concerned, but just as quickly the mask of weary cynicism dropped again; in the morning he was as morose as ever. On the night of the 28th, for the first time, Isobel witnessed Rudolf getting drunk—very drunk. It was not to be the last. The following morning he awoke with a splitting headache, but managed to pull himself together by lunchtime, when he had to attend a meeting in Schwandorf. He refused to tell Isobel what it was all about, merely muttering something about old comrades, ex-servicemen, matters that would be of little interest to a woman.

As her pregnancy advanced, Isobel tired easily and began to feel more and more uncomfortable. By the seventh month she was huge, and her womb felt like the venue for a boxing match. By now she knew she was going to have twins. It felt to her as though they were already fighting.

During the sheer, utter, unmitigated hell of the confinement, Isobel felt sure she was going to die. The first boy was delivered at 22.02 hours and his brother, whom the doctor had feared she was going to lose, at 01.17. The date was the 21st/22nd November.

The first son was christened Johannes Otto, and the younger boy Peter Ernest.

As was the norm in those days Isobel fed both the infants herself. Even after three months, Rudolf still shrank from all contact with her, apart from a dutiful good morning, good night, hello, or goodbye. To the outsider there was no sign of abnormality. Isobel was on reasonable terms with the staff, with the possible exception of Dietrich, who now nursed a bitter hatred for the English, or anyone else who had had a hand in the humiliation of the Fatherland. But between Isobel and the Baroness there was now open hostility. Her initial facade of affection for Isobel had now worn away entirely, and the old woman now had to make a conscious effort to extend to her daughter-in-law even the most elementary courtesies. Rudolf, meanwhile, simply remained sullenly detached.

Matters came to a head between Isobel and Rudolf in the middle of the following April. Rudolf had resumed something of his former vigour and was now extremely fit after a winter of hunting and shooting; his bronzed face and athletic figure were sufficient to turn many a female head. He was unusually attractive to women, the more so to Isobel who, though grieved by her husband's unpredictable, often irascible and even violent behaviour towards her, still felt there was a chance that his spirits would improve, given time. She also told herself that she was now the Baroness and, therefore, in theory at least, Mistress of Tahlmann. Her scant knowledge of German still gave her problems around the house, and the servants took full advantage. When they did not want to understand they would either shrug sullenly or smile patronizingly.

One night while the Baroness was away, Isobel seized her chance to arrange a quiet dinner just for Rudolf and herself. She summoned the housekeeper and in a three-part mix of English, German and gesticulation explained her wishes.

Rudolf had gone to Nuremburg and was not due home till shortly before dinner. Isobel still had plenty of time to dress for the evening, and selected the most alluring attire in her wardrobe. By 8.15 p.m. there was still no sign of Rudolf, and she was sitting in the drawing-room toying with a sherry while she waited for him to return. At last there was the sound of car tyres. Isobel looked out of the window. She bit her lip when she saw two cars parked outside. Who on earth could Rudolf have brought back with him? Why hadn't she been told?

Both Rudolf and the two men with him were drunk. It was raining outside and all three walked straight in without wiping their feet. Rudolf tottered over to where his wife sat, and kissed her on the cheek. Isobel did her best to welcome the guests in spite of their being unexpected and, as far as she was concerned, unwanted. Both men were in the army, part of the 100,000-strong Reichswehr permitted by the Versailles Treaty.

Slurred as his speech was, Rudolf began to try and introduce his companions, but in the confusion Isobel couldn't catch their names.

They had always been in the habit of changing for dinner, but Rudolf defied tradition, and after another few drinks, during which time Isobel was largely ignored, all four trooped into the dining room. The Captain was put on Isobel's right hand and, in deference to convention, she went through the motions of making conversation. But the Captain didn't speak English. The young Lieutenant could get by, and for a while acted as interpreter, an effeminate-looking youth with a girl's mouth, minimal beard and straight fair hair. The chin was on the weak side but his eyes were clear and blue. Isobel would have described him as pretty.

As the meal progressed Isobel hardly spoke but listened to the three men.

The Captain and Rudolf dominated the conversation, and to her surprise Isobel found herself able to understand quite a lot of what was being said. She studied them as they conversed. The Captain was on the short side, but thick-set, with a marked bull neck, small bright piggy eyes, and several scars on his face, the most noticeable being on his cheeks. He had no bridge to his nose, which had been shot away early in the war. An ugly brute of a man, Isobel decided; the thought of waking up in bed with him beside her sent a shiver down her spine. He spoke with fervour about the iniquities of the peace and of the November Criminals, those responsible for the surrender in 1918. He ranted about the weakness of the Berlin Government, and openly preached revolution—if necessary, the setting up of a South German State with Austria. As far as Isobel could make out, Rudolf seemed to be advocating a separatist Bavaria with the return of the Wittelsbach monarchy, to whom he was distantly related.

As soon as it was polite to do so, Isobel excused herself from the table and left them to their politics and brandy.

It was not until an hour later that the guests left, without having the good grace to thank their hostess. Isobel was delighted that she didn't have to face them again.

Sitting up in bed later that night, she heard Rudolf's unsteady footsteps coming up the stairs. By now very drunk, he reeled into her bedroom, a brandy glass loosely clasped in his right hand, a cigar in his left.

'Know who that man was?' Rudolf's tone was ugly and belligerent.

'No. Which one?'

'The Captain of course, not the pretty boy Lieutenant.'

'No. Why should I? You never gave me the courtesy of an intelligible introduction.'

'You'll know him soon enough. And so will all Germany. His name is Ernst Röhm.'

The name meant nothing to her.

Rudolf scowled. 'I'm going to bed,' he said, draining the brandy and casting around for a place to stub out the cigar.

As he lurched towards her, swaying on his feet, Isobel smelt the stink of brandy on his breath and couldn't repress the shudder of fear and disgust. On two previous occasions now, Rudolf's drinking bouts had been the signal for violence.

Through the haze of cigar smoke, Rudolf saw the look in her eyes, and knew it as the same petrified look he had seen on the faces of the animals he hunted. He moved in on his quarry, his features distorted into a grimace. Isobel shrank from him, pulling the eiderdown around her. Rudolf snatched it away and tore at her flimsy nightdress in a single violent sweep.

'I know what you want,' Rudolf smiled, 'You little bitch.'

'Rudolf, please—'

'You little *bitch*—'

A wild blow from Rudolf sent a china lamp-base by Isobel's bedside crashing to the floor.

'You want me to make love to you? Is that what you want?'

Isobel had buried her head in her pillow, her naked body spread out under her husband's gaze, waiting for the blow she knew would come. Rudolf started towards her again, unbuttoning his trousers—

'—I'll make love to you, you bitch. Look at me. *Look at me, bitch.*'

Still Isobel didn't move. Rudolf stepped forward in a rage of anguish and seized his wife by the hair, forcing her head round between his thighs. She had no alternative but to look. She wanted to scream, but nothing, nothing could be forced up through the waves of sickness and pain. In those few moments, all the love she had once felt for him died.

Horrified, she faced the stump of pinkish scar tissue. Shock and disgust fought with pity in her heart as now, at least, she understood the moods, the unpredictability, the drinking, the skulking evasiveness, the aloofness, the bullying. In her heart she cursed the absent Baroness whose scheming had brought her back to marry this monster.

For better for worse, Rudolf was still the father of the twins. Some things could never change. But as the months rolled by and turned to years, life became progressively more hideous for Isobel. The fundamental dislike of the two women for one another reasserted itself and turned to active hatred. The war between them turned into a slow, dreadful Chinese torture.

Johannes and Peter grew rapidly. Rudolf favoured the elder boy, on whom he poured all his frustrated, smothering affections. He would pay scant heed to Peter, who as far as he was concerned was simply the victim of an unfortunate birth. Peter, in compensation, sought his mother's company. Terrified that any favouritism for him would anger his father, Isobel forced herself to push him off with Johannes, but the two quarrelled continuously and could never safely be left alone.

Isobel tried on several occasions to talk to Rudolf, but the moment never seemed appropriate. She had almost left her husband on several occasions. Matters were usually brought to a head after a row following a visit to Tahlmann by friends of Rudolf from the rising National Socialist German Workers Party. Isobel particularly detested Ernest Röhm, who had now become a regular house guest at Tahlmann, but even he paled beside Julius Streicher, the editor of the violently anti-semitic local newspaper, '*Der Stürmer*'. That this filthy rag should be left lying around her home was bad enough. That its perverted editor should be a frequent visitor to her table was more than she could take. His manners were a disgrace, his talk repulsive.

Streicher appalled her. Without heed to the presence of a lady, and in labourer's epithets, he embarked on lurid descriptions of sub-human over-sexed Jews seducing innocent German Christian girls, mostly against their wills, and thereby polluting the purity of Aryan blood. Every detail recounted and gloated over. Isobel was speechless with disgust and outrage. Although she had never dared mention the fact to Rudolf, her own mother had been a Jewess.

On a similar occasion Streicher was seated further down the table, and the guest of honour, appropriately placed, was a man she had not met before. He had pleased her by his obvious delight in meeting the children. He also spoke with a pronounced Austrian accent, but seemed to lack the uncouth manners of his friends, talking quietly to Isobel and asking about England, about Esher, and about her father. Isobel studied the man's short dark hair, long pointed nose, the comical little toothbrush moustache, the eyes—those dark brown, hypnotic eyes. Adolf Hitler was not a bit as she had pictured him; she had to make a conscious effort to reconcile the comparatively mild demeanour of her guest with the real Hitler, the ruthless, ambitious Nazi leader, the megalomaniac who had already adopted the slogan "ein Volk, ein Reich, ein Führer". In the course of their conversation he hardly touched on politics, and when he did, he spoke only in the most moderate terms of his plans to make Germany great again, to restore something of the Reich's national pride and to unite the German-speaking peoples in one Empire. Isobel found herself agreeing with him: there was nothing wrong with a measure of national pride. In spite of living in Germany she was still proud, after all, to be English. As Hitler finally observed: 'A nation without pride is a defeated nation. Germany has no pride. Until it is restored we will remain defeated.' Abruptly he changed the subject.

By now Rudolf had graduated from Nazi sympathizer, to Nazi member. But ostrich-like, Isobel buried her head in the sand and chose to ignore what was going on round her. In public she played the dutiful wife to Rudolf. In private, to all intents and purposes, they led separate lives. Provided they didn't discuss politics, the arrangement seemed to suit them both. It was only his mother who caused the rows, and on occasions they were bitter and violent. It was almost as if the old woman blamed her daughter-in-law for her only son's emasculation. A more rational person would have cherished Isobel, who had borne not one but two sons to carry on the Tahlmann line.

Rudolf taught Johannes to shoot and, grudgingly, did the same for Peter, so that by the time they were twelve years old, both boys were accomplished wing shots. Of the two, Peter was marginally the better, but in every other sport there was little to choose between them.

Isobel made an annual pilgrimage to see her father from 1923 onwards, but Rudolf had refused ever to let her take Johannes with her. Peter was allowed to go, but not his eldest son and heir. Isobel saw no point in arguing. In any case, Johannes preferred to stay at home, where he was utterly spoilt by his father, and would probably have hated England.

In 1932 Isobel and Peter spent their Christmas at Esher, returning a month or so later to find the Weimar Republic in its death throes, but still intact. They arrived home on the 28th January, amidst considerable gossip and turmoil. That day the aged President Hindenburg had sacked the German Chancellor, General Kurt von Schleicher.

Rudolf was not at home to welcome his wife and son. That courtesy was left to the Dowager Baroness, who performed the task with a chilly punctiliousness. She apologized for her son's absence. 'Important business' was the excuse. Johannes was holding his grandmother's hand. He dutifully kissed his mother's cheek, and pinched Peter's arm when no one was looking.

That evening Isobel ate alone. She heaved a sigh of relief when her mother-in-law excused herself with a headache and retired to her rooms. Isobel also went early to bed.

The next day, Sunday, the nearby towns were filled with a constant stream of rumours and counter-rumours, but little of it filtered through to Tahlmann. Isobel went riding with Peter in the morning. In the afternoon, as usual, she went alone. Peter had gone out with Johannes and a keeper to shoot some rabbits. The old Baroness remained in her suite. Rudolf returned that evening.

On Monday 30th January, Rudolf invited a group of his cronies round to celebrate the momentous event which had taken place that day. Adolf Hitler had been appointed Chancellor of Germany, and the Third Reich was now officially born.

Early in the evening bottles appeared and the gathering soon degenerated into drunken revelry. Seeing the course the evening was likely to follow, Isobel had quickly decided to take no part in the proceedings and had retired upstairs to lock herself in her room. But the sound of raucous laughter, occasionally interspersed with the thump of heavy footsteps and the noise of breaking glass, made sleep impossible. Isobel attempted to shut her ears to the din and buried herself under the bedclothes. But in her nearby room the old Baroness could stand the racket no longer. Pulling on her dressing gown she made her way downstairs, determined to give Rudolf a piece of her mind.

Flinging open the doors of the drawing room, she marched inside. The earlier party of Nazis had now moved on, leaving Rudolf and the chauffeur Dietrich drinking alone together amidst a litter of broken bottles and cigar butts. Stale tobacco smoke and alcohol fumes hung in the atmosphere like a thick fog. The Baroness cast a stern puritanical eye over the debris, shocked not only by the devastated scene but the sight of her son drinking with one of the servants. She stormed up to Dietrich.

'Get out of here this instant.'

Dietrich staggered to his feet and lurched to the door, giving the Baroness an ironic Nazi salute as he passed.

The Baroness ignored him and turned to Rudolf.

'As for you, you disgust me. How dare you foul my drawing-room with this riff-raff? I will not have my house turned into a pig sty by those louts. Have you no pride?'

Rudolf shut his eyes and puffed a cloud of acrid cigar smoke in his mother's direction.

'I suggest you mind your own business, mother. If I choose to invite my friends here for a small celebration, that's my affair.'

The Baroness's temper flared.

'And am I supposed to stand aside and allow the Tahlmann home to be defiled by those scum? I have suffered their filthy manners and their scurrilous talk for long enough. I insist that they never set foot inside this house again. Do I made myself plain?'

'Abundantly, mother. Perhaps it would interest you to know that the men you so disparagingly refer to are among the most powerful in Germany today.'

'In that case my heart bleeds for Germany. To think of the Fatherland in the hands of those drunken upstarts!'

'The Fatherland? What does an old woman like you care for the Fatherland? Take a look around you, mother. Take a look at what the Führer has already done for this country of ours—'

The Baroness spat out her reply in a fury. 'Führer? Paul Hindenburg is my Führer—not your jumped-up Austrian house-painter.'

Rudolf suddenly realized how deeply he hated her, hated her domination of him. She had ruled him and she had ruined his life. Tottering on his feet he staggered towards her, intending to put his hand over her mouth, to quell further sedition against the party and the leader. His foot slipped and he lurched with outstretched hand, catching the Baroness a glancing blow to the side of her head. A slight woman, she was caught off balance and fell backwards, her skull smashing against one of the jutting friezes on the marble fireplace. With scarcely more than a faint gasp she collapsed on the floor. Her eyes were open, but she lay on the floor motionless. Rudolf stared at the prostrate form, watching as a pool of blood slowly oozed from the back of the old woman's head. It needed no second glance to realize that she was dead.

Rudolf was bending over the body when Isobel walked into the room having heard the row and come downstairs to investigate. Still swaying unsteadily, he turned round, stunned to silence, too drink-sodden to comprehend what he had done.

Isobel caught her breath and put her hand to her mouth. Rudolf looked back at the fallen body of his mother. Without a trace of emotion, he announced: 'The old lady must have had a heart attack. She just collapsed and hit her head as she fell.'

CHAPTER SEVEN

The same night violence erupted all over Germany with a series of pitched battles between Nazi troops and Communists. The next day Hitler broadcast a reassuringly moderate speech over the wireless. All would be well. The people were asked to remain calm.

The doctor who had been called to Tahlmann confirmed the cause of the Baroness's death as heart failure. Her funeral took place, in bitterly cold weather, on February 1st—the same day that Hitler obtained a decree to dissolve the Reichstag and declared that elections would be held on March 5th.

Rudolf had hardly spoken a word since his mother's death, not at any rate to Isobel. She did not accompany her husband to the large and lavish funeral. Rudolf played the role of the grieving son without difficulty. Only Isobel saw through his mourning and remorse; she knew that however much relief Rudolf may have felt now that the dominant influence in his life had been removed, his very real concern sprang from emotions of fear—fear that the truth about his mother's death might be discovered.

Rudolf made scant mention of his mother during the following months. He busied himself with work for the party and was frequently absent for days at a time. He never told his wife what this work involved; only when he was going away and when he would be returning. Loathsome associates of his from the Nazi top brass continued to be entertained at the house and Isobel, weakly rather than through politeness, continued to play the part of hostess.

There was something of a party at Tahlmann on July 2nd, the day after Hitler had summoned the S.A. leaders to a meeting at Bad Reichenall. The S.A., the brownshirts, the original Nazi storm troopers, had now been welded into a private army more powerful even than the Reichswehr, by its commander, Ernst Röhm. This onetime frequenter of Isobel's table was now second only to the Führer in power and influence.

Rudolf had begun to take delight in humiliating his wife at his little gatherings. This evening, with a dinner service set for twenty guests, the Baron insisted that a small, dark S.S. Officer, with silver insignia and death's head on his peaked cap, sit at his wife's right hand. Isobel was outraged to discover that her neighbour at table was none other than Dietrich the chauffeur, now resplendent in his Nazi regalia.

But this was not quite the final drama in their mockery of a marriage. One afternoon Rudolf and Isobel were taking tea together in the drawing-room. As usual, the conversation was politely banal. Isobel had been given no warning of what would happen when, to Rudolf's obvious delight, Johannes strutted into the room, proudly wearing his new Hitler Youth uniform, his arm raised in the Nazi salute. Isobel was aghast. She sprang to her feet and ordered her son to remove the uniform at once. Then she turned to Rudolf.

'I will not permit my son to join that disgusting organization.'

Rudolf was momentarily taken aback by her vehemence. But Isobel knew perfectly well that the Youth movement was a junior branch of the brown-shirted S.A. and had already sworn that no son of hers would have anything to do with it.

'How dare you, Rudolf? I presume I'm right in thinking this was your idea?'

Her husband smiled at her mockingly.

'On the contrary, my dear, the idea came from Johannes himself, although naturally I gave him every encouragement. I only wish that Peter showed the same eagerness to serve his country. But perhaps that's too much to hope for.'

Isobel flushed angrily and set down her tea-cup.

'I will not have it. I may not be able to prevent *you* making a fool of yourself with your filthy Nazi friends but I certainly intend to prevent Johannes.' She turned to face Johannes, who had been standing sullenly in the background listening. 'Johannes, I told you to go and take those clothes off.'

Johannes said nothing. He stood where he was, looking first at his mother and then at his father. Now he turned back to Rudolf.

'You're wasting your breath, Isobel,' said Rudolf, getting to his feet and placing an arm round Johannes' shoulder. 'The boy's mind is made up, and I doubt very much if anything you can say will change it for him.'

'We'll see about that. Johannes, I order you to go and change this minute.'

Johannes took one hesitant step, but his father checked him. 'Take no notice of your mother. Stay where you are. She doesn't understand.'

Isobel found herself barely able to control her anger and frustration.

'I understand—I understand only too well. I've listened to you poisoning the boy's mind with your perverted doctrines long enough to know everything I need to know. I've heard all I want to hear about your precious Führer and your precious Fatherland, and I despise every word of it. You're sick, Rudolf—your mind's diseased. And now you want to infect your son with the same filthy poison. But I won't let you. Johannes, for the last time, take that uniform off.'

Again Johannes turned to his father, torn between the two.

'Stay here, Johannes,' said Rudolf. 'You will do as I say.'

'Yes, father.'

There was silence while the boy sat down at Rudolf's side.

'Very well then,' said Isobel. 'I'm leaving. And I'm going to take the boys back to England with me.'

'When?'

'As soon as I can make arrangements.'

Peter had been out prowling round the the estate with his gun, his favourite pastime in the school holidays. The moment he entered the house he heard his parents' voices raised in heated argument. He hurried to the source of the commotion.

'We'll see about that,' his father said as the boy entered and rushed to his mother's side.

'There's nothing you can do to stop me, Rudolf, nothing. I mean what I say. I can't think why I didn't have the sense to leave you and this sick, sick country months, years ago. I only stayed because I actually thought you could provide a better life for the boys than I could. My God, I must have been mad.'

'You're a fool, Isobel. If you try to take Johannes from here I assure you I'll have you arrested. I have influence here. You would never get further than the end of the drive.'

'And I don't want to go to England,' interjected the elder boy. 'I want to stay here. This is my home, this is where I belong.'

'You won't have to, Johannes, don't worry,' said Rudolf. Addressing himself to Isobel again, he continued, a note of triumph in his voice. 'There you are. The boy wants to stay.'

Isobel, crestfallen, walked over to Johannes and put her hand on his shoulder, determined to give the boy a chance to make up his own mind.

'Come with me to England, Johannes. You would be happy there. It is a good country.'

'Our troop leader says England is a decadent country and we only lost the war because the Jewish Bolsheviks stabbed us in the back. He says the next time the Fatherland will not only conquer England but the whole of Europe.'

'He told you that?'

'Yes, mother.'

'Did he also tell you that you are half English?'

The boy hesitated, clearly out of his depth. Rudolf then turned to Peter, who had stood by silently.

'Do you want to go to England with your mother, or stay here?'

Isobel bit her lip as she waited for Peter to answer. She had always told herself that it was wrong to favour one son more than the other, but deep down inside her she knew that it was Peter for whom she cared the most.

Peter didn't hesitate. His voice now was that of a young man, conscious of the importance of his decision. As if to assert his approaching manhood, he adopted his most resonant tone.

'I shall go with *you*, mother. I think you will need me.'

'Very well, Isobel,' said Rudolf, 'I will permit you and Peter to return to England. You will need money, of course, and I will see that the family lawyers provide it. I propose to settle the sum of £50,000 upon you in trust for life, and a similar amount for Peter. I do not wish to be accused of turning a wife and child out to starve.'

'Very generous of you, Rudolf,' said Isobel, 'And the conditions? I assume there are strings attached?'

'Naturally,' said Rudolf. 'You surely don't expect me to give away £100,000 for nothing.'

'Naturally not,' countered Isobel. 'What are your terms?'

'They are very simple and, in the circumstances, I think you'll agree that they are sensible.'

'I'm waiting.'

'I will make over the money to you as soon as my solicitors advise me that you have complied with my conditions.' Rudolf took a deep breath and announced: 'I intend to arrange for a record of your death and that of Peter in a car crash to be officially registered in Berlin.'

Isobel gave a gasp of horror. She had heard of the methods that the S.A. and S.S. employed. Sinister names had started to be whispered abroad, among them that of Heinrich Himmler, Bavarian State Police President. With a chill of fear she thought back to the death of the Baroness; Rudolf had not hesitated to remove her when she stood in his path, and he would not hesitate now . . . But no, she was jumping to conclusions—she must get a grip on herself. Rudolf sensed the trend of her thoughts.

'No, Isobel. The idea had occurred to me. And it could be arranged, of course, but that is not what I had in mind.' He laughed. 'For your sake, Isobel, and for the records here, I shall arrange to fake the deaths. You see, when the Reich conquers England—and we will, believe me—I want no record of your existence to remain in Germany. As I say, it is for your sake and for Peter's. I don't have to go on, do I?'

'So you want our deaths registered in Germany. I suppose I have no option?'

'Not really.' Rudolf had played cat and mouse long enough and was getting bored. 'As soon as you get back to England you will destroy your German passports and travel documents. Then you will renounce the name and title of Tahlmann and adopt any other name that you may choose for yourself and your son. You will undertake never to mention the family name again, never to make contact with me, and never to make any future claim of any sort against the estate. If you agree, then I will let you go and assist you both to leave.'

Isobel heaved a sigh of relief.

'If that is all you ask, then I agree. Peter?' The boy looked at his mother and nodded.

Isobel saw no point in further argument. Why rock the boat which seemed to have stabilized at long last? She would always entertain doubts about doing the best by Peter, but as long as Johannes lived, the elder boy would get everything anyway, money, title, and land. She persuaded herself that Peter would not miss anything by renouncing the family name.

'It's agreed then, Rudolf. I shall re-adopt my maiden name and my son shall be called Peter Hutley.'

Within the week arrangements were completed, but not before Johannes and Peter had had a final quarrel. The trouble began when the older boy started to tease the younger. Peter tolerated it for a while in the vain hope that he and his brother might part friends. It was useless.

'I hate you, and I loathe my mother. I am ashamed of being half English,' Johannes hissed. 'We'll be glad to see you go.'

Peter turned away, and made to leave.

'You don't belong here any more, you know. You never did.' Johannes continued. 'One day, when I am older, I'll kill you both.'

Peter wrenched himself around and, summoning up all his strength, struck out at Johannes as hard as he could. The elder boy screamed in pain, blood streaming from his nose, and clasped a hand over his eyes.

'You swine,' he sobbed. 'One day I *will* get you. I'll get my own back, you'll see.' Peter moved to hit him again. Johannes cringed.

'No, no, don't hit me again, please,' he whimpered. Peter turned his back, but at once Johannes sprang on him from behind, fists flailing, nails clawing.

Before any more damage could be done the door burst open and in walked Rudolf. He pulled the two boys apart.

'Stop it at once, both of you,' he ordered. The physical hostilities were brought to an abrupt halt.

'What's all this about?'

'It's Peter's fault, he started it,' Johannes wailed.

'Is that true, Peter?'

'No, father.'

'Yes it is, he's a liar. He said he hated me and he hated you and . . .'

Peter didn't bother to deny the accusations. He knew from bitter experience that his father would only side with Johannes. In his eyes the boy could do no wrong. Peter knew what was coming. A stinging blow caught him on his left ear, nearly knocking him to the floor.

'You little cur, Peter. I had hoped that we might all part friends, but I see that is impossible. Now go to your room and stay there.'

Peter, seeing that protest was useless, didn't argue. Choking back his own tears, hating his father and despising Johannes, he fled from the scene and raced to his bedroom. Once alone, his tears flowed freely.

Two days later he and Isobel left Tahlmann. Johannes didn't even bother to say goodbye. Peter was glad for himself, and never wanted to set eyes on his brother again, but he was sorry for his mother, who he knew was deeply hurt. Rudolf drove them to the main station in Nuremburg. He at least made an effort to close the chapter with a veneer of affability. He wished Isobel and Peter luck and even made something approaching an apology for 'the way things had turned out', before seeing his wife and son safely on to the train.

Isobel reciprocated, but her heart was full of fear and foreboding. Something was brewing, she felt sure, though she had no idea what it might be. The train started to move. Isobel and Peter exchanged smiles, if only to reassure one another. Had Isobel looked out of the window and seen Rudolf standing on the platform, his lonely figure wreathed in smoke and steam, her mind might momentarily have been cast back to a similar parting after her first visit to Tahlmann. Now the circumstances were different, so very different. Rudolf remembered, though, and as the train disappeared, he wept. He wept for what might have been, had his body and his mind not been crippled those long years ago.

CHAPTER EIGHT

Isobel was firmly convinced that Rudolf would break his word and had planned all along to make their accident anything but a convenient fabrication. She would not relax until the train was safely over the border. Peter sensed her apprehension and did his youthful best to reassure his mother, but each time the train stopped at a station she would stare out of the window, waiting, waiting, until the engines started once more. Every time a ticket inspector or other official asked to see their papers Isobel would turn pale, her pulse racing.

Less than thirty minutes from the French border, the train made an unscheduled stop. Two armed, uniformed S.S. men entered the compartment and asked to see Isobel's papers. She opened her handbag and gave the documents to the senior of the two men. He scrutinized them for a moment or two. Isobel's heart sank as the man folded them up again and, instead of giving them back, put them into his pocket. Coldly he said: 'You will come with us, please.'

Desperately Isobel stood her ground.

'Is there something wrong with our papers?'

The S.S. man declined to answer and simply reiterated his command.

'You will come with us. We have our orders.'

'What about our luggage?' Isobel pleaded.

'That will be taken care of. Now come, please.'

Granite-faced, the men ushered Isobel and Peter from their compartment and out to a waiting car. They were unceremoniously bundled into the vehicle and driven off at high speed.

Isobel was convinced that their end was near and sat silently holding Peter's hand. She should have guessed. No, she should have known. A Nazi was not to be trusted. The £100,000 settlement was simply a bait—a bait she had stupidly swallowed. Why should her husband part with such a fortune when it was so easy to have her and Peter quietly done away with? She was not worried for herself. Her life was, and had been for some time past, quite meaningless. But there was Peter, scarcely yet a teenager, with everything before him. Somehow she must escape, she must get away to England and safety.

The car stopped at a building outside which dangled a red, white and black flag with the sinister swastika at its centre. Two sentries in black uniforms and steel helmets remained motionless as the party of four entered the police district headquarters. Isobel was now more certain than ever that neither she nor Peter would ever leave the place alive.

The boy and his mother were led with no preamble straight to a cell and the door was shut with a clunk behind them. The key turned in the lock and then they were left.

After an hour or so Peter wanted to relieve himself; Isobel, shaking with fear, could hardly contain herself either. She beat on the door for more than five minutes. At last it was opened, and an orderly inquired what might be the matter. Isobel explained without delicacy. The orderly pointed to a small cupboard and shut the door again, locking it before retracing his steps along the passageway.

Isobel opened the cupboard and took out a rather dirty and smelly enamel bowl. Peter turned his back whilst his mother used it first and then he too attended to the demands of nature. Once more they heard footsteps approaching.

Isobel found it impossible to reassure her son. She was so terrified that it was the boy who did his best to comfort his mother.

The door swung open. Isobel threw her arms around Peter's neck and kissed him. An S.S. officer stood in the doorway.

'Come with me,' he commanded. Meekly they followed him down the corridor and up a flight of stairs at the top of which was a shiny varnished door. The young officer knocked.

'Come,' a voice from inside responded. The S.S. man opened the door and held it, motioning to Isobel and Peter to enter. As they did so, a smiling man rose from the large desk at which he had been sitting.

'Ah, Baroness,' he began, holding his hand out in greeting. Isobel shrank back, clasping Peter's hand.

The S.S. man could see the terror on both their faces.

'Baroness,' he laughed. 'You look alarmed.' Isobel couldn't reply.

'Please sit down, Baroness, and you too, young man.' Isobel and Peter obeyed.

'A thousand apologies. There has been a mistake.'

At last Isobel found her tongue. A mistake? Then, they might yet be safe.

'What do you mean?' she asked tentatively.

'My dear Baroness, I mean just that. Some stupid

officer has confused you with a wanted person.'

'How? Why?'

'You need not concern yourself with that. It is sufficient for you to know that the emergent Reich has many enemies and would-be saboteurs. Believe me, I am sincerely sorry for the unpardonable inconvenience you have been put to.'

Isobel allowed herself a huge sigh of relief, but the S.S. man chose to ignore it.

'What about our luggage?'

'Do not worry, Baroness. Your luggage is downstairs in the general office. I see from your visa that you are travelling to England for a holiday with Peter. I hope you have an excellent vacation. England is a country I would love to visit one day. Is it as beautiful as we are told?'

'More so. In England you can say what you wish, without fear. There is beauty in freedom too, you know.'

'Come now, Baroness, the Reich is free enough,' the S.S. man countered. 'Such restrictions as we have are necessary to protect our freedom from Jews and Communists. Sometimes it is necessary to surrender a small measure of what we call freedom in order to protect ourselves from those who would otherwise destroy us. But let's not argue, Baroness.'

The officer turned to Peter. 'Now then, young man. Are you hungry?'

Peter nodded. Isobel shook her head and protested but the officer would not be put off.

'Then please allow me to give you lunch. Then I will drive you to the station and personally see you on to the 15.47, which will take you all the way to Calais and the steamer.'

Isobel tried to protest, but it was useless.

'Are you being met at the other end?'

'We were going to be—before all this.'

'My apologies again, Baroness. Tell me who is meeting you.'

'My father.'

'Where?'

'In London.'

'Leave it to me. Give me his telephone number and I will get a message to him. Is that fair?'

'Thank you.'

And so it was that Isobel sat down as a guest of the S.S. to the last meal she would ever have in Germany.

CHAPTER NINE

Later the next day Isobel and Peter arrived back in Esher. Isobel, with minimal luggage and stripped of all the Tahlmann jewellery, had very little to show for fourteen years of marriage. She could not even claim Peter as a positive result since he would have happened anyway. Isobel was approaching forty and the years had left their mark on her, but now she was away from the hate and the pain. Now she no longer had to entertain men she despised, or attempt to maintain a facade of harmony. She could relax at last. The relief was immense. Rescued from the brink of nervous collapse, Isobel quickly responded to the love and patient understanding that her father gave her and her son. Nobody could have been happier than Ernest when he received the news of their return. He made no attempt to disguise his relief and delight that the marriage was over.

Isobel kept her part of the bargain and called herself by her maiden name of Hutley from the moment she arrived home. Peter was sent to one of the less well-known public schools. To begin with, the other pupils were puzzled by his slight accent, but Peter, always a good mimic, rapidly lost any trace of the gutteral and soon passed for a perfectly normal English teenage schoolboy.

The small house in Esher soon became too cramped for two adults and a growing boy and in October 1932 it was sold and the Hutleys moved to a smart house in a private avenue in Maidenhead, Berkshire, with several acres of land. Isobel had been offered a job there by an old boyfriend in a local estate agent's office, and had accepted the position eagerly, not because she needed the money, since the income in 1932 from a six-figure sum was enough to ensure comfort, but rather to keep herself occupied, especially during the term, when Peter was away.

Peter came home to Maidenhead for the Christmas holidays, looking forward to a chance to potter around with his gun. A 16-bore made by Krupps of Essen, it had been intended as his thirteenth birthday present, but Rudolf had given it to his son as a goodbye gift. Isobel resumed her riding and kept a horse on a friend's farm—the same spot where Peter was given leave to rough shoot.

Johannes, meanwhile, was delighted to be rid of the twin he hated. Peter had won every physical disagreement they had ever had, and most of the verbal ones as well. Though born with a natural affection for his mother, he had cleaved to his father when the family became divided. The more his parents fought, the wider had become the gulf between Isobel and the boy, and the stronger grew his detestation for Peter, of whom he was insanely jealous.

By the time the split came between his parents, Johannes had no difficulty in choosing sides. He had already persuaded himself to look down on his mother, and felt a burning shame when he remembered that he had suckled at the nipple of a decadent English woman. With Isobel's departure the cause of that shame was removed, and Johannes' happiness was complete.

The new housekeeper, a young local girl by the name of Magda Ziegler, was strict enough, but with his father Johannes could and did get away with metaphorical murder.

Rudolf, his mind warped by his physical infirmity, continued to entertain his friends at Tahlmann, and the house soon became known as the infamous haunt of the very dregs of the Nazi party: the pimps and perverts, the thugs and murderers of the S.A. and their hangers-on. Once the scene of glittering high-society gatherings, the Tahlmann mansion became the venue for frequent orgies of drinking and homosexuality. The Gestapo carefully documented this activity.

For Rudolf, matters came to a head in June 1934, when the German Vice-Chancellor, Franz von Papen, made a sensational speech expressing the wish of the conservative middle-class that Hitler should clean up the party and, in particular, get rid of the more extreme elements of the S.A. Von Papen included a demand for the head of the leader of the brownshirts himself, Ernst Röhm, whose power was second only to that of the Führer.

Röhm sensed the danger, and to demonstrate his loyalty to Hitler he published a communiqué in the June 19th edition of the party newspaper, the *Völkischer Beobachter*, effectively dismissing the entire S.A. for a month by giving them 28 days' leave, commencing on July 1st. Many, if not most, of the senior S.A. commanders arranged to go away during the unexpected furlough, but before they dispersed Röhm arranged a special farewell dinner. He left for the Spa town of Bad Wiesse, south of Munich, and the Hotel Hauslbauer. Alarmed by Röhm's movements, S.S. leaders Himmler and Heydrich sent reports to Hitler that a *coup d'état* was going to be mounted in Munich.

On the 29th, Hitler arrived in Bad Godesberg to spend the weekend at the Hotel Dreesen. The same morning Himmler flew in from Berlin to bring him the latest reports, most of which were either faked or were mere figments of his own disordered imagination. Hitler was persuaded that he must act to pre-empt the conspirators. All day the Führer hesitated, while Göring, Himmler and

Goebbels urged him to act against his closest comrade.

The weather was oppressive, the air stifling, and the huge grey banks of a threatening storm formed a perfect backcloth for the tension of the hour. In the early evening there was a downpour, and the rain cooled the atmosphere sufficiently to encourage decisive thinking. In brief, clipped phrases, Hitler issued his orders. He and Goebbels would leave for Munich after dinner.

They landed at Oberwiesenfeld Airfield at 04.00 hours on the 30th June. At 05.00 Hitler, escorted by an armoured car of the Reichswehr, and heading a unit of the S.S. Liebstandarte, made his way to the Hotel Hauslbauer, where Röhm and his comrades were staying. Among the gathering at the hotel was Rudolf von Tahlmann.

In spite of the innocent scene which met his eyes at the Hotel Hauslbauer, it did not appear to occur to the Führer to doubt Himmler and Heydrich's dire warnings that a coup was about to be launched. The table in the hotel dining room was already set for Röhm's farewell dinner and it seemed odd, to say the least, that on the morning of a counter-revolution, the chief conspirators should still be asleep in their respective beds.

The S.A. guard on the door was arrested without resistance. The others faced a rude awakening. Almost all those present, including Rudolf, were summarily dressed and handcuffed. Within the hour they found themselves on their way to Munich and Stadelheim Prison. By 14.00 hours more than 200 people were being held under heavy S.S. guard. Later in the afternoon, Hitler studied the list compiled for him by the Gestapo and with a red pencil he marked 110 names, ordering that they should be executed immediately.

In the evening an orderly was personally instructed by Hitler to offer a pistol to Röhm. Röhm refused to take it. With ill-concealed contempt for the man whom he, more than anyone else, had helped to absolute power, he observed: 'If I am to be killed, then let Adolf do it himself.' Moments later two S.S. officers entered the cell and fired several shots point-blank. One of them was Theodor Eicke, later to attain notoriety as the Commandant of Dachau Concentration Camp. Bending one knee, he leaned forward over Röhm's body and administered the *coup de grace*.

Rudolf survived his old friend by less than one hour. He and five others were marched out into a courtyard, there to face a firing squad. Rudolf refused a blindfold. At a loss to know why he was being killed, he accepted his lot almost without protest, not caring particularly that his body was about to die and knowing now more clearly than ever that life had really ended for him with a hand grenade thrown in a Nuremburg street fifteen years ago.

The commander of the execution squad ordered his men to level their machine pistols. Rudolf did not flinch. There was hardly a moment's pause before a burst of automatic fire extinguished the lives of the six victims.

Nobody ever knew how or why the name of the Baron Rudolf von Tahlmann, an honorary Sturmbannführer in the S.S., had appeared on the Führer's death list. It could have been a genuine error—perhaps a confusion with an S.A. major called Tahlheim who was executed a week later. In his career in the S.S. Rudolf had certainly made enemies; perhaps one of them—one with the power to pull strings—had informed against him, drawing the Gestapo's attention to Rudolf's close links with Röhm, or to the notoriety of the Tahlmann home as a scene for drunken and frequently debauched gatherings. Whatever the reason, the fact remains that the Führer himself put a red mark beside the name of Tahlmann.

Rudolf's case was discussed subsequently at the very highest level. The name struck an immediate chord in the memory of Hermann Göring, who declared that he remembered the Baron as a fellow ex-fighter pilot. Though their acquaintance had been short, Göring claimed to have liked him well enough. The dossier on the family showed that Rudolf had been the father of two twin sons, one a fourteen-year-old schoolboy, and that the other boy, together with his mother, had been killed in a car crash whilst on holiday in England.

It is possible that Rudolf's death pricked what ever shreds of conscience the Nazi hierarchy may still have possessed in that summer of 1934. At any rate, Göring undertook to visit the boy and console him, out of loyalty to the orphaned son of an old comrade.

Göring and Johannes met for the first time about a week later. From the outset, Johannes became an ardent devotee of the fat and jovial "Uncle Hermann", as Göring told the boy he wished to be known. Johannes, who had been in the care of the housekeeper and the family solicitors since his father's death, was already over his grief and was thrilled to be visited by so important a national figure as the famous fighter ace who, like his own father, had been awarded the "Pour le Mérite" and had also belonged to the legendary Richthofen squadron. Göring for his part was impressed by the boy's smart bearing and the obvious pride with which he wore the brown uniform of the Hitler Youth, and took to him at once. Against his better judgement he told Johannes that his father had died a hero—that he had been killed fighting a rebellious S.A. unit, and that the boy could forever be proud of him.

From then on the young Baron found himself under a very special patronage. Without his father to spoil him, Johannes' character changed abruptly. He had tried throwing his weight about once or twice but had been speedily cut down to size by the strict Magda Ziegler, the Tahlmann housekeeper. Magda, the daughter of impoverished though aristocratic parents was a formidable young woman of twenty-seven, who now proceeded to run the house and Johannes with all the stern disciplinarian zeal of the late Baroness herself. The Tahlmann family solicitor had suggested Magda for the job soon after the death of the old Dowager. Rudolf's Nuremburg lawyer had picked the new housekeeper well. She was his niece, and shared his ambition.

If formidable was a suitable epithet to apply to Magda, it certainly referred to her will-power rather than her physical attributes. Though not unattractive, she did little to beautify herself. Average in height and build, she invariably wore her blonde hair in plaits over the top of her head. Her eyes were grey and cold, her nose verging on the large, and her mouth conveyed an impression of determination.

Johannes, in the meantime, did not object to being put in his place by Magda. On the contrary, he enjoyed it. His immature adolescent mind whirled with erotic fantasies, in which he saw himself stripping the dignity off this woman whom fate, in the person of his intestate father and her solicitor uncle, had seen fit to make his unofficial guardian. Johannes was quite certain that he was in love with Magda and would bed her one day—one day, when he was older.

He left school at the end of 1937 and volunteered for the Luftwaffe. The following February he was notified of his acceptance and ordered to report to a school of Military Training. The night before he left for Wildpark-Werder, near the holiday area of the Havel lake district, west of Berlin, he decided that he would throw a farewell party for a few friends. Magda had other ideas. Approaching her thirty-first birthday now, her future seemed suddenly far from secure. Firstly, there was Johannes' impending departure, and then all the uncertainties of approaching war. She persuaded Johannes to compromise. His friends would come for drinks. Then Magda would prepare a special dinner just for the two of them. Johannes gave in, but not without some show of truculence. He dared not upset Magda since he needed her to run Tahlmann until he could find a wife, but his dreams of bedding her were a thing of the past. Although she was certainly sufficiently well bred for his tastes, he saw no future in getting involved with a penniless woman, all but thirteen years his senior. But Magda had other ideas.

Johannes was far too self-centred to form deep or lasting relationships, and had been careless in his choice of friends—a score of assorted hangers-on who came either for free drinks or because it boosted their ego to claim the Baron as a friend. During the farewell celebrations Johannes got a little drunk, sufficiently so for his guard to drop. When the last guest had left, Magda appeared. Johannes blinked at her. He had never seen her dressed so alluringly. She was wearing an elegantly-cut full-length evening dress, showing just sufficient cleavage to titillate and not enough to give offence. And the hair. It was down, loose below the shoulders, a flowing golden blonde mane. Tonight Magda looked ten years younger, and ten times more beautiful.

When they had finished eating, they talked over coffee and brandy, and Magda controlled further alcoholic intake with accomplished artistry, knowing Johannes normally drank sparingly and was unused to brandy: too much would spoil her plans. Rising from the table Johannes thanked her for a marvellous evening and an exquisite meal, and announced he was going to bed: had to leave at the crack of dawn next day and had to get an early night. Magda pushed her chair away and followed Johannes to the bottom of the stairs. She stopped there and watched the young Baron climb the curving flight. When he reached the top Magda called to him.

'Good night, Herr Baron.'

Johannes stopped, turned round and looked down at her. Pausing for a little longer than was necessary to take in the plunge of her neckline, he smiled.

'Sleep well, liebe Magda.'

Slightly unsteady on his feet, he walked along the landing to his bedroom. He opened the door, entered and closed it behind him. In five minutes he was in bed, and in a further ten, fast asleep. He remained so for maybe another twenty minutes. He never heard his bedroom door open nor the quiet footsteps that tiptoed across to where he lay. He stirred when the sheets were pulled back. The long blonde hair was redolent with a heavy, musky scent. The full breasts stroked his cheeks. At once Magda started to work on Johannes with the touch of the expert, not wishing to wake him—not yet—not until he was fully erect. Johannes had never had a dream like this—never had his fantasies been quite so vivid, so deeply satisfying. By the time he came half awake, moaning softly with pleasure, he was already past the point of no return.

'Magda, Oh God, Magda . . .'

'Hush, liebling, relax,' was all Magda said, pausing for just an instant before her hungry tongue darted once more towards his loins.

CHAPTER TEN

Peter Hutley did well at college, becoming a house monitor and the youngest ever captain of the school rifle team. In the O.T.C. he reached the rank of Lance Sergeant and played rugger for the school 1st Fifteen, though not as a regular member of the team. On the cricket field he failed to fulfil his exceptional early promise. He had a fine eye and a natural talent for the game, despite never having seen a cricket bat until he was a teenager, but he incurred the constant wrath of the coach by persistently belting each and every ball out of the ground. His reaction to missing a place in the school eleven was to carry his bat for an unbeaten 137 out of 194, thus clinching the school's

1936 inter-House cricket cup. Though academically average, he had a natural flair for languages. His German could hardly be faulted and his French was not far behind.

In the summer of 1936 Peter spent the holidays shooting over 700 acres near Bray and riding with his mother. Now, too, he spent much time watching the flying at nearby White Waltham Airfield. Peter's passion for flying was kindled by an old friend of his mother's, Air Commodore L. E. O. Charlton, known as "Leo" by friends and family alike, who one unforgettable afternoon took him up for a joy ride in a Tiger Moth. Peter had decided there and then that he would get into the Royal Air Force, come what may.

White Waltham happened to be the site of the De Havilland Aircraft Company's School of Civil Aviation, and it was here that Peter applied for his training. He left school at the end of the Summer Term 1937, a few months short of his eighteenth birthday, but had to wait until September before he could attend the elementary three-month flying course. In the meantime he enjoyed the last long holiday he would ever have. All through the remaining days of July, all of August and the first half of September Peter waited restlessly, in a fever of anticipation. His was a restless spirit, and he had already developed a one-track mind. He bought a second-hand 350 cc B.S.A. motor bike, on which he commuted back and forth between his home and White Waltham, scrounging flights whenever he could, and occasionally succeeding in persuading Leo to take him up again.

At last the great day came. Peter was one of the earliest of the students to report in. Now he was on his own. He set out to prove that he was aircrew material, and succeeded admirably. He was the first to go solo, and in less than two weeks; it was routine, after all—Leo had shown him how, time and time again. If anything, Peter was a little too cocky and made himself rather unpopular. Two things cured him: first a bad landing, so bad in fact that he broke the tail skid on a Tiger Moth; and then the reprimand he got as a result.

Peter went on to pass the course, and with his confidence restored, he underwent two weeks of Officer Training before being posted in the early spring of 1938 to the R.A.F.'s No. 6 Flying Training School at Netheravon in Wiltshire, with the very temporary acting rank of Pilot Officer. On the way down from London, where he had to buy a few things, Peter stopped off at Maidenhead to see his mother and grandfather. His mother smiled and was happy for him, but Peter's youthful enthusiasm revived terrible memories in her. She had seen it all before—lives perfunctorily extinguished in an inferno of petrol flames, young bodies shredded by a hail of machine-gun bullets. When she kissed him goodbye, it was with the clinging affection of a mother desperately afraid for the future. She thought of Johannes too. God forbid that there should ever be another war. The thought of her own flesh and blood fighting on opposing sides was too awful to contemplate. She started to cry. Even the reassurance of Peter's enveloping arms was not enough to comfort her.

Life at Netheravon was very pleasant. It was an excellent area for shooting, natural partridge country, but Peter arrived during the closed season and so took up fly-fishing instead, spending many leisure hours casting the march brown or pale watery olive at the wild trout in the upper reaches of the River Avon.

The aircraft he flew in the Junior Term was the then obsolete Hawker Hart. In this reliable, relatively simple aircraft, he made steady if unspectacular progress. The memory of the busted tail skid was etched deeply into his mind, and he had sworn never to take that kind of risk again. At the end of his first term, Pilot Officer Peter Hutley was among those who attended the full ceremonial parade, stepping forward to have his pilot's wings pinned on his tunic by the Commander-in-Chief, Flying Training Command.

Cadet Johannes von Tahlmann was late in reporting for duty at the recruit training establishment at Wildpark-Werder, and found that his rather feeble excuses cut no ice whatsoever. His military career had begun inauspiciously. He was full of gloom as he lay in bed that night, pondering over the events that had taken place since he had said *aufwiedersehn* to his friends and sat down to that last meal with Magda. She had relieved him not only of his virginity but of his virility as well. Nearly twenty-four hours later he still ached. And he was embarrassed and resentful of the humiliation he had suffered as the Drill Sergeant browbeat him in front of the other recruits.

Sergeant Jungklauser was a stern disciplinarian who stood an inch under six foot tall. His head was almost square, his hair cropped so short that at first glance he appeared bald. His waxed moustache, bulbous nose and piggy eyes hardly improved his looks. He seemed as old as the River Rhine itself, and Johannes was not the only new recruit to conclude incorrectly that the man was a relic left over from the Franco-Prussian war of 1870.

Their antipathy was mutual. Johannes did not like Jungklauser any more than the old professional cared for the faintly foppish, arrogant young aristocrat of whom he had been instructed to take "special care". Unfortunately for Johannes, the higher authority responsible for the order had neglected to inform the Sergeant of the manner in which he was to interpret the request. He drew his own conclusions. The Fatherland needed men, soldiers and leaders—not cosseted teacher's pets.

During the next six months of basic military training, if the rest of the recruits were put through the mill, Johannes found himself put through a mangle as well. His feet ached from pounding concrete. His arms and legs were stiff from constant drill with an old model '98 Mauser. Jungklauser threw every dirty fatigue at him, every extra parade or picket duty, until Johannes could handle himself with a smartness that could not have been surpassed even by a member of the S.S. Liebstandarte Adolf Hitler.

At last the ordeal came to an end and Johannes was allowed home for a week's leave. Before he left, Johannes sought out the Drill Sergeant, his gaoler, his tormenter and taskmaster for the past half year, and offered him his hand. In that moment he found an acceptance and understanding of the seemingly senseless orders, the inane remarks, the blaspheming and cursing and, above all, the crushing conformity. His dislike of the old Prussian had been replaced by a grudging respect, and he realized that he owed his Sergeant a debt of gratitude. Jungklauser took the hand and shook it. He wished Johannes good luck, more as a matter of courtesy than from any sincere feeling of goodwill. He still did not care for the boy—and liked him even less when Johannes took a pace back and raised his arm in a Nazi salute. Jungklauser did not reply, but the expression on his face was quite sufficient to convey his feelings. Johannes, however, noticed nothing. He was already on his way home to Tahlmann.

Instead of sending the chauffeur, Magda came in person to meet him at Schwandorf station. As he alighted from the train she rushed towards him, both arms outstretched. Johannes forced a somewhat sickly smile but drew back, turning what had been intended as an affectionate embrace into a formal handshake. He was the first to speak.

'How nice to see you here, Magda. But you really should have sent Müller.'

'Of course, but I thought you'd prefer it if I came,' Magda replied.

'What do you mean? It makes no difference to me. Should it?'

Johannes certainly knew how to hurt if he wished. Magda was nonplussed for an instant. Then she took his hand and shook it limply. The Baron was right, she thought. Why should it matter whether it was Müller or she who met the train? It was she who had gone to his bedroom, she who had started the lovemaking, she who had set the pace. He could almost have been somewhere else. Why should she now expect to be treated as anything but a housekeeper? Magda inwardly recoiled. Then she recovered her poise.

'Of course, Herr Baron, I just thought we could discuss your domestic affairs on the way home rather than having to talk about them later. You only have a week. It's not long, is it?'

'I suppose not,' replied Johannes. Feeling a little foolish he added. 'A good idea, Magda. Where's the car?'

Magda led the way to the large Mercedes. Johannes then took her arm and solicitously opened the door for the front passenger. He settled himself down behind the wheel. The hood was down, the sun shining; it was a perfect day for a drive.

Magda assumed that the master of the house would be tired and would hardly feel like entertaining, so she had arranged a quiet dinner for the two of them. But Johannes surprised her by appearing to want to sit chatting till the early hours. He talked about everything he had experienced at Wildpark-Werder. When she cut in with a question now and then Magda conveyed great interest, but her eyes signalled apprehension. Johannes had changed. He was more grown-up, more self-assured, more self-confident and far, far better-looking. How was he going to treat her now? she wondered.

Why had she gone to his room on his last night at Tahlmann? Mostly, she told herself, because she had to make herself indispensable to him. What had she hoped to get out of it? Marriage? Out of the question, even if she had loved him. Perhaps it had simply been the challenge of fishing in forbidden waters.

Tonight Johannes was expecting her. He excused himself and went off to bed with a flurry of goodnights. Magda hesitated for a full thirty minutes before she made her move. Johannes lay silent and motionless in his bed, listening as the door was opened and a soft feminine voice inquired 'Are you asleep?' He wanted Magda, but he wanted her subjugated, abased and humiliated before him. It had to be her who gave *him* the pleasure. The poison spewed out by his father's perverted friends was running hot and quick in his veins.

Magda came towards the bed and quickly slipped out of her clothes. Once more Johannes felt the warm moisture of her tongue explore his body, but this time her attentions left him unaroused. He needed something more.

Despite Magda's experience she was unable to excite him; despite the darting, carressing movements of her tongue and fingers, and the warm suppleness of her body, Johannes had said not a word, had not so much as stirred. She sat on the bed, disappointed, wet for him and a little breathless. One eye flickered open, then the other, and Johannes sat up in bed, looked at Magda and smiled. Then he rose slowly and fetched his leather slipper, which he handed to her.

Magda shrugged. Then she too smiled.

'I must be punished.' Johannes said. 'I'm not doing as you wish.' Kneeling down he presented his naked back and bottom to her.

Magda had always looked upon herself as a fast learner. She stood over him, her breasts rising and falling as he squirmed with anticipation.

'Go on then, beat me. Hit me, damn you.'

'You'll be sorry for this, you bastard,' she said, taking the cue at last. As she gradually strengthened the blows, she found that nothing had ever given her quite such a feeling of exhileration. She was soaking wet, and when she looked at Johannes she found that he was erect and hard, and much bigger than she remembered. He lay on his back moaning. Magda could scarcely contain herself. She straddled him violently. Now at last she was playing the dominant role which had always suited her. She was on top, and there she would stay always, mentally and physically, till the end. She rode the young Baron fiercely, the sweat from their bodies, the pain and the pleasure mingling. In a short time he could take no more. It was he whose dignity had been destroyed, and when it was all over he cried like a baby. Magda cradled the tousled head in her arms until he was fast asleep and then crept silently to her own room.

The week's leave passed all too quickly, and housekeeper and master had no opportunity to repeat the adventures of the first night. There were always guests in the house, staying the night, arriving, about to leave. Magda began to wonder whether Johannes had arranged his socializing by accident or design. Even her plans for Johannes' last night were thwarted. He had said nothing about going out that evening until after lunch the same day, when he suddenly announced that he had been invited to a party in Nuremburg and would drive himself there. With a nonchalant shrug which gave no inkling of her bitter disappointment, Magda accepted the *fait accompli*. She would see him when he got back. Johannes, knowing what was surely in her mind, smiled broadly and said that would depend. He never said on what.

The supper party was an impromptu affair given by two of Johannes' friends to celebrate an engagement. Johannes sat between two enchanting females, Hildegarde Kreipe and Ilse Horcher, feeling that the holiday could hardly have ended more perfectly. Johannes was delighted with both girls' company, but it was Ilse in whom he showed the greatest interest. During their conversation he had found out that she had the better connections. Hildegarde seemed better endowed, but her father was merely an elderly Captain, appointed to a rather mundane administrative job in the army—a man who could be of no use to him. Ilse's father was a Colonel in the Luftwaffe and her mother was a cousin, albeit a distant one, of the Condor Legion ace Werner Mölders, who, flying the new Messerschsmitt Bf 109 single-seater fighter, had shot down fourteen Spanish Republican aircraft and thereby made himself the hero figure of every aspiring German pilot. To bask in even a glimmer of the great man's reflected glory would be an honour indeed.

Johannes returned home to Tahlmann long after the sun was up to find that Magda had gone to bed hours earlier. He was not in the least bit tired. He could not get Ilse out of his mind and he flattered himself that he too had made an impression. Why else should she have stayed on and on, talking, long after all the others had gone? On the drive back, Johannes had thought of Magda. He had enjoyed his little fling with her, but now he decided to push her out of his mind. He determined that he would think only of Ilse and paradoxically, because of her, of getting back to his new unit.

This time he arrived punctually at Wildpark-Werder. In fact he was the first to arrive at the airfield, which was situated just outside the little holiday town of Werder itself. As he entered the familiar surroundings he thought again of the Prussian Drill Sergeant, hoping that from now on his life would not be quite so hard, the discipline not quite so harsh. Above all, he prayed that there would not be another Junklauser waiting to make his every day a misery. He had resolved not merely to learn to fly, not merely to do well, but to be the best in everything. He would be top cadet for the Führer and for the Fatherland. And, of course, above all for Ilse.

Although life was much easier, Johannes drove himself relentlessly, tirelessly practising circuits and bumps under the watchful eye of a Flight Sergeant. After the eleventh time he went solo. At flying, he was above average for his class. But in the academic studies on technical and military matters, as well as on the advanced course that he had undertaken before he could be commissioned as an officer, Johannes was outstanding. For this and other reasons, he did not endear himself to his fellow cadets, preferring to keep his own company, avoiding the limited social activities so as to concentrate on his studies, and only allowing his attentions to be diverted occasionally in order to write to Ilse. He was awarded his wings at the end of the second term. Then it was back to the Military Training School again, but now as an officer cadet and therefore out of Jungklauser's range. Johannes caught sight of his erstwhile Drill Sergeant on a couple of occasions and smiled to himself. The old Prussian professional would be far too busy telling his latest charges that they were without doubt the worst bunch of deadbeats that he had ever set eyes on to bother with those who had already passed through his hands.

After being seconded for a spell to an operational unit, Johannes began to prepare for the passing out examinations. The questions were difficult and several of the class failed, but Johannes, as he had promised himself he would, passed with the highest marks. Promoted senior officer cadet, he was posted to the Fighter Weapons school at Werneuchen, north of Berlin. But first, he was allowed a week's well-earned leave. He had been invited to stay with Oberst and Frau Horcher in Berlin. Ilse had arranged everything, including a party attended by her cousin, Werner Mölders.

In May 1939 Johannes was commissioned Lieutnant and waited in hopes of a permanent posting to an operational squadron. Instead he found himself picked for special duties, mostly under the direct orders of Hermann Göring, helping to promote the image of the Luftwaffe. His aristocratic good looks and his undoubted charisma soon made him a considerable success in the job. He kept up his flying time. He practised mock combat and aerial gunnery at every opportunity. He attended scores of official functions and as many unofficial ones. He was feted and photographed, he was written up by the press and was the subject of more than one broadcast. His ego was flattered by all the attention from a public already programmed for war, already taught to admire the Nazi soldier above all others as the strength and sinew of the Master Race.

He saw a great deal of the Horchers, Ilse in particular. With everything to gain, Johannes was on his best behaviour towards the family. Ilse, too, was flattered by the dashing young Baron's overtures. Taken in, completely captivated, she fell in love, eagerly accepting the almost casual proposal of marriage when it finally came.

The ceremony took place in June, a fashionable affair which, despite the rapidly gathering clouds of war, was attended by many famous names. Hermann Göring had agreed to be best man, but had to excuse himself at the last minute due to sudden and pressing military matters. It might have crossed Ilse's mind to ask herself why Johannes had no friends of his own to do the honours, but in the rush of preparations she hardly gave the matter a moment's thought. Werner Mölders volunteered for the duty, even though he had only met the groom once before, at the cocktail party during his last leave in Berlin.

Colonel Horcher had good reason to be proud of the events he oversaw at the altar that day. His daughter looked a picture, her hair flowing freely over her shoulders, her clear blue eyes, tinged with mauve, at once conveying innocence and an infinite softness, her nose straight, her mouth firm and generous enough to hint at hidden passion. Ilse Horcher was, indeed, an unusually pretty girl, and Johannes had begun to be extremely thankful that he had forsaken the more obvious charms of her dinner companion on the night they had met.

The best man, Werner Mölders, was dark and lean and of medium height, his features finely chiselled. Unlike Johannes, however, the apparent effeminacy of his profile was deceptive. One look at Mölders' eyes, drilling into you, was sufficient to show that this was a man who could command the attention of his superiors and the obedience of his subordinates.

Mölder's witty speech at the reception was well received. But even Johannes noticed that the veneer of charm with which he coated his words to the company—and to the bridegroom—concealed an uncompromising shrewdness. Whether or not Werner Mölders approved of his cousin's choice of husband, he recognized Johannes as potentially a first-class fighter pilot. Mölders was Squadron Commander of Jagdgeschwader 53, and it was to that unit that Leutnant Baron Johannes von Tahlmann was to be posted when he returned from his honeymoon.

After the wedding Johannes felt able to put behind him all the toil, the tears and sweat of studying, and the strain of being permanently in the public eye. At last he could relax and be himself. He took his bride back to Tahlmann, where he spent much time resting.

But at the end of the week's leave the marriage remained unconsummated. Ilse was as puzzled as she was disappointed. She felt sure that it was a mistake to have spent a honeymoon at what was to be her future home. To begin with, she did not care for Magda Ziegler at all. The woman regarded her with sullen resentment and refused to accede to her requests. Ilse demanded that she be sacked. Johannes changed the subject. Ilse brought it up again the same night. Johannes flew into a rage and, sitting up in bed, struck his wife across the face. Ilse burst into tears. She had started to realize the extent of the mistake she had made.

After lunch the next day Ilse had a horse saddled and went riding herself on the estate. Whilst she was out Johannes and Magda went riding too—the first chance they had had in months. The whip Magda used on her master drew blood before he reached his climax.

Ilse tried to make it up with Johannes that night, hardly able to believe that there could be strife and bitterness between her and her handsome fighter-pilot husband.

Johannes, at his most charming, apologized profusely for his behaviour and asked for her forgiveness. Ilse readily accepted the apology and did forgive. But she would never forget. She avoided the painful subject of Magda altogether in future and suggested evenly that she would stay no longer at Tahlmann, preferring instead to return to Berlin and her parents until Johannes was settled in his unit and could provide married accomodation.

War intervened once more in the Tahlmann fortunes. At the beginning of September 1939, Hitler unleashed his Blitzkreig on Poland. Johannes' first confirmed victory came in October, when he shot down a Morane 406 single-seater fighter of the French Air Force. A week later he scored another hit and later that same day he might have added a fat Blenheim bomber to his tally had his Bf 109 not been grounded by an overheating engine when the rest of his outfit was ordered up to intercept a squadron of the British-made bombers. Johannes was not pleased.

He did not score again until March 1940. Werner Mölders, who had been made Group Commander of III JG-53* the previous September, was leading a fighter sweep, when Johannes spotted a lone Potez 63 reconnaisance aircraft. Mölders ordered him to attack and Johannes, with his wingman sticking to him like a barnacle, peeled off and pounced on the unsuspecting Frenchman. A single burst from two hundred yards was more than enough to send the twin-engined Potez on its final plunge to earth. Johannes waggled his wings, banked and climbed steeply back to reform with the rest of his outfit, his wingman following.

On the 2nd April came victory number four, Johannes' first British aircraft—a Bristol Blenheim. Again, it was a single aircraft flown rather badly by an obviously inexperienced pilot. This time the crew were lucky. They hit the silk and would live to fight another day. In view of

*3rd Group, 53rd Fighter Wing

what was to happen later to Johannes' victims, they had every reason to be grateful.

Johannes shot down two more Moranes in one mission towards the end of May. Mölders bagged three in the same action, a whirling muddle of a dogfight.

On the 4th June, as Dunkirk was passing into history, Johannes showed up in his true colours. Returning from an abortive mission, he spotted a road jammed with retreating French soldiers and hoardes of refugees. Seeing civilians, old people, men, children, women, some with babies in prams, jostling on the road beneath him, a pathetic flotsam of fleeing, frightened innocents, Johannes immediately resolved to strike a blow for the Fatherland on his own initiative, making four or five passes down the length of the road and slamming machine gun bullets and cannon shells amongst the terrified humanity. Those that could leapt for cover in the ditch or flattened themselves on the ground; others who could do neither perished in the hailstorm of bullets and shells unleashed by the fighter's guns. Johannes was delighted with himself. Not only was the sport new and enthralling—it was utterly without risk. He watched the herds of people below scattering like terrified cattle and imagined the screams and curses of the decadent Frenchmen, choking in the clouds of billowing smoke. Only one old man stood his ground, shaking his impotent fists at the Bf 109 as it banked before making a final pass. Johannes watched his bullets spurt on the tarmac, yellow splashes indicating the point of impact of the cannon shells. Still the old man stood there, a defiant speck rapidly getting larger as the fighter swooped: a woman was grabbing at him, trying to pull him to safety. But this time a cannon shell tore into him, the woman screaming as blood and tissue from her father's shattered body burst onto her meagre clothing. Johannes banked his fighter into a turn and waved from the cockpit to those below. His magazines were empty. The sport was over.

He looked for his wingman, Sergeant Dörr, but of Dörr there was no sign. Contrary to the strict orders to which the Luftwaffe fighter pilots flew, the Sergeant had left the Leutnant to his own devices. Johannes returned to base alone, angrily composing in his mind the dressing-down he would give his wingman when he landed.

On the ground, Dörr stood at dispersal and waited. Johannes taxied in and he watched the familiar figure emerge from his cockpit as the propellor stuttered to a halt. The enlisted man respected the Baron's ability as a pilot, but after the massacre he had so recently witnessed he despised the man. He had already decided that he could no longer fly with the likes of von Tahlmann and would inform the Squadron Commander accordingly.

Johannes had approached, and was about to issue his official reprimand when he noticed the anger taughten Dörr's features. Dörr cut in first.

'You murderous bastard. I hope I never see butchery like that as long as I live. You can find yourself another bloody wingman—*Sir.*' Dörr saluted contemptuously, turned on his heel and strode off. For ten seconds Johannes was speechless, fumbling for a suitable retort. He felt the hot flush of embarrassment rising from his neck—embarrassment that a mere Sergeant should dare to speak to him in such a way. Then he found his tongue.

'Dörr,' he began quietly, 'Come back here.' The Sergeant paid no heed, continuing towards the Squadron Office.

'Come back here, Dörr—that's an order.' Johannes' shout echoed amongst the station buildings, but had no more effect than before.

'Sergeant, I order you to come back here at once . . .' Johannes began to run after his recalcitrant wingman. Catching him up, he laid a hand on the man's shoulder, and lowered his voice once again.

'You're a damned fool if you think you can get away with this, Dörr.'

The Sergeant pulled away silently and reached the Squadron Office door. Two other pilots emerged at that moment and exchanged salutes. Both were in a hurry.

'Any luck?' one asked casually as they passed. Johannes held out a hand as if to seek their aid, but found all he could do was shake his head.

Other Luftwaffe personnel were about now. Even Johannes did not dare to quarrel with an N.C.O. in public—especially Dörr, who was well-liked and respected.

'Right, Dörr,' he hissed through his teeth as the wingman disappeared into the building. 'Have it your own way.'

Shaking with fury and frustration, Johannes headed for his quarters. He had to deal with Dörr. He would have him arrested. He could even have him shot for insubordination, refusal to obey orders, and insulting an officer. The Group Commander would hear of his behaviour. Werner Mölders would know just how to deal with the fellow. Johannes sat on his bed for a full ten minutes, mentally composing a report that would place his wingman in the worst possible light. He mulled over the words, polishing and perfecting his choice of phrase, and finally deciding that Dörr should be charged with desertion in the face of the enemy and summarily shot. Just as Johannes was warming to his theme, the tannoy crackled: a click, then a voice—

'*Leutnant von Tahlmann report to the Group Commander's office immediately . . . Leutant von Tahlmann . . .' The message was repeated.*

Johannes' fantasy began to dissolve. It puzzled him that he was being sent for. Perhaps Mölders had already heard what Dörr had to say and now wanted to hear his side of the story. So much the better. His knock on the Group Commander's door was firm and confident. Immediately it opened and Sergeant Dörr emerged. He saluted unsmilingly and walked down the corridor. Johannes limply returned the salute, suddenly fearing the worst. So Dörr had got to Mölders first. But surely Werner would take his own word before that of an enlisted man?

Werner Mölders was sitting at his desk. He stared stonily at Johannes as the young Leutnant approached. Johannes stopped and snapped his heels together to attention. There was no smart click since he was still wearing his flying boots, and the parade-ground stiffness merely made him look ridiculous. To mask a blush of embarrassment, he gave the Nazi salute. Mölders ignored it.

'You sent for me, Herr Major?'

'Yes. Yes, I did.'

Johannes stood rigidly at attention, surprised and injured by the fact that Mölders had not told him to stand easy. For what seemed an eternity, the Group Leader said nothing, and sat silently surveying him. At last Mölders continued.

'I suppose you know why I have sent for you, Leutnant.'

'Well no, not exactly, Sir.'

'It is to inform you that I am sending you home on leave, prior to your being posted to another unit.'

Johannes was shattered, but no emotion flickered across his face. He made a supreme effort to keep himself calm, logical.

'May I be permitted to ask the Herr Major why I am being transferred at this particular time?'

'Because simply, I do not wish to have a man like you under my command. You can commit cold-blooded murder in another unit. I can't stop that. You might even get a medal for it.'

'But the refugees—Sergeant Dörr . . .'

'The refugees, yes, Tahlmann.'

'But Sir, you haven't heard my side of the story—Dörr's insubordination, his desertion—'

'Leutnant, do not interrupt me.'

Johannes caught his breath. He felt as though he had been punched in the stomach without warning.

'Dörr did nothing less than any decent man would have done. We are soldiers, Herr Baron. Not assassins.'

'But Sir, I don't understand. It's less than half an hour since this happened—'

'I have warned you once before, von Tahlmann, do not interrupt me. This time it's an order.'

Johannes fell silent.

'I know exactly what happened because I was there. I saw you make five sweeps over those wretches, killing and maiming. What for? Why? Do you think your murdering brutality will help the Reich win the war?' The question remained unanswered.

'Dörr told me nothing. He came here because I sent for him. I ordered him to leave when I heard you knock. It is not my policy to reprimand my officers in front of enlisted personnel, however much I may despise the offender. So let me just tell you again: you will never fly with JG 53 again.'

'I'm sorry, Sir,' Johannes muttered feebly.

'Sorry for the innocent civilians murdered? Rubbish. You're sorry, perhaps, that your act has been discovered—but that's not quite enough.' Molders was having difficulty restraining his scorn.

'Murder, Sir? This is war.'

'To some of us, Leutnant, there is still a difference. Now get out of my sight and be off this station within four hours. Your papers will be ready for you when you go.'

Miserable and deflated, Johannes suddenly found he hated Mölders, hated his heroism, his honour, his reputation. He would not forget the ignominy he was suffering now. Or forgive. Near to tears, he saluted and turned to go. He was halfway to the door when the Major stopped him.

'One more thing, Leutnant.' Johannes turned.

'Sir.'

Mölders had opened a drawer and pulled out a package, placing it on the desk. He pointed towards it.

'This is for you. It arrived this morning. Normally, we would have a party to celebrate the event. This time you'll take it and go. You have four hours.'

Johannes took the package and guessed at its contents, the adrenalin racing through his veins. He threw a final defiant Nazi salute at the Group Leader.

'Heil Hitler,' said Johannes, before making for the door again. Mölders did not respond.

Just over three hours later Johannes sat in a passenger seat of a tri-motored Junkers 52 transport plane, en route for Berlin. On his left breast pocket he had pinned the Iron Cross 1st Class. He read the citation over and over again until he could remember it word for word. '*By order of the Führer, Adolf Hitler, the award of the Iron Cross, 1st Class, to Leutnant Baron Johannes von Tahlmann, for conspicuous gallantry and devotion to duty . . .*'

The next day, the 5th June 1940, whilst JG 53 were on a fighter sweep over the Chantilly Forest, the Group lost its commander, albeit temporarily. A French pilot pulled off a classic ambush from out of the sun. His Bf 109 caught a full burst at short range and was riddled with bullets. Mölders was unhurt and parachuted to the ground where he was captured by the French Army. His sojourn as a P.O.W. was, however, of just two weeks' duration, after which time France surrendered and the ace was released. Promotion to Kommodore of JG 51 awaited him and in this capacity he was to fly through the thick of the fighting during the Battle of Britain.

JG 51 would be stationed on the Eastern Front when Hitler attacked Russia on the 22nd June 1941. Mölders' score of kills would rise steadily and at the age of 28 he was to become General of Fighters and the first pilot in history to tot up a century of victories. Johannes wished him dead. It was to be barely five months later that his wish was fulfilled.

Luftwaffe Colonel-General Ernst Udet, a veteran ace of the 14-18 war, shot himself on the 17th November 1941, and Göring ordered Mölders back to Berlin to attend the funeral as one of the Guard of Honour. Mölders, deeply affected by the suicide of Udet, was determined to get back to the funeral despite the worsening weather conditions. A day or two later he took off as a passenger in a Heinkel III which had to fly into the teeth of a gale-force wind. Running short of fuel near Breslau, the pilot decided on an emergency landing. He couldn't make the airfield and the plane stalled on its very edge. Both Mölders and the pilot had been veterans of the Condor Legion in Spain. Both were killed instantly.

CHAPTER ELEVEN

Ilse was waiting for Johannes when he landed later that evening at Tempelhof, Berlin. Her thoughts had been full of him that day, full of the new life they would lead together in Berlin, far from the oppressive shadows of the Tahlmann estate and the influence of Magda: Ilse had resolved to put the memories of their unhappy honeymoon behind her, to make up for past disappointments, and had bought herself a new dress to mark the occasion, a pale garment, light and summery in colour and texture.

She noted the drawn look on Johannes' otherwise youthful face as he approached; she had also spotted the Iron Cross 1st class pinned to his tunic, and was proud of him. She kissed him gently.

Johannes was surprised to see her. How could she have known at such short notice? He returned her embrace, noticing how lovely she looked and fervently wishing that things could have been different—that some more happy occasion could have brought him back to her.

'Ilse. How did you know I—'

'Excuse me, Sir.' The reunion was interrupted by the voice of a Corporal who had run across to the couple. 'You're wanted at Headquarters.'

Johannes extricated himself from Ilse's arms.

'What for?'

'It's the Reichsmarschall, Herr Leutnant. He's been waiting for you.'

Johannes swallowed. So Göring had already heard of his expulsion from JG 53—those bastards Dörr and Mölders must have acted quickly. He turned towards Ilse: could that explain why she was there to greet him the moment he stepped off the plane? Had she been sent by Göring to soften the blow?

Ilse sensed her husband's mood as the pair of them were escorted to a waiting Opel, but she asked no questions of him. They clambered inside and she reached tentatively for his hand, not knowing the cause of his anxiety but seeking to reassure him. His palm felt cold and moist with perspiration. The couple exchanged hardly a word on the journey.

The door was opened the moment the car came to a halt. Ilse stepped out first and two steel-helmeted guards snapped to attention as Johannes followed. An airforce Captain hurried out to meet them and after a brisk exchange of salutes and introductions instructed the couple to follow him inside.

Johannes was taken straight to Hermann Göring's office. The Captain knocked on the door and ushered the visitors in. Göring rose from his desk, where he appeared to be studying some papers. He beamed at Ilse.

'Baroness,' he said, advancing towards her. 'Delighted you could make it. If I may say so, you look even lovelier than usual. If only I were a younger man, Johannes, eh?' The flab on his face glistened in the humidity of the summer evening.

'Heil Hitler,' said Johannes, anxious to postpone the

evil moment when the blow would fall, for another fraction of time.

Göring responded, impatient with such formality, nonchalantly raising his right hand.

'Johannes,' he continued, putting his arm round his adopted nephew's shoulders. 'Good to see you too . . . But my dear boy, whatever's the matter with you? You look frightened to death.'

'Herr Reichsmarschall, I have been thrown out of my Group by Major Mölders. Did you not know?'

Göring beamed.

'Yes, yes, of course. But a little disagreement between you and Werner is neither here nor there. I gather you used your remaining ammunition on the retreating enemy. Quite right, too. But Werner is a great pilot and a great commander and one of my favourites—I can't be angry with him. As for you, my fine friend, you did right. I have great faith in you too—always have had, since our very first meeting. I'm glad to tell you you've been promoted. As of now you are an Oberleutnant, and you'll be posted to a new unit after a week's leave. I'm only sorry that you'll probably miss the rest of the war. The French won't last out the month—they're a beaten, decadent rabble. And England will surely see the futility of continuing the struggle. The Führer is quite convinced that the British will give in. They know that my Luftwaffe can bring them to their knees within a matter of days.'

Later, Johannes and Ilse dined as houseguests of Herman Göring and his wife at their showhouse, Karinhall, close to the capital, where the highlight of the evening for their host was to conduct certain of his chosen guests to the enormous timbered attic, there to indulge in his favourite hobby—toy trains. Johannes was struck in equal measure by the size of the layout and the apparent puerility of his chief. Ilse remained below with the women, somewhat nervously anticipating the night ahead.

Once in the privacy of their bedroom Ilse tried again to consummate the marriage, but in spite of her kisses and endearments Johannes failed to respond. After an hour of fruitless fumblings he fell back on the pillows, angry at his own inadequacy, tired after a momentous day, and closed his eyes. Ilse, bewildered and hurt, lay back on her side of the bed, staring at the ceiling.

Then Johannes' thoughts started to roam. As he drifted into the twilight zone between wakefulness and sleep, he thought of Magda. He thought of the last wonderful night she had given him, of the exquisite sensation of her nails lacerating his flesh, and the indescribable thrill she had drawn from him as he reached his peak. Feeling his sex rise, he muttered her name softly.

Ilse sat up in bed.

'What did you say?'

Johannes was wide awake now and eager. He reached out to Ilse.

'Did I say something?'

'You said "Magda"—'

'I must have been dreaming.'

'You must get rid of her, Johannes—you must. She's evil.'

Johannes reached for her. He was demanding, and yet at first, disarmingly gentle. Momentarily deceived, Ilse melted at his touch. She remembered the terrible scene they had suffered the last time that woman's name had been mentioned, but as quickly as the memory arose, she pushed it out of her mind. Johannes was big and hard now and her fingers closed tenderly around him.

The sudden ferocity of Johannes' response took her breath away. Without tenderness, without a hint of fore-play, not even so much as a perfunctory kiss, Johannes pulled her to him and entered her with a savagery that amounted to rape. Too shocked to resist, too brutalized to respond, her eyes suddenly wide with alarm and fear, Ilse's body stiffened, her limbs tense and taut.

Johannes closed his eyes. The light was still on. As he thought of Magda his thrustings grew more urgent. He would punish and degrade Ilse as Magda had punished and degraded him.

Ilse started to struggle, but Johannes gripped her harder, his nails tearing weals into her buttocks. Ilse clawed at Johannes' back, but he was too strong for her. She shuddered and thrashed across the bed in an effort to escape. Suddenly it was over.

'Magda,' Johannes moaned.

For a few seconds the couple lay still. Johannes went limp. There were tears of exhaustion and horror in Ilse's eyes.

Göring had been wrong. In spite of the Führer's confident predictions, Britain did not sue for peace after the fall of France. As a result of renewed pressure from Werner Mölders, Johannes was posted to JG 51; but by a bitter irony, Mölders found himself ordered by the Reichsmarschall soon afterwards to take command of that very squadron. Göring fervently hoped that Mölders would forget the incident with the refugees and take a more tolerant view of the young Baron's zeal for the Fatherland. In a personal interview with the Commander-in-Chief, Mölders was ordered never to mention the incident again, and to behave towards Johannes in exactly the same way as he would to any of the other pilots under his command.

Only two others had known about the affair. One of them, Oberleutnant Helmuth Fiske, was conveniently shot down and killed by a French fighter on the 9th June 1940. The second, the unfortunate Sergeant Dörr, was involved, it appeared, in an unfortunate incident when it was suddenly discovered that his late mother had been a Jewess. He was arrested by the Gestapo on the 6th June, and nothing was ever heard of him again. The Nazis moved fast to protect their own.

Mölders had been angry and resentful when he found himself once more in direct command of the very man he had taken such pains to avoid. The irony was made the deeper when it was Mölders in person who, on the 1st September, saved Johannes' life by blasting a Spitfire from the young pilot's tail.

The Battle of Britain has been chronicled many times, so many, in fact, that the repeated clashes between the finest pilots of the warring nations in the azure skies of the Summer of 1940 have entered the realms of legend. Countless individuals played their part in the conflict—famous names such as Werner Mölders and Adolf Galland, Göring, Kesselring and Sperrle, Tuck and Bader, Dowding, Park and Leigh-Mallory along with them. The role played by Oberleutnant Baron Johannes von Tahlmann was a little-known but a distinguished one. Prior to the fall of France he had shot down six allied planes. By the 16th September 1940 his bag had risen to fifteen; five French and ten British.

On that same date JG 51 lost one of its most popular young pilots. He had been seen to parachute into the Channel. Dusk had been falling at the time, and no rescue could be mounted then. German Air Sea Rescue was not noted for its ability to pluck downed fliers from off the coast of Britain, but there had still been a faint hope that he could be found the next day. The weather continued to worsen, but it was Johannes who was the first to volunteer to go and look for his brother officer. He took off at first light. The search was fruitless and he returned to base. Within twenty minutes he was off again. Once more his search was unrewarded. Once more he returned to refuel. This time he delayed only fifteen minutes before he took off.

Eight hours later, Oberleutnant Baron von Tahlmann was officially posted as missing.

CHAPTER TWELVE

The mists of November were blanketing the Wiltshire Downs by the time that Peter Hutley passed out from Netheravon. He had stood proudly to attention whilst the Commander-in-Chief pinned the coveted pilot's wings on his tunic. As the final exams had drawn close there had been much speculation as to who would be posted where. In the event, only a few lucky ones were posted to operational squadrons. It was well known at that time that there was a surplus of pilots over unit requirements—a happy state of affairs that would be frighteningly reversed in less than two years. For the most part, therefore, the young men were all packed off to a Pilot's pool in the North of England. Peter fell into neither category and was ordered instead to report to Air Ministry Headquarters in London. Everyone else was given leave. Peter was instructed to present himself at 14.30 hours the next day.

On arrival Pilot Officer Hutley found himself seconded to Air Ministry Intelligence for "special duties". He found the work routine, mostly uninteresting, and badly wanted to get into a squadron, to be part of a front-line fighter unit, envying his friends who, in the last halcyon days of the Summer of 1939, flew and played cricket, practised gunnery and studied aerobatics. Like every jealous outsider in those days, Peter regarded being a member of a fighter squadron as a long weekend away from school. He continued to try every avenue of opportunity, every contact. Then the war started, and finally he was posted—to the Fighter Experimental Unit at Tangmere in Sussex.

It was there he discovered his ability with the Browning machine guns, the armoury of the Spitfires and Hurricanes of the R.A.F. Among the pilots of the combatant nations at this stage of the war Peter's record of accuracy was outstanding: aerial gunnery seemed to come naturally to him—to him, the judgement of the all-important deflection shot was a matter of instinct rather than learning.

But he had little chance to use his skills. Even though he should have been in the thick of the Battle of Britain, in theory at least, it always seemed that he was grounded from flying, or forbidden from combat on the slightest pretext. For the most part he had to create his own opportunities to do battle with the Germans. Had he not been thus checked, his personal score would certainly have exceeded the four that had been confirmed by the beginning of September 1940. It was not until a little later that he realized that his movements had been closely watched, and manipulated, by higher authority. Not until the 18th September 1940, the day after he had shot down his only brother and notched his fifth and, as it would turn out, final victory for the R.A.F.

PART II

THE BIRDWATCHER

CHAPTER ONE

Flying Officer Hutley awoke on the morning of the 18th September to a feeling of complete disorientation. His mouth was dry and stale. For some time he lay semi-conscious, unable to remember how long he had been in bed or even how he had got there in the first place. When his eyes flickered open and he registered the strangeness of his surroundings, he began to realize that the nightmare with which he had struggled so vainly was no dream, but stark reality. He felt the hair bristle on the back of his neck and he shuddered as he placed a rather unsteady pair of feet on the cold linoleum floor. He had barely taken a single, tottering step before a medical orderly walked into the room with a cup of tea in hand and a cheery smile on his face.

'Good morning, Sir. Slept well, I hope?'

Peter grunted, more as a form of politeness than a gesture of conversation, and got back into bed.

'Brought you a nice hot cup of tea, Sir. M.O. says you should drink it as hot as possible—wake you up, like.'

Peter managed a muttered 'thank you'. The orderly tried a new conversational gambit.

'Looks as if it's going to be a nice morning, Sir. The sun's shining.' He paused. 'Poor beggars in London got it again last night.'

Peter grunted afresh and sipped at his tea. It was hot, too hot, and burned his lips.

'Blow on it, Sir' advised the orderly, standing by. 'But get it down. I made it special myself, so it's strong—none of your usual gnat's piss.'

Peter blew into the cup and managed an embryonic smile, then at last remembered he had a tongue.

'Tell me, do I stay here or do I get up?'

'That I can't say, Sir. I'm only G.D.*—just a glorified tea boy, the ablution wallah round here. Thine is not to reason why but mine is to . . .'

Peevishly, Peter cut in. He had heard it all before and was not in the mood.

'All right, man, you've made your point. Get someone who knows the form to come and see me as soon as possible. Preferably Mr Crawford, if he's about.'

'Yes Sir, I will, but drink your tea first.'

'Oh yes,' Peter blew on the brew again and sipped. It was cool enough to swallow now and went down in half a dozen gulps. He handed the empty cup back to the orderly.

'I presume there's no objection to my proceeding to the washroom?'

'Not so far as I know, Sir. Do you want a hand?'

'I'm not a complete cripple, thank you. Just asleep on my feet.'

'Well I'll be off then, Sir. If there's anything you need, please ring.'

Peter nodded but did not speak again. He was still sitting on the side of the bed as the orderly left the room. Slowly the effect of the strong tea began to dispel the mists of drug-induced sleep. The long, long period of unconsciousness had done him a great deal of good. Like everyone else involved, he had been tired out by the anxieties of the last few weeks. He desperately needed the rest, and his need had been made the more urgent by the shock of his death-bed reunion with Johannes. He would have welcomed some leave, but knew he had no right to be so favoured with R.A.F. pilot strength stretched beyond breaking-point.

*General Duties

Feeling the call of nature more insistently now, he put both feet on to the cold floor. He was perfectly steady. It was the woolly feeling in his head that gave him an illusion of feebleness. He made towards the door, but before he could reach out for the handle it was turned from the other side, and Crawford walked in. His face was drawn with tension and fatigue, the black circles under his eyes proclaiming his own sleeplessness, the strain of working as often as not for twenty or more hours at a stretch. He, too, needed rest. Even so, he managed a smile of genuine concern.

'Good morning, Peter. How do you feel? Slept well, I trust?'

'Morning, Doc. Slept? You've got to be joking. I've never been out for the count for so long in my life. What the hell was in that shot you gave me?'

'Trade secret. Glad to see it worked, though.'

'Do you know, the last thing I remember is . . .' Peter scratched his head and mused for a moment. 'Come to think of it, I've forgotten.'

'Good. That's the effect that it was supposed to have.'

'Can I get up?'

'Yes and no.'

'What's that supposed to mean?'

'What it says. Have some breakfast first and then get up. Can you manage bacon and eggs?'

'Ugh.'

'Go and wash and shave in cold water, then you'll find your appetite all right.'

'If you say so, Doc.'

'I do.'

'What's the form?'

'Well, London got it again last night and the Krauts got away scot-free. We didn't bring one of the bastards down after dark. Hell of a mess in the West End. John Lewis completely burned down for a start. And there were others.'

'Mother had an account there.' There didn't seem much else he could say.

'Now look, Peter, when you've had a bite to eat and freshened up, you'll feel fine, I promise. We want you dressed and ready not later than 09.15. At 09.30 a Rapide will fly you direct to Northolt.'

'What on earth for?'

'My dear fellow, how should I know? I'm only a sawbones. Perhaps this'll fill you in.'

As he spoke he handed Peter a plain beige envelope. Peter glanced at it and noticed that it was handwritten, and addressed simply to F/O P. E. Hutley. There was nothing to denote who it had come from. Peter put it down on the bedside locker.

'Aren't you going to read your fan mail?'

'In a minute. What's the hurry?'

'None. But I've got to go. Don't ask me why, but I've got a feeling you and I may not be seeing each other again. Not for a while, anyway. So good luck, Peter. All the very best.' Crawford stuck out his hand and Hutley, surprised by the sudden gesture, shook it.

'Thanks, Doc. Thanks for everything.'

Without further exchange the Squadron Leader left the room. Peter followed, heading for the bathroom with the letter in his hand. As Crawford disappeared down the corridor, Peter opened the envelope and took out a single sheet of paper. It was a typical Air Ministry form, ordering F/O P. E. Hutley to present himself at noon that day at the Air Ministry Building in Kingsway, Room 43. It went on to stipulate that no luggage of any description should be carried. Peter put two and two together and came up with five, assuming that the latter order, underlined in red, could only indicate that he would return to Tangmere that same day. Otherwise, surely he would have been told to bring an overnight bag. Transport was arranged and he should wait in the sick bay until sent for. The orders were stamped *Top Secret—for addressee's eyes only*.

On the dot of 09.15 an elderly Flight Lieutenant wearing four campaign medals from World War 1 came into the room and introduced himself as the 'bus driver' for Northolt. Peter was in battledress and scarcely felt fitted out for a visit to Air Ministry, but orders were orders. He followed his senior, who though friendly enough, obviously knew nothing beyond the fact that a car would be waiting for him at Northolt Airfield. The flight was routine. As Peter walked down the steps from the aircraft, an L.A.C. approached him.

'Mr Hutley?'

'Yes, I'm Hutley.'

'Follow me please, Sir.'

A Humber staff car stood waiting. Peter had by now begun to suspect that his journey must be connected with the shooting down of his brother, but was still mystified as to what the connection might be. He remembered that he hadn't even finished filling in the 1151. Puzzled, he stared out of the window as the car sped along Western Avenue to Wembley, and thence via Shepherd's Bush and Notting Hill to Oxford Street. The effects of the Luftwaffe bombing were beginning to show. Gazing around, he saw damaged buildings everywhere. Firemen were still toiling in the smouldering ruins of the John Lewis store. At High Holborn the car turned down into Kingsway.

At 11.47 they drew up outside Adastral House, the Air Ministry Building. The L.A.C. driver opened the door to allow his passenger to get out and saluted as the Flying Officer emerged. Peter returned the salute and added his thanks. He showed his identity card to a sentry and then presented himself at reception. The Sergeant on the desk, engrossed in paperwork, did not look up. Peter cleared his throat. The Corporal looked up as Peter spoke.

'I'm Flying Officer Hutley.'

'Ah yes, Mr Hutley. Good morning, Sir.' The Corporal scanned the papers again and tapped his index finger twice by way of emphasis.

'Room 43. The Air Commodore is expecting you.'

The signature on his orders had meant nothing to Peter and he had no idea who he was going to report to, or why. As he travelled up in the lift and along the corridor to room 43, he wondered idly if it could possibly be Leo.

Air Commodore L. E. O. Charlton rose as his visitor entered. He had a round friendly face, close-cut light brown hair and hazel eyes. As they shook hands, Peter remembered something of what his mother had told him about the man: his training at Sandhurst, his experiences during the Boer War and eventual wounding at Spion Kop, his D.S.O., then the episode in Persia.

Leo's career had seemed set for glittering heights when in 1923 he was appointed Chief of Staff to the R.A.F. Commander-in-Chief, Lord Trenchard. Theirs had been a long and happy association, dating back to the early days at the Central Flying School. Charlton now found himself at Airforce Headquarters in Baghdad. It was the British Government's policy at the time to subdue rebellious minor Arab chieftains in the area by the simple expedient of the indiscriminate bombing of areas these recalcitrants were known to frequent. Such shows of force were designed to frighten them into submission. The original idea had been Lord Trenchard's, but Charlton had disagreed, informing his chief that his conscience would not allow him to countenance such barbarity. Finally he had pushed his disagreement to the point of resignation.

The Air Commodore had returned home, his career apparently in ruins. But after a short while he was sent to Grantham in Lincolnshire to administer a group of Air Stations stretching across the North Midlands to the sea.

In the winter of 1924 he was posted to Air Ministry in London, there to conduct a solitary enquiry into the best methods by which the Air Force might be rapidly expanded in the event of war. His thesis took three years to complete and was hailed as a masterpiece. It seemed to Charlton that his disagreement with Lord Trenchard had been forgotten. Unfortunately he was wrong. On completion of his task he found himself summarily retired.

His recall, which to this day few, including Peter, were aware of, took place as a result of a letter he wrote in the summer of 1938; in it he had acquainted Military Intelligence with the fact that Luftwaffe Leutnant Baron von Tahlmann had an identical twin brother, currently serving in the R.A.F., and drawn attention to the possibilities of using this unusual circumstance. Within a matter of days the Air Commodore was summoned back to the Air Ministry with a top-secret brief to plan for the day when there might be an opportunity to take advantage of the situation.

It had been a simple coincidence that Leo happened to be a friend of the Hutleys and knew the family history. It was equally coincidental that it had been Leo who had also helped kindle in Peter his own fanatical love of flying. But there was no coincidence in the fact that throughout his career in the R.A.F. Peter had been kept as far as possible away from active combat.

Today, unusually, Leo was in uniform. After ushering Peter to a seat, he spoke first.

'Peter, how very nice to see you.'

'Nice to see you, Sir.' Peter took in the Air Commodore's blue uniform and all the gongs at a glance. Remembering his own rather stained battledress, he made an effort to apologise for his appearance.

'I'm sorry, Sir, but I've had no chance to change my clothes. I expect you know all about it.'

'About your brother, yes. I'm so sorry, Peter, so sorry that it had to end like this. I realize it must have been an awful shock.'

'Does mother know?'

'No—and we've decided she shouldn't be told. What is it they say? What the heart doesn't know . . . ? Anyway, not a word to her about Johannes' death. That's an order, incidentally.'

'Yes, Sir, but why should I need to be ordered? I mean, why should I want to upset her?'

'I'm not suggesting you do. It's just a necessary precaution.'

'Precaution against what?'

'We'll discuss that over lunch. I'm taking you to the Savoy.'

'I can't go there like this, Sir. Look at me.' Peter gestured to an oil stain on his trousers and sweat marks on the collar of his battledress.

'I've thought of that one. There's a clean uniform for you in that cupboard.'

Peter sauntered over to the place indicated, opened the door, and discovered a brand new uniform neatly pressed and ready for him, with the single ring of a flying officer round each sleeve. He took off his battledress and tried on the clean jacket. It fitted perfectly, the trousers likewise. Then he noticed the single white medal ribbon with the diagonal dark-blue stripes below the pilot's wings. He turned to Leo, who had looked on approvingly.

'I must say, it fits perfectly. Whose is it?'

'Yours, Peter.'

'But the D.F.C.?'

'As I said, yours, my boy. His Majesty the King has instructed the Air Council to convey his sincere congratulations to you, but I'm afraid his Majesty regrets that it will not be possible to present the medal to you in person. My heartiest congratulations too.'

'But why me? I haven't done anything. There are plenty of chaps who have done much, much more without getting anything like this for their trouble.'

'Shall we say then that it's as much for what we hope you will do, as for what you've already done?'

'With respects, Sir, I don't quite follow.'

'You will, Peter. After lunch. I don't like talking shop

on an empty stomach. Do you mind if we walk? It's the only exercise I seem to get these days.'

After leaving the building the two officers strolled down Kingsway in the autumn sunlight, then turned right along the Strand towards the Savoy.

Peter settled for ale but Leo picked on a dry martini, a habit acquired by his father in America and passed on to the next generation. The meal and wine were excellent but the talk was mostly of family matters, and all mention of the war was confined to generalities. Even inside the fortress of the Savoy, a prominent poster proclaimed *Careless talk costs lives*.

They took a taxi back to Adastral House.

Back in his office Leo plunged the young man straight in at the deep end.

'Peter,' he announced, 'we want you to take Johannes' place.'

'You *what*?' exclaimed Peter. 'You've got to be bloody joking.'

Leo ignored his outburst. 'No, I'm not joking. Of course, I'm desperately sorry that it should have had to be you that shot your brother down. But whoever had done so, the result would have been the same. You must see that.'

'But it wasn't someone else, was it? It was me.'

Leo was silent.

'So what exactly do you have in mind?'

'Just what I said, Peter. We want you to fly to occupied France and take your brother's place in the Luftwaffe.'

Peter looked at the Air Commodore, sure that he must have taken leave of his senses.

'Right you are, then. Shall I go by scheduled Air Service, or do you think this evening's boat train might be more appropriate?'

'There's no need to be facetious, Peter. If you listen, I'll explain. Let me finish first, and then ask what questions you like.

'This is the result of a plan that British Intelligence has had in mind for some time—ever since your brother became a favourite of Göring and your own footsteps were guided into the Air Force. Peter, think what a coup it would be to have one of our men with direct access to the Chief of the Luftwaffe'

Leo looked at Peter and could see a question about to spring from his lips. He nipped it in the bud.

'You, Peter, are indistinguishable from your brother—we all saw that last night. You're a first-class fighter pilot, you speak German fluently, and you know the background at first hand. Until you find your feet, you can feign amnesia in any awkward situations—it's the perfect cover. Your first task will be to investigate and feed back to us all the information you can gather with regard to German progress with jet propulsion. We already know they have plans for a twin-jet fighter—the Messerschmitt 262. But we need to know more. For this purpose you'll need to get away from operations and on to experimental flying. Damn it, man, why do you think we put you in the Fighter Experimental Unit at Tangmere?'

Peter opened his mouth to speak, but Leo again held up his hand.

'No, no, don't answer that question, it was rhetorical. You won't be returning to your unit. Tonight your aircraft will crash near Tangmere. In it will be Flying Officer Peter Hutley D.F.C.—at least, that's what everybody will be told. In fact it'll be your brother's body dressed in your uniform. Vernon Keogh, one of three Americans with 609 Squadron at Middle Wallop, has volunteered to fly the plane with the body in it and jump out by parachute before it crashes.'

'That's charming. What is the plane comes down on somebody's head?'

'I'm afraid that's a risk we'll have to take.'

'What next?'

'Next we'll put you through a crash course in espionage

techniques and when you're ready—not before—your escape as a P.O.W. will be arranged. We have already reported Johannes' capture through the Swiss Red Cross.

'I suppose you've thought of everything?'

'I think we have.'

'If I may contradict, Sir, you haven't.'

'Oh?' The Air Commodore looked surprised.

'No, Sir. You didn't allow for the fact that I might refuse to play ball. I don't have to go, do I?'

'No, that's true. You don't have to go. Nobody can order you to become a spy, you have to volunteer for that. But I didn't allow for your refusal simply because I knew you wouldn't refuse.'

'You do take me for granted.'

'No, my dear boy, I don't. The system may, but I don't, believe me. You will go, won't you?'

'What about . . . what about my funeral?'

'I'm sorry, that's a sacrifice your mother will have to make. I'm afraid she can't be told the truth. But before you leap down my throat, remember this: your very willingness to undertake this hazardous enterprise will shorten the war and bring closer the moment when your mother will be able to hear the real story.'

'But that's bloody inhuman. So you mean to tell me you're simply going to send her the usual "Deeply regret" cable?'

'I'm afraid so. I have a copy of it here, ready to send off tomorrow morning.' Leo picked up a piece of paper and waved it in Peter's direction.

'She'll be heartbroken.'

'I'm sorry. I'm fond of your mother, as you well know. But there are other mothers too, thousands of them, not just in England but in Germany as well. The sooner this is all over, the better for all of them—mothers, fathers, brothers and sisters too.'

'And what happens if I can't get a transfer out of operations? What the hell am I supposed to do as a

Luftwaffe pilot if I find myself back on operational flying in a fighter squadron against R.A.F. aircraft?'

'We've thought long and hard about that, Peter. If necessary, you'll have to fire on our aircraft. If the maintenance of your cover depends on your shooting down R.A.F. planes, then you will do so. The Prime Minister regards your mission as being of the utmost importance to the allied war effort.'

'In other words you're asking me to shoot down my own men?'

'If absolutely necessary, yes.'

'My God, you brass hats play for high stakes, don't you? I suppose we lesser mortals are just pawns in the game.'

'We're all pawns, Peter, and the high stakes you speak of are nothing more or less than freedom for the majority. It's a simple mathematical equation.'

'I can't see anything simple about it.' Peter stopped to muse for a while. The Air Commodore did not push. Then he continued: 'I suppose I have to, though, whether I like it or not.'

'You'll do it, won't you?'

'You don't give me very much choice, really, do you?'

'I'm sorry, Peter, but . . .'

'Yes, I know. War calls for sacrifices.' The irony was not lost on Charlton.

'I'm afraid that's the way the cards have been dealt.'

'And I'm only just beginning to realize who's been doing the dealing.'

Charlton paused for a moment, and then continued.

'You'll be going straight from here to a destination that will not be made known to you—you'll be driven there blindfolded. If you're ever interrogated by the Gestapo, which God forbid, then you'll have nothing to tell them.'

A buzzer sounded on Charlton's desk. He broke off the discussion to answer it.

'Yes . . . thank you. We'll be right down.'

The Air Commodore released the switch on the intercom box and turned back to Peter.

'Shall we go, then?' Peter hesitated for a second. Then, with heavy reluctance, he rose to his feet and followed his superior from the room. The Humber car and L.A.C. driver that had collected him from Northolt a few hours earlier was waiting by the kerb. The driver saluted the two officers as they climbed into the back seat.

They drove westwards. Peter noted they seemed to be heading in the direction of Maidenhead, but just before they reached a roundabout Leo put a blindfold over his eyes. The driver drove several times in circles and then turned South.

Peter guessed that the journey took about an hour, estimating the distance travelled as approximately twenty-five miles, but it was impossible to know where he was. The blindfold was not removed until after both officers had entered a building and the doors, several sets of them, had shut behind him.

Leo Charlton removed the blindfold. He smiled at Peter and the two men shook hands.

'I must go now, Peter. But before I do, I wish you every good fortune and every possible success. I shall pray for you myself. May God protect you always.' The emotion in his words surprised them both.

During the night the dead body of Johannes was taken from its resting place, dressed in Peter's old uniform, and placed in the pilot's seat of Peter's own Spitfire. Pilot Officer Keogh, who had driven over from Middle Wallop specially for the job, climbed into the cockpit, sitting astride his ghoulish passenger.

Taking the Spitfire up to 2,000 feet, Keogh trimmed the aircraft to crash close to Tangmere. Then he jumped out and parachuted to safety. Two hours later he was back at Middle Wallop to rejoin 609 squadron, his minor but vital part in the affair concluded.

Easy Fox crashed approximately a mile and half from Tangmere and was soon reduced to little more than ashes in the ensuing inferno. The wreckage was, however, easily identified as that of a Spitfire Mark 1B and the misshapen remains of a Rolex watch, which Leo had thoughtfully taken from Peter's wrist, was positively identified as having belonged to Flying Officer Hutley. The cause of the crash was not known. There was no enemy activity in the area. Nobody could explain why the aircraft had suddenly and without authorization taken to the air. But accidents happened. Hutley was officially confirmed dead. The affair was soon forgotten. There were other deaths to attend to.

Isobel Hutley and her father were desperately proud of Peter's posthumous D.F.C., and Isobel eventually made the journey to Buckingham Palace to receive his silver cross from the hands of the King. She had cried a little when the telegram arrived, but life had taught her to expect such tragedies. She attended his funeral with courage and stoicism. Flight Lieutenant Barney Walker was, if anything, more miserable at the ceremony, and made a point of telling Isobel what a good fellow her son had been. Isobel gave the old Austin Swallow to Barney as a present. Neither he nor Squadron Leader Crawford had any idea of the truth.

In Germany, the news that Johannes von Tahlmann had been shot down and captured was greeted with shock and dismay. Many eyes were the wetter amongst Aryan womanhood. Ilse's were not among them.

In the secret enclaves of the Intelligence training establishment, Peter was put through his paces. Nothing was left to chance. Many of the things that had been so puzzling before now took on meaning. He was especially grateful for the days spent at Boscombe Down in Wiltshire, the R.A.F.'s Armaments Experimental Establishment, where he put in fifteen hours flying time on an authentic Messerschmitt Bf 109E3, which had been captured in France in May. He also spent hours familiarizing himself with the cockpit layout of the Me 110, the Junkers 87B and the twin-engined Junkers 88, as well as the Dornier 215 and Heinkel III.

By the end of 1940 Peter felt himself as ready as he would ever be for the mission ahead of him. By now he could pass anywhere as a genuine Oberleutnant in the Luftwaffe—but the real test was yet to come. He spent a terrible Christmas that year, thinking of the future, his stomach housing an entire squadron of butterflies. It was nearly time to go.

On New Year's Day 1941, Colonel Lovelace, the C.O. of the Intelligence training unit, reported that the preparation of the special project, code-named *Bird Watcher*, was complete, and that the subject was now sufficiently well-briefed to take the final irreparable steps. There could be none of the customary embarkation leave, no goodbyes to family and friends. Peter was officially dead, Johannes a prisoner of war. There could not even be a farewell meal. The project was too important to run the risk of Bird Watcher being recognized in a public place. Instead Peter would have to be spirited away under cover of darkness of the long winter nights.

Bird Watcher waited a whole week before the final arrangements could be made for his escape. On the afternoon of the 8th January Colonel Lovelace told his charge that Air Commodore Charlton would be coming to collect him that evening. In the meantime, he was instructed to change into his brother's German uniform and be ready to leave at 22.00 hours that night. Johannes' uniform had been cleaned of blood. The hole through which the fatal bullet had passed had been skilfully mended. On the back of the jacket, a large yellow circle had been patched on. There was another coloured patch on the right knee—the badges of the P.O.W. Bird Watcher looked the part in every detail.

Leo Charlton arrived an hour or so late, delayed by a

near miss from a bomb that had damaged his car. As a result he arrived a little after 23.05, driving an inconspicuous Hillman 10. With a minimum of fuss Johannes, as Leo insisted on addressing him now, was told to get into the car. After a brief goodbye and thank you to Lovelace, Peter was once again forced to submit to the indignity of the blindfold. He left, as he had come, in total ignorance of his whereabouts. It was, as he was told once again, as much for his own protection as for that of others.

It had taken several days to obtain a suitable aircraft for the escape, since no front-line fighters could be spared. A Lysander was considered, because of its very short take-off, but the idea was soon discarded. In the end, the ubiquitous and reliable De Havilland Tiger Moth—with which the Bird Watcher was extremely familiar—was chosen.* Earlier the same morning the bi-plane landed in a field near Dover. The pilot informed the farmer who owned the land that his engine had stalled and that the Tiger would be collected as soon as possible, regretting any inconvenience caused. The farmer thought nothing of the incident, nor were his suspicions aroused later when the machine was removed in the middle of the night. The pilot of the bi-plane was a little puzzled, to say the least, at being ordered to take off from Hawkinge in Kent and land again in a nearby field, but orders were orders. His was not to question them.

After an hour's driving, Leo told his charge that he could remove the blindfold. It was not too dark a night, but bitterly cold.

The plan was that Johannes should be seen to escape to occupied France. The airfield selected was Wissant in the Pas de Calais, a small field from which units of JG 53 had flown last autumn. This station was picked for its close

*There were a great many of these aircraft scattered around the country and in the event of a genuine escape such a machine would be very much easier to steal from a less well-guarded training establishment than a fighter from an operational station.

proximity to the English coast. Peter was to take off in the dark and, flying as low as safety would allow, cross the French coast as the approaching dawn brightened the sky, to facilitate a landing in strange surroundings.

Peter and Leo talked little on the journey. There was time in hand but not enough to make sleep worthwhile. Leo had thoughtfully laid on a package of smoked salmon sandwiches, the last of that delicacy that either man would be likely to see for a number of years, and while they ate they exchanged chit-chat and Leo cracked a few rather feeble jokes. Inevitably, the time came to drive the last mile to the field where the Tiger Moth had been parked. Leo became serious as the car began to move again.

'Johannes—' he began, only to be interrupted immediately.

'Must you call me that, Leo?'

'My dear boy, hasn't your training taught you to think Johannes, to *be* Johannes in every detail—except in so far as your allegiances are concerned? You surely don't expect me to put the clock back at this late hour?'

'I suppose not, but—'

'But nothing.'

'You know, I've actually begun to believe I *am* Johannes.'

'So much the better. Now remember: use amnesia in an emergency. You've been shot down and held prisoner—they won't know what might have happened to you in the meantime so it'll be nothing unusual. Remember the codeword and remember your initial contact in Wissant is Marie Leveque. Whatever you do, *remember that name*. She'll report your safe arrival to us and contact you when necessary. She's one of the best.'

Two R.A.F. Regiment sentries with rifles and fixed bayonets were guarding the aeroplane. The car pulled up at the edge of the field and as the two men stepped out were challenged immediately.

'Halt. Who goes there?'

Leo gave the password and the small ceremony was over in five minutes. The Bird Watcher, draped in an army greatcoat, climbed into the cockpit, put on a helmet and goggles, and went through the standard pre-take-off procedure. The Air Commodore swung the propeller, watched by the two astonished A.C.2. guards, neither of whom had previously been privy to the spectacle of so senior an officer performing such an apparently menial task. The engine coughed on the second swing. On the fourth it fired again and then caught. The revs picked up slowly as Peter opened the throttle. The pilot gave the thumbs-up sign before taxiing a short distance to face into the wind. There was a few moments' pause before, with a rising engine note, the Tiger Moth began to gather speed across the turf. Leo looked on as it climbed steadily before setting its nose in the direction of the French coast. Then it was swallowed by the darkness.

The small bi-plane droned its way across the sombre waters of the English Channel. Peter spent the flight peering into the gloom, fearful that he might be pounced on by fighters of either side, but reached the French coast without accident. The sky was brightening, and in the hazy dawn light Peter saw that landfall was a few miles to the west of the point intended. The Tiger banked to port and skirted the beaches, before Peter spotted the airfield at Wissant and a number of aircraft circling to land. At first there was no sign of opposition to his slow but steady approach, but then pinpricks of flaming tracer started to stream towards him, first from one point, then another, then a third. The aim was bad. Perhaps fingers were cold so early in the morning; more likely, nobody felt particularly threatened by a single English bi-plane trainer. The fire ceased abruptly when it became obvious that the intruder was intent on making a landing. Already the aeroplane was over the turf; now the wheels were touching down. Peter completed the landing and taxied towards what appeared to be the control tower and administrative area. His gaze flitted to one side as he became aware of a vehicle approaching out of nowhere and as far as possible, keeping pace with the aeroplane. A man, he looked like an officer, was standing up in the wagon and holding on to something with one hand. With the other he was frantically gesticulating at the aircraft to stop. Other men clutched rifles or machine pistols, and Peter saw they were keeping the British plane covered.

He stopped the Tiger Moth by the buildings and cut the motor, with a glance towards the officer who, pistol in hand, and accompanied by half a dozen others, was approaching cautiously. Calmly Peter turned off the fuel and unbuckled the safety harness. He felt something small and round and hard pressed into the back of his neck. At the same time a voice rapped '*Hände hoch*!'

Slowly he turned his head, raising his hands as well. He forced himself to smile, but the smile was not reciprocated. The officer took over now.

'Get down from your aeroplane,' he demanded. The pilot did as he was ordered. Then, under cover of the guns, he slowly unbuttoned the British Army greatcoat to reveal the blue Luftwaffe uniform with its P.O.W. insignia beneath.

'Greetings, Herr Leutnant. I am the Baron Johannes von Tahlmann, Oberleutnant late of JG 51, but more recently a prisoner of the British.'

For a lengthy period nobody moved. The guns remained raised, as Peter took off his flying helmet. Johannes' face was well known. Now he raised his hand in formal salute. 'Heil Hitler', Peter announced, with more confidence than he felt. The young Leutnant's face slowly creased into smile of recognition. He reciprocated the salute and the guns were lowered. At once the back-slapping and congratulations started as the group headed towards the buildings.

The Bird Watcher had arrived.

CHAPTER TWO

As Peter made his way towards the control tower surrounded by his now-jubilant Luftwaffe comrades, he was distantly aware of the remote drone of aircraft engines. The Leutnant who had greeted him seemed to hear the same sound. He stopped for a moment, standing perfectly still on the fringes of the group, straining to catch the far-off hum. For a couple of seconds the flurry of greetings and congratulations died down, and in the silence Peter could hear the noise quite distinctly. He hadn't been mistaken: there *were* aircraft approaching—the rumble of engines was getting louder. He had just time enough to register the panic-stricken faces around him as the group suddenly broke up and began to scatter for cover, when the ground beneath his feet erupted in a whirlwind of flying earth and stones, smoke and flame, and the air was rent by a deafening crescendo of explosions. Suddenly the sky seemed to be split open with the roar of racing engines and the staccato chatter of machine gun fire. A bomb blast only yards away picked Peter off his feet and sent him hurtling through the air.

The dawn raid carried out by the squadron of Blenheim Bombers, racing across at treetop level, had come entirely without warning, and the surprise had been total. Had Peter been in full command of his faculties, instead of lying bruised and unconscious in a muddy crater blasted out by the British bomb, he would no doubt have cursed his luck—particularly as the bombing raid had served no strategic purpose other then to kindle the hatred of one side for the other. But Peter was in no fit state, either physical or mental, to do anything of the kind. By the time the stretcher party reached him, picking their way through the rubble and the carnage, he was in a deep coma.

The aftermath of the raid on the Wissant airfield was chaotic: the bombs unleashed by the squadron of Blenheims had torn a series of gaping holes in the strip and one had scored a direct hit on the control tower itself, now reduced to little more than a smouldering ruin. The acrid smoke from the blazing aircraft hangar, the flames fanned by the stiff breeze sweeping across the flat surrounding countryside, billowed out over the field, burying the debris, human and otherwise, in a choking black shroud and severely hampering the efforts of the rescue workers. Of the party of Luftwaffe officers who had been standing with Peter when the Blenheims had struck, only two had escaped unscathed; but of the young Leutnant who had been the first to greet him, all that remained was a blackened corpse spreadeagled on the tarmac.

Gingerly, the two Luftwaffe survivors added their efforts to those of the stretcher bearers, guiding them to the spot where Peter's crumpled body lay. A steady German hand felt for his pulse: it was faint and irregular, but just discernable. Cautiously his body was lifted on to the stretcher and borne away to the waiting ambulance. Within a matter of hours Baron Johannes von Tahlmann had been transported to a military hospital in Berlin, there to be attended by Herman Göring's personal physician.

Peter lay in his bed in Room 15 for the rest of the day and all through the following night, dead to the world. He was unaware of the heavy guard posted at his door, the small throng of press reporters in the corridor, or the constant comings and goings of the medical staff. He remained motionless, never stirring, totally obvious too of the presence of the young woman who sat at his side as the hours ticked past.

That night Ilse who had rushed to the hospital the moment the news of Peter's return had reached her, stayed by his bedside until 9 p.m., only leaving after extracting a promise from the night sister that she should be informed immediately of any change in her husband's condition, and especially if he showed signs of regaining consciousness. She returned next morning to resume her vigil. In the middle of the afternoon her patience was rewarded.

The man in the bed stirred several times and then his eyes flickered open. Ilse immediately reached for the bell by the bedside. Johannes was staring at her, but his gaze seemed to hold no signs of recognition. To Ilse, it was as if he were looking straight through her, his brow furrowed by pain, his expression conveying a distress quite beyond his obvious physical discomfort. She reached for the bell a second time, but just as she did so a party of three doctors and two nurses entered the room.

Words were coming out now—faintly but audibly, in a bizarre mixture of English and German. At first surprised, Ilse realised then that in his delirium Johannes must be reliving the events of his early childhood. By the anguish written on his contorted features, she could see that he was suffering intensely, it was a sight she found hard to reconcile with her more recent memories of him. It seemed almost impossible to believe that the stricken figure she saw before her now was the same man she had married—the man who made *her* suffer. The news of his capture by the British had secretly delighted her; the news of his escape had filled her with dread; but now, for the first time, she found herself almost pitying him. It shocked her to discover that Johannes, always so disciplined, so taut with self-control, could suffer too.

As the man's delirious ramblings continued, Ilse turned away from him and faced the doctors, hoping for reassurance, but their faces were blank and impassive. Without a word to her, the senior of the three turned to the nurses and called for the patient to be sedated. Within minutes Ilse was watching her husband's haggard features relax into sleep.

The next morning the patient once again regained consciousness, but Peter's bewildered mind was as blank as ever. He could remember nothing. Once again he gazed at Ilse as if she were a perfect stranger. But this time he was sufficiently rational to give voice to his confusion. Minutes after he awoke, the questions started.

'Who am I? Where am I?'

—Over and over again the words were repeated, becoming more and more insistent. Ilse, who had spent the night watching over him in spite of assurances from the doctors that he would not regain consciousness until morning, suddenly panicked, as she felt Johannes' hand reach out to grip her own. The delirium seemed to be returning; her husband's body appeared to be undergoing a series of convulsions, his legs kicking wildly underneath the bedclothes. It was as if he were wrestling in the grip of some nameless fear, some terrible hallucination. Alarmed by the increasing violence of his spasms, Ilse rushed out into the corridor to get help. A party of white-coated medical staff immediately hurried past her into the room, and from inside she heard screams, heavy thuds and the sound of her husband's body being forcibly sedated. After a time the noise died down and the senior physician came out to her, brushing himself down.

Ilse was leaning against the wall, tearful and exhausted, still trying to control the shaking which had seized her.

The physician spoke.

'I'm afraid, Baroness, there's very little we can do for your husband. Physically he appears to be on the mend, but mentally—' He shook his head gravely. 'He seems to be suffering from amnesia.'

A week passed, but Peter's memory did not return, his mind remaining utterly void of detail. But his grip on reality seemed firmer now. He had accepted that his name was Johannes von Tahlmann and that he was a Leutnant in the German Air Force. He had even aquiesced in the revelation of his marital status and that the pretty woman who had hardly left his side was his wife. For that much he thanked—well, he wasn't quite sure who to thank at the time. He knew no God, any more than he knew Herman Göring, when the Chief of the Luftwaffe paid him a visit one afternoon.

The announcement of von Tahlmann's sensational escape from captivity in England might have signalled a veritable orgy of propaganda from Göbells' ministry, had it not been for the "regrettable" wounds this national hero had received in the course of a "cowardly British attack". Even so, the German Press and Radio cited the Oberleutnant as a shining example of the superiority of the master race, a credit to the dogged determination of the German people and to all that was best in the Third Reich. Daily medical bulletins reported his progressive recovery, but all mention of his amnesia was studiously avoided. As Göbells no doubt realised, hero without memory was a doubtful propaganda weapon.

To all outward appearances the man in room 15 was perfectly fit within the week, but it was decided to keep him in the hospital for a few more days in order that various tests could be carried out on him. The results were inconclusive. The fact that he spoke as much English as German was attributed to his mixed parentage. On the 24th January he was discharged, the doctors' hope being that a return to objects, places and people associated with his past might speed the process of recollection. Ilse was told to resume normal marital relations as soon as possible, but could not bring herself to tell the doctors that there had never been any such thing between her and her husband.

Ilse avoided going straight back to Tahlmann, even though she felt that the familiarity of her husband's family home might prod his memory back into activity. She simply felt unable to give Johannes' mental condition the attention it deserved with the spectre of Magda hovering in the background. Instead, she took her husband to the small apartment that she had taken in Berlin. There followed a two-week period for Peter of daily visits to the hospital, which Ilse was able to use as an excuse to postpone the dreaded though inevitable return to the family estate at Schwandorf. In so far as the medical regimen would permit, a number of friends and comrades, some under direct orders from Göring, came to visit. Among them was a reluctant Werner Mölders, but neither he nor anyone else sparked off the faintest gleam of recognition in Peter. Mölders still had not forgiven him for his barbaric conduct, but now felt a grudging respect for his fellow-pilot's exploits since the day he had sent him home in disgrace.

In the first week of February, whilst Peter was occupied by the medical routine, Ilse had to face a barrage of questions fired at her by doctors and psychiatrists concerning Johannes' psychological state. She felt for all the world as if she herself were on trial. She confessed that relations between her and her husband had often been strained in the past, but, surrounded by the formidable all-male assembly, she shrank from admitting just how bad things had been. At present, she explained, Johannes seemed understandably distant and detached. That was to be expected. But for her too the situation was a strain. It was very strange to be married to a man who professed not to know her.

Johannes, she realized, was profoundly depressed by his predicament, and constantly apologized for it. She had never heard him do that before. Gone was the arrogance and superficial self-assurance with which she was so familiar. To her, her husband was like a small boy, hesitant, shy, and not quite sure how to react to those around him.

Ilse recognized that he was utterly dependent on her—as dependent, in fact, as a babe in arms upon its mother. She began to enjoy his dependence on her and almost to dread the return to what she had learnt was normality. Later developments confused her even further.

After supper and a few glasses of wine one evening they

had been sitting together in the Berlin flat, by the fire. Peter spoke first.

'Ilse, you're so good to me. But I must be a terrible burden to you.'

Ilse looked puzzled. She hardly understood a word of English. This was one of the oddest things about Johannes now. As often as not he would start off in his mother's tongue. He apologized, and repeated himself in German.

'Johannes, you mustn't say these things. You mustn't worry. The doctors keep saying you'll get your memory back, but you must be patient.'

'Patient? Don't you think I've been patient enough? It's been a month, and that's as far back as my life goes. I'm twenty-eight days old. I'm a nothing.'

'Don't be silly.'

'For God's sake, Ilse, why must we pretend?'

'It won't always be like this.'

'Can you be sure?'

'Yes, in time.'

Peter was not convinced. Nor, for that matter, was Ilse, but if the past was erased from his mind, at least this gave the opportunity to make a fresh start. Ilse leaned across and gave Peter a reassuringly maternal kiss. The heady scent of her hair and the feel of it through his fingers, the soft touch of her lips brought memories suddenly flooding back to him. The recollections were not of people, but of feelings, sensations, emotions that he felt he knew, emotions he felt he must rekindle. Abruptly his mood changed. He reached out and stroked her cheek.

'Doesn't a husband who's returned from a long, hard war deserve a little more than that?'

Ilse hesitated, surprised. Then something made her relax.

'What do you suggest?'

The moment of truth for Ilse had arrived and she knew it. Peter took the lovely face in both hands and gently kissed her on the mouth. At once she started to respond. Then she seemed to freeze as the awful spectre of Johannes' rape rose up once more before her eyes. Peter stopped.

'I'm sorry,' he said, deflated. 'I've done something wrong.'

'No, no,' retorted Ilse, worried that she might be the one to offend, and struggling at the same time to sweep images of the past from her mind.

'It's just me being stupid. It's been a long time.'

'A month?'

'No, Johannes, much longer. But please, let's not talk about that now.'

Ilse took a deep breath and moved towards him once more. He saw her breasts rise and fall beneath the fabric of her dress.

'Kiss me again.'

Peter ran his fingers lightly across her cheekbones. He started even more gently this time, and his kiss seemed to last for ever. Ilse's mouth opened, her tongue beckoning his to do the same.

'More,' she demanded.

'Ilse, my love, you'll suffocate.'

'Never, never,' she purred, folding her arms around his neck and pulling his mouth to hers once more.

Suddenly a nearby air raid siren sounded its alarm.

Their love-making cut short, the couple rose from the sofa and Ilse turned out the lights. She drew back the curtains and they both stood by the window, gently caressing one another as they looked out at the fingers of light probing the darkness, searching for the Witney and Wellington Bombers of the R.A.F. that were surely up there with their cargoes of death. Göring had promised that not a bomb would drop on Berlin. Already the promise had been broken.

Without warning the room was lit up by a flare dropped to illuminate the target. A battery of 8.8 centimetre guns opened up in the distance and the couple could just make out a tiny, toy-like aeroplane caught in the apex formed by the meeting of four searchlight beams. Another battery opened fire nearby, its discordant symphony punctuated by the whistle and crump of falling bombs. Then the bomber caught in the beams escaped from their unwelcome glare, and melted back into the anonymity of darkness.

Peter and Ilse stood watching for two or three minutes. Neither spoke, excited by each other's closeness, the sudden feeling of vulnerability they felt before the onslaught of the raiders from the skies.

'It can't go on, you know,' Peter said. 'I must get back into action as soon as I can, memory or no memory.'

To Ilse, the statement was the last thing she wanted to hear.

'Not yet, darling. Please, not yet.'

'No, Ilse. Maybe not yet.'

A few other flares dropped from the sky. Although some distance away, their light, already augmented by the glow of burning buildings hit during the raid, was more than sufficient to pare the edge off the darkness. For eyes accustomed to the gloom, the interior of the flat became bathed in a soft orange light. In time, sirens announced the all clear, but by now a trail of discarded clothing ran from the vicinity of the window to Ilse's bedroom. Until this night Peter had slept in the spare room. He would not need to again.

Before the end of February, Peter was demanding to return to operational flying. So keen was he that Göring, despite the concern that he felt for his adopted nephew, was forced to agree, provided that a medical board would pass him as fit and that he could still match up to the rigorous standard demanded of all pilots. In the meantime, he was expected to do his bit for German morale by appearing in public at munitions factories and rallies. His scripts, as usual, had been carefully prepared, and as usual, he was quickly whisked away before anybody could ask any awkward questions. It was still a closely guarded secret that the young Leutnant's memory was only a few weeks old.

On the 3rd March, Peter presented himself at the hospital, and succeeded in persuading the medical inquisition that his memory had returned. The truth was that the facts, data and personalities of which he spoke were of very recent memory, the result of a carefully worked-out programme of reintroduction and re-familiarization with the past. Despite his continuing amnesia Peter was declared one hundred per cent. Physically he was perfectly fit to fly, which he now begged to be allowed to do. The matter would, he was promised, be considered. But first he was ordered away for a week's leave from Berlin and told to go home to Bavaria. He was overjoyed.

Marie Leveque did not share his mood. From her room in Wissant, she cursed the bombing raid which had dashed all her hopes of contacting Bird Watcher and thus ruined the operation. What possibilities had been missed, what hopes for France. In a brief radio message she reported that Bird Watcher was of no further use to the Allies. His mission would have to be aborted.

There followed a furious row back in London. Prime Minister Churchill himself demanded a confidential report on what had gone wrong. But neither Leo, nor anyone else in the Air Ministry, had any way of knowing how Peter Hutley had become Johannes von Tahlmann, or what could be done to reverse the process. Had Leo the ability to see into the future he might well have felt that Operation Bird Watcher could have been more appropriately coded Operation Boomerang.

CHAPTER THREE

The moment that Ilse had dreaded most of all had arrived. The time had finally come for the inevitable return to the Tahlmann estate, the huge house and the housekeeper, Magda. Among all her fears, Magda loomed largest, for Magda's influence over her husband might bring to life the very parts of his recollection that Ilse most wanted to remain undisturbed.

On the journey down by car, Ilse brooded silently, eventually persuading herself that it was not she but Magda who should have the most cause for apprehension. Assuming that her husband remained in total ignorance, as seemed most likely, then *she*, Ilse, would hold the upper hand. *She* would be mistress in her own house, and could act accordingly, especially in matters relating to the domestic staff. She smiled to herself, thinking of the relief she would experience when she was able to get rid of Magda once and for all. Then she looked at her husband. At last she was proud and happy to sit beside the man she had married. Peter sensed her gaze and glanced towards her. Just for a moment he took his eyes off the road ahead and touched her knee with his right hand. It was no more than a gesture, a fleeting reminder not of dependence but rather of love and trust. In a moment the hand was gone, and the car was turning the corner into the driveway of the estate.

Their arrival, and indeed the next four days, passed in total peace. Even Magda, sensing her own vulnerability, behaved with the utmost decorum, managing to assume a mantle of servility towards Ilse. But both women knew that, large as the house was, there would not be room enough in it for both of them. One of them would have to go.

Some of Johannes' old friends, carefully selected by Ilse, came to call and were re-introduced. During the day the couple rode together and visited as many of their employees on the estate as time would permit.

It was widely known that the Baron had been a prisoner and had been injured in the air raid, but nobody was told of his loss of memory except for Magda—and even she had no idea of the extent or depth of the mental void. She treated her master with punctilious correctness, but her vanity would not allow her to accept that what had passed between them was over and best left forgotten. Magda would bide her time. Sooner or later she would get him alone.

Her chance came on the fifth day of Johannes' leave. Ilse was out riding on the estate, alone, and Peter had decided to spend the morning rummaging through the family heirlooms, hoping that some memento of the past, some treasured trifle or other might jog his memory back to life. Quite by accident he stumbled upon a small photograph tucked into a silver frame and hidden at the bottom of a large trunk in the attic. He sat puzzling over it for a while. The young boy in the picture, dressed in the brown shirt and shorts of the Nazi Youth movement, was sure to be him. But who was the man who had his arm on his shoulder? The man dressed in the black uniform of the S.S?

Hoping Magda might be able to help, Peter rang the bell. The housekeeper appeared in moments, as if by magic. Peter had no reason to suspect that she had been waiting by the bell indicator from the moment that Ilse had left the house, waiting and hoping.

'Ah, there you are, Magda.' Peter greeted her as she came into the room, holding the photograph towards her. Magda took it and his hand at the same time and held it whilst she looked at the picture.

'That's your father. Don't you recognize him?'

'My father, an officer in the S.S.? Are you positive?'

'Of course I am. The late Baron Rudolf.'

'Ilse told me he was dead. But when exactly did it happen?'

'Some years ago now. 1934. In the summer.'

'My God, my father in the S.S. I—I had no idea.'

'I dare say there are quite a few things you don't remember.'

'Oh Magda, if you knew what it's like for me. I'm a total stranger to myself. I'd give anything to remember the past.'

'Can't you remember anything at all?'

'Nothing until I woke up in that hospital in Berlin. The rest's a complete blank. It's almost as if I hadn't been born at all—just thrust into this world fully grown.'

Magda realized that she was still holding Peter's hand. She tightened her grip and began to probe further.

'Johannes, my dear,' she said. A strange, puzzled look spread across his face, not of anger but of surprise at the sudden and totally unexpected familiarity. It needed little knowledge of his own past to realize that it was a little unusual, to say the least, for a housekeeper to address the Baron by his Christian name. He looked at Magda, wondering what was going to come next. But she had stopped in mid-sentence, unsure how far to go. Peter had to break the silence.

'Magda, why do you call me Johannes?'

'I always have done, when we were alone together. Because of what you and I have done.'

Now Peter looked genuinely taken aback. Magda realized that only one interpretation could be put on her last remark, but she was in too deep now to turn back.

'What do you mean?'

'Johannes, maybe one day you'll remember. I looked after you ever since your mother was killed; I used to come to your room. I made you what you are, I brought you up. We were happy, you know. Until that woman came along and spoilt everything.'

'What woman?'

'Ilse, the Baroness. Who else?'

Suddenly Peter flushed with anger. He looked straight at Magda, momentarily lost for words, furious at the insult to his wife. But what if she were speaking the truth? What had he done? What could he do now, what could he say? He needed time to think.

Magda had burned her boats and she knew it. 'I'm sorry if I've offended you, Baron. Please forgive me. You see, I loved you then. Perhaps things are different now.'

'I'm sorry too. But whether or not what you tell me is true, all I know is that I love my wife. She's the only person I'm absolutely certain of. She's my strength and my memory, and she's the one person I feel I can rely on.'

'But you can rely on me—I love you, Johannes. One day you'll remember and when you do, you'll want me. You'll need me to satisfy your cravings. Believe me, I can make you happy, I alone.'

'Magda,' Peter stated firmly, 'this conversation has gone on long enough. I don't propose to discuss my personal affairs with you.'

Magda was biting her bottom lip, attempting desperately to keep back the tears. She would have to go, and at once. The situation was intolerable.

'I intend to talk to my wife when she gets back. I don't see that we can keep you here after what you've just told me.'

'But you'll need me—'

'You flatter yourself, Magda.'

'No Sir,' Magda replied. 'No Sir, you flatter *yourself*. Who do you think runs this estate now? Your wife?'

'Magda, I've heard enough. You're discharged as of now.'

'You can't get rid of me just like that.'

'I think you'll find I can.'

'I'll make you regret it, Baron.'

Peter looked at Magda unnerved by the swiftness with

which her declaration of undying love had become a promise of bitter revenge. He was sickened by her performance, but undoubtedly she had something, a strange sort of hypnotic sexual attraction. Suddenly he felt desperately ashamed of himself, for the unhappiness he could not remember causing. His head began to throb.

'Get out,' he said. 'Please go *now*.'

Magda turned away, the tears started to well up in her eyes, and fled the room, slamming the door behind her.

She packed her belongings quickly, taking a few souvenirs that should not perhaps have been so classified. Some others she hurled across her room in one last defiant gesture of destruction. She left the house in less than two hours, before Ilse's return.

Peter was visibly shaken by the events of the morning, and his headache was unbearable. Lunch did not appeal. Instead he nibbled and drank, waiting impatiently, though not without some apprehension, for his wife's return. It was after six in the evening when Ilse at last appeared. Peter, though articulate, was less than sober and fell about her neck. Ilse could smell the drink on his breath but her anxiety for him came out in a stream of apologies. She had run into an old girl friend in Schwandorf and they had decided to make a day of it and have tea together. She had tried to telephone but there had been a fault on the line. She saw the pain in his face, but knew he had to be left to stand on his own feet emotionally if there was to be any chance of recovery. The doctors had so ordered.

Ilse's worries made it no easier for Peter to sum up his courage and explain what had happened. After listening to her rather breathless story he began his confession.

'You're going to be livid with me.'

'Why should I be? I'm sure you're not going to make a habit of this, are you?'

'I don't mean the drinking.'

'What have you been up to, then?'

'It's Magda.'

The name made Ilse's heart miss a beat. There had been a reluctant truce between the two women during the stay at Tahlmann, but Ilse still did not envisage any course of action other than getting rid of their housekeeper at the earliest possible moment. But she was not yet sure enough of her husband to do anything that might conceivably upset him.

Ilse looked up. There was no warmth in her expression, only something like fear.

'What about her?' she said, trying to sound as casual as possible.

'She's gone.'

'Gone?'

'I sacked her. I'm sorry.'

'You did *what*, Johannes?'

'I had to get rid of her. I'm sorry. I know I shouldn't have interfered.' Ilse's face was instantly transformed, but Peter was oblivious to the picture of radiant delight, busy as he was trying to justify himself. 'It's a bit difficult to explain and really rather embarrassing, but she was very rude about you.'

'I don't doubt it. What did she say?'

Peter hesitated. Ilse did not wait for a reply. 'Did she try and get you into bed?'

'How did you know? How could you possible know? Magda said you didn't . . .'

'Magda is a schemer and a liar. Of course I knew.'

'Then it *was* true. I mean the part about her coming to my room and . . .'

'Quite true.'

'Before we, before you and I were married?'

'Yes, mostly. But once or twice since, I believe.'

'Oh my God, please forgive me.' Peter sat down on the sofa, his head in his hands. Ilse stopped to comfort him. Peter shook his head slowly from side to side.

'It doesn't seem possible. It can't be. I simply don't feel that that's me. Can you ever forget or forgive?'

'It's all over now. It's in the past. Finished and done with.'

Ilse's confidence was, however, gravely misplaced. She had no way of knowing that on leaving Tahlmann, Magda had gone straight to her lawyer uncle, and poured out a bitter story, liberally spiced with innuendos and veiled accusations. Shortly after her visit a special dossier was opened in the name of Johannes von Tahlmann. The papers would be filed at Gestapo headquarters in Berlin. Magda Ziegler issued no idle threats.

From September 1940 onwards, the daylight assault on Britain was gradually reduced in scale until it was almost entirely left in the hands of the fighter pilots, whose 109s and 110s were now fitted with racks to enable them to carry small bombs. The bulk of the tactical bombers, the Heinkels, Junkers and Dorniers, were switched to night-time operations. In an effort to break the morale of the civilian population, the nocturnal intruders blazed a mighty trail of death and destruction. Under cover of darkness their own losses were minimal. By way of reprisal the R.A.F. sent their own Wellingtons and Hampdens to repay the enemy in their own coin.

Now, in 1941, Peter longed to get back into action. He felt it his duty to fight for his country, to fight for Germany. If he couldn't understand the reasons for the conflict, then at least he could repay the enemy for some of the damage. Returning to Berlin and noting for the second time the burnt-out buildings and the human suffering, Peter determined that he must do his share. Ilse, too, figured prominently in his decisions. He had sworn to do his utmost to ensure that never a hair on her head would be harmed.

Back at the hospital after his week's leave in Bavaria, Peter once more faced a medical board and demanded that he be sent back to operational flying. Part of his wishes were granted, but he was forbidden operations. Instead he was ordered to stay at the flat and report daily to the airfield at Gatow. At least by remaining in Berlin he would have the pleasure of being with Ilse.

Under conditions of considerable secrecy he underwent a series of refresher courses. He first flew in a Bf 108, the four-seater antecedent of the much more famous Bf 109 series, used as a communications and utility aircraft. The Taifun, capable of some 190 mph, compared with the 109's 350 mph, was the ideal machine in which to reintroduce the Baron to his craft. To fly it was a joy. Peter took to it at once and soloed later the same day.

Basic flying proved to be no problem at all; like driving a car, it seemed to be second nature to him. Correct procedures and methods are followed by habit rather than specific thought by the experienced pilot. Peter's only problem lay with the instrumentation and the location of the controls, which varied from one aircraft type to another.

In the first week of March, Peter graduated to the cockpit of Bf 109. But when he surveyed the instrument panel he was surprised not to find it more familiar. He checked and re-checked the position of the various dials and gauges. It was a puzzle to him, after he had been told that it would all be routine; but he dared not admit it, not wishing to tell his instructor that he somehow remembered things very differently. He bluffed his way through and after the standard check was given the all clear to take off.

The engine was started and Peter taxied to the runway. He opened the throttle and the engine note of the Daimler-Benz rose in pitch. Slowly at first and then faster the fighter moved across the concrete.

With its very narrow undercarriage and powerful engine torque, the Bf 109 had a nasty habit of veering off to the right long before the tail wheel was off the ground and whilst the pilot's forward vision was still obscured by the length of the aircraft's nose. Peter felt the pull, but resisted the temptation to accelerate even harder, the usual reaction of a beginner. He corrected and then increased speed, the tail wheel came up and the aircraft was clear of the ground. It felt good to be airborne again in a real fighter. He could not remember when he had last had that feeling but something told him he had been there many times before. He knew, though, that the flight could not be counted a success until pilot and plane were safely back on the ground. He came in too fast on the first approach and had to go round again; on the second, the error was in the opposite direction and Peter was dangerously close to stalling as he flopped down on the runway.

For days Peter practised, not just circuits and bumps, but aerobatics, formation flying, aerial gunnery and mock interceptions, desperately seeking to convince his superiors that he was ready once more for active service. Obstinately, his superiors refused to give their approval. But just before the end of the month Peter's persistent pestering and a personal appeal to Hermann Göring himself paid off at last. At his own request he was posted back to his old unit, JG 51, commanded still by Werner Mölders. In accepting the young Oberleutnant back once more Mölders showed the great chivalry and generosity of spirit for which he would be remembered long after his death.

Mölders welcomed Peter back and gave him the customary pep-talk. He insisted that men under his command fought as soldiers with chivalry at all times and with regard to the basic principles of fair play. At no time would he tolerate the strafing of un-armed refugees or the gunning-down of vanquished foes in parachutes or dinghies. Peter agreed wholeheartedly, though somewhat astonished that the Wing Commander should feel it necessary to deliver such an apparently pointed homily.

At that stage of the war it was a near daily chore for the Bf 109 pilots stationed on the Channel coast airfields to carry on the role of the bombers. For this purpose, each wing provided its own fighter escort for those of their fellow pilots carrying their single 500-pound or four 100-pound bombs. It was singularly unpopular exercise, especially as the impact that it was likely to make could in no way be expected to affect the war one way or the other. The normal procedure was to cross the coast at 18,000 feet and after unloading the bombs, mix it, on more or less level terms, with any attacking R.A.F. fighters that happened to intercept.

Peter safely avoided the missions for some time, but eventually his turn came. Following a morning attack on the small Sussex port of Newhaven, he and three others were instructed to fly across the Channel, this time at zero feet, and return to the target of the morning, drop their combined load of sixteen 100-pound bombs on the repair gangs that were certain by now to be hard at work, and then beat it back home again. If this seemed to be a reasonably safe way of carrying the war to the enemy, it was not what appealed to Peter. He felt by instinct that he had been trained as a fighter pilot. His mission was to do battle with the enemy aircraft, their soldiers and sailors—not their women, children and old people.

Mölders took a special interest in Peter, not simply on the orders of the Commander in Chief, but because he had become fascinated and intrigued by the miraculous metamorphosis of character that had taken place in the arrogant young Baron since his escape from Britain. It was, for all the world, as if his body was now in the possession of a different being.

On the last day of March 1941, Peter shot down his first R.A.F. aircraft, during a raid by a small number of Blenheim bombers. Three days later he added to his tally one of the new Whirlwinds, which he intercepted in mid-Channel. Next came one of the torpedo-carrying Bristol

Beauforts, which he caught strafing a couple of E Boats patrolling the French coast.

A party was laid on that night, as it invariably was whenever there was the slightest pretext for a celebration. Peter and his friends went down to the *Café aux Deux Canards*, famed for miles around for its *Canard à l'Albigeoise*. Another attraction came in the shape of three extremely pretty waitresses, who were known to be fairly liberal with their favours.

The café was a small one, typically French, boasting a bar, a dozen or so tables and a small floor space on which to dance. The atmosphere was friendly and relaxed on the surface, background music being supplied straight from the wireless or from an old wind-up gramophone. The Patron raised no objection to his girls partnering the men customers, always providing they did not neglect their duties. It was good for business, even if the business was with Les Boches.

The toast that night was Peter. Max, his friend, a fair-haired Leutnant who had appointed himself Master of Ceremonies, rose from the table.

'Gentlemen, I ask you to raise your glasses and drink with me to the health of Johannes von Tahlmann.' With much scraping of chairs the other pilots all got to their feet, chorused 'Johannes', and drained their glasses. From behind the bar there was a sudden noise of breaking glass. Peter turned round just in time to see one of the waitresses bending down to pick up the shattered fragments. The pilots gave a cheer for the broken glass and a wolf-whistle for the girl's shapely legs.

Peter rose to his feet.

'Thank you, gentlemen—thank you for your toast. Now I shall drink to you. To my good friends and comrades.' Peter disposed of his cognac in a single gulp.

The meal was a riotous affair, enlivened by frequent bursts of raucous singing, scurrilous stories and repeated calls for fresh bottles—though in the last case, the persistence of the Luftwaffe men had as much to do with their lecherous designs on the waitresses as with their thirst. All through the meal nudges and winks and nods were exchanged whenever one of the girls appeared. Walter, the young Leutnant on Peter's left, could hardly take his eyes off them.

'See that, Johannes?', he leered as one of the girls rather rashly leaned across him to remove a plate, 'I reckon I'm in luck tonight. Fancy your chances?'

'Me? A respectable married man?'

Walter snorted, inadvertently spilling cigar ash over his lapels.

'Don't give me that bloody nonsense. I've seen your respectable married men and there's damn all respectable about most of them.'

Peter laughed. By now the girl had retreated further down the table and out of earshot. Walter whistled softly.

'Just look at *that*. These French girls—what d'you say, Johannes? She may be all fingers and thumbs with the glasses but by God, I'll bet she makes up for it in other ways. Hello, I think she's giving you the look . . . Well I'll be damned, she *is* too. Johannes, you sly old fox, I reckon tonight's your lucky night. Just make sure you tell her, if ever she's feeling—'

'Walter, you're a bloody fool. Now shut up.'

Walter shrugged nonchalantly.

'Have it your own way. Just trying to do you a good turn.'

'Well don't.'

'Suit yourself. You're a loser. My God, I know what I'd do if I were in your shoes.'

'Walter, for the last time—

The pretty young waitress was about to leave the table, carrying a stack of dishes, but as she did so she seemed to stop and turn towards Johannes, fixing him for a brief moment with her deep brown eyes. While Johannes coloured slightly, the persistent Walter broke in again.

'See what I mean? Don't tell me I imagined that!'

Johannes came back to earth with a sigh of resignation.

'Oh well, I'm afraid I'll just have to leave her for you lechers to get on with.'

The meal over, the small trestle tables were pushed back against the wall, the chairs stacked in a corner, and the Patron appeared, wheeling in a trolley supporting a somewhat ancient-looking wind-up gramophone—the cue for the dancing to begin. Immediately the girls were besieged by would-be partners and dragged, somewhat reluctantly, on to the improvised dance floor, where they were whirled and spun to the hissing accompaniment of a well-worn selection of 78s.

Later in the evening, his head already reeling after heavy inroads into the cognac and several glasses of rather coarse Burgundy, Johannes was surprised and somewhat embarrassed to find himself tottering around the floor in the arms of the prettiest of the three girls—the brown-eyed waitress who had been so attentive during the meal. Ignoring Walter's broad winks from the opposite corner, he braced himself and made a brave stab at coherent conversation. The girl was attractive, no doubt about that, and she had a way of moving her hips—a supple, gyrating wiggle—that made him gulp every time he saw it. In company like that any man could be forgiven for thinking twice about the virtues of monogamy. They talked about this and that—conditions in France, Johannes' friends, life in the Luftwaffe,—and the girl seemed to draw him out, the closeness between them making him relaxed and easy. With a shock Peter realised how close he was coming to an act he might later have cause to regret. The thought of Ilse stopped him in his tracks. With a muttered excuse—something about the heat and the noise—he withdrew and escaped outside for five minutes in the cool night air.

When he returned the dance floor had thinned out, energies were flagging, and it was obvious the evening was coming to an end; only two couples were left dancing, and with a stab of something akin to jealousy, Peter recognised that one of them consisted of Walter and the girl—Walter, in a state of terminal inebriation, his arms draped languidly round her shoulders, was propping himself against her for support as the pair of them shuffled round the floor. The girl did not seem to be enjoying herself much. With a thrill of secret delight, Peter noticed her wrinkle up her features in distaste and shoot him a sly conspiratorial glance.

On the way back to base in the small hours of the morning, Peter found himself crammed in the back seat of the car with a very out-of-sorts Walter. Unable to bear the reek of brandy and cigar smoke on his breath a minute longer, Peter wound down the window as the car raced on through the sleeping French villages. The blast of night air did something to revive the young Leutnant's dampened spirits. Peter felt him stir and come to.

'Nice girl, that.'

Peter agreed.

'Reckon I had it made there.'

'You should have stayed and found out.'

Walter yawned, then gave a lackadaisical hiccup.

'No. Maybe some other time.'

There was a brief pause in which Walter seemed to be deciding whether or not to go back to sleep. He decided not to.

'Got her name and address, though.'

Peter felt a brief stir of curiosity.

'And?'

'She's called Marie. Marie Leveque.'

In April Peter continued to pile up his personal score, adding two Hurricanes, a Spitfire, a Wellington and another Blenheim bomber. Once, he even finished off a Hurricane for Mölders himself, for which the ace insisted that the younger man take all the credit. Peter's star was very much in the ascendant. His fame was spreading.

Peter was ashamed of himself when he thought back to his brief flirtation with the French waitress. He missed Ilse more than he could express. His love for her and the longing to return to her in peace, made him fight with a ferocious fanaticism, his one hope being to bring about the cessation of the war at the earliest possible moment.

On a late April afternoon in 1941 Peter found himself on the tail of yet another Blenheim. It seemed like a straightforward interception for him, and trusting his wingman to keep an eye on his tail, Peter tore into the R.A.F. plane. For a fatal moment, he allowed his thoughts to wander elsewhere and his concentration lapsed. He failed to notice that his wingman was no longer there. The two Luftwaffe pilots had been ambushed by a squadron of new Spitfire V's. There was a burst of gunfire and Peter stared in horror as his instrument panel disintegrated before his eyes. He felt a sharp pain in his left leg. He was too low to dive. He couldn't outrun a Mark V, nor could he hope to outmanoeuvre it. He thought of Ilse. So this was it. This was the end, the way it had to finish for so many young men on both sides. The old 109E still responded to the controls, but the engine was beginning to labour and the screen had clouded over with oil. There was an explosion in the cockpit, and a lump of cannon shell carved out a groove of flesh and bone from Peter's head. His mind went blank, like a wireless at the close of transmission. He felt he should get out but didn't know why, let alone how. The stricken machine bounced two or three times on the surf before smashing into a partially submerged sandbar. The tail rose in the air. The nose dipped, the engine disappearing with a hiss below the water. In the calm that followed the crash, little could be heard save the gentle lapping of the waves and the cries of the sea birds. Peter's head lolled forward on his chest, his face covered in blood, his body held erect by his harness. Slowly the cockpit began to fill with water.

CHAPTER FOUR

Above all, he must remember to think of himself as Johannes, but it was difficult, damn difficult, and his head, his poor bloody head. Ye Gods, he'd never had a headache like this before. Who the hell had decided to greet his arrival with an air raid? Surely Leo could have organized things a bit better? Peter did not open his eyes for a while but decided to lie low and give himself time to orientate his senses. He could feel crisp linen sheets. He breathed deeply and smelt antiseptic. A hospital. Slowly he opened an eye. It was broad daylight and the late afternoon sun was streaming in through the window. The curtains were partially drawn to shade his eyes. The room was sparsely furnished, typically institutional; a bedside table, another table, two chairs and a small wardrobe. There was a vase of tulips and narcissi on one of the tables and in one of the chairs a beautiful woman was sitting reading a book. Peter studied the face and idly wondered who she might be before he lapsed back into unconsciousness.

It was another eighteen hours before he finally came to. His headache was still there, but the pain was less intense. He had not been dreaming. The woman was still sitting in the same chair. As far as he could tell, she had never left it. She paused for a moment, as she had done every few minutes for the last two days, to glance at the recumbent figure for any sign of awakening. Their eyes met. The woman's face was soft, and brightened instantly with a smile, a gentle expression of infinite relief.

Ilse rose to her feet, crossed over to the bed and bent over him. The patient's head was bandaged but there was just enough bare skin to find a spot to kiss.

'Darling Johannes, you're awake at last.'

Peter didn't speak, but nervously returned the smile. This was the last sort of greeting that he had anticipated or allowed for, however pleasant. He studied the face and the figure with approval, but apprehension. They had told him about the wife, but until now he had never faced up to the problems she posed. Perhaps he had never really expected to get this far.

Ilse put her hand out to comfort him.

'Lie still and don't talk. I'll fetch the doctor.' Ilse pressed the bell. Peter lay back on the pillows. Now he was worried. It was all Leo's fault. He must have been mad to have ever dreamed that he could get away with the deception. In the alien surroundings he suddenly felt terribly alone.

'Where am I?'

'Back in hospital. In Berlin, Johannes.'

'How long have I been here?'

Ilse was about to reply but was interrupted by a nursing sister who had just come into the room. She took one look at the patient and seeing his open eyes, jumped to the correct conclusion.

'Good day, Herr Baron.' She paused for a reaction before continuing. 'How are you feeling?'

'I've got a headache.'

'I'm afraid you'll have it for several days yet.'

'My leg hurts, too.'

'We took a large piece of shrapnel out of your calf, but that will heal.'

'How long have I been here?'

'Almost exactly three days.'

'*How* long?'

'Three days, Herr Leutnant, three whole days. We didn't think you were going to survive the operation.'

'What operation?'

'Minor head surgery. I'm afraid you took a nasty knock, but everything should be alright now.'

'Head?' Peter's hand reached up and felt the bandages.

'Yes, but don't worry. The scar won't mar your looks and the hair will grow again.'

The two women exchanged smiles.

'Are you hungry?'

'I'm famished.'

'Good, good. That's excellent. It shows you're on the mend.'

Peter thought of bacon and eggs, and then remembered where he was. He'd be lucky to get anything other than frankfurters. Three days! No wonder he felt hungry.

'I hope you can wait long enough for the doctor to come and see you before you eat. What would you like?'

'Coffee and rolls, please.'

'I expect that can be arranged,' the sister replied, '—if the doctor says it's alright.' Thank God for small mercies, thought Peter. 'Baroness, I think you'd better leave for the time being.'

Ilse smiled again and kissed the same patch of bare flesh between Peter's bandages.

'I'll be back soon.'

As she turned to leave the room, Peter summoned up what energy he had and replied.

'Don't be too long, darling. I shall miss you.' There was little sincerity in the remark, though it sounded genuine enough. The two women left the room together. For a moment Peter indulged his mind with thoughts of England and his mother. He wondered idly if he'd ever see her again, ever see England again. Suddenly he knew he was utterly alone and very, very vulnerable. He lay back on the pillows, tired now, and closed his eyes. In moments was asleep again.

How long he slumbered, he had no way of knowing. When he woke up he saw a tray of food had been left on the bedside table. Unusually for a hospital, he had not been awakened to eat it, nor had the tray been removed. He lifted the lid of the coffee pot. The coffee was cold, and the rolls were as hard as brickbats. It was dark again outside. Peter rang the bell. In a while the nursing sister came into the room, followed by another woman wearing a white overall and a stethoscope round her neck. Peter shrank back. The woman doctor was blonde, hard and clinical. She looked too bloody efficient by half.

There followed a repeat of his previous conversation with the sister. Peter still had not eaten and he was starving. He longed for food. It came soon after the doctor had left. Then he lay still, his mind seeking refuge from the enormity of his problems. He thought of the pretty woman, now his wife. He wondered how long he would be able to deceive her, if at all. Then he fell asleep again.

'Good morning, good morning,' said a jovial elderly male orderly, bursting into the room with enough noise to awaken a corpse. For a few seconds the man in the bed was at a complete loss to know where he was. He stretched, his head was still sore, his leg hurt too. Then Peter remembered.

'Oh God . . . morning' he mumbled.

'Please?' The orderly excused himself. He hadn't understood. Peter had spoken in English. Apologising, he repeated himself in German. The orderly shrugged, too witless to think anything of it.

'Here's a nice cup of coffee for you,' he said, handing a cup and saucer to Peter.

'Thank you .. . By the way, what's the time?'

'06.00 hours, Herr Leutnant.'

The minion then withdrew, leaving the patient to drink his coffee. Peter regarded the brew with suspicion. He'd heard rumours about ersatz coffee made out of acorns, but this was the real thing—hot, strong and sweet. Surprisingly, it was excellent, and it acted on him like a shot in the arm, sending his reeling mind spinning back to reality. His thoughts were abruptly truncated by hospital routine. He was asked to get up and wash. Breakfast, they assured him, wouldn't be long.

The very dark rolls and margarine were not as inviting

as the second cup of coffee, but somehow Peter swallowed it all down. Not long after he had finished eating, the beautiful woman came into the room again—not the sister, but the attractive girl who he had fancied had been at his bedside whilst he was regaining consciousness.

Ilse was full of apologies and explained that having dashed back to their flat and sat down for a few minutes, she had simply fallen asleep and not woken until that morning.

Peter pretended fatigue and let Ilse do the talking. She rambled on about various people whose names were all unfamiliar to him. Peter said nothing at first, afraid of giving himself away. He remembered Leo's advice about amnesia: "*only use it as a short term expedient, as a last resort. You can only do it once.*"

In spite of the turmoil of his thoughts, he made polite noises, nodding "yes" and "no" and hoping each was in the right place. If he looked as bad as he felt, he concluded that due allowance would be made for him. He was prepared to accept that he might persuade the military machine of Nazi Germany into believing that he was Johannes, but looking at Ilse he doubted very much if he could take her in as well. He would have to cross that bridge when he came to it.

Peter felt the sweat gather at his armpits and in the small of his back. He felt like a rat in a trap, with no prospect of escape. He was, as he had already discovered, in Berlin, many, many miles from Wissant and Marie Leveque and far from any hope of getting airlifted back to England if the going got rough. *Damn* those bloody Blenheims!

'Damn who?' enquired a very startled Ilse, who had been in the midst of talking about her mother and father.

'Those bastard R.A.F. bombers that unloaded their bombs on me.'

'But Johannes, darling, it wasn't a bomb, not this time. You were shot down.'

'Come off it, Ilse, I reckon I'm the best judge of how I came to be in this bed,' countered Peter testily.

'I'm sorry, darling,' replied Ilse softly. 'I expect there was some mistake—they told me you'd been shot down.'

Further exchange was stopped by the entry of the newsvendor. Ilse bought the paper Johannes was used to and, walking across to the bed, she handed it to him. He took it with a polite 'Thank you.'

Peter glanced at the front page, not really taking it in—something about the German occupation of Athens and another paragraph headed "Rommel!" Time enough to read the thing later. He put it down, but as he did so his eye caught the date, May 2nd 1941. He snatched up the paper again to examine it, as if closer scrutiny might prove that his eyes had deceived him.

'What's the matter?' Ilse asked, noting Peter's expression of astonishment.

'Look at this, the papers seem to have got the date wrong. Here, see for yourself.'

Peter gave the paper to Ilse, who took it, puzzled.

'No, that's right. It is the 2nd of May today.'

'But it can't be—it's not possible.'

Ilse didn't know what to say. Peter began to frighten her. After a moment he asked quietly: 'How long have I been unconscious?'

'Off and on—four days.'

'Do you honestly mean to tell me that it's only four days since the accident? What year is it?'

'1941.'

'Well at least we can agree on that.'

Ilse laughed, but it was a hollow sound caused by a mixture of nerves and fear.

'Open the window, it's hot in here,' Peter asked desperately. Ilse went over to it. It was wide open already. She walked back and sat on the bed close to Peter. She kissed him. She felt him freeze. 'Johannes,' she demanded, 'please kiss me.'

Peter searched the face of the stranger. It was soft, gently possessive, and he saw in it an infinite capacity for kindness and patient understanding. Sooner or later she would find out the truth, but until then perhaps there was a chance. He reached his arms up around her neck and kissed her gently on the lips. Then she started to cry. At that moment Peter felt a lurking suspicion that she was on his side.

The female doctor entered the room and Ilse was again asked to leave. Everything else would have to wait. Ilse got off the bed and smiled wanly at the unwelcome visitor, wiping her eyes with the back of her hand and smudging her eye make-up. She left the room to repair the damage whilst the patient had his needs attended to.

The doctor asked a number of medical questions. None of them were of apparent significance, until she suddenly changed tack.

'Tell me, Herr Oberleutnant, who is your Group Commander?'

Nonplussed for a moment, Peter decided to play along.

'Major Werner Mölders.'

'Good. And your unit?'

'JG 51.'

'Where are you stationed?'

'Come now, doctor, you should know better than to ask me that.'

'What is your wife's name?'

'Ilse.'

'Where do you live?'

'In Bavaria, Schwandorf. I have an estate there.'

'Good. That's a long way from here.'

'We have a flat in Berlin.'

'Indeed? Tell me where.'

Peter was faced suddenly with a total mental blank. 'Look doctor, do we have to go on with this? I'm tired.'

'Rubbish, Herr Baron. You have been unconscious for over three days.'

'So?'

'So you shouldn't be too tired to answer some simple questions.'

'Well, I am.'

'I'm only trying to test your memory. You know what trouble you have had.'

Peter shrugged. 'If my memory had gone, then I couldn't answer any of your questions, could I?'

'That's not necessarily so.'

'I see. What you're saying is that anyone who can't remember the smallest incident must be suffering from loss of memory.'

'It's a matter of degree.'

'Then I'm an amnesiac, doctor.'

'Young man, you're hardly helping me to do my job. It's all down here in your case history, you know.' Airily she waved the buff-coloured folder in his direction.

'In that case why the questions? Look, I'm sorry, doctor, but I just want to be left alone with my wife.'

'Quite understandable. But you must realize you're not alone in that. There are millions of German soldiers with the same idea. There's a war on, Herr Baron, and my orders are to get you fit for action again, as soon as possible.'

The doctor was beginning to dislike her patient almost as much as he disliked her, but they were to have to put up with each other for at least another two weeks. During that time Ilse was in constant attendance, and in their conversations together many of the details of Peter's history over the previous few months filtered through. Peter was horrified to learn that he had shot down several British aircraft. Although Ilse broke the news gently enough, he still had difficulty in concealing his dismay. He pondered long and hard on the way fate had treated him. First he had killed his own brother, and then within months he had slain a further score of his own countrymen. Leo's cold-blooded words were ringing in his ears again. '*If it's necessary for you to fly combat missions and to shoot down our aircraft in order to maintain your cover, then you're to do just that.*' God knows, he had maintained his cover beyond Leo's wildest expectations.

Peter did his best to conceal his lack of knowledge about the time between his accidents, succeeding by the simple expedient of avoiding questions dealing with the past and talking as little as possible, even to Ilse, of whom he still could not be absolutely sure. Naturally though, Ilse told her father of Peter's second mishap; through him cousin Werner Mölders and the Reichmarschall himself came to be informed.

As a result there were a number of visitors to the hospital bed. All were carefully selected and came strictly by appointment only. All except Hermann Göring. From the start, the Luftwaffe Commander in Chief had accepted Peter as Johannes. Why, indeed, should he have had the slightest inkling that his adopted nephew was an imposter? Thanks to the documents recording the deaths of Peter and his mother, Göring had not the slightest idea that Johannes had a brother, let alone an identical twin. Göring continued to think of him only as a hero, the first member of the German Armed forces to escape from allied imprisonment in England.

Despite the knowledge that his potential contact with Göring was the real reason he was here, Peter was stunned to near incoherence when, without a word of warning, the Reichsmarschall walked in through the door. Though able to stay only a few moments, he had felt it his duty to see how the patient was getting on. He kissed Ilse on the cheek and, after a few words of small talk, he addressed himself to the bandaged man in the bed.

'Johannes, my dear boy, how are you?'

'Better, thank you.'

'This memory of yours is rather inconvenient for us all.'

'Yes indeed, Sir. I'm sorry.'

'Never mind. We can do your remembering for you.'

'Thank you,' said Peter, wriggling uneasily in the bed.

'You remember me, don't you?' Göring enquired.

'Yes, Sir. You are Reichsmarschall Göring.'

'Come, come, Johannes, why so formal? The Führer, by the way, sends his best wishes for your speedy recovery. He also, of course, sends you his warmest greetings and congratulations.' Peter wondered what was coming next. He had not long to wait.

'And I am proud of you too, my boy.'

The Luftwaffe Chief was wearing his pale, powder-blue uniform and from one of the pockets he took out a small box. Removing the contents and approaching the bed, he announced: 'I'm sorry that we cannot have a more formal presentation, but the Führer felt that you should have your award now, as it might possibly help your recovery. As I said, he sends best wishes.'

Peter watched fascinated as the broad black, red and white ribbon unfolded and the heavy black cross with the silver edging was revealed. Göring leaned over the bed and placed the medal around the patient's neck.

'I would like to add my heartiest congratulations too. Very well done, Johannes.'

'What's this for?' Peter enquired, without thinking.

Göring laughed.

'Come now, Johannes, you may have lapses of memory for detail, but surely you must remember? You have earned your Knight's Cross. Your escape from England was enough, but now the enemy planes that you have shot down or damaged have scored more than 40 points for you. As you know, the award of the Knight's Cross is automatic to all Luftwaffe fighter aces who score so highly. Considering what you have been through, you have done remarkably well. Especially since you came back from England.'

Göring's words struck Peter with stunning force. He, an R.A.F. pilot granted the King's Commission as an officer, had been so successful in shooting down aircraft from his own side that he had now qualified for one of the enemy country's highest awards. A cold sweat broke out on his forehead. The palms of his hands were damp with fear.

Ilse covered what she perceived as rising panic with a kiss.

'Well done, darling,' she said joyfully.

'Johannes, I must go now,' Göring said. 'I understand you will be out of here before long. You must come and have dinner at Karinhall as soon as you are fully recovered. It will be nice to have you and Ilse there again.'

Ilse and Peter both nodded their thanks and then with the most informal of waves, and another kiss for Ilse, this time on both cheeks, Hermann Göring was gone. Peter and Ilse looked at one another. Neither spoke. They listened to the sounds of the visitors departing down the corridor. Göring's aides had waited outside the room. Peter removed the cross from his neck and replaced it inside the little presentation box. He lay back on his pillows and, closing his eyes, sighed long and deeply. Ilse took his hand and held it gently. The physical contact provided some reassurance for Peter. He did not want to talk, and Ilse sensed it. He wanted to lie with closed eyes, to try and pull his thoughts into some sort of order and to come to terms with himself.

In a while Peter fell asleep once more.

As Göring had predicted, he was able to go home before long. By the 18th May the head wound had healed sufficiently to enable the stitches to be taken out. Peter was told to change the dressings daily and return to the hospital as an out-patient during the following week. The days at the little Berlin flat passed quietly. While there was still danger of the wound re-opening Peter slept in the spare bed, grateful for the time alone. He was afraid of becoming close to Ilse and revealing his duplicity, and in a shared bed he felt sure the deception could not be kept up. But he also feared that if he did not share a room with her soon he would only arouse her suspicions. There was also a further factor to consider: already his feelings for her went deeper than mere carnal desire.

Peter began to think of his duty to the others, to his companions, his country, his mother and his friends. How could he ever face them again after what he had done? Yet he was a prisoner of circumstance.

Then one evening everything seemed to become very simple. As Peter made his way to the spare room after dinner, Ilse intercepted him, a smile in her eyes. Peter stopped and looked at her, his questions remaining unspoken as she gently led the way to their room and the big bed. After undressing one another, slowly, cautiously, each frightened that they might hurt the other, they made love, naked on the bed as the moonlight streamed in to the darkened room through the open blackout curtains.

Then they lay back on the bed holding each other close, and Ilse drifted into sleep. Peter whispered to her gently, stroking her hair. Strangely calm, he lay awake, sure now after feeling their bodies moving against one another and the familiar ecstasy rising and enveloping them both, that he had loved this woman before. He remembered the sensations that she had imparted to him, mental as well as physical. He was in love with Ilse. It was a love stronger than any other emotion that he had yet experienced, and it had engendered a protective instinct that would transcend all previously cherished loyalties.

CHAPTER FIVE

The next night, Ilse was in a mood for celebration. All her worries about her husband had been beautifully swept aside, and she was certain of him at last. She suggested to Peter that they should eat out—they hadn't dined out together for months. Ilse telephoned the reservation: a table for two for 9.30 at Horchers, one of Berlin's smartest rendezvous, famed for its cuisine, even at that stage of the war. It had been a favourite haunt of the young Baron before his recent misfortunes, and was run by cousins of Ilse's family.

The couple arrived at the restaurant little more than ten minutes late, but already their table had been taken. Peter started to protest but, as if in explanation, the head waiter jerked his head nervously in the direction of their table.

Peter and Ilse both had a clear view of the man and woman who had usurped their places. Both were blonde, the woman much more so than the man. She wore a nondescript evening dress which exposed a substantial and obviously well-explored cleavage; her face was pretty but forgettable. But her male companion was the very opposite of a nonentity. His fair, gingerish hair was cut short and smoothed back against his scalp. His eyes were small, grey and cold, and set close together. A large Roman nose dominated the thin face. The mouth was cruel and licentious. Only the ears, which stuck out slightly, mitigated an otherwise wholly sinister appearance.

Ilse recognized him at once and shivered, but Peter, aware only of the man's rudeness, started to move towards the table, aiming to eject the couple as swiftly as possible. The waiter, hoping to avert a scene, put out a restraining, apologetic hand.

'A table will be free very shortly, Herr Baron. Would you and the Baroness care to have a drink at the bar in the meantime?'

As he spoke he made a bid to propel Peter in the opposite direction. Ilse needed no persuasion.

'That would be lovely,' she replied diplomatically.

'On the house, of course,' added the waiter.

'Thank you very much.'

Peter said nothing, his face darkening with anger. Even if he was not absolutely certain who he was, he was not going to let some damned Nazi upstart push him around. He was sure the arrogant Johannes would have done the same. Ilse saw the look in his eyes and knew he would have to be restrained, physically if necessary. She ordered a gin for both of them. That in itself was something that had changed since the accidents. Johannes had never drunk much in the way of spirits and when he did, it was invariably Schnapps. The Head Waiter murmured a few quiet words in the barman's ear and the refreshments were hurriedly served.

'Sit down, Johannes,' Ilse said quite forcibly. He did as bidden, but positioning himself so as to watch the couple's every move. They clinked glasses and Ilse started chattering away. Every so often Peter grunted, but he was not really listening, his concentration riveted on the other man. He was obviously trying to impress his companion and she, poor fool, appeared to hang on his every word. Peter's anger combined with intense dislike. They had a second gin and then a third, at which point the Head Waiter, still full of apologies, announced that a table was now ready for them.

During the meal Peter occasionally looked towards the spot where he and Ilse might have been sitting, but his feelings of animosity towards the man were rendered less urgent now. Besides, he persuaded himself, it might be as well not to draw attention to himself. His stomach had stopped growling. Once or twice the man brushed past their table as he danced with his girl friend. Peter and Ilse danced too.

Around midnight Peter felt the call of nature and excusing himself he set off slightly unsurely in search of the men's room. Coincidentally, the man's blowsy companion had had the same idea. Peter passed her on the way. When he returned to the restaurant, he was not immediately aware that anything was wrong, but quickly saw that Ilse was not at their table. She must have followed in his footsteps. He reached the table and sat down, his eyes wandering across the room. The woman had returned to her table but she was also alone. He followed her eyes, and then he spotted Ilse. She was on the dance floor, but plainly she was being invited to do a good deal more than dance. Judging by the pained look on her face, she was loathing every minute of it. Her partner was the man who had taken his table. She was struggling but the man was holding her in a grip of steel.

One look was enough for Peter. He got to his feet, and in doing so pushed his chair back so rapidly it fell backwards on to the ground. The restaurant was suddenly silent and the band stopped playing. A few couples had remained on the dance floor but they too suddenly shifted towards its edge. With the crash of the falling chair the focus of everyone's attention had shifted to Peter. Ilse looked at him, her eyes pleading at once to be rescued but at the same time to warn of danger. Only the other man seemed unaware of what was about to happen. As he tried yet again to force Ilse's face to his, Peter caught hold of his arm and pulled. As the man spun round Peter's voice rang out audibly above the whispered exclamations of Horchers' clientèle.

'Let go of her, you thug.'

The man looked at Peter for a moment but then contemptuously waved him away.

'Your wife will return to you as soon as we have finished this dance.'

The silence was punctuated only by Ilse's urgent whisper.

'No, oh please, *no*.'

Peter retained his grip on the man's arm. 'I told you to let my wife go. I'm not going to warn you a second time.'

The man swung a clenched fist at the side of Peter's head. Peter ducked and the man was thrown off balance, loosening his hold of Ilse and barely managing to stay on his feet. In the packed audience, one or two people started to laugh. The man looked at Peter hard. Half scowling and half smiling, he whispered: 'You Sir, are a dead man.'

'Herr Heydrich, you mustn't . . .' Ilse pleased.

'We will meet again, my friend. Very shortly, believe me.' Then he turned to Ilse and clicked his heels. 'Baroness,' he said, and was gone. His companion, seeing him make for the exit, got to her feet and followed, forgetting the unpaid bill.

'Arrogant bastard.' Then Peter too, began to realize the extent of their danger, the meaning, for the first time, of the onlookers' reluctance to get involved. Ilse started to cry, suddenly afraid for their future. The man he had humiliated in front of a hundred or so strangers, was none other than Himmler's deputy, the feared and sadistic head of The Central Security Office of the Reich, S.S. Obergruppenführer Reinhardt Heydrich.

Peter paid their bill and, feeling distinctly embarrassed, the couple prepared to leave the restaurant. The doorman hailed a taxi. Ilse got in first. Peter was about to follow when he felt a restraining hand on his shoulders. He stopped, his heart nearly following suit. Turning round, he saw two men in civilian clothes. Neither was smiling. The nearest demanded: 'Your papers.' There was no "please", no "by your leave", simply the staccato command.

'Who wants to see them?' Peter snapped.

'Geheime Staatspolizei.'

Peter did not argue further. Reaching for his wallet, he handed over his identity card and sick leave authority.

Carefully the two men scrutinized the forms by the light of a torch. Then the spokesman handed them back.

'What's it all about?'

'Routine, Herr Baron. Just routine.'

'May I go?' Peter asked, his sarcasm thinly veiled. The doorman was still holding the cab door open. The gestapo man nodded.

'Of course.'

Peter didn't wait for any further exchange. With a great sense of relief he got into the taxi and sat down beside Ilse. She had stopped crying but was still visibly shaken. He put his arm round her to comfort her. She clung to him like a frightened animal.

'There's nothing to worry about, my love,' Peter said with more confidence than he felt as he kissed the damp cheeks.

'Oh dear God, Johannes, you don't know what the Gestapo are like. They're monsters.'

The taxi pulled away from the kerb as a bolt of lightning lit the sky, heralding the first squall of driving rain that lashed the streets as they made their way back to the apartment.

Several days passed, and both Ilse and Peter began to hope that the incident at the restaurant had been forgotten. But even though nothing had happened, they could not assume that Heydrich had pocketed his pride and decided to declare the matter closed. News had spread swiftly from Horchers', and even Werner Mölders, normally so keen to keep a low profile where Johannes was concerned, was anxious for details of the incident.

Peter did not return to his unit; instead he was ordered to take three months on light and restricted duty. He was permitted to stay in the capital for most of the time but always remained under the direct orders of Göring. Ilse was happy that their life together in the little flat could continue a little longer. The day the orders had arrived, they had had a quiet celebration at home and afterwards made love. In bed later that night, Peter's thoughts returned to the episode with Heydrich. The fact that a week had passed without incident did little to lessen his growing concern. He had been finding out a few facts about the man, and he did not like what he had discovered. He cursed his stupidity, wishing he had paid attention to Ilse's warning. Even then, she had tried to protect him. That, too, had begun to puzzle him.

Peter grunted and Ilse made a suitably affectionate reply.

'You're awake.'

'Of course.'

For a moment, they were both silent.

'What are you thinking about?'

'You.'

'Me? What about me?'

'Just you. How much I love you.'

Ilse stretched in the bed, luxuriating in the pleasure of hearing his words. But the anxiety, the hesitance in his voice had not escaped her.

'What's the matter? What have I done?'

'It's not something you did. It's something you said.'

'Johannes, darling, have I said something to hurt you?'

'No, no. It's nothing like that.'

'Then what is it?'

Peter paused. He had to get this thing out into the open. He had to trust somebody. In the lingering atmosphere of fear and uncertainty he felt he was losing the last shreds of his identity. And if he could not trust Ilse, he was as good as dead in any case.

'What did I say, darling? Please tell me.'

'It was outside the restaurant, after those men had looked at my papers.'

'Oh dear God, don't remind me. I don't think I've ever been so terrified in my life.'

'But you said a strange thing—I remember it exactly. You said I didn't know what the Gestapo were like. You said they were monsters.'

'What's wrong with that?'

'Nothing, I'm sure you're right. But why did you think *I* had to be told? Why shouldn't *I* be aware of it just like everyone else?'

Ilse faltered.

'You—you had lost your memory.'

'But it went deeper than that, didn't it?' Peter paused and gazed at her searchingly. 'You know, don't you?'

'It doesn't make any difference, I swear. I love you.'

'Ilse, darling, answer me. You know . . .'

Peter switched the light on and saw she was looking at him earnestly.

'Yes, I know. Does it worry you?'

'How long have you known?'

'Known for certain, or just suspected?'

'Both.'

'I suspected . . . No, suspected is far too weak a word. I was convinced there was something different before you even left hospital the first time. But if I had any lingering doubts, they disappeared the first time we made love.'

'And you allowed me into your bed, knowing . . .?'

'There's nothing very strange about that. Didn't your Intelligence reports ever tell you that Johannes and I hadn't been happy together? What contact we had was a painful, terrible experience for me. It was something I wanted to forget. You see, against all the odds, you've given me great happiness and fulfilment. I came to you believing you were the husband I hated and feared, and yet you broke through that barrier. I've grown to love you. I didn't tell you before simply because I didn't know what you might have to do—I didn't know whether I could survive if I showed you I shared your secret.'

Peter was horrified. Ilse seemed to be suggesting that he might have to take steps to prevent her from revealing the truth; the thought appalled him.

'Ilse, my darling. I'd go through hell and damnation to protect you. Why on earth would I want to silence you?'

'Isn't that what you do? Isn't that what you've been trained for? To eliminate people who might reveal who you are?'

Peter laughed. 'I'm afraid the hardened secret agent image doesn't really suit me. Even if I tried to kill you, I'd probably mess it up.'

'You're Peter, aren't you? His brother.'

Peter nodded.

'*Peter.*' She repeated the word, as if trying out the sound of it. 'Somehow, I think Johannes would enjoy the irony. He always told me he had a twin brother, but he said you had been killed with your mother in a car crash in England.'

'It wasn't strictly true. As you can see.'

'Where's Johannes now?'

'Dead.'

'How?'

'He died of his wounds after being shot down over England.'

Ilse nodded briefly, then turned away. When she turned back, there was no trace of grief or sadness in her eyes. Peter was somewhat taken aback by her reaction.

'Your husband is dead and you say nothing?'

'I'm sorry, of course,' she replied. 'I mean I'm sorry for him, not for me. You must understand, Peter, it was as if we hardly knew each other. The fact that he's dead doesn't change that. How could it? He did things to me that no friend, no lover would have done.' Tears of memory clouded her eyes.

Peter raised his hand to wipe them away, his emotions torn between sadness for the brother he had lost and hatred for the man that brother had been.

'It was I who killed Johannes.'

'You?'

'I shot down Johannes' plane.'

'Am I supposed to think any the worse of you? Do you think it would have made that much difference to Johannes who squeezed the trigger?'

'I've asked myself the same question a thousand times since it happened, but I still reproach myself. And you see, it's worse now. I can't explain it away as an accident of war any longer, because—'

'What was that?' Ilse interrupted, sitting up in bed. Both listened and the noise came again. A rustle of footsteps, then a sharp tap on the door.

'Who the hell could that be at this time of night?' Peter asked irritably, as if Ilse could possibly know any better than he. The knocks on the door were repeated. This time they were more insistent, more urgent, and clearer in their message to those within.

'Blast,' said Peter, slipping on a dressing gown and making tracks for the front door of the flat.

'All right, all right. I'm coming,' he shouted, hurrying to slide back the bolts and open the door.

There were two men standing there on the landing, both wearing grey uniforms and peaked caps. They were not regular army, and certainly not civil police. The distinctive triangle on their left sleeves bearing the two letters S.D. identified them. Sicherheitsdienst. Peter's heart sank. So Heydrich's men had come to call at last.

'Johannes von Tahlmann?'

'Who wants to know?' Peter asked.

'You will come with us.'

'In the middle of the night?'

'Who is it, darling?' Ilse's voice was calling from the bedroom.

One of the S.D. men took a PPK from its leather holster, as if daring Peter to reply.

'Police, Ilse. Just a social call—' The rest of the words were cut short as the larger of the two men put a hand across Peter's mouth. The other placed the muzzle of the Walther pistol to his temple.

Ilse ran to the door as the two thugs started to march Peter away. She caught up with them and started to pummel at them, arms flailing wildly. A powerful blow across her chest knocked her to the ground and left her gasping for breath, feeling suddenly helpless in her nakedness. By the time she had struggled to her feet again the men were gone. Ilse reached a window just in time to see Peter look up from the street. If ever a face pleaded for help, it was his. Still in his dressing gown, otherwise naked too, Peter was pushed into the car by the man with the pistol. In a few moments the car started, doors slammed and it was gone.

She dressed as quickly as she could and taking her bag and some money she left the flat and stepped out into the darkness.

CHAPTER SIX

Peter sat quietly between the two uniformed men. He shivered a little, but whether from fright or cold he could not tell. All he hoped was that it didn't show.

The car journey took about thirty-five minutes, weaving its way through the unlit streets. It might have been shorter but for a detour to avoid an unexploded bomb. Peter already knew the building they were bound for: No. 8, Prinz Albrecht Strasse. All Germany knew it as the Headquarters of the Gestapo, housing the offices of both Heinrich Himmler and Reinhardt Heydrich. The S.D. was the security service within the S.S., and Heydrich was its Commander. Peter tried to summon up a morsel of relief, the tiniest crumb of comfort, from the knowledge that an argument with the deputy chief of the S.S. was hardly in itself a capital offence, even in Nazi Germany, but the comfort was of short duration.

He was taken into a small room on the fourth floor and left there. On one side of the room was a single window and under it a chair and a desk; on the left hand side, a small cupboard. It was locked. Peter paced up and down the room, each minute seeming like an hour. At some point in the proceedings—Peter had quite lost track of time—somebody came and took his finger prints. That's torn it, he thought. If they have a different set on file under the name of Johannes von Tahlmann . . . Peter asked what the hell was going on. The petty official's reply was totally predictable: 'just routine'.

In due course the need to relieve himself, exacerbated by fear, became an urgent necessity. He put up with the discomfort for as long as he could, but soon he was in agony. Hammering on the door brought no response. Unable to bear it any longer, he urinated on the wall by the cupboard. The relief was immense, an almost exquisite sensation that for a few nostalgic moments took him back to gentler times—to the day at school when a master had refused to allow him to leave the class. Then, as now, he had simply done it where he was. That time the worst that he received was a public upbraiding by the Headmaster in front of the school. He was in no doubt that Heydrich had something considerably more unpleasant in mind.

Peter tried to look out of the window, but found it was a false image fastened to the brickwork. A small light bulb glowed feebly over the desk. Whatever hour of the day it might be outside, it was permanent night in the poky little room. He sat on the chair and tried to sleep, but couldn't. His increasing fear easily overcame the excruciating boredom.

Ilse turned left outside the flat, then walked in circles for ten minutes before making her way to a friend's house. She was not followed. The door was opened by a very frightened man. When he recognized Ilse the look of relief on his face was clear enough. She apologized for banging on the door in the early hours of the morning: as she had so recently discovered, nocturnal knockings usually meant only one thing. Breathlessly she explained what had happened and asked if she could use the telephone, then seized the implement and rapidly dialled a succession of numbers. Her father was "not available", nor was Werner Mölders; her ultimate potential source of help, Hermann Göring, was incommunicado. It was June 22nd 1941. In a few hours Operation Barbarossa was due to be launched, in which Hitler would hurl three million German soldiers, three army groups and most of the Luftwaffe into battle against the U.S.S.R. Without Göring's intervention Ilse could do nothing. The family lawyer, understandably, was powerless as well.

After three days of solitary confinement in Prinz Albrecht Strasse, with nothing to occupy him but the infrequent visits of a guard with a tray of inedible prison food, Peter was getting to the end of his tether. The hours seemed interminable, and the waiting only served to aggravate his own morbid thoughts and fears. There was no way of knowing what charges he would have to face, but Peter felt sure that whatever hideous punishment was in store for him, Heydrich's vindictive wrath would ensure that it was long and agonising. His only chance of salvation now lay with Ilse—Ilse, whom he loved, and who, through sharing his secret, had now become as vulnerable as he was. If Ilse could contact Göring and persuade him to step in, then there was a chance that he might escape with his skin. But as the hours turned into days and still no word came, that single slender chance seemed to recede further and further into the realms of impossibility.

Repeatedly Peter tried to collect his thoughts and thrash out some intelligent explanation for his arrest; he had made a fool of Heydrich in public—stupid of him, but hardly indictable. It could worsen his ordeal, but on its own it hardly amounted to a reason for arresting him. Unless, of course, there was some prior evidence against him, some scrap of rumour or hearsay which, when added to the incident in the restaurant, might be cobbled together into some kind of case. Given a man of thoroughness and good memory—and everything Peter had discovered about Heydrich suggested that he had those two qualities in abundance—that might be enough. *Might be.* The uncertainty was a torture in itself.

With an effort, Peter set about searching his patchy memory for the chance remark or gesture, the overlooked detail of speech or action that might have alerted a suspicious observer to his true identity, but it was a fruitless quest. His own recollection of the months that had followed his flight to France, those blank, grey weeks with the Luftwaffe, the incessant to-ing and fro-ing between home and hospital, was far too hazy; he only had Ilse's account to go on. And Ilse had been with him for only a fraction of that time. Who knows what he might have said or done to betray himself when he was away from her?

The agony of not knowing receded briefly: if there had been evidence against him, surely it would have surfaced before now? Was it even possible that the Gestapo would have allowed a known imposter a free hand, letting him loose among top brass like Mölders and Göring and, for all they knew, sending detailed reports back to England through the resistance? Surely no Gestapo man worth the name would have let him get away with *that*?

But what if they were playing a waiting game? After all, what little scraps of information he had managed to pick up here and there about the German war effort could hardly be classed as military secrets. Even if he had managed to get them back to Leo—and of course, to his shame, he had done nothing of the sort—even then, there would hardly have needed to be tears shed at the Sicherheitsdienst. Military secrets? They were chickenfeed. The Gestapo could quite happily sit back and watch, safe in the knowledge that at the slightest sign of him stumbling on anything remotely likely to put their beloved Fatherland in jeopardy—a pretty feeble hope, on his past record—they could have him safely behind bars in a matter of minutes. Witness the events of three nights past.

Peter smashed a fist against the wall. With a renewed sense of impotence and fury he realised he had come full circle, back to his first question, and it was still unanswered. *What could have tipped them off in the first place*? Again the desperate ransacking of his memory. Again the same tantalizing uncertainty. He knew finally the utter hopelessness of his dilemma: so long as he remained in ignorance of the event, or the person, that had betrayed him, there was no chance—not the slightest, remotest chance—of building a defence for himself. What he didn't know, he couldn't hope to deny.

Time was running short for him now, and he knew it. There were footsteps outside in the corridor and the sound of voices approaching. They could mean only one thing. The steps came to a halt outside the door and there was a pause in which he heard the jangle of keys and a grating sound as one of them was thrust into the lock. The door was flung open and two heavily built guards stood waiting for him.

'On your feet.'

Peter hesitated a moment.

'*Schnell.*'

With a last, almost fond look round the tiny cell, Peter followed the two men down the narrow corridor. This time he had no need to ask where he was being taken.

Heydrich looked up from his desk as Peter was led in and signalled for the guards to leave. Peter was left standing alone in front of him, nervously stroking his three days' stubble.

'Aha, Baron Johannes von Tahlmann. I trust you're enjoying your little stay with us. I take a very close personal interest in the welfare of all my guests here, you know.'

Peter remained silent.

'I fear I must apologise for the poor standard of the

food, however. No doubt as an habitue of Horcher's restaurant you are used to better things.'

Heydrich's mouth had twisted up into an icy smile. Still Peter did not answer. Heydrich went on.

'Of course, sadly, even standards at Horcher's seem to be declining. Not so much in the food, perhaps, as in the loutish behaviour of some of the clientele. I dare say you have some thoughts of your own on the subject, Herr Baron.'

Peter fixed him with a stare. 'Indeed I do, Herr Obergruppenführer. I have heard that a man can hardly leave his wife alone in the place for five minutes without her being molested.'

Heydrich gave a low, mirthless chuckle.

'Of course, Herr Baron, but there is a certain class of woman who brings such unfortunate attentions upon herself. Would you not agree?'

'I'll take your word for it.'

Peter suddenly felt a stinging blow across the cheek, the force of it almost knocking him off his feet. Recovering his balance he slowly straightened up and dabbed a finger at the spot: Heydrich had drawn blood. Under his breath, he muttered, 'Congratulations, Herr Heydrich—your aim's improved.'

Either Heydrich had not heard or he chose to ignore the remark. He had retreated behind his desk and had taken out a large manilla folder, spreading it open in front of him. With a shock of trepidation Peter noticed it had his name on it. The crunch had come. He felt the hair on the back of his neck prickle and had to make an effort to prevent the sudden tension in his body from becoming visible.

'I have been interested in your case for some time, Herr Baron—as you can see.' He lifted up a thick sheaf of papers from the file. 'It has been relatively easy to follow your movements, since you appear to have a talent for arousing publicity. First your dramatic escape from captivity, then your lengthy hospitalization; then I gather you met with a second slight accident.'

Peter mustered his courage and chipped in.

'I was shot down, Herr Obergruppenführer—shot down in the service of the—'

'—Thank you, Herr Baron,' Heydrich rasped, tapping an impatient finger on the folder, 'I am well aware of the details. I have all I need to know here before me. But let us go back to your much-lauded escape. A quite remarkable feat. One is almost tempted to describe it as miraculous. According to the records, you were the victim of a bombing attack immediately afterwards and when you regained consciousness you were found to be suffering from amnesia.' He looked up. 'Amnesia, Herr Baron? Perhaps you could describe the symptoms to me.'

Peter cleared his throat, conscious of Heydrich's close-set eyes drilling into him.

'I'd lost my memory. I found I couldn't remember my past—it was all a blank.'

Heydrich pounced on the words.

'How very unfortunate—a problem I find myself constantly faced with here at Prinz Albrecht Strasse, as I expect you know, Herr Baron. So many of those who pass through my office claim to have lost their memory. They cannot remember a name, a face, a detail. Often, of course, there is little I can do to help them, but occasionally, just occasionally, I find that my methods help their memory to return.'

Peter's anger suddenly erupted.

'You murdering bastard—you don't need to tell me what goes on in this hell-hole. The whole of Germany knows.'

Heydrich continued, quite unperturbed.

'In your case, however, the loss of memory appears to be of quite a different kind. When you awoke in hospital you suddenly found yourself in a new and unfamiliar land, surrounded by new and unfamiliar faces. You spoke, let me remind you, Herr Baron, in a mixture of English and

German. It was as if the life you came back to was entirely foreign to you.'

Peter saw the direction in which Heydrich was leading and attempted, vainly, to head him off.

'But I tell you, I—

Heydrich slammed a fist down on the desk.

'*Silence*! I have heard your explanation. You say you lost your memory. *I* say there was another reason: your life in Germany seemed strange to you because it *was* strange to you; your house, your wife, your friends—they seemed unfamiliar, not because your memory was playing tricks on you, but because *you had never known them before*. Your so-called amnesia was nothing but a simple-minded ploy designed to blind the eyes of your associates here in Germany to the obvious truth: that you are an enemy agent—an impostor.'

Heydrich's voice had risen to a crescendo, and on his final words the heavy fist once more pounded the desk. Peter knew now that the situation was hopeless, that Heydrich had discovered everything. In his heart he had accepted defeat the moment he had stepped inside the room, but his mind and his spirit told him there was still time for one last, desperate protest. It would be his last chance to clear himself of the charges. He had better make it good.

'I demand to speak to Reichsmarschall Göring.'

Heydrich looked up, clearly somewhat taken aback.

'Out of the question. The Reichsmarschall is engaged on the most pressing military business. He has better things to do than consort with British spies.'

'In that case I insist on hearing the evidence against me. I assume I have not been arrested and detained for three days on your mere personal whim?'

'The evidence comes from a source close to the Tahlmann family. Beyond that, the details need not concern you.'

Peter's mind whirled back over the events of the last

few months in a bid to identify his betrayer—but with no immediate result. His memory was as blank as ever. Unless—

'Magda Ziegler.'

He muttered the words at first to himself, then repeated them louder for Heydrich to hear. A picture was beginning to shape itself in his mind: a picture of himself and a blond-haired woman alone in an attic at Tahlmann. The two of them seemed to be staring at an old family photograph; suddenly there were bitter words, an angry scene, and in his imagination he heard the slam of the door as the woman fled the room. Magda Ziegler: the name had sprung to his lips from nowhere, but now a host of images and words seemed to be chasing it across his brain. Piece by piece they were assembling themselves, like a jigsaw puzzle, into a single coherent memory. The irony was not lost on Peter, even in those frantic few moments: Heydrich had claimed to have ways of refreshing the memory of his suspects—perhaps here was a way of forcing his methods to rebound on him.

The Obergruppenführer was reclining on his chair, studying Peter intently and drumming with his fingers on the desk. The sound recalled Peter to the present.

'I trust you will not be so foolish as to deny the charges, Herr Baron. There is no hope for you now, as I'm sure you must realise. Had it not been for that unfortunate incident in the restaurant, your masquerade might have passed undetected; but now I'm afraid—'

A violent outburst from Peter suddenly cut him short.

'Deny the charges? Of course I deny the charges.'

Heydrich looked startled and Peter, scenting the advantage, pressed it home.

'I've spent half the week locked up in this filthy tomb with nothing but the smell of my own piss for company; I've been starved of all contact with the outside world until I felt I was going out of my mind; I've not been allowed to speak to either my wife or the Reichsmarschall—and on what charges? The trumped-up insinuations of my own housekeeper! A woman whose mind's so cluttered with nymphomaniac fantasies I wouldn't trust her with a grocery bill! By God, I wouldn't like to be in your shoes when Göring gets to hear of this. Your *methods*, Heydrich. Your methods stink in the nostrils of all civilised people. Save them for the Jews!'

Heydrich's face had darkened at the mention of Göring and Peter had the faintest sense of having hit a raw nerve. He had already heard that relations between the two men were strained; at first he'd feared that it would work against him, but now he saw a way to turn it to his advantage. Heydrich's voice was thundering at him now.

'My methods are my own affair. Do you imagine I give a damn what you think of them—a paltry British play-actor? *Guards*!'

He gave a shrill command and two SS orderlies entered the room, dragging by the arms a bleeding, bedraggled thing scarcely resembling a person any more, its head hanging limply between its shoulders, its heels trailing along the ground. The two men let go, and the body sagged onto the carpet in a heap. What had once been the pretty face of a young woman stared up at Peter from the floor, her skin caked with blood, her gums toothless and bleeding. Peter made a fly for Heydrich but the two orderlies were quick to restrain him.

'You *bastard*!'

Heydrich smiled, frankly enjoying the scene.

'What's the matter, Baron? No stomach for our type of work? You poured scorn on my methods. This woman is in the process of discovering just how effective they can be. She is a member of the French Resistance. We caught her in the act of sending a message by radio to England. Unfortunately she persists in refusing to tell us what that message contained. She is being very obstinate; but in time—and we have all the time in the world—she will no doubt come round.'

Peter tried to avert his gaze from the pitiful creature on the floor, but was helpless to prevent an agonised cry of compassion from rising in his throat.

'Now then, Tahlmann, or whatever your name is—' Heydrich began again, but he was interrupted by the sudden entrance of an aide. Through the mist of angry tears which had clouded his vision, Peter had time to register that the man looked agitated.

'Herr Obergruppenführer, the Reichsmarschall is on the telephone and demands to speak to you at once.'

A sudden look of alarm crossed Heydrich's face. He turned his back on Peter and reached for the telephone on the desk. He picked up the receiver, hesitated for a moment, and then announced himself softly into the mouthpiece. 'Heydrich speaking.'

At once Peter could hear a stream of voluble invective pouring out of the instrument. The Luftwaffe Chief's words were inaudible, but from Heydrich's expression it was obvious what was being said. The Obergruppenführer's interjections were infrequent and ineffectual.

'Yes, Herr Reichsmarschall . . . No, Herr Reichsmarschall . . . I apologise . . . But I must insist . . . There was a question of treas— . . . Yes . . . Very well, Herr Reichsmarschall . . . Yes, at once . . . Yes, Sir. Heil Hitler.'

'It seems,' announced a red-faced, perspiring Heydrich as he replaced the receiver, 'that the Reichsmarschall has ordered your release. He is sending a car to collect you as soon as possible.'

'What else did he say?' asked Peter.

Heydrich did not reply. Instead he turned to the guards.

'Get that filthy little whore out of my sight. Goodbye then, Herr Baron. I think we will meet again before long. Heil Hitler.'

As he left the room, leaving the two orderlies to follow

him with the girl, a chill shiver coursed the length of Peter's spine.

'I'll see you in Hell first,' he thought out loud.

Peter did not have long to wait after Heydrich's departure. An SS orderly, his voice shorn of all deference to rank, ushered him out of the building. Two Luftwaffe officers were waiting for him at the entrance with a large Mercedes. Ilse was getting out of the car, arms outstretched, tears of relief in her eyes. Peter did not look back as they drove off, praying with all his heart that he would never set eyes on the evil building again.

By the time the pair of them arrived back at the flat, Peter had collapsed in a state of exhaustion. The initial relief had passed, and for the first time he was fully aware of the terrible danger from which he had just escaped. The memory of Heydrich's savage tauntings and the bleeding face of the young French girl returned. He felt too tired to sleep and spent the next two hours pacing up and down, vainly trying to work out his next move, his mind besieged by questions. One of them at least he succeeded in answering: he had managed to put a name to the broken female form that Heydrich's guards had dragged into the office. By now there was no doubt in his mind that it had been Marie Leveque.

S.S. Obergruppenführer Reinhard Heydrich, Chief of the R.S.H.A.*, the self-appointed Reich Protector of Bohemia and Moravia was mistaken once more. He and Peter were never to set eyes on each other again, though it would prove to be a close run thing.

Peter discovered the full story behind his release from Prinz Albrecht Strasse from Isle early that evening. Hermann Göring had kept his word to take a personal interest in the young Johannes von Tahlmann, a commitment he had entered into, a commitment in blood. But it had been three days before Ilse's frantic message had reached him.

*Reichssicherheitshauptamt (Reich Central Security Office).

Despite his preoccupation with the invasion of Russia and the heady scent of the overwhelming early victories for his Luftwaffe, Göring found the time to turn his very considerable anger on Heydrich and a furious argument ensued. Peter had heard only part of it in Heydrich's office, for its implications went beyond Albrecht Strasse. Göring had complained of the high-handed behaviour of the S.S. direct to Hitler, but the Führer would brook no criticism of his beloved elite force. Himmler, on the other hand, lent a much more sympathetic ear and confided to Göring that Herr Heydrich was becoming dangerously big for his boots, and that he and Martin Bormann were determined to deal with him, in good time. The events that took place less than a year later removed the need to settle with their dangerously ambitious rival.

In spite of Ilse's reassurances Peter remained in a state of the utmost fear; he had been horrified at the extent of Heydrich's suspicions, and to add to his anxieties, there was now the extra risk that Marie Leveque might betray him.

The following day he had a brief personal interview with the Reichsmarshall. To his relief, Göring seemed to entertain not the slightest doubt of his innocence. The Luftwaffe chief insisted that, whilst the row between the S.S. and himself was in progress, Peter should keep a low profile. Perhaps the answer was for the young ace to return to active service. For Peter it was the worst thing that could happen. Though his loyalties were increasingly divided, he had no desire to fly against his former comrades, despite the orders he had been given in England that he should not shrink from doing so. He still had a little time. In order that he could live at home and make periodical visits to hospital for outpatient treatment on the insistence of his doctors, he was posted as an instructor to the Air Academy School at Berlin Gatow. But in the weeks that followed, Peter lived a nightmare existence. The hardships of the war and the mounting strength of the British bombing of German cities only added to his dilemma. Both he and Ilse lived with the constant dread that sooner or later Heydrich would find the evidence he needed, and strike again. Göring's intervention had brought a temporary respite, but in their heart both of them feared that it would be short-lived.

The winter came early in 1941, and the headlong advance of the Wehrmacht into Soviet Russia froze to a halt. December brought momentous events. The European War became a global conflict. Japan attacked the American Fleet at Pearl Harbour on the 8th, and Germany's immediate response was to declare war on the U.S.A.

As the memory of his lost months returned, Peter's mood slowly changed. Ilse sensed it almost before it happened. It weighed heavily on his conscience that he had killed so many of his fellow countrymen. Now that he could remember quite clearly how it felt to be a fighter pilot for both sides, he convinced himself that he was becoming something of a Jekyll and Hyde. The agony of not knowing exactly who he was was a thing of the past now, but it was replaced by another uncertainty. He no longer knew in his heart which of the two sides he truly belonged to. To whom, therefore, did he owe his allegiance? In England, so far as he knew, he had a mother and grandfather, many of his friends, most of his memories. But here in Germany there was Ilse, whom he loved above all else. He despised the Nazis and everything they stood for, but their days were surely numbered. Hitler's gamble to knock out the U.S.S.R. in a swift summer campaign, "a war of destruction" as the Führer had described it, had patently failed. Now England was supplied by a mighty arsenal of men and weapons from the United States. Despite himself, Peter could only hope that the land of his father would not be utterly destroyed in the final conflict.

He argued endlessly with himself about what he should do. He had to accept that he was just as much a German as he was English. And, as he turned things over in his mind again and again, he came to a number of conclusions. It was the British who had seen fit to regard his life as expendable, who had been ready to send him off to near-certain death in the greater interest of the nation as a whole. It was an Englishman, who on orders from the highest political level, had commanded him to shoot and kill his own side if such actions became necessary. Paradoxically, Hermann Göring had shown considerably more concern for his welfare than Leo Charlton.

Then Peter thought of his mother, and the very close relationship they had had. He even thought of the old days at Upavon, happy carefree days, a lifetime ago. His mind dwelt once more on Ilse, her father, Werner Mölders, his comrades in JG 51 and new-found friends at the Air Academy—all good people with whom he had much in common, for the most part drawn into a conflict in which their only concern was to do their duty by their comrades. Damn the politicians, the prejudices and petty jealousies. Damn them all and their internecine war. Resort to armed conflict by his respective countries should have been as unthinkable as war between Britain and America.

Finally, when all other ways out of the deadlock had seemed to fail, Peter examined his predicament on a simple mathematical basis. As Ilse was wholly German and he half so, then between the two of them they were three-quarters of stock. Peter knew that ultimately his duty was no longer to a country but to an individual. But for her love and loyalty he would, even now, be a dead man. Such deliberations, however, were soon to be taken out of his hands.

Some months after Peter had been arrested by the Gestapo, Leo was informed of the events. From the fact that Marie Leveque had sent no further messages after her last report, describing her abortive rendezvous with him, Leo guessed that she must have met the same fate. Peter he knew, had been released—but Marie had not been so lucky. Soon after, a British agent in Berlin was despatched to gain access to the hospital where Peter had been treated, and managed to get a sight of the medical file in the name of Oberleutnant Baron Johannes von Tahlmann. Charlton knew now that Marie Leveque's report of her brief meeting with him had been accurate in its assumptions: Peter *had* been suffering from amnesia, and the amnesia was genuine. At other times Charlton would have been able to appreciate the irony. Now, he began to understand better the terrible tightrope which Peter had been forced to tread. Clearly Herr Reinhard Heydrich posed a formidable threat. Perhaps Marie had told him nothing—but even so the risk to Peter remained: if the dreaded head of the S.D. was crossed, he did not generally forgive and forget. It was then that Leo decided that Operation Bird Watcher still had a chance of success, if certain barriers were raised. The first, and most obvious, was Heydrich. The onrush of events necessitated the activation of a plan Leo had been developing for some time.

In 1942, Heydrich spent most of his time in Prague, as befitted the Reich's Protector of Bohemia and Moravia. Leo sought an audience with the Czech Government in exile in England. He was listened to with interest and sympathy. By the close of the meeting, Reinhard Heydrich's fate was sealed. He would no longer have to wait for Himmler, Bormann and a still furious Hermann Göring to finish plotting his downfall in Germany. Britain would strike first. Leo had brought the strongest pressure to bear to expedite the matter at an early date.

On the 27th May 1942, two Czech partisans, Jan Kubis and Josef Gabeik, were specially parachuted from England for the purpose of carrying out the assassination, their plan being to ambush Heydrich's Mercedes en route to his office in Prague. In true German style, the car appeared punctually at the appointed spot and was easily recognizable. There were two pennants on the mud-guards: the flags of the S.S. and of the Reich Regency. As the driver slowed to negotiate a sharp bend, a purpose-built bomb was rolled down the road to explode under the car.

Heydrich was severely wounded by steel fragments which entered the area of his lungs and stomach. He was rushed to the Bullovka Hospital where he underwent emergency surgery, and appeared to be making a good recovery when he suffered a sudden relapse. The medical staff struggled to save his life but septicaemia set in. Obergruppenführer Reinhard Heydrich, the infamous deputy head of the S.S., died within hours.

There followed the most terrible retribution against the Czechs, themselves largely innocent of the killing. Furious at the murder of their deputy leader, the S.S. executed thousands or transported them to concentration and extermination camps.

It was the village of Liddice that suffered worst. On June 9th, a detachment of the S.S. division, "Prinz Eugen", under the command of one Haupsturmführer Max Rostock, moved in. All the inhabitants were ordered to be confined to their homes. The following day, the men were taken out in batches of ten and summarily executed. By 16.00 hours 172 had been killed. A further nineteen who worked outside the village, together with eight women, were taken to Prague and similarly despatched. The other 195 women of the village were packed off to Ravensbruck Concentration Camp. The 90 children were, so far as is known, adopted by German families as a racial experiment. Finally, each and every building was dynamited and the whole area razed to the ground.

Reinhard Heydrich had made the von Tahlmann affair very much a private concern, his own personal vendetta. The details he left on file did not go beyond the record of the arrest and subsequent release. Hermann Göring personally demanded the destruction of the file from Heinrich Himmler, and his request was granted. The greatest menace to Peter Hutley had been removed. But a terrible price had been paid.

The von Tahlmanns eschewed what little remained of the social life of Berlin at the time. The couple kept to their own company, prefering simply to be together. Peter read a great deal, including *Mein Kampf* and certain of the works of Marx, Engels and Lenin, rapidly becoming more and more alarmed at the prospect of a Communist-dominated Europe—the inevitable result of the defeat of Germany.

Throughout the first half of 1942 he was content to keep a low profile. The Heydrich affair had taught him its full value. But, by the middle of summer, whilst the Panzers amidst renewed optimism smashed their way ever deeper into Soviet territory, Peter began to experience increasing feelings of conscience. He felt he could not remain on the sidelines forever.

New types of Russian aircraft, vastly superior to the semi-obsolete machines that had been crushed by the Luftwaffe the previous summer, were beginning to make their presence felt. Replacements were constantly required by the Germans both in terms of personnel and planes.

Ilse read his mood, as she always did. Deeply concerned for his safety, she did everything in her power to dissuade him from once more seeking a posting to an operational unit. She knew full well that he would volunteer for the Eastern front. It was the only logical battleground for him. Up to a point she was successful, but she knew better than anyone that her luck could not last. It was only a matter of time.

CHAPTER SEVEN

The news of the assassination of Heydrich reached their ears as sweet music, but the couple continued nonetheless to live in constant dread that irrefutable proof of the masquerade would be discovered. Each and every time there was an unexpected knocking on the door of their flat, particularly at night, they would experience that terror afresh. In Peter's mind now, there was no question of carrying out his orders to obtain information for British Intelligence. If he had failed in that task, it was, he argued to himself, no fault of his. The British had risked his life, then destroyed his effectiveness, and, subsequent events had produced a major shift in the focus of his allegiances. Even if he had felt more than a passing loyalty to the man who had willingly sent him on this path, he knew there was no practical chance to obey them. Göring's personal protégé was the very last man that the Reichsmarschall would permit to engage in the dangerous job of experimental flying. Peter had already requested such an assignment and had been met with a flat refusal.

Apart from a continuing risk of Gestapo investigation, Peter lived in dread of two other eventualities. The first was a fresh posting to a fighter squadron on the western front. The second was direct contact with another British agent.

As it turned out, Peter had to face both eventualities on the same day.

In the morning he received orders to proceed the very next day to the Messerschmitt factory at Regensburg to collect a replacement Bf 109. Much to his relief he was not instructed to fly west, but was posted to Maykop, deep in the Russian Caucusus. There he was to join up with JG

52, the 52nd fighter Geschwader of the Luftwaffe.

The Russian front had always seemed to him to be his salvation, his one chance to fight for the future of both his countries of origin. The British might not understand at this stage, but surely they would later, when they woke up to the Soviet menace.

Peter was thankful that at last he could do something constructive, and resolved to throw himself into the fray with a maniacal, desperate fury. Ilse was crestfallen at the prospect of Peter's departure, but the strain was beginning to tell on both of them. Peter insisted that they have a farewell dinner that night, as well as a belated salutation to the passing of Heydrich. They decided this time to avoid Horchers. Unfortunately Hermann Göring telephoned late in the afternoon, insisting that they join him as his guest. Peter had no choice but to accept gratefully, but the truth was that it was far from his idea of a pleasant evening.

The heavy burden of his responsibilities and the deteriorating military situation were evident in Göring's mood and appearance. He was, if anything, even fatter than the last time he and Peter had met. For the most part, Frau Göring and Ilse exchanged small talk whilst her husband dominated the conversation.

Outwardly he was full of enthusiasm for the ultimate victory of the Reich over her enemies. But he spoke in subdued tones for the most part, and strictly for his young guest's ears. Peter found himself feeling almost sorry for the man who had saved his life. The swaggering Nazi was now reduced to a pathetic parody of a man, a fanatical devotee to the cause of National Socialism, which he swallowed like the drugs on which he was so dependent. Drinking copiously, his tongue loosened, he became more expansive.

'My boy,' he suddenly whispered, dribbling wine down his tunic, as he spoke. 'I have endorsed your assignment to the Russian front, because I thought you would prefer it—with your English background.'

Peter froze.

'But Herr Reichsmarschall, an English mother who left my father and in any case died years ago, is scarcely worth consideration, surely?' Peter paused before continuing. 'Besides, I can hardly remember her or my brother. They died together.'

'I realize that, Johannes. I simply thought you would prefer it that way. You might not have liked to think that perhaps you were fighting a relative—a cousin of yours, maybe. Besides, for my Luftwaffe boys, the Russian front is much the safest posting at the moment. The standard of the Russian pilots is far inferior to that of the English. I want you to take great care of yourself. I know you will acquit yourself with distinction out there. I wish you every good fortune.'

'Yes, Herr Reichsmarschall. Thank you.'

Göring switched the conversation to the ladies and to subjects less painful. Soon Peter and Ilse found an excuse to bring the evening to an end. They thanked their host for the meal and returned to their flat for their last night together, collapsing on the sofa in the little sitting room to listen to some music before retiring.

They had scarcely settled down when they were interrupted by a sound within the apartment. Peter released his hold on Ilse and listened. Ilse froze.

Peter tiptoed over to the kitchen door and flung it open. Their visitor had clearly not entered the building from the front.

'Herr von Tahlmann?'

A nondescript man with a thick sallow face was framed in the doorway. Peter surveyed the small man. He had steel-framed spectacles and a strangely high-pitched voice. Something about him was familiar, but Peter couldn't put his finger on it.

'Who are you?'

'The code word you require, is, I believe, Birdwatcher.'

The blood turned to ice in Peter's veins. He stood, wanting to speak, but no words came. The visitor took in the look of anguish and fear.

'Don't worry, Flying Officer, I'm on your side. You'll find the Gestapo generally knock on the front door.' He managed a smile. Peter still didn't say a word.

'I think I'd better come in, Mr Hutley, don't you?' The man spoke in English for the first time. Peter nodded helplessly and held out his hand to usher the man into the living room. At the same moment Ilse appeared.

'Who is it . . . .?' Seeing the man and noting with relief, that he was alone, she went no further.

'Allow me to introduce myself. My name if Helmuth Crisinger. At least, that's what my papers say.' He pulled out his identity card and showed it to them. Peter noted that the man was a clockmaker. He handed it back to the visitor.

'Actually, my real name is Barry Neale. I'm with British Military Intelligence.'

Peter said nothing, but walked towards the telephone.

'Of course, I don't expect you to accept that at face value. I know what you're thinking. But let me assure you: this is not an S.S. plot to trap you. I've tried to contact you on several previous occasions.'

The two men exchanged glances, each sizing up the other.

'You haven't been well, I gather,' said Neale.

'You could say that. Now what's this all about?'

'I'm here on the direct instructions of Air Commodore L. E. O. Charlton. I'm charged with making contact with you. The Air Commodore wishes to know how the mission is progressing. You are, of course, pursuing your targets, I assume . . . ?'

'What mission?' Peter said angrily. Something in the man's bearing made him uneasy; he wanted further proof.

'My dear Mr Hutley, you know that just as well as I do.' The visitor gave a rather high-pitched, nervous laugh.

'You tell me then, if you know so much.'

'Come now,' Neale whined again. 'If I were from the Gestapo—if they knew what I know—you would have been arrested ages ago.' Peter didn't reply. The visitor continued.

'You were specifically sent here to discover all possible details and data concerning German progress with regard to jet propulsion. Regrettably, we are still, shall we say, a trifle in the dark in this respect. Now are you satisfied, Mr Hutley?'

'I suppose so. But what you're asking is out of the question.'

'Indeed? Do I take it then you intend to disobey orders?'

'Frankly, yes. I think it's a little late in the day to go chasing after the Reich's military secrets.'

'Come, come, I'm sure you'll find a way.'

'I tell you it's impossible. I've already requested Göring to post me to experimental flying and he turned me down flat. You see, my late brother Johannes, ironically enough, was just a little too close to the Reichsmarshall for comfort. Now he's concerned for my safety. The devil, you might say, looks after his own.'

'Perhaps if you were to see Herr Göring in person . . .'

'If you must know, my wife and I were his guests at dinner tonight.'

'Well, you're going to have to do better than that, you know. The Air Commodore has quite an investment in you. He even had to push forward Heydrich's death to protect you.'

'I find that hard to believe. You know as well as I do, he was killed by Czech partisans.' Peter smiled confidently, but had begun to dislike the turn the conversation was taking.

'Correct. But they were specially trained in England to do the job, and sent out to Prague for the purpose. You owe the Air Commodore a great deal for that. I have it on good authority he had to argue the toss with Churchill himself. You should be very grateful.'

'Grateful?' Peter snapped back. 'And who got me into this bloody mess in the first place, may I ask? Who dropped a bloody great bomb on me? Who decided arbitarily that I was expendable and conned my mother into believing I was dead? Who did all that, Mr blasted Neale?'

'There is such a thing as duty. Or had your infatuation with your brother's wife made you forget that?'

'My brother is dead.'

'Don't count on it. He's alive and well and living behind barbed wire in England—a kind of guarantee of your good behaviour.'

'You're a bloody liar.'

Peter was getting angrier. Ilse was getting worried. From what little she could understand of the conversation she knew all was far from well. She looked, pleadingly, from one man to the other. Peter turned to her.

'I think you'd better go to bed, Ilse.'

'I'm staying,' she insisted.

Peter nodded, then continued.

'In that case we'll carry on this discussion in German so my wife can understand.'

'As you wish,' Neale conceded. Then he delivered his ultimatum.

'My instructions are to give you direct orders. Not, I might add, from the Air Commodore, but from higher authority.'

Ilse and Peter exchanged glances but neither made any comment.

'I am to instruct you to do as you have been told, or—'

'Or nothing,' Peter cut in. 'I've already told you, it's impossible.'

'Please let me finish,' Neale insisted. Peter lapsed into silence.

'I'm giving you twenty-four hours to think it over. If, after due consideration, you still refuse to co-operate I have orders to eliminate you. In other words, I've been appointed your executioner. If I fail, somebody else will be sent; if they fail you can be sure that your brother will make an unscheduled appearance on Mr Göring's front doorstep. That should put the lid on this charming little love nest of yours.'

Peter was unmoved. He knew Johannes was dead. He had seen him on that bed at Tangmere, dying of his wounds.

'I really don't see that you have much ground to stand on. The S.S. would be very grateful for the gift of a British agent. And it would strengthen my position immensely.'

Neale shifted uneasily, his hand in his raincoat pocket. It was not difficult for Peter to guess what it was holding.

'Twenty-four hours, you say?'

'You heard.'

'And, I take it you won't choose to rid yourself of me until the 24-hour period is up?'

'Not unless you force me to.'

'Then I'll tell you, once and for all, why I can't help you. By this time tomorrow, I shall be on my way to a posting to a front-line squadron in Russia. Now, Mr Neale, what do you suggest I do? Refuse to go, and get the chop from the Germans? Or do I go and do my best for both our countries on the Eastern front?'

'I don't follow you, Hutley. I thought you were supposed to be serving the interests of England. Didn't anybody tell you that the Russians are our allies? That must have been one hell of a blow on the head.'

'Allies, my arse. The Russians are the enemy. Or won't you believe that until Germany is defeated and the Red Army comes trampling all over Europe?'

Neale was furious. 'You're a bloody traitor.'

'Do I surmise, then, that your loyalties lie closer to Moscow than to Mr Charlton's precious Military Intelligence?'

Neale's hand emerged from his pocket with the pistol.

Peter sprang at him and seized the weapon. The two men struggled. Ilse stood aside, her hand over her mouth in mute horror.

Peter was the bigger, but Neale fought like a man possessed. Peter forced the pistol from his grasp, and it fell to the floor with a clatter. Neale broke free from Peter's grip and kicked him hard in the knee. Peter felt the pain shooting up his leg like slivers of ice. He fell back against a chair which splintered beneath him, then dived to one side as Neale advanced again. Ilse picked up the nearest weapon to hand, a heavy silver candlestick. With it, she aimed a blow at Neale, but was brushed violently aside. But it gave Peter the moment he needed to gather himself. He launched another attack and both men sprawled heavily to the floor. Again Neale lashed out, and succeeded in smashing Peter's head on the corner of the table with such force that he was knocked senseless. Neale's outstretched hand reached for the pistol, but Ilse got to it first. She picked it up and held it unsteadily with both hands, pointing it at Neale. He rose slowly to his feet. Peter lay motionless on the floor.

'Give it to me, please. Give me that gun.' Neale asked gently.

'Stay where you are, you bastard,' Ilse cried in German.

'You wouldn't shoot a man in cold blood?' Neale took a short step towards her.

'I promise you,' she said, 'if you come any closer I'll kill you.' Ilse wiped the sweat from the corner of her eyes with the back of her left hand, still pointing the pistol directly at Neale, who now remained rooted to the spot. Peter groaned on the floor. Ilse glanced in his direction. For a second her attention was diverted. Desperately Neale lunged at her. Her reaction was mere reflex, an instinct of self-preservation. The pistol was cocked. She tugged hard on the trigger, pulling the hammer mechanism through the double action peculiar to the Walther automatic, and the little 7.65 mm leaped in her hand with an ear-splitting report.

Neale stopped dead in his tracks. For a moment he stood there, a look of utter amazement on his face. Ilse saw a small, angry hole just above the bridge of the man's nose as he toppled backwards and collapsed across a table.

Peter groaned again and sat up. Slowly he got to his feet. His head ached and there was blood on his cheek. His brain was fogged from Neale's blow. He moved unsteadily, nearly fell over again. Then the mists of unconsciousness dispersed and he remembered. Ilse was standing, as if etched in stone, the pistol still in her hand.

'I've killed him. My God, I've killed him,' she said at last, a note of total disbelief in her voice. Peter walked to her side and gently took the pistol from her hand. Gingerly, he uncocked the hammer before placing the weapon on the window sill. Ilse continued to stare at the body that lay at her feet. Peter put his arm around Ilse and led her to their bedroom. She was rigid with fright, her eyes huge and staring.

'I've killed him,' she whispered. 'What are we going to do?'

Peter had no medical training, but it didn't require specialist knowledge to realize that Ilse was in a severe state of shock. For some time he sat on the bed, reassuring her that there was nothing to worry about. Slowly she regained her composure, her sense of proportion. Suddenly she sat up on the bed. When she looked at Peter, her huge, haunted eyes were clouded with tears.

'Oh dear God in Heaven, what are we going to do now?'

'Call the police, of course,' said Peter. 'I've just killed a British agent.'

'But you didn't kill him, my darling . . .'

'No, Ilse,' he said patiently. 'Please let me do the talking. I had to do it. I had to kill him, he was trying to kill me. That's the truth.'

'The police aren't stupid; they'll never believe you.'

'I think you'll find they will. It will be quite obvious to them that the British, hoping to destroy Johannes von Tahlmann, Göring's propaganda weapon, despatched an assassin to do the job. Baron von Tahlmann averted disaster and killed the man—who, incidentally, probably worked as much the the KGB as MI5.'

Ilse found some relief from tension and shock in tears, and tried to convince herself that Peter was right. Then Peter went back into the sitting room. He picked up the pistol and wiped it clean of finger prints. He put it in the dead man's hand and closed the fingers round the butt. Then he picked it up and held it firmly before laying it on the table beside Neale's prostrate body. Only his prints and those of his attacker would be on the weapon, in accordance with the story he would tell the police.

Peter went over to the telephone. He started to dial and then changed his mind. He dialled again, but not the police. A good Nazi would not hesitate to opt instead for Gestapo Headquarters at Prinz Albrecht Strasse.

In a surprisingly short time there was a familiar knock on the door. This time, perhaps the only time, they would be on his side, Peter hoped. He suddenly thought: could Neale have left evidence to incriminate him? Evidence that could prove who he really was?

He need not have worried. The two men from the Gestapo were friendly and full of congratulations. Neale, it appeared, had already been uncovered, and had been followed for the past two weeks. The Baroness and he would, of course, have to accompany them to Gestapo Headquarters to help in the enquiries, but the questions would be a formality. And so it turned out. Ilse was trembling, sure that the urbane, black-uniformed officer who treated them with such deference as he pieced their account together knew the truth already. But she was wrong. After an hour they were free to go.

Peter's mood appeared positively buoyant on that last extra night before he set off for pastures new. Ilse and he even marked the occasion with a night out at Horcher's, but beneath the facade of jocular optimism, a terrible doubt now nagged at his very soul. Carefully, he concealed his thoughts from Ilse. She had suffered enough. Over and over again he asked himself, had Neale really spoken the truth? Was Johannes still alive?

During a restless night he struggled with the dark threats Johannes's existence could present. He finally lapsed into a fitful slumber with the spectre of his mortally wounded, hate-filled brother, lying on a blood-soaked bed—and he hoped to God Johannes was dead.

CHAPTER EIGHT

Peter's departure for Russia had been delayed by 24 hours, but after the assassination attempt had been reported and capitalized upon, Peter said goodbye to a tired, tearful Ilse and travelled by train to Regensburg. There he duly collected the Bf 109 before taking off for the Eastern front. The flight was uneventful and Peter was delighted with the Gustav—the G. Model, a vast improvement on the old but reliable Emil which he had flown the previous year. He made one stop for refuelling before heading for Maykop, which lay some 150 miles north-west of Mount Elbrus, the highest mountain in the Caucasus. On landing he reported to the Wing Adjutant, a dapper man in an immaculate uniform. After exchanging salutes and a firm handshake, Hauptmann Kuhl took Peter to an underground bunker which served as headquarters.

The Wing Commander, Colonel Dietrich Hrabak,

presented a stark contrast to Kuhl. His uniform was crumpled and oil-stained, his boots mud-bespattered. Hrabak was on the short side, stocky, his blond hair receding. As he shook hands with the new arrival, Peter was struck by the piercing blue eyes which seemed to look right through him. Momentarily he was unnerved by the gaze, but such reservations as he felt at first were soon dispelled. Hrabak was a warm and generous man, universally loved and respected by all his pilots. Notwithstanding the Knight's Cross that hung at Peter's throat, Hrabak treated him to the standard pep-talk that he gave to all newcomers.

'Living to serve with the Luftwaffe in Russia,' he told Peter, 'is a question of learning to fly as fast as possible with your brain, not your brawn. To survive in Russia, you must develop your strategy. Act aggressively, of course, but temper your fighting spirit with cunning, judgement and intelligence.'

Hrabak went on to tell Peter that he would have to start slowly; he would detail an experienced man to be his leader, probably a Sergeant or a Leutnant, and his subordinate in rank would at all times, in the air, be his superior. He should do exactly what he was told.

For the next few days Peter familiarized himself with Group routine and met many of the other pilots before being posted to III JG 52, which had its main field at Soldatskaya, north of the Caucasus. Just before he left, he received two letters. One was from Ilse; the other, a message of congratulation personally signed by Heinrich Himmler for his actions with regard to the Neale affair.

The journey was made in a Junkers 52 transport aircraft, and from it Peter was able to study the area. Mount Elbrus, even in summer, was capped with a roof of snow which shone brilliantly in the sunlight. The plains at its feet stretched to infinity and brought home to the newcomer the forbidding vastness of the terrain.

Soldatskaya was the home of some sixty Bf 109s, but

permanent buildings were non-existent. The men slept in tents and the Group was directed by Major Hubertus von Bonin from an underground bunker similar to the one in which Peter had met Colonel Hrabak.

In manner, von Bonin bore the same stamp as Hrabak. He was a thirty-two-year-old veteran of the Spanish Civil War and had fought through the Battle of Britain with JG 26. Peter smiled to himself, wondering if he had ever tangled in those early encounters with the man who was now his C.O. If he had, he was glad that neither he nor von Bonin were the worse for it. Peter had heard much about von Bonin, and liked what he heard.

'We do not judge men by rank or protocol. Only victories count here. On the ground we have to have military discipline, but in the air the top ace leads, even if he happens to be an enlisted man. Believe me, Tahlmann, that dictum applies equally to me. It is important that you should understand this from the outset. I am glad to have you in my unit, but if you happen to think you are a special case just because of your Cross, forget it. You start again from the bottom, like everyone else. I have assigned you to the 7th Squadron. You will fly as wingman to Sergeant Tagg. He is a first-class flier and he will look after you.'

Von Bonin proved his point a little while later when he was flying as wingman to a young Leutnant. During a whirling dogfight with a strong force of Soviet fighters, the Leutnant became rather agitated when von Bonin did not acknowledge his radio instructions. 'If you won't listen to me, then you can kiss my arse,' roared the young Leutnant. Still not getting any answer, the man continued to curse and blind at his ranking superior.

After they had returned to base, von Bonin grinned broadly and told his subordinate that he had heard every word, but had been unable to acknowledge due to a defective radio. He added with a laugh: 'Now that we are on the ground, Leutnant, you will surely agree that your arse is far too grubby for me to kiss.' Everybody fell about with mirth, much to the young Leutnant's embarrassment.

In appearance, Wolf Tagg was a quiet, studious young man with a shock of unruly, apparently ungroomable fair hair. He wore glasses to read by, but in the air his long sight was quite phenomenal and he was invariably the first to spot hostiles. Peter didn't take to him immediately, but soon realized that the Sergeant's apparent reticence sprang from shyness. The youngster had a proven record of over 40 victories, considerably more than that of his charge. Wolf would soon prove himself to be the antithesis of his studious image; a dedicated, talented and ruthless fighter pilot. As the two men got to know one another a warm relationship developed between them.

Peter first saw action on the Eastern front early in October 1942. He was patrolling the area between Groznyy and Digora when a voice crackled into his earphones.

'IL2s* attacking transport near Prokhladnyy. Intercept and attack.'

Tension rising, Peter followed Wolf down the line of the Terek river to Prokhladnyy. The two planes levelled off at 10,000 feet and in just less than a quarter of an hour his headset came to life again. It was Wolf's voice.

'*Achtung, achtung*! Bandits ten o'clock low. Close up to battle formation and follow me down.'

Peter did as he was told, but search as he might he could not see any sign of Ivans. He closed to within 150 feet of his leader and after diving three thousand feet spotted them at last, a group of several dark-green aircraft. Flat out, the two Bf 109s hurtled towards the enemy, both opening fire from about 200 yards. Peter was so intent on what he was doing that he overshot Wolf's aircraft. His shells were having no apparent effect. Then he realized he'd lost his leader. Exactly what he had been told not to do.

*Ilyushin-Schturmovik—Russia's equivalent to the Stuka dive bomber.

Wolf accelerated and wagged an admonishing finger at Peter. A cool customer, this one, he thought. Enemy fighters were on their tail. Wolf had shot down his IL2 but Peter's target, together with the rest of the hostiles, had turned for home.

Von Bonin's orders to fight with the head rang in Peter's ears. There were two of them now and they were outnumbered by at least six to one. Fuel was running low. But Wolf knew what he was doing, and nosing his Bf 109 into a steep curving dive, he raced down to near ground level, Peter following. The Russian fighters were left far behind. Climbing once more, they found Mount Elbrus and set their course for base. Peter expected a sharp reprimand for overtaking Wolf, but the Sergeant never mentioned it. Instead, Peter grumbled at the apparent ineffectiveness of the Gustav's guns. Then he began to wonder if perhaps his marksmanship was a trifle rusty.

'No,' explained Wolf, 'We'll make something of you yet, I think. There's nothing wrong with your shooting. Just try and slow down a bit.'

Peter was indeed starting at the bottom again, just as he had been told he must. His first victory came three days later. An almost carbon copy of the previous encounter, same time, same place. Perhaps even the same opponents. The difference was that this time Peter spotted the Ivans first.

'You lead,' ordered Wolf over the R/T. The Sergeant took up his position as wingman.

Discussing tactics with regard to the IL2, the most difficult of all the Russian aircraft to knock down, Peter had been struck by the suggestions of another acknowledged ace, Leutnant Grislawski. He repeated his words to himself now: '*Drop below the enemy and squirt him from underneath.*'

The 109s bounced the ILs from up sun. The two fighters came screaming down in a long dive, flattening out again just above ground level. Even Wolf had never tried this manoeuvre at such low level. It was dangerous, very dangerous, but it worked. The two German pilots felt themselves slammed back into their seats, the ground rushing along beneath them. They opened up as one. Cannon and machine gun bullets tore into the unsuspecting Russian aircraft. Simultaneously, the ILs that Wolf and Peter had selected as targets began to pour dense black smoke from their oil coolers. Both broke away from their formations wreathed in flames. One plunged to earth. The other exploded in mid-air. Banking and turning and elated with success, the 109 pilots came roaring back for more, but the rest of the Russian aircraft had turned again for home. As they flew off down the road, grateful German soldiers waved from below.

'Horrido, Horrido*', the pilots called to one another on their RTs. Wolf was just as delighted as Peter and the two embraced each other on their return. The partnership had been christened and would go on from strength to strength. Wolf suggested that he should fly from now on as Peter's wingman and would be honoured to do so.

'Wolf, I appreciate the offer,' he answered, 'but the old man's right. You can fly as my wingman when I've beaten your record. And I will, believe me.'

'As you wish, Herr Leutnant,' Wolf replied with a laugh.

It was pure luck that Peter should have scored his first Russian victory simply by being the first to spot the opposition. Wolf didn't miss much, and as Peter insisted, he continued to fly as the Sergeant's wingman. By the end of the year he had only scored one further victory, a Lagg 3 single-seater fighter.

News of Wolf's promotion to Leutnant came through in time for Christmas that year, giving the men an extra reason to celebrate, apart from the customary festivities. But the onset of the Russian winter had again brought the

*Victory cry of Luftwaffe pilots

German advance to a freezing halt. Things began to look bleak for the Wehrmacht once more. Like his fellow pilots, Peter found it hard to settle down, due to the continuous movement of the squadron from landing strip to landing strip, as the Soviets made fresh advances. In January 1943 the squadron was forced to move every few days, each time keeping only one jump ahead of the Red Army. After brief stays at Amavir, Krasnodar, Maykop itself, Timeshevskaya and Slavyanskaya, the outfit moved to Nikolaev, where it joined up once again with the rest of III JG 52. On the 18th January Wolf secured his 50th victory, which at one time would have qualified him for the automatic award of the Knight's Cross. But now it was refused. The ante had been raised. Wolf was bitterly disappointed.

Towards the end of February 1943, the leader of the 7th squadron was replaced by a new commander, the redoubtable Oberleutnant Walter Krupinski. Peter had met him briefly the previous year when he was at Maykop. The loudspeaker that relayed radio chatter from the fighters suddenly burst into life. A calm but authoritative voice demanded: 'Clear the field. I've been hit, I'm coming in now.' There was a pause before the voice was heard again. 'I hope I can make it. Engine's on fire.' Somebody—probably Colonel Hrabak himself—was heard to say: 'It's Krupinski.'

The duty officer fired a red flare to clear the grass field as a single 109 made its approach, an oily plume of smoke marking its passage. The landing gear was down and Krupinski got the stricken machine on to the ground, but it only taxied a few yards before it slewed over and exploded. The fire crews could not get near to the inferno for the crump and flash of exploding ammunition. The pilot's escape was a miracle. From the apparently all-consuming inferno he suddenly appeared like a phoenix from the ashes, racing to safety.

Hrabak looked at the young pilot in near disbelief.

'Krupinski,' he said, 'tonight we'll throw a birthday party for you.'

One of the young pilots, not familiar with the custom, asked what he meant . Hrabak explained that whenever a pilot had a narrow escape from death, as Krupinski just had, he was thought of as being reborn. If he had been killed, then they would have had to drink to his skin.* A birthday party was better. And rarer.

Peter had been struck by the mercurial and magnetic personality of Krupinski from the time of their first meeting. He was a strongly built five-foot-niner, one of the outstanding characters in the Luftwaffe, with an unparalleled record of mishaps and narrow escapes. By now his fellow-pilots had almost lost count of the times he had been shot down, crash-landed or taken to his parachute. He had also been wounded more than once. Krupinski was a veritable tiger of a fighter pilot and would wade into his opponents almost without a care.

'Count Pinski's' reputation as a dare-devil was not confined to the cockpit. He was also a ladies' man, from the top of his head to the tip of his toes, handsome, debonair, loving life and living it to the full. But as always, it was hard finding a wingman to fly with him. None of the Sergeants wanted the job. In the end the young, then unknown, second Leutnant Erich Hartmann volunteered. Not yet twenty-one, Hartmann, destined to become the top-scoring fighter ace of all time with 352 confirmed victories, was so youthful in appearance with his fresh complexion, blue eyes and blonde hair, that Krupinski referred to him as Bubi. The name stuck. Krupinski and Hartmann formed a truly formidable combination and, under the senior man's leadership, Bubi's score rose steadily.

Peter counted himself fortunate to move in such illustrious company. There were other famous aces in the

*'*Sein Fell Versaufen*'

outfit too, amongst them Güther Rall, Willi Batz, Hans Dammers, Alfred Grislawski and Josef 'Jupp' Zwernemann. They played hard and they flew harder.

Wolf continued to lead Peter. It was as if the former R.A.F. man was frightened to let himself go. But fear of a fight was not an emotion that he would normally show and certainly not one he would admit to. By the beginning of July 1943 Wolf had notched his 63rd victory and Peter, contrary to his promise to overhaul his friend, lagged far behind with a total of 18 Russian aircraft. He had been shot down once and parachuted to safety behind the German lines. He had also crash-landed once, through fuel shortage, but had been snatched by the army from the very clutches of a Red Infantry unit.

On the 5th July, in a whirling battle over the 7th squadron airfield, Wolf made his final kill. He and Peter had downed a Lagg 5 each, but in the ensuing mêlée Wolf's 109 was damaged and started to burn. Peter heaved a sigh of relief as he saw his friend pull back the canopy and roll the Messerschmitt over on its back to let gravity shake him free. His parachute opened and he gave the thumbs-up sign to his wingman as he drifted earthwards.

But now another Lagg 5 came storming in on his helpless comrade, guns hammering. Peter watched, horrified, but there was nothing he could do. Wolf died instantly, his body riddled with bullets. In a fit of blind fury, Peter banked in a steep turn to take immediate revenge, but the Lagg pilot had given him the slip. Four other pilots did not return that day, a full third of the squadron strength. Another casualty was Krupinski, who fractured his skull on his gunsight after executing a violent swerve during an emergency landing to avoid hitting another aircraft taking off. Krupinski would recover, but he needed six weeks' medical attention first.

Peter was inconsolable at the death of his friend. He dutifully drank his skin that night, but the ritual was a dreadful melancholy affair. He could not get his last sight of Wolf out of his mind, Wolf being ruthlessly, fatally, strafed whilst his wingman, his insurance policy, was helpless nearby. Peter was certain that he had let his leader down.

Günther Rall, now the Group Commander, ordered Peter back to Germany for leave and a well-earned rest. Peter refused to go and protested that he had to avenge his friend's murder. Rall was sympathetic, but he knew the signs. A pilot devoid of caution and thirsting for revenge was as likely as not a candidate for an early coffin.

Peter flew back to Berlin in a Junkers 52 on the 1st August. Ilse was waiting for him at Tempelhof and together they travelled by taxi back to the flat.

Peter looked tired and drawn, and spoke very little, obviously shocked and depressed to see the mounting toll of damage to the city. The Allied raids had increased in intensity, and Berlin, now a beleagured war-torn skeleton, was strewn with wrecked houses, cratered roads, and burned-out shops and offices. The faces of the people they passed in the street were grim, but determined. Everywhere there were queues, mostly of women, waiting patiently at shop doors, while workmen, old men for the most part, toiled away to repair essential services. Peter was struck by the utter futility of it all: another air bombardment that night or the next, and their efforts would have to begin all over again. In one year, Berlin had changed dramatically. And, as Peter knew only too well, this was only the beginning. The Führer had sown the wind and now the German people would reap the storm.

Ilse had saved her rations and was able to provide a welcome-home meal of near pre-war quality, if not quantity, but Peter couldn't really do it justice. Later they talked over coffee, real coffee. Ilse's father telephoned just as they were going to bed, to invite the pair of them over to lunch the next day. Ilse had a hurried word with her husband. Peter grimaced. He would have preferred to rest, but dutifully nodded assent. Ilse picked up the receiver again.

'Yes, we'd like that.'

'Good. I have a few influential friends that I'd like Johannes to meet.'

'All right, Father, thank you.'

'About twelve, then.'

'About twelve.'

Around midnight they were awakened by the wailing of sirens and shortly after they heard the crump of high explosives falling on another part of the city. The crashes drew closer and the 8.8 centimetre anti-aircraft guns in the square below the flat opened up with a thunderous cacophony.

Ilse and Johannes got dressed as quickly as they could and made their way to the shelter beneath the block of flats. They found two seats and sat together, listening to the surrounding chatter. Curses were being heaped on the heads of the Englanders, uttered with a rugged, stoical sense of humour that Peter had last heard in London. The bombs were now very close indeed. Without warning, there was an earth-shattering explosion. The lights flickered and went out. Somewhere, a woman screamed; a child started to cry. The darkness was absolute. Someone struck a match and then lit a candle. The shelter was full of dust, but it had remained intact. The child continued to cry—a tiny piece of falling plaster had slightly cut his forehead. He was the only casualty.

For another quarter of an hour everybody remained calm, seated where they were. The noise of exploding bombs moved further away and then the all-clear sounded. The occupants of the shelter slowly filed out. A bomb had exploded close by the entrance to the front of the flats and a great deal of damage had been done to most of the apartments. Ilse's flat was at the back, overlooking the square with its gun emplacement. It was undamaged. They made their way back to it.

The bombing raid decided Peter once and for all.

'Ilse,' said Peter as soon as they got back into bed, 'you must leave Berlin. I can't have you in the middle of this.'

'Where would I go?'

'To Schwandorf. Back to Tahlmann. You know how glad they'd be to see you down there.'

'The place reminds me of that woman.'

'Ilse, Magda has gone.'

'I know. But somehow her memory still pervades the place. The last I heard of her, she had become an S.S. orderly at Dachau.'

'Where?'

'The concentration camp.'

'And?'

'Oh Peter, I keep dreaming she'll return. They say things about that place, things too terrible to believe.'

'Darling, Magda has gone. As far as we're concerned, she's a thing of the past.'

'But I can't leave my father.'

Peter would not be put off.

'I'm sorry, Ilse. I don't care what you say, you can't stay here. Sooner or later they'll hit this flat or your father's apartment, and I'd never forgive myself.'

Peter stopped for a moment, his thoughts turning suddenly to the all too recent past. Again, he remembered Wolf.

'You'd have liked Wolf so much, Ilse . . .'

Ilse felt herself suffering his pain.

'I don't want to have your death on my conscience as well.'

He looked at her, tears gathering in his eyes.

'I blame myself for his death. I should have done something.'

'My darling you could do nothing.'

'It was my job to protect him, and I failed. I'm not going to fail you as well.'

A pale watery dawn was beginning to leak through the partly drawn curtains. From somewhere down in the square a blackbird bravely sang its liquid notes to the echoing silence that had followed the chaos of the raid. Ilse buried her head in the pillows.

'Come here,' said Peter, turning her over very gently. 'You talk too much.'

They decided to walk to her father's apartment. As they passed some fresh rubble from last night's bombing, Peter recognized the same group of workers he had seen at one spot the day before, and stopped to talk to them.

'English bastards,' the foreman said. 'This is the third time, in exactly the same place. It's ridiculous.'

Then the old man noticed Peter's youth, and the civilian clothes he was wearing. Abruptly his tone changed.

'And what makes you so damned special that you can laze around while the rest of the Herrenvolk are fighting for their lives?' The foreman spat at his feet. Peter made no answer. Perhaps the old man was right. Here he was, making love to Ilse when he should have been back in Russia avenging Wolf's murder. Ilse opened her mouth to spring to his defence, but Peter put his fingers to her lips.

When they had walked out of earshot she asked, 'Why didn't you let me put him in his place?'

'What good would it do? Telling him I'm a fighter pilot with the Cross wouldn't help. He'd probably ask me why I'm walking along the pavement here instead of stopping the Englanders blowing holes in his road. And he'd be right.'

'Peter, you were ordered home on leave. I know you wouldn't have come without coercion, but what about me? Aren't I more important than that man's precious road?'

'You really don't understand, do you?'

'No, I don't. I sometimes think you men enjoy all this—you see us women as an audience, rapt onlookers to your heroic deeds.'

'That's hardly fair, Ilse.'

'It's not meant to be . . .' She hesitated for a moment, remembering suddenly the short, so very short time they had together. They had stopped walking. Looking up at Peter, she smiled with difficulty. Did he know how she felt when he was flying at the Front? 'I love you so much. Please try and understand what hell it is for me when you're away. I feel so helpless.'

'What about the flat. Will you leave it?'

She hesitated. 'Alright.'

'We'll both go to Tahlmann tomorrow. I know your father will agree.'

The Colonel greeted Ilse's decision with relief. He had been trying to persuade his daughter to leave Berlin for some months and was delighted to hear that Peter had succeeded where he had failed.

Apart from Ilse, there were no other women present. She and Peter were introduced to the other guests who had called in for drinks. One or two of them Peter had heard of, others he had not. The most senior officer present was Admiral Wilhelm Canaris, Chief of the Abwehr, the Intelligence Bureau of the Army High Command. Another name Peter remembered later was a certain Caesar von Hofacker.

The talk was of the inevitability of defeat and, quite openly, the need to be rid of the Führer in order to seek an honourable peace as soon as possible. In Russia the previous February, after enduring the most bitter hardships, the German VI army, under the command of General Feldmarschall Paulus, had surrendered 91,000 men to the Russians, all that remained of the 285,000-strong force that had been surrounded two months before. The place was Stalingrad. On July 4th, Hitler had launched Operation Citadel, which would turn out to be the last great offensive in the East. The élite of the Wehrmacht, more than half a million men, including seventeen panzer divisions, many equipped with the new Ferdinand tanks, had been hurled against the Russian positions at Kursk. Hitler was convinced that he could not only trap more than a million soldiers of the Red Army and avenge the Reich's honour after the previous defeat, but could then advance again to the River Don and even to the Volga, eventually heading north west towards Moscow.

The Russians had been expecting the attack and another massacre of the Germans had followed. By the middle of July, the Russians were moving forward again, their first summer advance since the war had begun. By the 22nd, the Germans had lost half of their armour. The battle at Kursk, the greatest in the history of armoured warfare, was over. The entire German front had begun to crumble. From now on, except for local counter-attacks, the war was drawing ever nearer to the soil of the Fatherland. Now, it was only a matter of time.

This last defeat was much in the minds of Colonel Horcher's lunchtime guests. Peter found himself closely questioned by Canaris about the morale of the Luftwaffe personnel in Russia. He replied that their morale couldn't be higher, but that severe shortages of supplies of spares, of food, aviation spirit and ammunition were becoming more serious by the day. As regards loyalty, his answer was more guarded.

'I think I can assure you, gentlemen, of the utmost loyalty of all the officers and men to the cause of the Fatherland.'

He was careful not to indicate whether or not their loyalty was to Hitler. Although among Peter's comrades there were some who still passionately believed in the crusade of National Socialism, and a few who even yet believed in ultimate victory, by and large they were soldiers, air soldiers, whose duty was to obey orders. And that meant doing their utmost to hold back the Soviets for as long as possible.

Soon after, old Colonel Horcher excused his daughter and son-in-law, explaining to his friends how short a time they had to be together, and that they were off to Bavaria the next day.

Ilse and Peter shook hands with the others, and Ilse kissed her father tenderly and long. There were tears in her eyes as she watched Peter give the Colonel an affectionate hug, and she couldn't resist giving her father another embrace. The emotion she felt was more than that of a casual farewell. She knew, as did all the guests, which way the words shared by the assembled company were taking them.

'What's this? Tears, Ilse?' laughed Colonel Horcher. 'It's not like you to cry. We'll meet again, quite soon.'

'Yes, of course. I'm being silly,' she sniffed, and wiped her nose and eyes with the back of her hand, 'Of course, I'll see you again soon.' But as she once more brushed a soft damp cheek against her father's wrinkled old face, it was as if she doubted her own words.

Admiral Canaris instructed his aide to drive Peter and Ilse back to their flat. The car took the same route that they had walked some hours earlier. Sure enough the bomb crater in the road had been filled in. Peter wondered idly how long it would be before it was blown open once again.

The next day the couple travelled down to Tahlmann, and were fortunate enough to catch a lift in a Junkers 52 that was travelling from Tempelhof to a small airfield south of Nuremburg. The rest of the journey was completed by car. The couple of days that followed were as restful as Peter had promised they would be. But they were never really clear of the knowledge of the meeting they had just witnessed.

CHAPTER NINE

During their second night in the country the R.A.F. returned once again to Berlin. Heavy bombers dropped large quantities of incendiaries and high explosives, one of which hit the Horcher home and completely demolished it. Not a trace of the Colonel's body was ever found. Ilse could so easily have shared his fate.

To begin with she put on a brave face and, superficially at least, accepted her father's death. Peter had expected tears—there were none. His wife was numbed, already drained of overt emotion by the awesome mental burden under which they both lived.

After Colonel Horcher's death, Peter applied for, and was granted, extended leave on compassionate grounds. Both he and Ilse would later have cause to feel a profound relief that her father had died in the air raid. For had he not done so he would undoubtedly have shared the fate of his friends, Canaris, von Hofacker, and their fellow conspirators in the unsuccessful bomb plot on the Führer of July 20th 1944.

Despite his preoccupation with the conduct of the war, and beset with internal strife at top level, Göring attended the hastily arranged memorial service for Colonel Horcher. Afterwards, the Reichsmarschall invited Peter and Ilse to travel to Karinhall with him. This also was to be a last meeting.

The Commander in Chief had originally incurred the contempt of his Luftwaffe as long ago as the summer of 1940, when, after his failure to overwhelm the British, he had lashed out at the aircrews as a scapegoat, accusing them not only of letting him down, but of actual cowardice.

Peter was struck now by the further mental and physical deterioration in Göring's general condition. Gone was the jaunty self-assurance of the man who had brought the Knight's Cross to his hospital bed. Instead Peter saw an invalid, increasingly dependent on drugs, the fearful responsibility of his position forcing him to retreat into fantasy. In the middle of August 1943 another disaster had befallen Göring's Luftwaffe. Chief of the Air Staff, Colonel-General Hans Jeschonnek had been upbraided by Hitler for the lack of success of the fighter defences. Four days later, on the 17th August, a large force of American B17 Flying Fortresses bombed the ball-bearing works at Schweinfurt and the Messerschmitt factories at Regensberg. Although the Luftwaffe succeeded in destroying sixty of the raiders, once again Jeschonnek was ordered to report to the Führer for yet another berating. The very same night, the R.A.F. turned its attention to the Rocket Research Station at Peenemünde on the Baltic coast, the vital complex engaged in perfecting the Führer's Vergeltungswaffen*, the V1 Flying Bomb and V2 Rocket. Considerable damage was done and 750 personnel lost their lives. Air defence that night proved to be a shambles. Due to an error in assessing the intended target, 200 Luftwaffe fighters rendezvoued over Berlin. General Jeschonnek knew only too well who would have to shoulder the blame. The Chief of the Air Staff took the time-honoured way out, following in the path trodden by General Udet less than two years earlier. Jeschonnek took his own life with a pistol and left a note claiming the responsibility for the failure was Göring's, with whom he had found it utterly impossible to work.

A further illustration of the Reichsmarschall's ostrich-like refusal to face reality was given only a month later. After the death of Mölders, Adolf Galland was appointed to fill the vacant position of General of Fighters. At a

*retaliation weapons

meeting with Hitler he informed him that American escort fighters had been shot down over Aachen and that incursions ever deeper into the Reich could be expected as fuel capacity increased.

Göring was about to board his private train when Galland came to see him off. Immediately he took the fighter ace to task.

'Why did you tell the Führer that American fighters have reached German territory?' he demanded petulantly.

'Because they will soon be landing in Berlin itself, Herr Reichsmarschall,' Galland replied.

'Rubbish, Galland. That's pure fantasy,' snapped Göring.

'With respect, Reichsmarschall, it is a fact. American fighters *have* been shot down over Aachen.'

Göring would not yield.

'It simply cannot be true. Absolutely impossible!'

'Go and see for yourself,' Galland suggested. 'The wrecked planes, as I said, are there.'

'Come now, General, I too am an experienced fighter pilot, and I know full well what you say is not true.' With a smile of triumph he continued: 'No doubt the planes were crippled a long way further off and glided to Aachen.'

Galland could hardly believe his ears.

'Glide? In an easterly direction, Sir?'

Göring lost his temper.

'I am informing you officially that they were *not* there. Do you understand? No American fighters were there. I shall report the fact to the Führer.'

Göring turned his back, leaving the still unruffled General of Fighters standing on the platform, and went to board his train. As he stalked off, he half turned his head for a final admonition.

'You have my official order.'

Galland, totally bemused, merely shrugged.

'Orders are orders, Herr Reichsmarschall.'

Peter returned to the Eastern front at the beginning of September, but had some difficulty in locating his unit. III JG 52 had been constantly on the move throughout August. He finally caught up with them on the 8th. They had just moved to Boguslaw and the same day had to move again, this time to Dnjepropetrowsk.

During Peter's absence, Leutnant Hartmann had increased his tally dramatically. On the 17th August he passed the 80 mark—the total achieved by Baron Manfred von Richthofen in World War I.

Peter was still intent on avenging Wolf's death. But to have shown it openly would have been to render himself temperamentally suspect. It was time to get back into the fray, and this time to lead rather than be led. Wolf was dead, but Peter would score for both of them. He also needed to prove to himself, as well as his dead comrade, that he was fit to wear the Knight's Cross. He made a deep study of the Hartmann methods and carefully selected his wingmate. At the end of August 1943, Leutnant Tahlmann became a Rottenführer again, for the first time since 1941. He selected a promising newcomer as the other half of his team, a young Sergeant named Hans Kriegshauser.

Hans was dark and not unlike the dashing Count Pinski to look at. He could certainly have doubled for Krupinski, whom he loved to mimic during moments of relaxation. He too liked the good things in life, women included, and the mails nearly always brought a number of letters from female well-wishers and admirers from his home town of Stettin. Though a devil-may-care flyer, Hans was soon to prove his reliability.

Throughout September and October the progress of the couple was marked by steady success. By the 29th October, Peter had brought his score to 50 Russian aircraft, which, when added to his late brother's and his own previous successes, made a grand total of 73 victories. Now there was really something to celebrate. His achievement was, however, eclipsed by Erich Hartmann, who had scored his 150th victory on the same day, a figure that merited the award of the Knight's Cross. Erich's feat had put him almost on a par with Count Pinski, who had himself passed the 150 mark just four weeks previously.

Throughout that winter, in temperatures often as low as 40 degrees below freezing, the Tahlmann/Kriegshauser partnership continued to score steadily. The cold was terrible. It gnawed at the pilots relentlessly, freezing them in their cockpits. The Daimler-Benz engines of the 109s were almost impossible to turn over, let alone start. The lubricating oil froze near solid. Only the help of a captured Russian pilot solved this problem. He instructed the maintenance staff to mix petrol with the sump oil. Despite their initial fears of sabotage, the Luftwaffe pilots found the method worked. The engines started immediately, and as they warmed up the petrol evaporated. No longer did frustrated pilots have to sit it out whilst their airstrips were destroyed by hordes of Russian fighters. If only they could have found such an effective heating system for the men themselves.

By the beginning of March, Peter had increased his victory tally to 80 Soviet aircraft, and Hans 29. The Führer awarded four JG 52 aces additions to their Knight's Crosses. Gerhard Barkhorn was to receive the Swords, whilst Johannes Wiese, Erich Hartmann and Walter Krupinski, would receive the Oakleaves. They were ordered to travel to Salzburg by train and then proceed by car to the Eagle's Nest at Berchtesgaden. Whilst they were away Peter made another error, a mistake that nearly cost the life of his new wingman. That morning Hans had had a gut feeling, a totally illogical but disturbing presentiment that something out of the ordinary was going to happen that day. He told Peter about it as they made their way to their aircraft.

'Nonsense,' countered Peter. 'You just need a rest.'

'Maybe. But so do you.'

'You could be right. But then we all do.'

It wasn't like Hans to be so gloomy. Peter slapped him on the back.

'Anyway, *Hals und Beinbruch** my friend. Just you watch our arses and we'll be fine, you'll see.'

Peter was desperately tired, worn out with the constant strain of living on his nerves, and this morning he was careless. He had had two letters from Ilse in the last three days and she seemed cheerful enough, despite the increasing privations that had to be endured in the beleaguered Reich of 1944. Peter thanked God for his good fortune.

He climbed into the cockpit of his 109, still puzzled by Hans' melancholy. Shrugging it off, he began his pre-take off procedure.

Fuel switch on, throttle open one-third, prime one, twice, three, four, five times, close water cooler, set propeller to automatic, main ignition on both. Two mechanics cranked the inertia starter and when the whine had reached its peak one of them signalled "free". With that, Peter pulled the clutch and the propellor started to turn, coughed once, a second time, then burst into life. A swift check on oil pressure, fuel, electrical and cooling system and both magnetos in turn. Peter had done it all hundreds of times before. It was just routine.

Hans' 109 was warming up too. Tightening his safety harness, Peter gave a final wave to his wingman. Slowly, he opened the throttle, and the fighter began to taxi towards take-off. Turning into the wind with Hans at his tail, he opened the throttle all the way and roared across the hard ground.

Feeling the slight jolt as his undercarriage retracted, he checked flaps and trim, turning towards the east, into the brilliant sunrise. There was often a bit of trade to cope with on these dawn patrols. Today would be the rule rather than the exception.

*Literally, 'Break your neck and legs'. a traditional Luftwaffe greeting.

'Achtung,' called Hans through the intercom after they had been airborne for less than ten minutes. 'Achtung; single Ivan, two o'clock low.'

Peter scanned the area from side to side but he could see nothing. The sky below was empty, and equally void above, a vast, lonely area topped with a canopy of orange candyfloss. He instructed Hans to attack whilst he remained aloft. Hans dropped into a shallow dive and as he did so Peter spotted the Russian at last. His wingman was rapidly closing the gap on his adversary, a Bell P 39 Aeracobra, an American-made fighter with a performance considerably inferior to that of the Bf 109 G. It was a sitting duck. Hans was not renowned for his marksmanship and liked to get in close. Peter watched as flashes along the side of the dark-green Russian aircraft marked the effectiveness of the cannon shells. The Aerocobra started to slow down, its propellor whirring erratically. In moments it would stall. Peter glanced in his mirror for the umpteenth time. Nothing. Then, as if from nowhere, an entire squadron of Lagg 5s was diving down on his unsuspecting comrade, who was relying on his leader to protect him.

'Break. Break, Hans. For God's sake, man, break *now*. Ivans coming at you nine o'clock high.'

The Laggs banked as they dived, hot on the tail of Hans' immediate and violent evasive action. But even before the P39 had commenced its death spiral, the pilot slumped over the controls, the first of the Laggs' shells were thudding into Hans' 109. Peter saw fragments fly off the wings and tail plane. Then, the inevitable smoke. At this moment the two Germans were, Peter guessed, several miles behind the Russian line. Frantic now, he watched in horror as Hans' plane began to lurch out of control. There was little he could do at this stage. He should have done it earlier. He should have seen. Peter dived on the last of the Laggs. One burst finished it, and an even shorter burst the next. Then a third burned, and still the Ivans did not cover their rear.

Hans raced down to ground level and then firmly pulled up the nose of his 109 sufficiently for a wheels-up forced landing. The Russians had followed him down, intent on killing their fallen foe, as they had his predecessor. They roared down as a fourth fighter, still apparently blissfully unaware of the danger that threatened him, exploded, debris flying past Peter's 109, uncomfortably close. The bastards were shooting at Hans who had, to Peter's utter joy, pulled back the canopy and was running away from his furiously burning machine. In a moment it blew, sending a mushroom cloud of oily smoke and flame skywards. Hans made the cover of what looked like scrub trees and disappeared from view. Now the Russians suddenly woke up to the loss of four of their number. A furious fight followed between the six Laggs and the lone 109.

Hans watched from the ground as Peter out-turned, out-manoeuvred and completely out-flew the Russians. A fifth burst into flame, and then a sixth. Turning for the seventh and getting it in his gunsight, Peter pressed the firing button. The guns fired a couple of rounds and then stopped dead. Ammunition exhausted. Sweat prickled on Peter's forehead, and began to seep from beneath his flying helmet into his eyes. There was only one thing he could do: bank steeply and then turn back towards his enemy. Both aircraft approached each other head on. At the last moment, Peter shut his eyes, and the Russian's nerve broke. He turned too tightly, stalled, lost control and bounced across the landscape below.

Peter turned his attention back to Hans, who emerged from the bushes by his burning plane. Peter decided to risk a landing. He was not having yet another comrade's life on his conscience.

The landing was surprisingly smooth and the 109 touched down in the middle of a relatively flat stretch of ground. Peter could see soldiers running towards them as he taxied up to where Hans was waiting. Flinging back the canopy, he was greeted by a grinning Hans with: 'Welcome to Russia.'

'Shut up and get in.'

'With you?'

'For Christ's sake, we can't stick around here.' Peter pointed at the advancing infantry and then shouted: 'Plant your arse in my lap and you can fly the bloody thing.'

The soldiers opened fire. Hans climbed in. It was not going to work, he was sure. There was no room.

'Get out, quick,' said Hans, his tone suddenly urgent and serious. Peter didn't ask why. He knew. He stood on the wing whilst the Sergeant crawled into the area behind the pilot's seat. How he managed to cram himself into the confined space neither of them knew. Peter didn't have time to find out. He jumped straight back into his seat and fastened the safety straps. He gunned the throttle, slewing round into the wind, and glanced in the direction of the soldiers. They were very close indeed. Any moment he expected the bullets flying overhead to start slamming into the Messerschmitt before he could get up into the air again. There was a crash as the side of the cockpit starred, but in seconds they were up and away.

'You all right behind there, Hans?'

'Funny man, Johannes. Pretty soon I'm going to crawl out of here and nip back down.' A pause. And then: 'Thanks. Thanks for not letting me down.'

Peter didn't answer. He pointed the nose of the 109 towards the west and streaked off in the direction of base at full speed.

When they arrived back, Peter went straight to his quarters and lay in his bunk. The combat report could wait. He felt like a wet rag, limp with exhaustion, wrung out from the sheer physical and mental strain of the rescue and the Russian roulette.

The release from the tension left him totally debilitated. He needed a rest. Six months of continuous fighting had tired him out. He thought of Ilse, and wondered what she might be doing at that moment. Then his memory wandered further back, to Netheravon. He had been a Pilot Officer, or had he still been a cadet? He couldn't exactly recall.

He was back in action at first light. Conserving his meagre resources of energy, he played it safe. He didn't score again until four days later. Unusually, his target was a British-built Spitfire. Odd it looked, too, the familiar, graceful lines of the fighter daubed with alien red stars. Peter's victory had nothing to do with superior flying skill. He moved like an automaton. And the Russian pilot was good. Somehow, some unknown instinct gave him the seconds necessary for a long burst raking his enemy from below. He banked the Messerschmitt and circled his stricken enemy. The Russian pilot thought his last moment had come. But Peter waved wearily and the man released his hold on one of his parachute straps and saluted. The 109 waggled its wings and flew off into the setting sun.

News of Peter's rescue of his companion and his single-handed battle with half a Russian squadron reached Berlin, with the strongest recommendation that the pilot should be decorated for his conspicuous gallantry. The Group Commander had described his courage as 'a shining example of the unquenchable will of the German people to fight on to ultimate victory.' Shortly after Peter was astonished to hear that the Führer himself had ordered that Leutnant von Tahlmann should travel to Salzburg to be awarded with the Oakleaves to his Knight's Cross.

Peter left the next day, following the same route taken a short while before by Krupinski and Hartmann, puzzled only by the fact that the wing adjutant specifically instructed him to behave himself.

He boarded the waiting Heinkel III in which he would

make the uncomfortable first part of the journey. The remaining distance he would cover by train.

The Reichsbahn, a prime target for allied bombers, suffered to an ever-increasing degree from wartime pressures and privations—far more so than the railways in Britain. The train that Peter boarded looked as though it had been dragged out of a museum. The old Henschell engine wheezed, huffed and squeaked as it struggled to pull nine over-laden, equally antique coaches from the station. To sit down was out of the question and Peter had to content himself with standing in the corridor, despite his first-class warrant. Such seats as were available all seemed to be occupied by members of the Waffen S.S. or senior Wehrmacht officers. Refreshment facilities on the train appeared non-existent but after an hour or so Peter determined to get himself a beer at the first opportunity. The corridors were crammed with civilian workers, Todt organization officials, and a vast throng of exhausted or wounded soldiers and airmen. The air was rank with the odour of stale sweet, cheap tobacco smoke and disinfectant. Peter stood out like a sore thumb in his immaculate blue uniform, tunic and breeches, his field boots brilliantly polished.

The Knight's Cross at his throat should have been enough to show that he was no slouch. But more than once, ordinary private soldiers took as long as they dared before making way for Peter to pass down the corridor. A one-legged Sergeant demanded to know where the hell Peter had been at Stalingrad. Peter didn't reply.

It took him the best part of another half hour and several more such exchanges before he managed to elbow his way to the guard's compartment. The old railwayman, a veteran of the Kaiser's airforce, looked up at the handsome young pilot who tapped at his window. He took in the Knight's Cross at a glance and opened the door.

Peter spoke first.

'Is there any chance of getting a beer at the next stop?'

The old man smiled politely, eyeing the coins in Peter's hand.

'It's against regulations, Herr Oberleutnant,' he replied evasively.

'*What*?'

'I'm sorry. I have my orders.'

Peter switched on the charm.

'Just one glass of beer, that's all I ask. I really have got a hell of a thirst.'

The guard changed the subject.

'What outfit are you with, Herr Oberleutnant?'

'You should know better than to ask me that.'

The guard smiled, an expression of genuine warmth and admiration.

'You're with JG 52, aren't you?'

'And if I am?'

'Unless I'm mistaken, you're Oberleutnant Baron Johannes von Tahlmann.'

Peter nodded.

The guard beamed and thrust out a huge hand for the shaking.

'Allow me to congratulate you, Sir.' There were tears of pride in the old man's eyes.

Peter took the hand.

'Now what about the beer?'

'Now then, Sir, I've already told you, I have my instructions direct from your unit.'

Peter was mystified.

'Do you really mean to tell me that you have been specifically ordered not to give drinks to members of my unit?'

'No, Sir, just you.'

'Me?' Peter pointed to himself in disbelief.

The old man nodded.

'You must be joking!'

'No, Herr Oberleutnant. I assure you I'm not. But orders are made to be disobeyed . . .' The train was beginning to slow down. The guard looked out of the window.

'You stay here, Sir. I suppose one beer won't hurt you.'

Peter pushed the money at the guard again as he left the compartment, but the man held up his hand in horror.

'No Sir, it will be my pleasure, my honour. Think how I'll feel when I tell my grandchildren I bought a drink for the Baron von Tahlmann!' Then he eased himself on to the platform, as the train squeaked and groaned to a halt. A final escape of steam and more banging of doors followed. Peter sat on the guard's seat, staring out of the window at the jostling crowd on the platform.

Suddenly something caught his attention. He noticed a thin and emaciated creature hurriedly weaving in and out of the throng. He seemed to be heading towards him. In moments he had reached the steps to the guard's van and their eyes met, just for an instant. In that split-second Peter saw the traces of thread where the Star of David had been torn from his jacket and knew the reason for the terror in his dark, haunted eyes. The Jew spun round for a glance down the platform and tried to dive under the train. From twenty feet away, two soldiers in field grey were levelling their Schmeissers at the fleeing man. Suddenly there were screams and a burst of gunfire. At least three of the 9mm bullets found their target. Others ricocheted off the platform and two more hit the train, one of them embedding itself in the woodwork round the window of the guard's compartment. Peter had withdrawn his head the moment he had seen the soldiers raising their weapons, but when the burst of fire and the echoing reports had abated, he cautiously peered out of the window again. The Jew was lying half under the train. Peter could not see his head. There was blood on his back and one leg, shattered by the bullets or the fall, was twisted at a grotesque angle. The man was whimpering softly, trying to draw his broken body under cover like a wounded crab.

The two soldiers from one of Heinrich Himmler's Einsatzgruppe units were standing at the window. One muttered: 'Filthy Jewish bastard,' and spat on the dying man. The other S.S. man finished the job with a single bullet in the back of the neck. When they straightened up, grinning with delight their eyes met those of the Luftwaffe officer.

'Your papers,' Peter rasped at them, having taken the precaution of pulling out his own pistol. The S.S. men looked at the blunt muzzle of the Walther in amazement.

'Who the hell are you to ask for our papers?' demanded the uglier of the two.

'I am Oberleutnant Baron Johannes von Tahlmann, and I shall be reporting your behaviour direct to the Führer in person. Your papers. *Now.*'

The old guard was approaching the compartment again with a bottle of beer held in each hand, but he stopped dead when he saw the confrontation. He was used to this sort of thing. Hardly a day went by without some 'Jewish saboteur' being caught at the station in a last, hopeless, dash for safety.

The two S.S. men shouldered their machine pistols and fumbled in tunic pockets for their identification papers without further protest. Peter holstered his own pistol and made a note of the names, serial numbers and unit. Satisfied, he handed them back. Finding his tongue again, the more unprepossessing of the two, an S.S. Standartenführer, squared up to Peter.

'You're in a great deal of trouble, Herr Oberleutnant. When Haupsturmführer Geller hears of this you will regret your rashness, believe me.'

For a moment the Standartenführer smiled; Peter saw a film of wetness on his upper lip. Then he added: 'You know what happens to people who interfere with the work of the Reichführer's special units?'

Peter was not to be put down.

'Shut up' he spat. 'You and your kind sicken me. Now

get out of my sight and take that, that . . .' Johannes stammered over the words, 'take that wretch away with you.'

The S.S. men did not argue further. Grabbing a leg apiece they dragged the corpse back up the platform, through groups of curious onlookers, those to whom such an incident was commonplace enough but mesmerizing nonetheless. They parted to let the men through.

The train had been held up for ten minutes, but now the guard waved to the driver, blew a whistle and once more the aged engine clanked into life.

The old guard put the two bottle of beer down on the table but neither of the men opened them.

'Has this sort of thing happened before?' asked Peter, visibly shaken.

'Oh yes, Sir. Quite a regular occurrence, I'm afraid. We're used to it. Only two weeks ago a railway official was shot dead and two passengers wounded by S.S. men shooting at an escaping prisoner.'

'This is what we fight for?' Peter muttered.

'And they call themselves soldiers, Herr Oberleutnant. Bah.'

The guard spat out of the window, his fingers touching the jagged wood where the bullet had narrowly missed his guest. He hadn't noticed it till then, but drew back and pointed. Peter nodded. The old man took out a penknife and prized out the bullet.

'Here's a souvenir, for what it's worth,' he said handing the bullet to Peter. 'Now what about a drink?'

'Thank you.'

With a glint in his eye, the guard produced a bottle of Schnapps along with the beer, and the two men drank in silence. They said goodbye at a station a few miles from the Eagle's Nest and with a final wave Peter disappeared from view.

CHAPTER TEN

Hitler's Luftwaffe adjutant, Major Nicolaus von Below, was waiting at the ticket barrier to conduct Peter to the Mercedes, the car that would convey them straight to the Führer. The two men had only met once before, but Peter had no trouble recognising the tall, blonde-haired Major. They saluted and shook hands. At first Peter thought he was mistaken, but as the Major prolonged the handshake he realized he was not: his guide was trying to smell his breath. Von Below's first question removed any further doubt.

'Have you been drinking?'

'My God,' exclaimed Peter. 'What the hell's going on here?'

Von Below didn't respond. Peter continued, angry at being treated like a juvenile. 'If you must know, yes, Herr Major. Like a fish. In fact I've downed an entire half-litre of beer since I left Russia.'

'Half a litre, Oberleutnant?'

'Half a litre, Major.'

'That's all right then.'

'Look, Sir,' continued Peter, thoroughly perplexed by the whole business. 'Just what's this all about? I had the devil's own job even to get that one beer.'

'It's nothing,' von Below replied. 'There are much more important things to discuss. The Führer is looking forward to meeting you again. I understand he has not seen you since you were a youngster. But I don't expect you remember.'

'Of course I do,' lied Peter. 'Not well, though. It was a long, long time ago.'

'Yes, indeed. For many, more than a lifetime.'

Von Below did most of the talking during the drive. He

informed Peter that he was the only man to be decorated that day. Arrangements perforce had been rushed and the holding of a top-level conference of the Führer's Generals had, on Hitler's specific orders, been postponed for half an hour so that he would have time to confer the honour himself and talk to the recipient. He especially wanted to meet the fighter pilot because of his half-English background. Apparently he still remembered that dinner party at Tahlmann back in the early 1930s when he had sat at Isobel's right hand.

The Eagle's Nest was an impressive building, heavily guarded by black-uniformed S.S. guards. Dutifully they snapped to attention and presented arms as the Mercedes came to a stop and the two Luftwaffe officers approached the main entrance. On entering the foyer Peter was instructed to take a seat and wait. The room was sparsely furnished, what furniture there was being functional rather than decorative. In one corner stood a hat stand. On a peg hung a single peaked cap, unusually large, with golden badges and braid. Peter rose from his chair to examine it. He had taken only two or three paces towards the stand when von Below appeared in the doorway through which he had passed a few minutes ago.

'Come this way, Tahlmann. The Führer will see you now.'

Peter followed the Major, his stomach churning with confused excitement.

Hitler was standing in front of an enormous map which covered almost the whole of one wall. On it, flags and plaques and arrows depicted the movements and identities of the units involved on the entire European theatre of operations.

'Oberleutnant Johannes von Tahlmann, mein Führer,' von Below announced as they entered the room.

For a few agonizing moments Hitler did not move. Then he turned to face the two men. Peter clicked his heels together and saluted.

'Heil Hitler.'

The Führer smiled and, with his arm bent at the elbow, raised his hand to shoulder height, returning the ace's greeting. As Peter had expected, the dictator of Nazi Germany was wearing black trousers and a simple grey double-breasted tunic. On the left breast he wore the Iron Cross and on his left sleeve the Nazi Party emblem, an eagle clutching a swastika. Apart from these two insignia his uniform was spartanly simple and devoid of the frippery with which many of his minions, Göring especially, were wont to decorate themselves.

Hitler proferred his hand.

'Herr Oberleutnant, it is a great pleasure to meet you again. You were only a small boy when I came to your late father's house as a dinner guest so many years ago.'

'I remember, mein Führer.'

'That is good. You must have an excellent memory.'

Peter was struck at once by Hitler's extraordinary powers of recall—or diplomacy.

Von Below stood by the Führer with a black leather case in his hand as Peter modestly answered questions about the action for which he was about to receive the Oakleaves to his Knight's Cross. As he spoke, Hitler took the case from the adjutant and removed the prized cross with its cluster of silver oakleaves. He walked towards Peter, who bowed slightly to enable the dictator to put the ribbon over his head.

'Congratulations, my boy. The Reich is proud of you.'

The ceremony was simple, brief, but personal. Peter could hear the Generals, amongst them Keitel, Jodl and panzer expert, Guderian, starting to assemble outside, but Hitler appeared unconcerned. They would have to wait. Their Führer was far too much taken by this half-English, half-Bavarian son of the Reich.

Peter found himself questioned at length about the morale of the Luftwaffe pilots and the general situation on the Eastern front. His Generals, Hitler complained, always told him what they thought he wanted to know, rather than the truth of the situation.

Peter was honest. He took his life in his hands. He too cared for what was to become of the German people.

'Mein Führer,' he answered. 'The fighting spirit and devotion to the Fatherland of my comrades is great, but we believe that the war is lost. Everywhere we are in retreat, short of essential supplies and replacement equipment. We need thousands more planes and the men to fly them if we are to defeat the Russians in the air.'

Peter expected an outburst. None came. Quietly, at first, Hitler explained that top priority orders had been given to Feldmarshall Milch and Herr Speer to maximize aircraft production and that the figures were improving by leaps and bounds, despite round-the-clock Allied bombing. Then the Führer's voice began to rise, not in anger but with the excitement of his theme.

'Herr Oberleutnant, believe me, we will win through to absolute victory in the end. Very soon now, Von Braun's miracle weapons, the pilotless bomb and the V2 rocket, will destroy the British spirit. Soon, too, we shall have the new generation of jet aircraft, the Me 262 blitz bomber, and the 163 rocket fighter.' Hitler's voice rose to a crescendo. 'With these weapons we will regain mastery of the air and sweep our enemies from the sky. We will flatten their cities and raze their factories to the ground.' He took a deep breath and then added, more quietly: 'I am surprised, Oberleutnant, to hear of talk of defeat. There will be no defeat. We are going to win.'

'Indeed, my Führer. But the 262—you referred to it as a blitz bomber. Surely it is a fighter plane, the best in the world?'

'It is a bomber. I have given orders that it shall be made to carry bombs.'

Hitler wiped a fleck of sputum from the side of his mouth with the back of his hand. Peter was too flabbergasted to speak. The one plane the Luftwaffe had to have was the twin-jet, heavily armed 262, the aircraft that made all those flown by the Allies obsolete. And now Hitler planned to deny his airforce the only weapon that might yet save them, even at this late hour.

Just prior to the July 1944 bomb plot, as a result of which his health and questionable mental stability would be finally undermined, Hitler's personality was little short of hypnotic. Well did Peter understand why those closest to him told him what he wanted to know, rather than the facts. His grip on events, his detailed knowledge of weaponry and his astonishing memory for names and faces, were formidable. But it was plain to Peter that a major cause of the total defeat that he saw inexorably drawing closer, was the Führer's stubborn refusal to accept a *fait accompli* and act accordingly. To insist that the fitting of a fighter aircraft with bombs rendered it by definition a bomber, was little short of ludicrous.

Peter had to get a grip on himself. He felt as if he were falling under the spell of this extraordinary paradox, this perverse and perverted genius. Then he remembered the Jew at the station and the two grinning gangsters who had nearly shot him at the same time.

'My Führer, one more thing, please.' Peter withdrew the still shiny 9mm bullet from his pocket and showed it to Hitler, explaining what had happened at the station. Hitler expressed both surprise and concern. He promised that the S.S. men would be punished. The interview was over. Hitler shook hands with Peter, but his grip was weak and his hand trembled.

'Goodbye, young man. Look after yourself. Germany will need men like you when we have won our final victory.'

Peter nodded. Major Von Below and he saluted, and the two men left the room.

The interview had lasted almost ninety minutes. The Generals were not pleased at being kept waiting this long by two junior officers.

Von Below drove Peter back to the station and waited to see him safely aboard the train that would convey him to Schwandorf. From there it was but a short trip to Tahlmann, to Ilse and a week of peace and relaxation.

Ilse was out when Peter arrived. She did not come to the station to meet her husband for the simple reason that she had no idea that he was coming, let alone that he had earlier in the day been decorated by Hitler in person.

Peter hired a somewhat decrepit Opel taxi to drive him home. The cab rattled and shook in a manner reminiscent of the railway guard's van. Petrol was virtually unobtainable for "non-essential purposes", and the taxi engine had been adjusted to run on gas, supplied from a large cylinder towed on a trailer behind. Whilst speed and acceleration were scarcely enough to excite a motor enthusiast, the car reached its destination nonetheless.

Peter paid the driver and walked in through the front door. After a moment or two, a middle-aged, greying woman met him in the hall.

'Good afternoon, Fräulein,' Peter acknowledged. 'I—'. He got no further.

'Good gracious . . . you must be the Baron, Sir.'

'Yes I am.'

'The Baroness, she, we . . . er, nobody had the slightest idea that you were coming . . . Oh my goodness.' The woman flapped and fussed like a mother hen. 'This is an honour, Sir.'

'I don't think we've met before.' Peter smiled indulgently at the fidgeting female.

'No, of course, Herr Baron. I am Griselda Stopf, the new housekeeper.' Peter stuck out his hand and Fräulein Stopf darted forward, bird-like, and shook it nervously.

'Now, Fräulein, where is my wife?'

'She's not here, Sir.'

'Well where is she?'

'She's out, Sir.'

Peter smiled.

'If she's not here, then she must be out. But out where?'

Stopf tittered uneasily.

'Oh, of course, Baron. The Baroness has gone out with the Major.'

'Gone *where*? *What* Major?'

'They have gone riding together. His name is Major Gunther Strauch, I believe, Sir.'

'Who the hell's he?' demanded Peter petulantly, with the first stirrings of jealous doubt.

'I don't know, sir. But he's a frequent visitor here.'

The housekeeper could hardly have made a more tactless remark if she had said that the couple were upstairs in bed together.

'They'll be back any time now. But his wife is here. I think she's in the drawing room.'

Spared any further agonized guess work, Peter heaved an audible sigh of relief. Why, he thought, hadn't the stupid woman said so in the first place?

'Shall I take you in, Sir?'

'Thank you, but that won't be necessary. I'm sure you have more important things to do. Thank you anyway, Fräulein.'

The bird-like creature flitted back to the servant's quarters, leaving Peter to walk to the drawing room on his own.

'I'm von Tahlmann,' he said as he entered the room. His eyes widened as the figure turned from the fireplace and revealed herself to be a stunningly beautiful woman.

'Johannes,' said a startled voice. 'Johannes, what a marvellous surprise. Where did you spring from?' The elegant, fair-haired beauty flung her arms round Peter's neck and hugged him. Peter was speechless with surprise.

'Darling, don't you remember me?' she queried, releasing her hold on his neck and stepping back a pace. Peter, worried now, was wondering whether his memory was at fault again, or—.

'Really, Johannes. You don't remember me, do you?'

'Well, I . . .' Peter stammered.

The blonde pouted.

'I should be very hurt. I'm not the sort of woman that men forget, am I?'

'Good God no,' Peter said, too quickly. 'But . . .'

The woman was tactful, she had teased enough.

'I'm Hildegard Strauch. You knew me as Hildegard Kreipe. We last met at your wedding in Berlin.'

'Of course. How very stupid of me. Of course I should have remembered your name, but . . .' He fell back on his usual line of defence. 'Much of my past was blotted out after the accident.'

'Yes, you poor dear,' sympathized Hildegard, brushing a manicured hand across his furrowed brow. 'Shall we sit down?'

Peter made for the sofa, as Hildgard launched into an impromptu monologue about times past. She and Ilse had met Johannes at the same supper party that evening in Nuremburg before the war. He must remember. Of course, in those days Johannes had only been a hopeful young Fahnenjunker*, but she had fallen in love with him at first sight; it had taken her months to get over the fact that he had chosen Ilse instead. Generously, she added: 'But I'm sure it all worked out for the best. I have my Gunther. He's a dear man—you'll like him.' She paused and took a deep breath before suddenly changing direction. 'Ilse, dear Ilse. If you don't actually know it, let me tell you now: she worships the very air you breathe. She seldom talks of anything but you.'

'Yes, I do know. Bless you, Hildegard, I do assure you that the emotions are entirely reciprocated.' Peter was smiling now, wondering how he could possibly have entertained even a momentary doubt about his wife.

About two hours later, Ilse and Gunther returned from their ride and came straight to the drawing room to see

*Cadet.

how Hildegard was faring. They had not encountered any of the household staff on the way. Hildegard heard voices. Always one for drama, she motioned to Peter to stay where he was.

'Let's surprise her,' she whispered to him.

Ilse had nearly reached the door. Gunther, making slower progress, followed. Hildegard shot out of the room, barring her hostess from further progress.

'Now then, Ilse,' she commanded. 'Shut your eyes, follow me, and I'll give you a nice surprise.'

Ilse did as she was told and Hildegard led her into the room.

'Now keep them shut tight, won't you, darling?'

Ilse, entering into the spirit of things, screwed up her face, her lips pursed, half expecting some tasty morsel to be popped into her mouth. She heard footsteps approaching and then she felt a familiar kiss, gentle at first, then more passionate. Her eyes flickered open.

'Johannes!'

The couple hugged and kissed and Ilse was left gasping for air and delirious with delight. 'Oh, please God, tell me I'm not dreaming. Is it really you?'

Half crying, half laughing, she at last released her husband. Gunther had entered the room close behind.

'Let me introduce Hildegard's husband. I don't think you two have met before.' A tall, balding man with a black patch over his left eye was standing on one leg in the doorway. The other he had left somewhere on Russian soil during the previous summer's campaign.

'My dear fellow, I have heard so much about you and read much of you too. I'm honoured to make your acquaintance at last.'

The two men shook hands. Peter knew at once that Hildegard was right. The two men struck up an immediate rapport.

For a while they all sat talking until Gunther and Hildegard, sensing that the couple would appreciate some time alone, simultaneously glanced at their watches, excused themselves and made a diplomatic exit, leaving Peter to break his momentous news.

CHAPTER ELEVEN

Günther was still officially in the army, but he was due for discharge on medical grounds very shortly. The papers were expected to come through any day. Pending the arrival of his formal release, he was on extended leave. He and his wife had had a lucky escape when their house in Nuremburg had been bombed out, but had lost most of their possessions. Ilse had offered to put up the homeless couple at Tahlmann, *sine die*, or at least until they could find other accommodation. She was glad of the company since Tahlmann was a big place in which to live alone. Ilse had felt sure Peter wouldn't mind. She was right. In fact, Peter and Gunther got on increasingly well as the week progressed. Despite the loss of a leg, Gunther was an accomplished horseman, and they rode together with Ilse every day. Hildegard, however, was only persuaded to come out once, and immediately fell off. Laughing, she refused to join the others after that, saying that she only made herself look foolish.

In the evenings the men talked, into the small hours about the war and about the future of their country. Gunther had been an ordinary infantry officer in the Wehrmacht, an average soldier doing his duty by his country; but his descriptions of the privations and horrors he had to suffer during the icy Russian winters defied belief. Peter was only too well aware of the appalling conditions the army had had to endure, but he had never had such graphic and articulate descriptions before. He also learned from Gunther of the horrors perpetrated by the S.S. Einsatzgruppen, and of the barbaric treatment of German prisoners that the Reds meted out in return. Günther finally agreed with his host that the war was lost, that it had been since the moment the Americans had entered the conflict. But like Peter, Gunther's dread was not defeat at the hands of the Western Allies but the thought of the sacred soil of the Fatherland falling under the boot of the Bolsheviks. Now it seemed altogether inevitable.

The week ended all too quickly. Once again it was time for Peter to return to the front. Ilse cried a great deal when the moment finally came, imploring him to return to her soon. Hildegard cried too, and Peter fancied he even saw Gunther wiping away a tear. He had made a good friend. Another one worth fighting for to the last.

CHAPTER TWELVE

JG 52 was in the thick of the fighting again when Peter returned. This time he had been lucky enough to cover the journey by air, albeit in three separate hops, arriving at his unit with the rations and mail in a transport aircraft. The field was in the process of being sprayed with machine-gun and cannon fire as the lumbering JG 52 tri-motor, with its strange, corrugated fuselage and wings, came in to land. The big plane was only superficially hit, and the moment it stopped Peter opened the door and leapt to the ground. Racing twenty yards or so, he sprinted for the cover of the nearest slit trench, as bullets hissed and spurted in the dirt all round him.

In his last dash for safety he suddenly felt a searing pain in his calf. Fighting for breath, he dived for the trench, completely flattening and winding its only other occupant. After heaving himself up he examined the wound. Blood had started to ooze through the hole in the boot leather.

Are you all right?' questioned his startled and rather breathless companion.

Peter grimaced, then managed a smile.

'I think so.' He waggled a leg. It moved. 'Just a flesh wound, by the feel of it. Damn the Ivans. What a bloody awful way to return to work.'

The man, a Corporal, nodded resignedly.

It was only a nick. The bullet had travelled right through his leg, clean as a whistle, miraculously, missing the bone. A few days and it would be as good as new.

When the raid was over, Peter hobbled off to the medical quarters where he was attended to at once. He was the only casualty, and was walking with less of a limp now that he knew the worst. Then he reported his return to the Wing Adjutant.

'Welcome back, Tahlmann,' he said. 'Sorry about the reception committee.'

'Not your fault, Sir,' replied Peter. 'By the way, there's something I want to ask you.' Peter had not forgotten the business of the drink on the way to the Führer's headquarters.

The Admin officer looked up.

'What d'you want to know?'

'Quite simply, why you told me not to misbehave on my trip. Do you know, I found it well-nigh impossible to get even one glass of beer on the train. Has everybody gone crazy? Are we all to be treated like school children? Damn it, even Major von Below said he was glad to see I was sober.'

The adjutant smiled. 'There's a perfectly reasonable explanation, but it's not for me to tell you. No, I think Krupinski should do the honours.'

Walter Krupinski was out on a mission at the time. He came back safely, but his 109 had collected some scars on its tail fins. Several bullet holes and jagged tears in the metal attested to the accuracy of a Russian pilot's shooting. But his aim had not been quite straight enough.

Krupinski was in excellent form, none the worse for his narrow escape. He had nailed a couple of Ivans that day and Hartmann had scored twice too. The unit had operated without loss. Back in the mess, Peter waited until throats were oiled and tongues lubricated before putting his question.

'Now look here, Sir. I gather you can explain why I found it nearly impossible to get even a single solitary glass of liquid sustenance on my journey west?'

The announcement was greeted by roars of mirth and sustained cheering.

'My dear Johannes, do you mean to tell me you don't know?'

'Know what?'

More mirth.

'God in Heaven,' screeched Krupinski, scarcely able to speak for laughter. 'You must be the only man in the whole Luftwaffe who hasn't heard the story. My poor ignorant friend.'

'Shame,' chorused the company.

Peter stuck out an admonishing finger and prodded Krupinski in the chest.

'Come along now, Graf Pinski. Out with it, then.'

'Well,' the other began hesitantly. 'It's like this—or rather it was like this. Once upon a time—'

'Get on with it, man,' interrupted Peter amid the laughter.

'As I was about to say,' Krupinski continued, 'when I was so rudely interrupted . . . Four of us—Erich here, Gerd Barkhorn, Johannes Weise and I, were on our way by train to see the Führer and, like you, we had a bit of a thirst. So we sought out the guard, who we soon found out had been in the mob in the other war. Of course, there was no bar on the train, so we persuaded the fellow to stop at the next station. Probably it was the Knight's Crosses that did the trick. Anyway, he duly stopped the train, just for us. And almost as soon as it started again he brought out a bottle of Schnapps. Well, you know us.'

'I do indeed,' interjected Peter.

'The Schnapps didn't last long,' Krupinski took a deep breath, 'so the train had to be stopped again and again to take on supplies—beer, wine, cognac and more Schnapps. You missed a right regal piss up, old boy.' Krupinski smiled and patted Peter sympathetically on the shoulder. 'As you can imagine, we were in cracking form when the guard finally poured us off the train. We shambled to the ticket barrier, where we fell into the arms of a very shocked von Below, who was waiting to take us to the Führer. But do you know what that bastard did to us then? You'll never believe it.' Krupinski gave a mock shudder. 'Seeing what he called "our unseemly condition" he ordered the driver to put down the hood of the car. Well, you know what it's like up there in March—it's bloody cold. And there was snow on the ground, several inches of it. Every time there was a breath of wind, fresh flurries were sucked off the mountainsides. I thought we were all going to freeze to death! Anyway, von Below still wasn't certain of our sobriety, so he ordered us to get out and run about to warm ourselves up and clear our heads. After all that we arrived with minutes to spare before our appointment with the Führer and von Below took us into an ante room and told us to wait. In that room was a hat stand with a single hat on—I expect you saw it.'

'I know the one you mean,' said Peter.

'Well then, Bubi here,' Erich Hartmann's boyish face creased into a broad grin, 'spotted the hat, and, seeing the gold braid on it, stalked over to the stand and took it off. "Ah, my hat, I believe," he said, "I think I'll promote myself to General"—and put the thing on his head. The cap was umpteen sizes too large for him, so of course it slipped way down over his ears. I hadn't seen anything so damned funny for years. But old von Below wasn't amused. He took one look at Bubi and hissed at him: "Hartmann, take that hat off at once and put it back where you found it. That is the Führer's hat." So you see, Johannes, that's why they wouldn't let you at the booze.'

The mess erupted with renewed mirth, and the mystery solved, Peter was able to join in.

'I reckon you bastards owe me a few drinks after that.'

'You could be right, Johannes,' said Hartmann. 'Let me be the first in the chair.'

Not for the first time, or the last, Peter appeared on duty with a splitting hangover the next day. He was far from being the only member of JG 52 to be so afflicted.

Ten days later he began operational flying again, but now he had stepped up the ladder of command. Within a month and eleven more victories, he was leading a squadron.

The Allies opened a second front in June, when the biggest amphibious force in history, under the command of General Eisenhower, landed on the beaches of Normandy. For the German forces the end was now clearly in sight.

Consequent to the successful landings in France, a number of Luftwaffe units were transferred from the Russian front. To Peter's intense relief, JG 52 was not amongst them. By the 22nd November 1944, Peter, recently promoted to Captain, had raised his tally of victories against the Soviets to 132. On that day he scored his 133rd and, as it would turn out, his final success of the war. In a confused skirmish with U.S. escort fighters, his first combat against American-flown aircraft, he shot down one P.51 Mustang, more as an act of self defence than of aggression. Heavily outnumbered and outgunned, he found his plane riddled with .50 calibre machine gun bullets. Before he could abandon the stricken machine, it blew up in mid-air. The force of the explosion hurled him clear of the debris, and his body plummeted to earth. Some last, desperate reflex action saved him. He had no recollection of what urged him to pull the ripcord on his chute. He drifted to earth, a sagging bundle, his head on his chest, arms dangling at his sides. Some hours later he woke up in hospital, his body racked with pain, his left arm broken in two places, and with two severely sprained ankles to add to his woes.

PART THREE

THE PRISONER

CHAPTER ONE

The arm took longer to heal than was expected. The limb did not bind together as it should have done and had to be rebroken the following January. For Peter, it seemed, the war was over. But at the beginning of May 1945 he received orders to rejoin No. 1 Group, JG 52, now commanded by Major Erich Hartmann, who had become the ace of aces with 351 confirmed victories.

Not unnaturally, many of the familiar faces had disappeared from the scene during Peter's absence. Some had been killed, a few were known to be prisoners of the Russians; and Krupinski and Barkhorn had both been posted to JG 44, the squadron of experts commanded by General Galland, where with devastating effect they flew the few Messerschmitt 262 jets assigned to fighter operations against the American bombers in the closing months of the war.

JG 52 was, at this time, based at Deutsch Brod, where Peter reported for duty at 08.15 hours on the 8th May. At 08.30 hours Hartmann and his comrades took off on what would be their last mission. Peter was forced to stay behind and watch them go. Their object was to ascertain the depth of Russian penetration in the area of the nearby town of Brünn. A huge cloud of smoke hung over the area and Soviet lorries and tanks were advancing into the outskirts. Hartmann spotted a formation of Yak II fighters flying below him, one of which appeared to be performing victory rolls over the oncoming troops. Hartmann signalled to his wingman his intention to attack, and the two 109s came screaming down on the unsuspecting Russian. Waiting till the enemy machine was close enough to fill his gunsight, the ace of aces pressed his gun button. A single well-aimed burst was enough. The Yak began to burn immediately, and flipping over on its back it plunged to the ground, exploding in a fountain of orange flame and billowing black smoke.

The two German pilots soared away and prepared for another attack. Then they noticed a squadron of American-flown P.51 Mustangs approaching from another direction. They turned their noses to the west and gunning throttles, tore back towards their base. Glancing in his rear-view mirror Hartmann was pleased to see that the Russians, not by any means for the first time, had mistaken the P. 51s for Bf 109s and were already engaged in a furious dog-fight with their so-called allies.

Hartmann had scored for the last time. His 352nd victory made him the most successful fighter pilot in the history of aerial combat, a brief spark of triumph against the funereal backcloth of Hitler's suicide in the Berlin Bunker and the dying days of the Third Reich.

The 109s landed safely back at Deutsch Brod and Hartmann went immediately to report his mission to JG 52 Kommodore Harmann Graf. The Leutnant Colonel's face was a picture of dejection.

'The Russians,' announced Hartmann, 'are already occupying Brünn, Sir.'

Graf nodded but said nothing. He prodded a finger at the town of Strakonitz on the map.

'American armoured units have arrived. We also have reports that some elements of the American spearhead have advanced as far as the Moldau river. The war is over. At least for us, Erich.'

'Surrender, Sir?' Hartmann queried.

'Just that. I have the order here.' Graf passed him a slip of paper.

'Graf and Hartmann both fly immediately to Dortmund and surrender to British forces. All other JG 52 personnel

will surrender at Deutsch Brod to Soviet Forces. Signed: General Seidemann, Air Fleet Commander.'

Graf's face creased into a grin at last.

'It seems that our masters still care enough for *our* skins not to want us to fall into Russian hands. We've shot down a hell of a lot of Ivans between us.'

'Yes, indeed,' agreed Hartmann, smiling briefly at the thought of their combined total—well over 500.

'So it looks as if we'd better jump into our 109s and push off,' Graf said. 'At least, that's if we decide to obey the General's orders.'

They looked beyond the raised flap of the tent, the canvas structure that served as the Kommodore's last H.Q. for the outfit. The two men surveyed their faithful 109s, the planes that had served them so well and which would now have to be destroyed. But what of the personnel—not only the members of JG 52, but their comrades in arms, their families? Women and children, old people, refugees, helples people, 2,000 of them all desperately trying to escape from the Russians, were camped out, for the most part in the open, waiting patiently for the next move. The ragged outline of their muddy, overcrowded encampment was visible through the flap of the Kommodore's tent.

'We cannot obey our orders, Erich.' Graf said quietly.

'No Sir. Our duty is to them.'

'I didn't think you'd give any other answer,' Graf added, and pointing his finger once more at the map he went on. 'Pisek here, in the American area—we'll try to reach it. I'll organize the people; Erich, you attend to the destruction of the equipment.'

Hartmann gave orders immediately. The twenty-five 109s were to be burned, together with all their spares, fuel and ammunition, as well as all the other stores and equipment.

Peter was kept by Graf for assistance, and before the funeral pyre of JG 52 was ignited, the sad and vanquished column had started to move to the west. After a while, a burst of cannonfire was heard which heralded the igniting of the huge bonfire. The air was rent with the pop and crump of exploding ammunition, and pillars of smoke and flame rose out of the stillness behind the shambling refugees.

An hour later Hartmann made his way to the head of the procession, where he joined Hermann Graf and Major Hartmann Grasser, the C.O. of JG 210, who had brought his wing staff and joined up with JG 52 just before the end. Peter had not seen Grasser since his early days as Adjutant to Werner Mölders.

In the early evening of the same day they ran into the Americans. Hartmann was the first to spot the drab, khaki-painted Sherman tanks with their conspicuous white stars. The 75 mm guns were pointing menacingly towards them. The Germans poured across the fields waving and shouting, their hands raised in surrender. Graf and Hartmann saluted the officer who was perched in the turret of the leading tank.

'I am Leutnant Colonel Graf, C.O. of the 52nd fighter wing of the Luftwaffe. This is Major Hartmann, who had command of No. 1 Group. The people with us are JG 52 personnel and civilian refugees. On behalf of us all we surrender to the United States Army.'

The American officer saluted before contacting his H.Q. on the tank's R.T. The Germans did not have long to wait. In less than a quarter of an hour a truckload of soldiers slewed to a halt behind the tanks. The Germans were relieved of their weapons, except for the officers, who were permitted to retain their pistols and instructed to keep order. JG 52 had surrendered to elements of the 90th U.S. Infantry Division.

Encountering for the first time the Americans' insatiable greed for trophies and souvenirs, the Germans were angered when their wrist watches were removed. But it was a small price to pay for their escape from the jaws of the Red Bear. Some of the G.I.s cast lascivious glances at a few of the more obviously attractive women, but made no move.

The 90th Division, operating in conjunction with the 60th Armoured Division, had advanced well beyond the eastern limits agreed with their Russian allies. Blissfully ignorant of the situation, the Luftwaffe men heaved sighs of relief that they, and more especially their families, would be spared the horrors that Russian troops were known to have already inflicted on captured Germans. The prisoners were equally ignorant of the fact that under an agreement reached between the Allies at Yalta, all military personnel who had fought on the Eastern Front would have to be handed over to the Soviets.

The refugees were conveyed to a hastily-erected enclosure at Schuttenhofen in Czechoslovakia, where they were joined by hordes of others until their numbers had reached the staggering figure of 50,000. The compound was guarded at each end by a single Sherman tank. Conditions were barbaric, toilet facilities non-existent. American guards began to turn a blind eye towards whole families, who, taking their courage in their hands, calmly walked out and began to make their way westwards.

After eight days without proper food, living on what they had brought with them, their meagre supplies barely supplemented by unofficial handouts from the Americans, the prisoners were told that they were to be transported to Regensburg in Germany for "processing". At 4.00 p.m. they were loaded into trucks and driven away. The journey was unexpectedly short. Some five miles down the road the lorries turned into a field where they halted. Tailboards were lowered and the occupants ordered to get out. Peter recoiled in horror when he saw that the field was filled with Russian soldiers, who had already begun to segregate the women from the men.

Before they drove away, the American truck drivers

were given a glimpse of the fate to which they had, albeit unwittingly, delivered their prisoners. The men were forced to stand in line by a party of swaggering Red Army soldiers, who covered them with rifles and machine pistols. Other Red Army men seized some of the girls and began to abuse them. Neither the German men nor the handful of Americans that were left could do anything at all to help. They could only stare, mouths agape, at the scenes that followed.

Two girls managed to escape from the clutches of their assailants and clawing at the sides of the truck, were hauled to temporary safety by the Americans, but this single show of defiance did not please the Russians, who approached the truck, firing their weapons wildly in the air. The G.I.s, who had kept their engines running, thrust gear-levers forward and sped away down the road. It was not their fight.

With all vestiges of opposition now removed, the Russians took the women with a maniacal savagery. A pretty girl in her thirties begged for her twelve-year-old daughter to be spared. Her pleadings fell on deaf ears. Mother and daughter were taken repeatedly, their screams bringing tears to the eyes of the helpless onlookers.

Some of the German men made as if to move to the rescue, but soon found gun muzzles thrust in their stomachs.

'Nazi pigs, this is all you deserve,' a Russian Corporal shouted at a grey-haired woman, a grandmother well into her sixties. The German tigress fought back with unusual ferocity and succeeded in gouging the Corporal's left eye clean from its socket. With a shriek of pain he released the woman and, with his trousers round his knees, staggered to his feet. Cupping his hand to his left eye-socket, blood streaming through his fingers, he fumbled for his holster. He withdrew his TT 33 pistol and shot the woman repeatedly in the head and torso before staggering off, still screaming, into the arms of a comrade.

The twelve-year-old child appeared suddenly from behind the truck where she had been dragged. Stark naked and whimpering helplessly, she collapsed like some dis-discarded plaything, her body crimson with her own blood.

When the medic had attended to the injured Russian he had the decency to see what he could do for the girl. There was nothing. After a short while her whimpering subsided and she died.

At length, their lusts satiated, the Russian soldiers relieved their comrades who had kept the men covered with their guns, and a fresh wave of horrors began. A number of women were herded into trucks and driven away, never to be heard of again. The rest were returned to their grief-stricken menfolk.

That night, thirty Russian tanks surrounded the prisoners, who had to sleep on the bare ground where they were. When the first rays of the dawn began to illuminate the scene, a large number of the prisoners did not stir.

Peter gained some small consolation from the fact that Ilse, safe in Bavaria, had been spared this fate. He had been amongst those who had wept openly, helplessly. Sleep had not come easily, but in the end he had lost consciousness through sheer mental and physical exhaustion. He had lain down on the grass beside his long-time friend, Sergeant Pieter Ostertagg, his former chief mechanic, together with his wife Joanna and their two daughters Heide and Ursula. They were still asleep when Peter awoke, so he did not move lest he disturb them. As the light grew stronger he looked hard at Pieter. A dark stain coloured the grass by his head. He didn't appear to be breathing. Peter crept towards him and felt the body. Cold. His wife and daughters too. Speechless with this new horror, he examined the family and discovered that Pieter had cut his own throat after slashing the wrists of his wife and children with a piece of broken glass.

Slowly, dazed, people got to their feet. Graf and Hartmann were not far away. There were many who remained where they were, who would never stand again. Men had suffocated their whole families and then cut their wrists or throats with any pieces of glass or jagged metal they could lay their hands on. Some had hanged themselves from the sides of trucks with lengths of knotted material.

If Peter had not been certain before, he knew now that he had done the right thing in opting to fight his captors rather than doing battle with his own kith and kin.

Later that day, a Russian General appeared, evidently a civilised man and a stern disciplinarian. One look at the pathetic flotsam in his charge told him all he wanted to know. Prisoners and soldiers alike were paraded. The General ordered that the German officers should be separated from the other ranks and the women placed in their charge. The Russians were ordered, on pain of severe punishment, not to molest the women further.

During the next night, one girl was dragged from the officers' compound and raped by three men. In the morning, on hearing of the incident, the General ordered an identity parade at which the girl was able to point out to the soldiers who had assaulted her.

What followed was swift and merciless. In front of the entire company, Russians and Germans, the three men had their hands tied behind their backs and were summarily hanged.

After this salutory lesson, captors and captives kept an uneasy distance. But some of the women, creating virtue out of what they saw as the necessity to survive, gave of their favours freely to the soldiers, in return for a little extra food or other small luxuries such as cigarettes and chocolate.

From the makeshift stockade, the officers and women were taken to another camp at Neubistritz. Here the men were categorized: names, ranks, serial numbers and brief career details. Towards the end of June, the clerical work at Neubistritz was completed and rumours began to spread concerning the next move, but the Germans still had no idea where they were heading, even after they had been assembled and marched out of the camp. After four days of mounting speculation, which included dread whispers of "Siberia", nobody yet knew for certain what awaited them. At the town of Budweis the column was halted and a Russian officer smilingly told them not to listen to the rumour-mongers. To the joy of all the prisoners, he announced that they were not going to the Soviet Union, but were to be put on a train bound for Vienna, whence they would all be sent home.

Peter, his commonsense overwhelmed by immense relief, was near to delirium with happiness when he boar- the ramshackle train the next day. Erich Hartmann, almost alone, was sceptical of the stated destination, but like everyone else his spirits soared too as the locomotive headed steadily south.

Then the train halted, timbers heaved and couplings jolted as it shunted backwards and forwards. A Russian officer explained in halting German that they would not be travelling on to Vienna now, as originally planned, since the city was in a state of anarchy: they would be going to Budapest instead. The train did indeed take the prisoners to Budapest, but it did not stop there. Instead, it rattled on eastwards for several more hours. When it finally stopped, the men were ordered out and marched away to a camp at Maramures, run by Rumanian Communists.

Another week passed before Peter and his companions were marched back to the train again. It was now stiff with Russian guards bristling with rifles and machine pistols. Sixty Germans, including Peter and Erich Hartmann, were herded into one small freight car. It was insufficiently ventilated and the air soon became unbearably hot and stale. Erich, showing his natural flair for leadership, organized a rota which permitted one third of their number to lie down for two hours at a time. Rank was forgotten as officers and Sergeants alike took equal share of the hardships.

This terrible routine continued for a fortnight as the train moved ever deeper into the Soviet Union. They passed through Kiev, Moscow and Vologda, and at length reached Kirov, the centre of an endless mass of peat bogs and swamps. In this desolate spot they detrained, grateful at least for the luxury of clean air once more.

The men were assembled and addressed by a Commissar. Anyone who wished to escape was invited to try, should he so wish. The prisoners were ordered to build their own shelters and shovels and axes were provided. With these they dug holes in the ground and hacked down branches to make makeshift canopies. The food was appalling, hardly enough to sustain life, but even so the prisoners were expected to work from dawn to dusk cutting blocks of peat, which were stacked in enormous piles to be removed each day by the one train that plied backwards and forwards from the camp.

After a month, morale began to crack. Peter was close to despair, his only respite from the gruelling routine being an occasional dream of happier days past. A week later all the officers of the rank of Major and above were ordered to the camp at Gryazovets. With them, of course, went Erich Hartmann, whose presence had been an inspiration to them all, as well as Hermann Graf. Peter shook Erich warmly by the hand.

'Pray God we meet again, Bubi,' Peter said sadly.

'We will, Johannes. Don't despair, this can't go on forever.'

For another week Peter laboured on, becoming weaker by the day. He knew he could not take much more. His face was gaunt, his body emaciated.

As he paraded for work on the 9th day after the departure of the senior officers, Peter was instructed to remain behind by the Commissar. He was taken to an office where he was invited to sit down and was even offered a cigarette.

Peter took the cigarette and the Russian gave him a light.

'I have good news for you, Tahlmann,' he announced. 'We're sending you to Gryazovets camp. I'm sure you'll find it a very much more pleasant place than this.'

Peter nodded and took another drag at the cigarette.

'Cheer up, my friend,' continued the Commissar, looking at the picture of misery sitting opposite him. 'Things will improve. Good food, good conditions, entertainment. You'll soon put all this behind you.'

'Why am I being sent there?' queried Peter, suspicious that he was to be plucked out of the frying pan only to be thrown into the fire.

'Don't look so suspicious, Tahlmann. We're not all animals, you know.' Peter still looked glum, unconvinced.

'We're sending you to Gryazovets because you're rather a special case.'

'What's so special about me?'

The Commissar laughed. 'Tell me, how many German officers with the Oakleaves to the Knight's Cross can say they're half-English?'

Peter felt the skin tighten on the back of his neck. The truth was out—they knew. He felt certain that he was either destined for a firing squad, or would be handed back to the English and tried for treason.

'My mother was English, that's true. But she died long before the war. I don't see that that makes me so special.'

'Perhaps not. But plainly some of my superiors think otherwise.'

Peter didn't reply. The Russian looked steadily at him as he spoke.

'Our agents in England have told us that you were shot down in September and that later you escaped from captivity. You should be congratulated.'

Peter, inwardly relieved by the thought that he was still being taken for his brother, managed a smile at last.

'That's better, young man. You are, you know, not so much special as unique.'

'Oh?'

'You see, we also know that you had a twin brother. Do you know what happened to him?'

'Naturally I do. He was killed in the same car accident as my mother.'

'Wrong.'

'What do you mean?'

'Just what I say. You are wrong. Your twin brother, an officer in the R.A.F. was killed just two days after you yourself had been shot down. Surely you must have known that?'

'How the hell should I know?' Peter snapped.

'I just thought you might, that's all.' The Commissar was probing. He added: 'You don't seem unduly upset.'

'I have no reason to be. I hated him.'

'I see,' the Russian replied.

The noise of a train whistle and the clanking of couplings brought the interview to a close.

'It's time to go,' the Commissar said, giving Peter a couple of cigarettes for the journey.

'Thank you,' he replied, with exaggerated politeness.

Peter was marched off by two Russian Privates, each with drum-fed Shpagin tommy guns slung round their shoulders. He was ushered into a van, where he sat on the floor, the two Russians eyeing him suspiciously. After a while the guards relaxed, joking with one another and ignoring the prisoner, who sat in silence throughout the journey. Peter was trying hard to convince himself that things would look up, but his mind was sorely troubled by the apparent extent of the Russians' knowledge of his past.

CHAPTER TWO

The Gryazovets camp was indeed all that the Commissar had promised, and more. Conditions were better than he had dared to hope, even in his moments of wildest fantasy. After a brief period in hospital for tests screening him for signs of contagious disease, he soon sought out his erstwhile JG 52 friends. Erich Hartmann at once took him to one side, warning him not to be taken in by the superficial comfort of the place after the festering bog that he had just left.

Gryazovets was a permanent camp. Apart from the barracks, admin offices, a hospital and so-called "convalescent unit" housed in wooden buildings, there was provision for recreation, for football and athletic activities. A stream which froze over in the winter was used for skating and ice hockey. There was also a band which gave concerts or played popular western dance music, and even a cafe where cups of real coffee could be purchased for a rouble at a time.

To Peter, in spite of Hartmann's warnings, the place still seemed like a holiday camp. But appearances were deceptive. Its *raison d'être* was to "soften up" the German prisoners and screen them politically for potential Communist sympathisers who would be likely to be of use to the Soviet Union in the furtherance of their post-war expansionist aims.

Erich Hartmann told Peter what he could expect at the hands of the Russian interrogators. He did not have long to wait before the process began, a near daily routine involving a mixture of intimidation, threats and cajolery.

One of the most odious of the N.K.V.D. men, an object of universal hatred by the prisoners, was one Captain Klingbeil, a German renegade. The former officers of the Reich had grown to expect bad treatment from the Russians, but to receive it from one of their own kind was that much harder to endure.

Klingbeil's first major success was no less a person than Hermann Graf, the former Group Commander of JG 52, the holder of the diamonds to the Knight's Cross and the victor of 212 aerial combats. Erich Hartmann, the first to hear the news, was shattered by Graf's defection, but refused to be subverted himself. Hartmann told the others what had happened. Peter heard about it just before he was once again ordered to report to a triumphant Captain Klingbeil.

'Please sit down, Captain,' Klingbeil began, his oily politeness clearly indicating his confidence that Peter would be a push-over. 'Have a cigarette.'

Peter took it without thanks and Klingbeil rose from his chair to offer the prisoner a light. Peter inhaled and blew the smoke across the room. For a few moments each man surveyed the other, neither speaking. Then Klingbeil paced slowly round the room and at last began his diatribe. Peter had heard it all before. First the soft approach, then the threats.

'Your commanding officer has, at last, agreed to see things our way. There's no point in you and Hartmann and the others continuing your defiance any longer. Be a sensible fellow and sign the confession. As soon as you do, you'll be able to go home to your wife.'

'You don't say?'

'You have my word on it. Just sign the papers and hand over your Cross. By the way, where's your medal?'

Peter was silent.

'I'm waiting, Captain.'

'You don't think I'd let scum like you lay your hands on it?'

Klingbeil looked grim for a second but then smugly held up the Knight's Cross with Diamonds lying on his desk.

'If only you had the commonsense of your Commander Graf, things would be so much easier for all of us.'

'Is that so?'

'Yes, damn you,' Klingbeil snapped. 'This is Graf's Cross. He gave it to me. Graf had the wit to confess that what he had done during the war was wrong; he admitted to his crimes against the Russian people. For your sake, Tahlmann, I strongly urge you to do the same.'

'I don't take my lessons from traitors, thank you Klingbeil. The only confession you'll get out of me is to doing my duty as an officer in the German Air Force.'

Klingbeil scowled and approached his prisoner's chair. Peter stubbed out the cigarette.

'Now look here, Tahlmann, let me put you in the picture. If you don't do as we ask, then you'll stay in Russia as our prisoner until you rot. You will never go home. *Never.*' Klingbeil leant closer to Peter's face for emphasis. '*Do you understand what that means*?'

'Thank you for the cigarette,' Peter muttered. 'May I go now?'

'Yes, yes. Get out and send Hartmann here to see me again.'

The interview was over, short and sharp; but it was to set the pattern for weeks of similar confrontation.

As the result of his continued truculence, Peter was informed that he and his friends would be confined to a segregated part of the camp and all contact with other prisoners would be denied them.

Erich Hartmann defiantly complained about the ill-treatment meted out to those in his group direct to the N.K.V.D. Commander in the camp, one Captain Uranov. To all the prisoners' delight, Uranov overrulled his underlings, to the point of removing the Politburo's representative in the camp. A day or two later Peter was summoned to appear before Uranov in person.

'Please sit down, Johannes. Relax. Have a cigarette.' Uranov was beaming. Peter scowled but took up the offer. More soft soap for openers, he deduced.

'Now that I've got rid of those of my subordinates who have been making life difficult for you and your friends,' Uranov began, 'perhaps you will believe my good intentions.'

'I'd believe them more if you let us all go home.'

'It's not as easy as that, Johannes, as you know. If I had my way, that's just what I'd do. But first there are certain formalities to be gone through.'

'Yes, I know—sign the papers.'

'Johannes, be reasonable, please. You must understand that you have destroyed many of our aircraft and killed hundreds of our people. We can only forgive that if you co-operate.'

'I will not sign the paper admitting to war crimes. Never,' Peter countered.

'I am not asking you to sign anything at the moment.'

'Then what do you want?'

'That's better,' Uranov beamed. 'Do you want another cigarette?'

'No thank you.'

'Now, there are, amongst your friends, a number of officers who have committed war crimes against the Russian people; they have killed civilians and destroyed our villages. Even here, they continue to spread hatred against us.'

Uranov handed Peter a clip of paper on which he had written a number of names. Peter studied them: five Colonels and a number of Majors, amongst them Erich Hartmann. Peter returned the paper without comment.

'All I ask, Johannes, is that you help us bring these criminals to justice. I want you to find out what they did during the war, report everything to me about their past, their home life, and what crimes they committed.'

Peter had seen enough. He had grown to respect his comrades in the Luftwaffe. They were honourable officers doing their duty by the nation of their birth.

'What's in it for me if I do as you ask?' he asked.

'When you've finished the job, we'll put you on the first train home to Germany.'

'That would be nice. I'd like to go home.'

'Good, then it's settled. When can I expect your first report?'

'Give me thirty years.'

Uranov was livid, but Peter stood his ground.

'What you ask is impossible. I will not bear false witness against my comrades and friends. I will never do that, for you or anybody else.'

'Then you will sign this paper,' Uranov demanded, pulling a document from a drawer in his desk and thrusting it towards Peter, who noticed at a glance that it was written in Russian.

'I thought you said you weren't going to ask me to sign anything?'

'Sign it, damn you, and sign it *now*.'

'I cannot.'

'Why?'

'It's in Russian and I don't understand your language.'

'It's just a routine document to say that you have been interrogated without being threatened.'

'I'm sorry, Captain, I refuse to sign it unless it's in German.'

'You have my word as a Soviet officer as to its content.'

'I still will not sign it unless it is in German.'

Uranov lost all control of himself. 'You have insulted me and insulted the Soviet people and for that you will be punished. Seven days in the bunker.'

Two guards entered the N.K.V.D. Captain's office, and Peter was led away and bundled into a damp, dank, smelly cell, nine feet long, four wide and six feet high, lit only by a small shaft, less than three inches in diameter, located in one corner of the cell. A bucket served as a latrine. There was no bed and no furniture of any description. The daily rations, delivered each morning, amounted to 600 grammes of bread, 2 litres of water and 5 grammes of sugar.

Peter began to suffer from claustrophobia. He was a creature used to freedom and open spaces. To be hemmed in on all sides, with no escape, was the worst torture that could have been conceived for him. He was chilled to the marrow in the coldness of his own sweat and began to admit despair. He prayed that he might die and escape the torment. He prayed as he had never prayed in his life, summoning up all the angels and saints he had learned of in his youth, and trying to lose himself in memories of happier days past. He thought constantly of Ilse and gained some comfort from the thought that she would be waiting for him. He must not lose his will to endure. One day, he promised himself, this ordeal at the hands of the Soviets must surely be over.

Time passed and the months rolled by. Hermann Graf was sent to Moscow for further political education. Erich Hartmann, who symbolized the prisoners' spirit of defiance against the tyranny of Russian Communism, was sent to another prison and from there to another and another.

The interrogations and the threats, the ill-treatment and the privations continued, until Peter's life seemed to dissolve into one interminable round of question and answer. Angered by his obstinacy, his captors' methods became cruder and more brutal each time.

'You filthy Nazi swine,' an N.K.V.D. officer began one day. 'How would you feel if we presented you with your wife's head on a tray, just like your John the Baptist?'

Peter was stupefied; his stomach contorted in agony, partly out of fear, partly from pains brought on by weeks of inedible prison food.

Gloatingly the N.K.V.D. officer continued: 'It would be a simple matter for us to seize your wife, no matter where she is. Do you remember how we dealt with Trotsky?'

Peter nodded feebly. Although on the verge of tears, he somehow found the courage to acknowledge the chilling reality without displaying the torment within.

'You can do as you like, I can't stop you. But I will not spy on my comrades, nor will I admit to crimes I have not committed.'

'Damn you, Tahlmann. You will rot here for ever.'

Now a second N.K.V.D. officer took his turn.

Peter gripped his stomach. A terrible paraxysm of pain seized his guts and he doubled up. Beads of sweat dribbled off his forehead and trickled down his face. He wanted desperately to go to the latrine. The Russian officer surveyed the pitiful wreck who still defied them. The spasm passed and Peter sat up.

'Would you like to go home?' the second officer enquired, his tone soft and disarming. Peter nodded feebly.

'Well, you can. We will make you an officer in the East German Airforce, if only you agree to co-operate with us. Captain Tahlmann, you must understand that nobody gives a damn about you or the other Nazi prisoners here. There is no one who is interested in you in the West; not a soul cares whether you are dead or alive. We are your only friends now. Why can't you see it? Why do you persist in defending your colleagues? Can't you see that they have abandoned you?'

The pains came on again and with renewed venom. Peter passed out and awoke some time later in the camp hospital. He spent a week there, suffering from dysentry and malnutrition. With medical treatment and an altogether better standard of food his health improved but the respite was of short duration. As soon as he was discharged, the cycle of interrogations began afresh.

Mail was infrequent and was held back by the N.K.V.D. as a further and most potent weapon of mental torture. Peter was permitted to write only twenty-five words per month to Ilse and even they, as he knew, were heavily censored. Ilse's letters were infrequent, and they too were usually heavily mutilated by the censor's scissors.

In the middle of 1947 Peter was moved from the camp at Gryazovets to another prison. From then on, it seemed, he was constantly on the move. Some camps were better than others, but in all of them the purpose was the same: to break the prisoner's will to resist. Soon all the faces—prisoners, guards and N.K.V.D. men—as well as the routine of interrogation, seemed to merge into one endless, agonizing regimen of brainwashing and mental torture. Peter was on the point of giving up when news began to circulate of the outstanding bravery of Major Erich Hartmann, who, after being classified as a war criminal in a mockery of a trial, had now been sentenced to twenty-five years imprisonment in the slave labour camp at Shakhty, alongside Russian criminals.

As Hartmann had arrived at the camp, the first thing he had noticed was a huge hoarding announcing simply: "Our Labour makes the Soviet Union strong". On the first day, all the prisoners were paraded outside their barracks and were then marched off to work in the local coal mines. The lone figure of Erich Hartmann remained behind. A guard ordered him to move. The German stood his ground and told the guard that he was a German Staff Officer and was therefore not required to work under the terms of the Geneva Convention, to which the Soviet Union had been a signatory.

The Russian prodded Hartmann with the muzzle of his rifle.

'Move. You will follow the others.'

Still Hartmann refused to be intimidated.

'I demand to see the Camp Commandant.'

The Sergeant of the Guard was called, but Hartmann would not bend to his threats either; eventually, as he had demanded, he was marched off to the Camp Commandant's office.

'You refuse to work, Hartmann?' the Commandant

asked, with something approaching disbelief.

Hartmann once again quoted the Geneva Convention and demanded his rights.

'You are a convicted war criminal, and you *will* work. For you, the Geneva Convention does not exist. The Soviet Union has seen fit to spare your life—you should show gratitude by working for those who have shown you mercy.'

The slight blonde figure would not give in. He stared stonily at the Russian Colonel.

'We were defeated by your country more than five years ago. I am a Luftwaffe officer, and not a criminal in any way. Lenin taught that a country which keeps prisoners of war for more than six months is an imperialist degenerate.'

'So you've read the works of Lenin then, Hartmann?' the surprised Russian Colonel replied.

'Yes. I've read every word he wrote. I believe he also said that a nation that forces prisoners of war to work is a leech and an exploiter of the defenceless.'

The Colonel changed the subject.

'You refuse to comply with our requests?'

'I do, and I demand an International Tribunal to investigate the disgusting and inhuman conditions at this camp.'

The Colonel didn't reply. Scowling with fury he summoned the guards. In a minute two armed privates entered his office.

'Put this man in solitary confinement,' he barked.

News of Hartmann's defiance and incarceration acted like a spark to a keg of gunpowder. Five uneasy days passed with the scent of rebellion hanging in the air. Returning from the mines, the prisoners saw the door to Hartmann's cell wide open. He was tied up to a chair, and two guards were force-feeding him.

The next morning a great roar of rage arose from among the prisoners. En masse the men overpowered their goalers and burst into the Colonel's office. He too was seized. Others broke down the door to Hartmann's cell and released him from his bonds. The revolt had been engineered by Colonels Wolf and Prager, but now that Hartmann was free, the prisoners looked to him for leadership. None of the Russians were harmed during the uprising, though a few known informers amongst the Germans were punished appropriately.

Hartmann, showing an incredible nerve, quietly ordered the Commandant to telephone the area headquarters at Rostov.

'The soldiers will come and shoot you all,' the Commandant protested.

'That's as may be, Colonel. We'll risk it. Please make that call now.'

The Colonel obeyed and soon the voice of an incredulous Russian General was heard on the other end of the line.

'General,' he began. 'The Germans have overpowered us and we are being held prisoner . . . No, we haven't been harmed.'

'Give me that telephone, Colonel,' Hartmann demanded. Reaching for the receiver he informed the General in Russian: 'The conditions here, Sir, are appalling. The accommodation is not fit for cattle. We are expected to work twelve hours a day on food that an animal would refuse to eat. This treatment will kill all of us. We demand that Moscow inspect this place and permit an investigation by an International Tribunal.'

A torrent of invective poured down the line, in the course of which the General threatened to hold Erich Hartmann personally responsible for the safety of the Russian prison officials.

'We are officers, not criminals, General,' Hartmann countered. 'Your men have nothing to fear from us.'

Thirty minutes later, truckloads of Red Army soldiers arrived at the camp, some two hundred in all, bristling with weaponry. As they poured out, a huge jeering cry of derision arose from the local populace, ordinary, decent Russian civilians, outraged by the ill-treatment of their former enemies by their political and military masters. Led by Erich Hartmann, the prisoners also ran to the wire and taunted the Russian troops.

Shortly after, the General himself arrived, and cautiously the Red Army troops herded the Germans back to their barracks. The revolt was over. Changes would be made. But for his part in the defiance, Hartmann was sent to another camp at Novocherkassk, where he was destined to spend the next nine months, five of them in solitary confinement. There, he faced a tribunal and was accused of inciting the civilian populace to revolt. He denied all the charges, vainly trying to defend himself. He was permitted to sum up his case and, choosing his words with care, he addressed the military judges:

'I have been accused of war crimes by your government, a charge of which I am wholly innocent. This claim has been based on spurious and contrived evidence which would have been quite unacceptable in any civilized nation. You have defied the dictates of the Geneva Convention and have sought to divest me of even my basic rights.

'In the name of humanity and justice I asked only for a tribunal to investigate the plight of the thousands of German soldiers who you hold at your mercy. Your Government talks of peace, and yet you refuse to end the war. One day, your Soviet Officers may suffer the same fate.

'Your government, suspicious of everyone, seems intent on waging war with the whole world. I have never spoken to the civilian population of Shakhty and therefore it is patently false to accuse me of inciting them to revolt against the Soviet Government. One day you may have to face up to them, and were it now their prerogative, we Germans would be free and our countries at peace once more. Beware your own people. One day, they will rise up and be done with you—and what you dare to call justice.'

Hartmann spoke quietly and deliberately, a touch of desperate eloquence in his delivery. The judges sat in stony silence and heard him out. The sentence pronounced was a further twenty-five years' hard labour.

CHAPTER THREE

As news of the events that had taken place at Shakhty prison camp, and details of Erich Hartmann's outstanding bravery in defiance of Soviet tyranny spread throughout the German prisoner population in Russia, it acted as a tonic on their resolve. Even those on the point of giving in somehow found the courage and will to continue their resistance.

Peter was one of the exceptions. He was a sick man and he yearned for his freedom. As the years had rolled by he had watched better men than he felt himself to be break under the strain. He had seen Colonels steal trifles from brother officers, Majors inform on their own comrades and Captains beg for forgiveness from their Russian masters. Under the hideous system, civilized men had been reduced to the level of primitive savages.

It was now 1952, seven long years since Peter had surrendered to the Americans with the rest of the JG 52 personnel; years of privation and loss. Ten per cent of an average life span had passed him by. Bluster and bullying had failed to break him. Now he was ready to crack. And the Soviets recognized the signs.

In the autumn of that year Peter was transferred to yet another camp, one quite unlike any he had experienced before. The accommodation was reasonable, the barracks not unduly overcrowded, and the food was adequate if plain. For three days Peter had nothing to do except attend morning and evening muster parades.

On the fourth day he was ordered to present himself at 20.00 hours to the office of a Lieutenant Colonel Kuznov, an officer in the N.K.V.D., for an apparently routine interrogation.

Peter had not met the smiling and smartly uniformed Kuznov before. The Colonel ushered the emaciated figure to a seat. He offered the inevitable cigarette. Peter took it and Kuznov, impeccably mannered, rose from his own seat and offered a light. Peter inhaled deeply. The N.K.V.D. man remained on his feet and started to pace casually round the room. Peter stared at the picture of Stalin that hung on the wall behind the Colonel's desk.

'You really are a stubborn fellow you know, Johannes.' Kuznov's tone was genuinely friendly. 'If only you could bring yourself to see our way of things, you could go home to your wife and child tomorrow.'

'*Child*? What child?' Peter burst out.

'Why, didn't you know? Ah, no, of course not. You have a son who is now seven years old.'

For a moment neither of the men spoke. Stunned by the bombshell, Peter was on the verge of tears and pleaded: 'Have you Russians no humanity, no sympathy, nothing? My wife must have written to me with the news?'

'Indeed she did, but all letters refering to the boy were withheld. I have them here.' Kuznov withdrew a bundle of letters from a drawer and put them on his desk. There looked to be over twenty. Peter reached out to snatch them, but Kuznov blocked his move with a restraining hand.

'Not so fast. You shall have them later, I promise.'

'You promise?' Peter spat the last word. 'Since when did a Russian keep his promise?'

Kuznov, a disarmingly gentle man in appearance, was in his late fifties, his dark hair, grey at the temples, giving him an aura of distinction. His nose was straight and his bone structure finely chiselled. Everything about the man attested to the aristocratic roots from which he had sprung.

'I always keep my promises,' he replied. 'Here, see for yourself,' he added, taking the top letter from the bundle and handing it to his prisoner. Peter, his hands feverishly trembling, removed the letter from the envelope and started to read:

'My love, I did not want to worry you with my troubles but now that it is all over I can tell you that we have a son. I have had a difficult time, but I am quite all right again now. I have called him Ernst, after your grandfather. He is a fine boy and looks just like you. I am very proud for both of us. No matter how long it may take, we will be united again one day, that I promise. God willing, we will be allowed to live our own lives together in peace and happiness. I love you, darling.
Your Ilse.'

Peter could take no more, and started to cry. Physically and mentally he was a broken man, putty in Kuznov's hands. He read the letter again. It was dated the 8th December 1945. Only now, after all these years, he had found out that he was a father.

'You bastards. You callous, calculating bastards,' Peter raged, in a final futile show of defiance.

'Yes, Johannes, I think that's a fair comment,' Kuznov admitted. He sat down again and offered Peter another cigarette.

'Off the record,' he went on, 'I fail to understand the methods of our masters—in fact, I cannot help asking myself whether in the end they will merely be seen to have prolonged the death struggles of capitalism and delayed the victory of the working classes.'

Peter pulled himself together, surprised that his inquisitor could actually admit to such doubts. Kuznov read his thoughts and continued.

'I would have acted in an entirely different way, if the choice had been mine. Instead of all the physical privations and mental tortures that you and your comrades have had to endure, I would have packed you all off to the best hotels in the holiday resorts on the Black Sea and given you the finest food and wines and a thumping good vacation before sending you all home. Had we done that, I honestly believe that the Soviet Empire would stretch across Europe to the Atlantic Coast and that the former soldiers of the Reich would now be our brothers in arms.'

Peter didn't reply, but he did manage a wry smile.

'My dear Johannes, just like you, I come from an aristocratic background. My parents were big landowners—personal friends of the last Czar and Czarina of Russia. When the revolution came they were executed, and I was threatened with the same fate as you have suffered. But I was young enough to be malleable, and old enough to recognize where my personal interests lay. You have a saying in the West: "if you can't beat them, join them". That's exactly what I did. Whilst I have not been able to match the luxury that my parents enjoyed through exploitation of the working classes, I have been given privileges and preferences, which few, if any, of my more idealistic aristocrat contemporaries have enjoyed.' The Colonel stopped to observe Peter's reactions. His expression was deadpan.

'Worldwide Communism, Johannes, is as inevitable as death itself. Life is too short and too precious to fritter away in a futile struggle to bolster the rule of the decadent exploiters—men who continue to thwart the legitimate aspirations of the working classes. Be sensible, now, and stop this pointless defiance.' Still Peter didn't say a word, he merely leant forward and stubbed out his cigarette.

'All you have to do is to agree to work for us and you can go home, almost at once.'

Peter found his tongue at last.

'What do you mean, *almost* at once? What sort of

"work" do you want me to do?'

'Almost at once means just what it says. Not tomorrow, but within a few days—a week at the most.'

'To my wife and son?'

'Yes, within one week you can be together.'

'Oh God, please help me,' whispered Peter.

'There is no God to help you,' said Kuznov quietly. 'God is for the feeble-minded. To believe in Him is merely a sign of weakness.'

'I still believe.'

'Then you are a damned fool. I put your so-called God to the test. I prayed for my mother and father to be saved. Much good it did them, or me.'

'You seen to have come out all right,' countered Peter.

'Enough.'

'You still haven't told me what I have to do by way of work for you.'

Colonel Kuznov coughed to cover his own pricking conscience. He resumed his smooth demeanour and smiled again. 'The Soviet Union requires nothing of you now. Only that you return to your home and go about whatever employment or occupation you may wish. When we need you, we will make contact and you will receive your instructions.'

'And if I refuse?'

'You will remain here indefinitely.'

'Do you mean to tell me that you'd keep me a prisoner for the rest of my life?'

'Yes, Johannes. And you would never see your wife again or set eyes on the son that you have fathered.'

'That's inhuman.'

'The needs, even the life, of the individual must be sacrificed, if necessary, to the—'

'—All right, all right, Colonel. I don't want a sermon. So long as I can get back to Ilse and my son, then I . . .' Peter paused, still torn between the alternatives. He felt some last vestige of conscience nagging at him, urging him not to sign, but the promise of reunion with Ilse was too strong. 'No,' he said at last, 'you're right. My God has done nothing for me. I'll sign your paper. But if you're lying—'

'—That's more like it,' beamed Kuznov. 'Now you must have something to eat.'

Peter felt his stomach churn with anticipation as the N.K.V.D. man pressed a button located behind his desk. In a moment an orderly appeared with a tray, carrying a bottle of Vodka and some caviar.

'Put it down on the desk, here,' Kuznov ordered the moon-faced youth. 'Comrade Tahlmann here and I have a little celebrating to do.' The lackey did as he was bidden, his face expressionless.

Peter attacked the caviar with scant respect for its status as a delicacy. Kuznov nibbled politely. They both drank the fiery Vodka in one gulp and then recharged their glasses.

Peter was soon very drunk. He had not tasted a drop of alcohol since he had been taken prisoner, and was quite unused to its effects. He relaxed utterly with the N.K.V.D. man, whom he now dared to call Alexei.

'I hope you don't mind me calling you by your first name?'

Kuznov smiled.

'Johannes, in Russia all comrades are equal. Rank has no meaning, except where duty is concerned. I am happy that you should wish to call me Alexei. Prosit.'

'Prosit,' Peter replied, downing another glass. Kuznov saw his opportunity and handed his prisoner a pen. Peter instantly took it up and signed the form.

The interview was at an end, Kuznov pressed the button again and the moon-faced orderly re-entered. The Colonel ordered him to conduct Comrade Tahlmann to the special quarters. The two men shook hands and Peter, in a state of drunken euphoria, paused to invite Kuznov to come and stay with him and Ilse in Bavaria. The Colonel thanked him and said that he hoped such a visit might one day be possible.

'Good luck, my friend,' were his last words as Peter left his office, firmly clutching the bundle of letters. Kuznov had at least kept one promise.

The special quarters to which Peter was taken consisted of a small self-contained suite—an absolute luxury after the years of filth and degradation—in which he found a sitting room with two easy chairs, a desk with paper and pen, a wireless set and even a vase of flowers. The bedroom with a comfortable bed, clean sheets and a sprung mattress, led to a bathroom with its own flush lavatory and, joy of joys, hot, running water.

The orderly ushered Peter inside and then left him. Peter was lost in admiring wonder at the small electric cooker, cups, saucers, coffee, milk and sugar. He staggered towards the stove and made himself a strong black coffee, hot and sweet. He drank it and his head began to ache. He knew he was in for the grandfather of hangovers, but he didn't care. He cast off his filthy, threadbare garments and ran himself a hot bath. He relaxed in the almost forgotten comfort of hot water, soap and a fresh, clean towel. When he had finished he wrapped a towel around himself and lay on the bed. He read Ilse's letters, one by one, over and over again, despite the difficulty he had in focusing his eyes on the writing. Then he fell asleep.

How long he slumbered he did not know. He awoke in the middle of the night, thirsty and hungover. His whole body was in a muck sweat and the bed felt clammy and damp. Peter lay there for a while, unable to collect his thoughts or even to orientate to his surroundings. At first he imagined that the dysentry that had plagued him from time to time was with him again. The sweating and the thirst and the disturbed dreams were all familiar symptons. The image of his home haunted him, as it had throughout his years of captivity. Would he be returning there? Or had he succumbed, after all, for nothing? He would have willingly sold his soul at that moment to be home with Ilse; even worse, he would happily have faced the wrath of the British. Perhaps in his heart he still feared that he would one day have to.

Slowly, Peter's head cleared. He realized that he was in a bed, a real bed, a comfort that he had thought he might never see again. He opened his eyes and felt around. His hand blindly groped for the bedside light and knocked it to the floor. The bulb broke with a dull plop. Peter lay back in a state of delirium, still sweating profusely, his heart pounding at his ribs. He wanted to cry out for help but no sound came. His head ached and his eyes were stinging. It hurt every time he blinked, as if his tear ducts had frozen and the lids glued themselves to the retina. A searchlight swept across his window, illuminating the room for a fleeting moment. In a while it came again and again, at regular intervals. Peter noticed a switch on the wall. Judging his moment, he staggered from the bed and pressed it. He gasped at the sudden brightness. He felt awful. His mouth tasted like a midden. He stood there, trying to sort out his muddled thoughts. The lamp lay on the floor, the shattered remnants of the bulb scattered around it, and there too were the letters. Ilse's letters. Still he thought he was dreaming. His thirst was intolerable. He must have a drink of water. *Home*. The feeling was too vivid, too real, for it to be a dream. He found the bathroom and turned the tap on—cool, fresh water. He drank and drank till he felt bloated and then reeled back to his bed.

He lay there shivering until his body heat overcame the chilling effects of the damp sweat. The room was still whirling around him when he fell asleep once more.

From sheer force of habit, combined with the demands of a bursting bladder, Peter awoke at the very crack of dawn the next morning. His head still ached, but less now.

His hangover was almost gone. Many of the events of the previous evening were at first a complete blank. Peter climbed out of his bed and walked to the bathroom. He relieved himself and then drank some more water. He looked in the mirror, his eyes bloodshot and bleary from his alcohol-induced slumber. Then he returned to his bed, and lay awake listening to the sounds of his fellow-prisoners mustering outside prior to being marched off to their various work duties.

So he was going home. But why?

Why was he to be released after all these years?

Then suddenly he recalled the meeting with Lieutenant Colonel Kuznov, the signing of the paper. He broke out once more in a chill sweat: *why* had he signed their confession after this long, long fight? There was no going back now. He had broken faith with those who would continue to resist and hocked his honour—just to get home to Ilse. And what would she think of him when she discovered the price of his freedom? She would despise him. First a traitor to the English, now a turncoat from the Germans; how low he had sunk. Peter knew then the meaning of despair.

Over the years, he had often tried to imagine how he would fare at the hands of the British, if and when he made it back to Germany. Time and time again he told himself he had sound and valid excuses for his failure. He could hardly be blamed for losing his memory, nor for failing to make the rendezvous with his initial contact, Marie Leveque; the British Bristol Blenheims had to answer for that. No, the real problem, then and now, was Neale. Peter had begun to reassure himself: it had been Ilse who had killed the man—though he would certainly have done so himself had he been able to. But then he remembered: he had rigged the evidence and taken the onus of guilt upon himself. And the English would never believe that it was an act of self-defence. After the killing, and during his early days as a prisoner of the Russians, he had pondered endlessly what view the British would take, but as the years had rolled by, he had dwelt on the subject less and less. Now it would have to be faced, and soon. But what about the Statute of Limitations—seven years, wasn't it? He felt better. He had been a prisoner of the Soviets for longer than that.

One thing was for certain: he would never work for the Soviets as a spy. As soon as he was safely over the border he would wave the Reds goodbye. Somehow he would clear his name with the British and return to Tahlmann to live in peace with Ilse and his young son, Ernst. A merciful Almighty God could not demand more.

Breakfast was brought to him in his room: bread, real butter, jam and coffee. Even an East German paper was provided, although it was several days old; Peter read it from cover to cover.

Later that morning Kuznov came to reassure himself that his latest conquest had been truly won over. He need not have doubted. Peter greeted him with a beaming smile.

'Good morning, Colonel.'

'Good morning, Johannes. I thought we agreed on Christian names?'

'Sorry, Alexei.'

'Comrade, we can arrange for your wife and son to join you in the Peoples' Democratic Republic of Germany. If you wish to volunteer for the new modern airforce we are building up there, you will be re-appointed to your rank of Captain.'

Peter frowned.

'I'd rather go home to Bavaria,' he replied, suddenly fearing a double-cross.

'Then you shall do just that, as I promised. It's all arranged.'

'And then what?'

'Then nothing, my dear fellow. You are free to do as you wish; when you can be of service to the Democratic

Republic, you will be contacted and given your instructions.'

'What exactly did I sign yesterday?'

'The paper said only that you admitted to a political error and would place your services at the disposal of the movement for the victory of the working people over the forces of the capitalist imperialists. Prisoners are no longer required to admit to war crimes.'

'Does it guarantee me a change of clothing?' Peter was still draped only in a bath towel.

'Damned idiots,' answered Alexei. 'Haven't they given you new ones?'

'No.'

Kuznov left and reappeared a few moments later carrying a new suit, rather a rough baggy affair, new shirt, tie and black shoes.

'Here you are,' he said, flinging them on the bed. 'I hope they fit. Now the good news. I said you would be going home soon. We leave tomorrow afternoon.'

'We?'

'Yes, Johannes, *we*. I have some business to attend to in East Berlin and I will travel with you.'

'That's splendid.'

Peter already tingled with the anticipation of seeing Ilse again, and scarcely knew how to fill up the rest of the day. He turned in early, but slept very little. He could not recall ever having been quite as excited in his life, but at the same time his emotion was tempered with dire apprehension for what the future held in store.

The following morning, breakfast was served again in his room. He was up and had bathed and shaved at the same early hour as the previous day. After eating he sauntered round the small area outside his quarters and breathed deeply of the crisp morning air. Lunch at noon. Ilse's letters read once more, and another Communist German Daily perused and digested.

Alexei came to fetch him around 14.00 hours. The two

men walked to a large car which was waiting to take them to the station. As they arrived at the main gate another vehicle was just entering the compound. Both cars stopped at the same moment. A guard whispered a few words to Alexei, who turned to Peter.

'Excuse me one minute, I have to make a telephone call. You wait here.'

Peter's heart missed a beat; a last-minute hitch. Oh no, please God, no, he prayed. The N.K.V.D. Colonel got out of the car and disappeared into the gate house. Peter switched his gaze from the doorway through which Alexei had gone and turned his eyes towards the other vehicle.

A thin, gaunt figure, his face drawn but his eyes still brightly defiant, his blond hair making him quite unmistakable, emerged from the other car. The man shuffled towards the car where Peter sat. He wound down the window.

'Bubi! Bubi Hartmann!' Peter cried out. Major Erich Hartmann looked at the man in the car. For a moment he didn't recognize the face. It seemed to have aged, but the features were still vaguely familiar. And then he remembered.

'Johannes, it is good to see you.' The two shook hands, then Erich noticed the other man's clean clothes and saw that he was sitting at the back of the car unguarded. He hastily withdrew his hand. Peter knew at once that the ace of aces had guessed.

'Give it up, Erich, give up this pointless struggle.'

'Never. Never,' replied Hartmann, no trace of bitterness or reproach in his voice. With an expression of generous understanding on his face, he continued: 'You've made your decision, Johannes, like Graf and many another before you. But I can't give in to a tyranny which I've fought against all my life. To do so now would be a betrayal of everything I believe in—and of my wife who waits for me.'

Peter took this as a stinging rebuff, though Hartmann

had not meant it as such, and blushed a fiery red with shame. Hartmann noticed.

'It's not as bad as it looks, Erich, please believe me.'

'Goodbye, Johannes,' Erich answered. 'I don't suppose we'll meet again.'

Peter didn't reply. He had nothing to say. There was no going back now. The Russian soldiers prodded Hartmann away from the car and towards the cage where large numbers of prisoners, some of them Peter's former comrades in arms, were housed. First one, then another and another, recognized the blond ace of aces as he walked slowly towards the cage. A cry went up: 'It's Hartmann!' Other voices called, and slowly the name was lost in a rising crescendo of cheers. Peter had to look away, his gaze fixed steadily in front of him.

Colonel Kuznov reappeared, and the car was driven off at once, the sound of the cheering growing fainter by the second. For some time Peter remained silent.

'Cheer up, my friend. Hartmann's a fool. He'll see things our way in the end. They all do, you know, sooner or later. Believe me.'

'You're wrong, Colonel. You'll never break Erich Hartmann. Never. That I can promise you.'

The N.K.V.D. man smiled.

'I won't hold you to that promise, Johannes. We shall see. Now enough of Hartmann, forget him. He has to crack one day or he'll stay here for ever—it's that simple.'

Peter didn't comment and sat tight-lipped until Kuznov said: 'How about some good news?'

Peter grunted.

'My dear fellow, can't you guess what that telephone call was about?'

'Me?'

'Of course. Our agents in Western Germany have contacted your wife and she will travel to Berlin to meet you.'

Peter's face lit up at this announcement and he pushed his recently rekindled feelings of guilt to the back of his mind. Home and Ilse could only be hours away.

They travelled by train as far as Frankfurt on Oder, where another Zil limousine was waiting to carry them along the autobahn on the remaining leg of the journey to the crossing-point at Marienborn, on the southern outskirts of Berlin. As the last few kilometres slipped away, Peter began to ache with anticipation. And he still felt sure something was going to go wrong at the last minute.

Now, seven years after the war had ended, East Germany was still very drab, and was littered with reminders of the frightful destruction wreaked on most of the towns and cities. In places, grey barrack-like blocks of flats had risen from the rubble, some of them still in the process of construction. For the most part the populace, the ordinary working people, the housewives queueing for their meagre rations, the labourers, went about their daily business unsmiling, as if in a daze. Occasionally a spark of jollity would be provided by children, who, starved of consumer luxuries such as toys, improvised their own games on the street corners.

The car travelled up a slight hill and rounded a right hand bend. There were trees to the left, clawing skywards through mountains of barbed wire.

'We're here, journey's end. This is where we must say goodbye for the time being,' said the Colonel, pointing ahead of the driver to the barrier and the sinister look-out tower from which two *Volkspolitzei* men stared stonily.

The Zil halted just short of the barrier and the two men walked towards it, Colonel Kuznov resplendent in uniform and Peter, in his ill-fitting baggy suit, trailing along beside him.

They had to walk a hundred yards or so to the border itself. The *Volkspolizei* sprang to attention and saluted. A Lieutenant demanded tonelessly: 'Your papers.'

Kuznov opened his briefcases and produced the required documents.

Peter looked about him. Shielding his eyes he could just

make out a single woman standing by the barrier beyond which lay West Berlin and freedom. The image was a little blurred. Peter's eyesight had deteriorated during the last years. It looked like Ilse, but he could not be certain.

The Leutnant took his time scrutinizing the papers.

'Wait here,' he ordered, leaving the Colonel and Peter under the watchful eye of another policeman with a machine pistol slung over his shoulder. Apparently the Leutnant was not satisfied with the exit permit. Peter could see him through the window of the guardhouse talking to another officer, who then lifted the telephone.

'You see, Johannes, we leave nothing to chance,' Kuznov observed. 'Do not imagine you can go back on our little arrangement when you get home. Our agents can reach out to any place in the world to punish those who betray the cause. You'll remember that, won't you?'

'I don't suppose you'll let me forget.'

'You're a good man, Johannes. I'm glad I've been able to persuade you to see sense. Just remember that the wise man is not he who fights for a lost cause but he who is on the winning side.'

Peter nodded as the young East German officer appeared.

'Comrade Tahlmann, you may proceed,' he announced.

'This is it then, Alexei,' Peter said, offering his hand.

'Yes, indeed. My best wishes go with you and to your Ilse. She must be a fine woman.'

The two men shook hands stiffly, then Peter turned away.

Slowly he walked through the pedestrian gate and saw Ilse walking towards him from the opposite direction.

Within feet of her he stopped and, turning briefly, he waved a final goodbye to the Russian Colonel. Then he flung himself into Ilse's outstretched arms. Tears of joy, of happiness and infinite relief, were coursing down Ilse's cheeks.

Peter held her very close, savouring emotions long dormant, feelings he had so often despaired of experiencing again.

'My love, my love,' was all he could manage to say.

Ilse and Peter walked hand in hand back to the barrier at the western end of the checkpoint. He didn't look back again, and with each step he held his head higher. He was free.

The formalities at the Allied end of the checkpoint were quickly disposed of. Peter was surprised by the lack of official interest that his homecoming had engendered. At the best he had expected some sort of reception committee. But there was nothing, not a single, solitary person.

Ilse had hired a car which she had parked just across the road, and the couple, still hand in hand, made their way slowly to it. A room had been reserved at the Adler Hotel for the night.

Peter seemed reluctant to let go of Ilse's hand, lest the breaking of physical contact might snap the spell. When he did, he slumped into the passenger seat, looking at her through misty eyes. There was so much to say, so many long years to make up for. Ilse started the car and drove off.

'I thought it would be wonderful just to be alone together for the night before we go home—I hope you don't mind?'

Peter smiled. He watched her as she drove. Somehow, it made her nervous.

For a few moments neither spoke, and Peter sensed a sudden uneasiness in his wife's manner. After some minutes Ilse broke the silence.

'Darling, there's something I must tell you.'

Peter's spirits sagged; he knew it couldn't last. Some damn thing would have to go and mar his happiness. He looked at Ilse, eyes wild, like some sort of hunted beast.

'I can see by your face it's not good news.'

But Ilse sought to warn—not to alarm.

'There's a man waiting to see you back at the hotel.'

'What do you mean, a man? Who? Why should anybody be waiting at the hotel?'

Ilse started to explain. Peter cut her short.

'I suppose they've sent him instead of having a reception committee at the barrier. I thought it was too good to be true.'

Ilse started again.

'It's more complicated than that. It's a long, long story and I can only give you some details now.' Ilse took a deep breath. The car had stopped at some traffic lights and she took the opportunity to get a cigarette out of her handbag. Peter lit it for her. She inhaled quickly and blew out the smoke. The lights turned to green.

'Things were very difficult at the end of the war, you must understand. There was no food, no money; it wasn't easy for a woman without a man, and with a young child to fend for.'

Peter shivered, guessing at what was coming.

'I found myself in trouble with the occupation forces. I was given food and clothes by a British officer, who then accused me of stealing them. Looking back on it now I know it was all set up. I was threatened with imprisonment and separation from my son, our son. Whilst I was being held in custody a man called Cave-Browne came to see me; he said that he was from the British Embassy in Bonn. He said he'd known you in the R.A.F. and wanted to help. Do you remember him?'

'I've never heard of him.'

Ilse took another drag on the cigarette and then threw it out of the window.

'Cave-Browne told me that if I signed a document he would see that all the charges against me were dropped and that the Embassy would look after Ernst and me.'

'Oh Christ, what the hell did you sign?'

'I'm sorry, my love. I was so afraid—they looked innocent enough, but Cave-Browne didn't give me time to read the small print.'

'Please Ilse, you must tell me. What have you signed?'

'I admitted to our collaboration with the Nazis, and to our personal friendship with some of their leaders.'

Peter swore under his breath.

'So the British, damn them, are using the same methods as the Russians.'

'What do you mean?' Ilse asked pitifully.

'Ilse, the only reason I'm here now, the sole explanation for my sudden release, is that I couldn't take it any more. I also signed papers. I've agreed to work for the Russians.'

Ilse didn't speak for a moment or two. The expression on her face was one of utter horror.

'I don't believe it. Peter, not you. There must have been something else, some pressure,' Ilse insisted.

'Please try to understand. I was desperate. I knew that if I didn't sign I would never be released and never see you again, never meet our son.'

Ilse didn't answer. Of course she understood. Every man had his breaking point.

'Now, I have no intention of helping them, but I may have no choice when it comes down to it. We'll just have to cross that bridge when we come to it.'

'Right,' agreed Ilse.

'Please go on about Cave-Browne.'

'Well, after I signed the papers, the charges were dropped and I was free to go. I was given food and clothing and allowed to go back to our estate. But ever since my release, Cave-Browne has been following me, constantly reminding me of my guilt, of the incriminating papers and my obligations. It was he who arranged for your entry through the Western checkpoint. He laid on the car and the hotel. Peter, darling, I'm so frightened of him.'

Peter was now reliving all the terrors of his seven years of captivity—the stabs of fear, the clanking of cell doors, the measured tread of the guards, the treacherous, sibilant voices of his interrogators. Oh God, would it never end?

The car drew up at the front entrance of the Adler Hotel. A Commissionaire opened the door for Peter to get out. Ilse followed.

The couple took a lift up to the fourth floor and walked slowly down the carpeted corridor. The door of their room was slightly ajar. Peter pushed it open, standing aside to let his wife precede him.

CHAPTER FOUR

A man in his early forties rose to greet them as they entered. He ignored Ilse, approaching Peter with outstretched hand.

'Good afternoon, Flying Officer Hutley.' Peter took the hand diffidently. 'My name is Cave-Browne, Basil Cave-Browne.'

'And mine is Johannes von Tahlmann.'

Cave-Browne burst out laughing.

'My dear Hutley, don't give me that old story. Your brother Johannes is dead. Has been for years. But I don't want to rake over ancient history, old man. You know why I'm here, so let's get straight down to business.'

'If I may, I'll have a drink first,' Peter said.

'Certainly, old boy, my apologies.' He poured out a whisky and water and handed the glass to Peter.

'Cheers, then,' he said, raising his glass. He took a long draught and set the glass down on the table with a rap. 'Alright then, Cave-Browne, what do you want?'

'Basil, do call me Basil.'

'Just tell me what you want.' Peter repeated, further irritated by the man's false bonhomie.

'I think a little explanation is called for first.' Turning to Ilse, he said: 'I'm sure you have some shopping to do, Ilse.'

'The devil she—' Peter started to say, but Ilse cut in defiantly:

'No, I do not.'

'Let me put it this way, Ilse,' Cave-Browne said. 'I'm sure you can find something to do.'

'She stays,' said Peter.

'Then so do I—all night if necessary, and all tomorrow as well. How's that suit you?'

'All right, all right,' Peter conceded. 'Ilse, you'd better do as he says.'

'How long?'

'Give us an hour, my dear.'

Ilse nodded and left the room, her drink unfinished. Peter watched her, hating to see her go. He was frightened to be left alone with this creature and worried and apprehensive about what he was about to hear. He finished his whisky the moment Ilse left, then walked over to the side table to recharge his glass, trying to remain calm.

Cave-Browne took the initiative at once.

'First, you'd better know—'

Satisfied with his drink, Peter countered: 'What's in the sandwiches?'

'Beef.'

Peter took one and started eating it.

'As I was saying, you'd better know one or two things. I am, and have been for some time now, the head of a small section in our Embassy dealing with counter-espionage.'

Peter noted that Cave-Browne had dropped his exaggerated upper-crust accent. His speech had become classless, his delivery clipped.

'OK, we footle around under trade cover—but our

business is the K.G.B. The war has never ended for us. Only the enemy has changed. Some people say that the real enemy has always been Russia. Since 1945 and even before Germany surrendered, we've been engaged in what is now popularly called the "cold war". It's just as vicious, just as brutal as a shooting war, if not more so, but it's conducted in more subtle ways—by much smaller groups of people with different weapons: sabotage, corruption, subversion, defection and assassination, espionage and counter-espionage. After you've been in Germany a while you'll soon learn how things are shaping up.'

Peter picked up another sandwich.

'Go on,' he invited. Cave-Browne took a swig from his glass and cleared his throat.

'A long time ago, we and the Americans decided as a matter of top-level policy to rebuild Germany into a major European power, economically at first, and later militarily. The purpose of a resurgent Germany is to act as a buffer state against the spread of Russian Imperialism further west. France, Italy and the smaller countries were considered far too weak or corrupt for a major role of this nature. In fact, it was predicted that either France or Italy or both, with their large Communist parties, could be taken over by the Marxists. But not Germany: she fought the forces of the extreme left too hard and too long. Hence, the Marshall Plan and Germany's economic recovery.'

'The Marshall Plan?' Peter enquired.

'The brainchild of General George Marshall: America's method of financing the operation.'

'I see.'

'As part of the strategy, the German forces, including the Luftwaffe, will be rebuilt. If we let it happen, which we will, you and your friends will be required to resurrect the German Air Force and mould it once more into an efficient fighting machine. In due time it'll be equipped with the most modern aircraft. Jets, of course—the piston-engined aircraft is obsolete.'

Peter was listening with gloomy resignation, but his thoughts were elsewhere. He was thinking of his shattered hopes of living in peace with Ilse and his son and wondering how he could ever have believed that life could return to normal. How he had deluded himself.

'We know already,' Cave-Browne went on, 'that the K.G.B. are busy penetrating the top Government bureaux. They're in the process of establishing a formidable espionage and subversive terrorist network in Germany. This is what you'll have to combat in the future. You, my friend, are very much part of our plans.'

'What the bloody hell do you mean?' rasped Peter. 'I have absolutely no intention of playing your stupid games any longer. I've already had enough of them to last me a lifetime.'

'Make no mistake, my friend, you will work for us. Of that there's no shadow of doubt.'

'That's what you may think Mr Cave-Browne. But what if I refuse?'

'You'll do exactly as you are damn well told because you have to—you have no choice.'

'What the devil's that supposed to mean?'

'Just what I said. We know full well that you bought your freedom by agreeing to become a Russian agent—how's that for openers?'

Peter felt the blood drain from his face.

'How the hell could you possibly know that?'

'An inspired guess.'

'Come off it—you can to better than that.'

It was a stroke of indiscretion Cave-Browne could not resist.

'Alexei Kuznov, my dear fellow, who else? He's one of our best. He's been working for British Intelligence since the early thirties. It's a miracle he's survived so long, but he's a brilliant man and the supreme master of his job. He knew perfectly well you'd crack, but he also knew your sort well enough to see that you'd break your word to the Soviets as soon as you were out of their clutches. He had to get you to sign the paper for the record before he could get you out.'

Peter was staggered. *Alexei Kuznov*.

'Then what took you so bloody long? I've been through more than seven years of hell at the hands of those bastards.'

'I'm sorry, but your release couldn't be arranged until you were fortunate enough to find yourself in a camp at the same time as Kuznov. It might have happened earlier. It could just as well have never happened at all.'

'Very ingenious—but it doesn't alter my position in the slightest. I have no intention of working for the Reds or you, or anyone else. So your threats are useless.'

Cave-Browne laughed condescendingly.

'Innocent as a newborn babe, aren't you? Surely you don't think you can buy your freedom as you did without mortgaging your future! Listen, you don't need me to tell you what the Russians are like. They'll contact you all right—and if you don't do as they say, they'll eliminate you without a murmur. We're asking you to work for us as well—as a double agent, the most difficult role of all the intelligence game. One slip and you're dead. One side or the other will wipe you off the board. But it'll be worth it for us both. The Russians intend to keep you as a sleeper for a while, but one day the K.G.B. will activate you. If we get you the right jobs in the Defence Ministry, as we plan to, then that one day will probably be sooner rather than later. Then, dear boy, you will work for us like a good, well-manipulated little puppet. We'll pull the strings and, believe me, you'll dance.'

'Oh, you bastards,' Peter cried out. 'Haven't I done enough already?'

'I'm sorry for you, old boy, I really am, but you're a victim of circumstance. You have no choice, except perhaps prison, or death.'

'Suicide seems just about the only way out.'

'Even if you were serious, I should put that notion right out of your head. If you thwart our plans then we'll take it out on Ilse. Do please remember that she's signed some rather incriminating papers: amongst other things, she's admitted to being an active Nazi supporter. With the testimony we have of a certain former S.S. orderly, one Magda Ziegler, we should be able to put dear Ilse away for a very long time indeed. And I wouldn't like to think what might happen to your son in the meantime.'

At that point Peter went wild, shouting and cursing at the British and at Cave-Browne in particular. Cave-Browne sat silently in his chair waiting for the storm to blow itself out.

'I told you it was a vicious business, Hutley. The weapons of intelligence are the dirtiest of them all. No quarter is asked, no quarter is given, and no rotten lousy trick is too foul to play. The stakes are high. We've been waiting for a long time for you, and if you do what we want, you will, at least, be able to enjoy some sort of life with your wife and son.'

Cave-Browne's remark reduced Peter once more to despair. All he could whisper was: 'Alright. You leave me no choice. What do you want me to do?'

'For now, nothing. Tomorrow you'll go home and for the time being you'll pick up the threads of your old life. In due course we'll see that you get a Defence Ministry posting. I'll be your guide and master, and you'll make no move unless I tell you. You'll receive, unknown I trust to the Russians, very careful and confidential training in all our latest intelligence procedures and gadgetry. If you blow it, then I fear, as the saying goes, that'll be your lot. Ilse and her son will only know the disgrace you have brought on them.'

'May I ask a question?' Peter enquired, subdued.

'Certainly, anything you want to know I'll do my best to tell you.'

'Am I wanted in England?'

'What on earth for?'

'Some might think I had committed treason—I mean, I was sent over to do a job, to take my brother's place. As it happened, I failed dismally, but it was hardly my fault some R.A.F. idiot dropped a bloody great bomb damn nearly on top of my head.'

'Hardly,' agreed Cave-Browne. He smiled. 'Of course we could drag you back to England and put you on trial. No doubt you would be found guilty of treason and executed. We had no qualms about hanging William Joyce, you know, and he wasn't even British. If that's what you'd prefer I'm sure it could be arranged.'

'No, I was merely curious,' Peter conceded.

'Look, old boy, as far as we're concerned right now, F/O Peter Hutley was killed on active service in September 1940. His grave is in England to prove it. Let sleeping dogs lie, I say. Don't you agree?'

'Is there anything else?'

'A thousand things—hundreds of questions.'

'For instance?'

'What about Neale?'

'Who?'

'Barry Neale, the agent sent to order me to carry out my mission.'

Cave-Browne scratched his chin and looked pensive.

'Neale, Neale, let me think. I remember now—what about him? Did he ever see you?'

Peter instantly regretted mentioning the name, and backtracked.

'Not exactly. We arranged to meet over the telephone, but he didn't turn up.'

'Just as well, in that case. The Gestapo were on his trail, as well as that of his wife. So far as we know, they were both arrested and executed for espionage. After contact ceased we unearthed evidence in England proving conclusively that the Neales were both doubles. You see, even in those days, our dear Soviet allies were busy beavering their way into our firm. You never know who your friends are, do you?'

'Absolutely,' Peter agreed.

'Next question?'

'How is my mother? Can she be told the truth now?'

'I'm sorry, Peter, it's too late. Your mother and grandfather were both killed by a doodlebug in 1944. Your mother died believing that you lost your life in a flying accident. According to Air Commodore Charlton, she was intensely proud of you and went to Buckingham Palace to receive a posthumous D.F.C. from the King.'

'Poor woman,' Peter murmured, wondering how the mother he had once been so very close to would have felt about him now. 'Poor mother, she didn't have a very successful life.'

'I'm sorry,' Cave-Browne added uselessly. 'Any more questions?'

'What about Charlton?'

'He's a sick man—cancer, I understand. When your show misfired he was finally retired and settled somewhere in the south. Later he moved up to Northumberland and stayed there, so far as I know.'

'I wish I could say I feel sorry for him.'

'That's a little ungracious, old boy.'

'I didn't notice your black armband.'

Cave-Browne changed the subject.

'Next question?'

'What's the hurry?'

'Save it, then. We'll be in touch relatively soon—ask me later. One more thing. If you take my advice, you'll not make too many plans for the future. They might not work out.'

Peter said: 'I'll think about it.'

'Give your dear wife my regards. Tell her I was sorry not to see her before I left, and give her my apologies for invading your privacy. For what it's worth, I'm rather sorry that your hand of cards adds up to a bag of nails. Console yourself with the knowledge that we're working for a happier, healthier world. It'll make it much easier for us to work together.'

Basil Cave-Browne emptied his glass and got to his feet to leave.

'Enjoy yourself tonight, old boy. You know, Ilse is a damned attractive woman.' Cave-Browne smiled broadly as he opened the door to let himself out. Peter decided he didn't like him at all. His approach, his manners, and least of all the departing leer.

CHAPTER FIVE

Tahlmann, on the face of things, was much as Peter had remembered it during the war, though many of the faces on the estate had changed. The place was in surprisingly good order despite the cataclysmic collapse that Germany had suffered. A factor, appointed fortuitously by Magda Ziegler's uncle before the war, and who still held the position, had run the place with considerable success. The farms were profitable, going concerns.

Peter was able to take his ease and relax. His health improved rapidly and his emaciated frame soon filled out to something approaching its normal shape. He and Ilse were as happy as they could be under the circumstances. The son she had borne him was his pride and joy. Peter and Ernst took to each other at once. The seven-year-old boy had heard much about his father, and was unprepared for the gaunt, wasted figure that he first encountered. But Ernst was gentle and generous-natured and did not, as might have been expected, shy away in horror from the stranger. Peter noted the look of sadness and compassion on his son's face and was troubled. He was the image of his mother.

Throughout the rest of 1952 and for most of the following year as well, the Von Tahlmanns led the life of any normal couple with a small son and the advantage of money behind them.

Gradually, the memories softened and the future seemed to offer hope. Peter took a great interest in the farming and the estate management. He had a lot to learn and he enjoyed learning it. The war was a thing of the past. Cave-Browne had not been seen or heard of again, nor had there been any contact from anybody even remotely connected with the K.G.B. Western Germany was well on the way to its economic miracle, under the leadership of Chancellor Konrad Adenauer. Things looked good. If Russia menaced from the east, the nation could draw comfort from the protection of the Americans.

Peter's dreams still haunted him: terrible nightmares from which he would wake in a cold sweat of terror. But even these were getting less frequent and far less intense.

Peter made new friends, and renewed his brief acquaintance with Günther Strauch, the one-legged veteran from the war in Russia, and his wife, Hildegard. The Strauchs were their nearest neighbours and most frequent visitors. After a visit to England for physiotherapy and the fitting of an artificial limb, Günther was now fully mobile and, though a little ungraceful on the dance floor, he took most other activities in his stride. He and Peter became inseparable and spent much time together shooting, riding and fishing. Günther was not in the same league as Peter financially, but he was adequately provided for through his ownership of a smart leather shop in Nuremburg, one of a small chain that was now expanding fast, carried forward by the consumer boom and helped by an injection of capital from Peter who, with Ilse, became a major shareholder in the company.

Then one day in the Autumn of 1953 an envelope bearing a Bonn postmark arrived with the morning mail.

Peter and Ilse were finishing their breakfast when the letters were brought to them. Ilse sat opposite him, glancing up from time to time. Peter had invited Günther round to shoot a few pheasants that morning, something that both men enjoyed immensely, and was looking forward to the sport. But as Peter opened the buff envelope the expression on his face altered. Ilse noticed the sudden change.

'There's something wrong—'

'Damn and blast them,' he muttered, rising from the table and starting to pace up and down.

'What's the matter?' Ilse asked.

'Here, see for yourself,' Peter responded, handing the letter to her.

'I thought it was all too good to last.'

Ilse started to read. The letterhead was of the Federal Ministry of Defence.

Dear Baron von Tahlmann,

Your application for a position with this Ministry has been accepted and you are required to present yourself at this office at 10.00 hours on Monday next, the 16th November. You will be working as liaison officer between the American and British Air Force on advance planning for the future reforming of the Bundesluftwaffe.

A flat will be provided for the use of yourself and your family.

It was signed by one Karl von der Schulenburg. The name meant nothing to Peter or Ilse, though Peter had heard of Count Siegfried von der Schulenburg, whom he had met once or twice whilst both men had been in Russian captivity.

'So they've made their move,' Peter burst out. 'The nerve of it. What application? I never made any application.'

'There must have been a mistake.'

'There's no mistake. I detect the sticky fingers of Cave-Browne in this. I actually thought he and his henchmen had decided to leave us in peace. I should have known better.'

'Do you have to go?'

'I can always try to refuse, I suppose.'

But they both knew that the years-old trap was beginning to close around them once more.

Peter went off to get his gun and cartridges ready for Günther's arrival.

Günther appeared, punctual to the second as usual. He noted that Peter was not quite his usual affable self, and soon found out why. Peter felt touched by his concern, but his efforts to console only made matters worse. Günther had no idea of what lay behind the letter from the Defence Ministry, and Peter could hardly explain the whole story—even to his closest friend.

The two men collected seven brace of pheasants between them. Günther had shot all but three of the birds. Peter was decidedly off his shoot, his mind elsewhere, his reactions unusually slow.

Hildegard had come to Tahlmann for lunch and was waiting with Ilse when the two men returned from their morning's sport. Peter greeted Hildegard dutifully but his mood was sombre, made the worse by his poor shooting. Ilse had warned her guest that Peter was liable to be a trifle testy, so she was forewarned of a cool greeting.

There was a message waiting for him in the hall. Someone had telephoned shortly after he had gone out. He didn't leave a name but asked the housekeeper that the Baron should call him back as a matter of urgency. Peter dialled the number he was given

At the other end of the line, the instrument was picked up immediately.

'Hello.' It was a man's voice. Peter recognized it immediately.

'Cave-Browne. What a surprise.'

'Yes, old son, right first time. Clever of you to recognize my voice.'

'How could I forget it?' Peter muttered.

'No doubt you know why I'm in touch with you?'

'I haven't a clue,' Peter said.

'Surely you've heard from the Federal German Ministry of Defence?'

'I had a letter from them this morning.'

'Who do you think got you the job?'

'I think you've got a bloody nerve. I'm writing to tell them I won't take it.'

'The holiday is over, old son. It's time to get back to work. It's taken me a long while to arrange things to our satisfaction. Be thankful for small mercies—you've had over a year's holiday.'

'Thanks a million.'

'Now look, Hutley, I don't want any damn trouble with you. You'll do as you're bloody well told. Your job will be vital to the interests of Western Defence. And I guarantee that your Russian friends will be in touch with you shortly after you start work. That's what we want. We'll give you information that we mean to reach them, but your real job will be to ferret out the Communist agents and sympathizers at work in the Bureau.'

'Look,' said Peter desperately. 'Let's face it, I was absolutely useless as a spy. Why don't you find yourself another patsy—somebody who wants to do the job, somebody who'd make a success of it. Just bloody well leave me alone.'

'Not a chance, old son. You're our man.' Cave-Browne was becoming more patronizing by the second. 'You'll play ball, won't you?'

'Try and make me, damn you.'

'Firmly if rather indelicately put. Is that the good Baron's last word?'

'What do you think?'

'What a pity. I had so hoped that you'd co-operate.'
'You hoped in vain then.'
'A pity.'
Cave-Browne hung up. Peter's spirits lifted. He'd write later and tell Herr von der Schulenburg the bad news, but that could wait. First there was lunch, and with a great weight lifted from his mind he decided to try a few more pheasants afterwards. He felt a need to show Günther that his poor shooting in the morning was not going to be repeated.

After a relatively relaxed luncheon, Hildegard returned home, leaving the men to their afternoon's sport. Ilse remained behind in the big house.

The two men shot another three and a half brace and a blackcock that afternoon. Peter only fired five cartridges but killed four pheasants and the cock. His skill with the gun had returned.

Peter asked Günther in for tea but his guest excused himself. He explained that he had best get home as he and Hildegard were going out to dinner that night and had a long drive ahead of them.

Peter saw Günther off in his car, and walked into the house. There was no sign of Ilse. He cleaned his gun and put it away before going in search of his wife. He hunted around for a while but Ilse was nowhere to be found. He rang for the housekeeper to enquire where the Baroness might be. It was most unlike Ilse to go off without saying where she had gone.

The housekeeper arrived in a few seconds, in response to the bell.

'Ah, Fräulein—do you know where my wife is?'
'She's gone out, Sir.'
'Do you know where to?'
'No, Sir. She left with a gentleman.'
'Who?'
'I don't know, Sir.'
'Can you describe him?'

'Yes. He was tall, middle-aged, and walked with a slight stoop. I think he was English.'

'My God.'

'Pardon?'

'Nothing, Fräulein. Never mind. I know who the man is. Did the Baroness appear to be in any distress?'

'Distress? No, not really. She did look worried though.'

'I should have known—didn't they leave any message?'

'No, Sir. Nothing.'

'All right, Fräulein. Thank you, that will be all.'

The housekeeper withdrew, leaving Peter to ponder the implications. Why on earth had Ilse gone off with Cave-Browne? What could the man want with her?

That evening, there had still been no word from Cave-Browne or Ilse. Peter stayed up till late into the night, growing more frantic by the hour, sleep an impossibility. Eventually he went to his room around 3 a.m.

Peter watched the hands of the clock creep slowly but inexorably on. As soon as it was light, he abandoned his fruitless efforts to sleep and took a bath, shaved and dressed. He ate a light breakfast and retired to his study to await events. He thought of telephoning Günther but knew he couldn't help. He contemplated contacting the police, but soon rejected the idea. Finally at around nine o'clock the telephone rang. Peter grabbed it at once.

'Hello,' he snapped.

'Good morning to you, old son. I trust you've had plenty of time to think. Perhaps you're feeling more sensible after a good night's sleep.'

'Where's Ilse—what in Hell's name have you done with her?'

'She's quite safe. There's no need to worry—for the moment.'

Cave-Browne stressed the last phrase. Peter broke out in a sweat and began to shake from a mixture of fear and frustrated rage.

'You bastard, you've kidnapped her.'

'Very bright, dear boy, quite right on both counts.'

'I'll call the police.'

'I wouldn't advise that. It would only complicate matters, I assure you.'

'Isn't it time you gave me an explanation?'

'Ilse will be released just as soon, dear boy, as you see sense and agree to co-operate.'

'And if I don't?'

'Surely I don't need to go into the details?'

'Alright, I think I get the message.'

'That's better. You know, this sort of thing—kidnapping and so on—it really goes against the grain. But I hope you see now how easy it would be for me, now or in the future.'

'Can I speak to Ilse?'

'Just as soon as you give me your word that you will co-operate and take up that job.'

'All right, blast you. I'll do it. Now please let me speak to her.'

'Just one more thing, old boy. You should be flattered that we're paying so much attention to you. But don't imagine you're indispensable. You'll be well paid for your work and we'll look after you in every way. But from now on, one false step . . .'

Peter didn't reply. After a pause he heard Ilse's voice.

'Peter?'

'My darling, are you all right? Where are you?'

'I've honestly no idea— I was brought here blindfolded.'

'When are you coming home?'

'Hang on—'

Peter could hear Ilse talking to Cave-Browne, but couldn't catch what was being said. Cave-Browne came on the line again.

'I'll be releasing your wife immediately, old boy. I do hope you've learned your lesson.'

'I've already told you I'll co-operate,' Peter snapped

back. 'What more do you want?'

'Nothing. Just don't get any more funny ideas, and don't mention a word of this to anybody—not a single solitary person. That's an order.'

Peter paced and worried for the next hour and a half, glancing frequently out of the windows overlooking the entrance to Tahlmann. At last his vigil was rewarded by the sight of a car coming up the drive. It stopped short of the house. Peter was out of the front door like a shot, in time to see his wife standing on the gravel, blindfolded, as the black, nondescript limousine disappeared back through the gates. Ilse removed her blindfold just as Peter, running towards her, took her into his arms.

With the administration of the estate in good hands, as it always had been, Peter and Ilse were able to move with Ernst to the flat in Bonn with no worries on that score. Peter's work in the Defence Ministry was more than interesting; to his surprise, he found it fascinating. But the spectre of Cave-Browne and his Russian counterparts cast a long shadow over his new life in the Federal capital. For his first few months in the Ministry, Peter seemed to be living with one eye constantly over his shoulder.

In early February 1954 the Soviets made their move, in the person of a Ministry filing clerk. The Reds had come to claim their pound of flesh, as Cave-Brown had predicted. Peter played along, but although he reported the existence of their agent in one of his periodic bulletins to Cave-Browne, care of a P.O. Box number in Bonn, nothing was done and the Soviet agent remained in place. Peter continued to pass information to the filing clerk at regular intervals and the year passed without any untoward incident.

Peter and Ilse spent as much time at Tahlmann as his duties would permit, and it was during the long Christmas vacation of 1954 that he received notice that he would be moving the following March to an Office in Nuremburg, where he would be on liaison duties with the American Air Force. This was Peter and Ilse's best possible Christmas present for that year. They could return home permanently. Peter could commute to work each day by car. The holiday became a real occasion to celebrate.

In March 1955 the transfer to new duties was effected. With Peter safely out of the way, the Communist filing clerk was swiftly dealt with. With him fell another two of his ilk, whom Peter had uncovered by sheer accident during his last month in Bonn. None of the three were brought to trial; instead they were simply "eliminated", and Peter's cover effectively guarded. As far as the Russians were concerned, their agents in Bonn were expendable; Johannes von Tahlmann was not. They were agreeably surprised that their most potent espionage weapon had escaped detection.

The small office on the outskirts of Regensburg where Peter was to work existed for the purpose of liaising with the U.S. Air Force base at Erding, 100-odd kilometres away. The work involved close co-operation with the Americans and concerned the planning for the reformation of the fighter arm of Luftwaffe—due to take place in the early days of 1956. But increasingly now, Peter's first and foremost concern was to keep his balance on the tightrope.

The K.G.B. were soon in contact with Peter once again. On April 12th 1955, he received a call to a meeting with a man calling himself Petlyakov, who congratulated him on the excellence of his work to date and the value of the information that he had passed on. Petlyakov ordered Peter to volunteer for commissioned rank in the Luftwaffe, to avail himself of every opportunity to evaluate the performance and capability of the aircraft types coming into service. The K.G.B. man then went on to give Peter the names of three good comrades who would render him every assistance. One of them, a Captain in the U.S. Air Force stationed at Erding, was a veteran of the war in Korea who had been turned during an eighteen-month spell as a prisoner.

The following day Peter reported to Cave-Browne, who was delighted at the last success. In two days he came back with instructions that Peter should do exactly as the Russians required.

The Soviets now observed their man return to active flying in his new capacity as aviation adviser to the Federal Ministry of Defence. More than a decade had passed since Peter had last taken the controls of a Bf 109. He started gently in small training planes before graduating to jets. Slowly but steadily his confidence in the air returned.

He flew the Lockheed T.33 trainer, in which he soloed on jets, moving on to the Lockhead F.94 Starfire, an all-weather fighter, the mainstay of the N.A.T.O. Air Defence forces in Europe at the time. In almost every respect Peter was ready by the turn of the year to step into command of a front-line jet fighter unit. But that was not his mission.

Meanwhile the Russian operatives he had uncovered were wiped off the board, but not until Peter had passed on to them a quantity of suitably laundered material. The Russians were again agreeably surprised that Peter had managed to escape the purge, but this time they were suspicious. Peter, meanwhile, had no idea that anything might be amiss.

His problems were brought to a head by a series of events. The first was a letter from a firm of solicitors in Frankfurt, which arrived in December 1955. It was addressed to Baron Johannes von Tahlmann and announced that he had been favoured in the will of a distant relative, of whom, moreover, there was no mention in various family records. A substantial sum was said to be involved, and the Baron was asked to make an appointment at his early convenience. Peter said nothing to anybody except Ilse, and told her merely that he had to go to Frankfurt on business. To Ilse, who was already used to his movements, there was nothing out of the ordinary in Peter's absence.

On arriving at the Frankfurt solicitors' office, Peter was met by a grey-haired senior partner in the firm and ushered to a seat in the lawyer's comfortably furnished chambers. The solicitor dispensed with preliminaries and came straight to the point.

'The will in question, Herr Baron, involves a considerable sum—something in the region of 20 million marks.'

Peter, who had only just settled in his chair, suddenly sat bolt upright in astonishment. The figure was larger than he'd dared to hope for—enough to keep Ilse and Ernst provided for years.

'But naturally before the money can be made over to you there are one or two formalities to be dealt with.'

'Yes, yes, of course.' Peter stammered.

'As I'm sure you will appreciate, our first concern is that you should be able to prove your identity. Presumably you have papers—birth certificate, marriage licence and so on—to show that you are who you say you are?' The man's tone was brisk and benign, but Peter had the uncomfortable feeling that his piercing eyes were studying him closely.

'Well, yes . . . I—I'm sure I have them somewhere. They're probably in my study at home.'

The solicitor leaned forward at the desk.

'You seem hesitant, Herr Baron. I trust there will be no problem in locating the documents?'

Peter made an effort to sound more confident. He had no doubt the papers could be found, but at the same time he was troubled at the turn the interview seemed to be taking.

'No—there shouldn't be any problem.'

'Good. In that case matters should be considerably more straightforward. You see, Herr Baron, the reason I ask is that I understand your family circumstances are, shall we say, somewhat unusual.'

'Unusual? How do you mean?'

'You had a twin brother, I believe.'

Peter gave an ill-disguised start: the conversation was beginning to bring back unpleasant memories.

'That's right—he was killed in a car crash with my mother. They were on holiday in England at the time. But I don't see what that has to do with—'

The solicitor interrupted him.

'Perhaps I should explain, Herr Baron. Since writing to you I have already made enquiries with your family solicitor in Nuremberg. Naturally, it was a matter of some importance to establish that your brother and mother had in fact died in the manner you describe.'

'But I don't see why. Surely the will was made out to me, not to them?'

The solicitor wagged a finger.

'Ah, I'm afraid it is not quite as simple as that. In fact the will was made out originally to your brother Peter. But in the event of his death, the money reverts to you. Hence the necessity of authenticating the exact manner and time of your brother's death.'

Peter was fidgeting nervously with his tie; suddenly the 20 million marks had become relatively unimportant to him. What mattered far more was the damage the lawyer could do by nosing through the family history. The grey-haired man continued:

'When I contacted your solicitors in Nuremberg, I was of course told exactly the same story as you told me: that your mother and twin brother had died in a road accident. But there appeared to be some kind of gap in the records: for some reason no copy of the death certificates had been forwarded from England, merely a handwritten letter from your grandfather Ernest Hutley. So I contacted the English authorities via the British Embassy in Bonn and asked them for confirmation of the story. Unfortunately the information I received from England only served to complicate matters further. You see, according to the British records, your brother Peter was killed while on active service in the R.A.F. in 1940, and your mother—well, your mother seems to have been killed during a Luftwaffe bombing raid in 1944.'

He looked up, studying Peter's reaction.

'A peculiar discrepancy, wouldn't you say, Herr Baron?'

Peter was too bemused to reply. He waited a moment, thought, and then blurted out:

'But look here, what the hell difference does it make how or when they died? The fact is, they're both dead. Isn't that enough?'

The solicitor gave a sigh and raised an indulgent eyebrow.

'I'm afraid not, Herr Baron. It may be a distasteful subject to you, but for the legal process it is vitally necessary to establish the exact circumstances of your relatives' death beyond all reasonable doubt. We are dealing here, let me remind you, with a very large amount of money; it is my duty to take all possible steps to confirm that the original beneficiary of the will in fact died in the manner set down. I fear that until I have done that no money will be forthcoming.'

Peter left the solicitor's office in a mood of gloomy apprehension. The prospect of further enquiries by the lawyer, of more ferreting around in his past, more questions to answer, filled him with an all too familiar dread. Although the man had promised to treat the matter with the utmost confidentiality, there was no guarantee that compromising information about his English background might not leak out. Suddenly the 20 million marks seemed hardly worth the risks.

The following day, a Saturday, the telephone rang. Ilse answered it.

'It's for you,' she said passing the handpiece to Peter.

'Who is it?' Peter whispered. Ilse covered the mouthpiece with her hand.

'I didn't ask.'

Peter took the receiver from his wife's hand.

'Von Tahlmann,' he announced.

As soon as the caller had established that he was talking to Peter he dispensed with formality.

'You blithering bloody idiot! What the hell are you playing at?'

'Cave-Browne?'

'The same. I'm coming to see you. I'll be with you in an hour or two. I've got to talk to you before you do any more damage.'

'I'm afraid I won't be here. I have appointments.'

'Then cancel them. Just be there—that's an order.'

'Very well—where are you now?'

'In Nuremberg, trying to cover up your gaffe.'

With that, Cave-Browne slammed down the receiver, cutting Peter off in mid-protest.

An hour and forty minutes later, Cave-Browne arrived at Tahlmann. He stormed straight in through the door to the study, shaking an admonishing fist at Peter, who backed away in alarm.

'You really are a bone-headed bugger,' Cave-Browne yelled at him. 'Why in God's name did you let those solicitors try and prove your title to the estate?'

'How on earth did you get to hear about that?'

'Me? I should think just about every intelligence man in the Western hemisphere knows about it by now. Have you gone raving mad? Can't you see that as far as everybody in England, Germany and especially the Soviet Union is concerned, you are Johannes von Tahlmann, a German fighter pilot, returned from years of captivity in Russia? If the Reds get one sniff of your real identity, you're a dead duck. Damn it man, even Kuznov didn't know the truth. We only told him to get you out—we didn't tell him why.'

Cave-Browne's face was red with fury. Peter sank down into the nearest chair and held his head in his hands.

'But you still haven't told me how the whole thing leaked out. The solicitor said it was confidential—he promised he wouldn't tell a soul!'

Cave-Browne gave a snort of utter exasperation.

'Are you really that witless, Hutley? Do I have to spell it out in words of one syllable? You can't trust *anybody*—the K.G.B. have got men everywhere. I shouldn't think there's a public building in Bonn without its resident Russian stooge. Let me explain. The first thing your solicitor did was to go to the British Embassy and ask for all legal documents relating to your family history to be forwarded to him from England—death certificates, travel permits, the lot.'

'Yes, but the documents don't mean a thing—they only cover Isobel and Peter Hutley, not Johannes von Tahlmann. And besides I still don't see—'

Cave-Browne raced up to Peter and shook him by the lapels.

'*You don't see*! By God, you'll see when I've finished with you. The man your discreet solicitor friend spoke to at the Embassy was a Russian agent—we've had him under surveillance for weeks now; he's small fry of course—that's probably why he's always managed to slip through the net. But for the past week, just about every scrap of information about your wretched past flying to and fro between England and Germany in diplomatic bags has been fingered by that man!'

Peter's head was spinning.

'But surely, that doesn't necessarily mean he's discovered who I am? God knows, Charlton went to enough trouble to hush things up. All he'll know is that Peter and Isobel Hutley didn't die when the German records say they did.'

Cave-Browne stared at him in disbelief.

'Hutley, for Christ's sake get a grip. Put yourself in the

shoes of that Embassy spy: all he knew was that Johannes von Tahlmann was a German fighter pilot, a national hero, captured by the Russians at the end of the war, broken, turned and put back into play as a Soviet spy—probably the best one they had. When suddenly—what's this he hears? Even the man's family solicitor is raising doubts about his identity, and asking for legal documents to be sent over from England. *England*, Peter. Don't you see what that means?'

Peter nodded hopelessly. 'So how much do you reckon he knows?'

Cave-Browne looked grim.

'Just about everything there is to know. You don't have to be a genius to work it out. Think what those records would have told him: Johannes is shot down over England, September 1940. His twin brother Peter, who's been carefully kept out of combat all through the war and trained as a fighter pilot, dies in a mysterious accident the following week. Three and a half months later—just about enough time to put a man through a crash course in intelligence techniques—Johannes effects a miraculous escape from British Prisoner of War camp and returns triumphant to the Fatherland conveniently suffering from amnesia. Christ, with the information he had I should think he turned the whole story inside out in five minutes.'

Peter sat for a full minute staring blankly into space as the full extent of his plight began to dawn on him. Finally he said: 'So what do we do now?'

Cave-Browne shrugged.

'Well you can forget about the Embassy agent for a start. I've dealt with him.'

'You've killed him?'

He nodded. 'But it doesn't end there. We still don't know how much he managed to pass on to his masters.'

'You mean he might have squealed before you got to him?'

'We can't rule it out. He had the goods two days ago.'

Cave-Browne paced up and down for a few minutes. His anger had abated by now, but his expression still retained its fierce determination. He hadn't finished with Peter yet.

'Now listen to me, Hutley. Is there anybody else at all—and I mean *anybody*—who knows the truth about you?'

Peter remained silent.

'For God's sake, *think*, man. Your life depends on it.'

Once again he gripped Peter hard by the shoulders. Peter tried to look away, but knew that resistance was useless. He shook his head feebly and struggled to free himself from Cave-Browne's grip.

'Come on, Hutley. It's no use trying to hold out on me. You must know who you've told?'

Peter shook his head again. Furious, Cave-Brown lashed out at him with his fist; and Peter felt a trickle of blood run down his chin. He put up a hand to ward off further blows.

'Alright, alright. You've made your point. There are two friends of mine—Gunther and Hildegard Strauch. Gunther knows, so I suppose Hildegard must know too. Ilse told them everything. It was while I was away in Russia—I suppose she saw no harm in it; for all she knew at that stage, she might never set eyes on me again.'

'And what did they say when they heard?'

'I don't know—apparently Günther thought it was a huge joke. Listen, Cave-Browne, do you think they're in danger? Because if they are—'

'That's my problem.'

Peter suddenly felt desperately afraid.

'I couldn't bear it if I thought I'd put them at risk. If anything happened to them I'd go out of my mind.'

Cave-Browne turned on him in a fury.

'Your sanity is the least of my worries just now, Hutley. *I'm* the one who has to carry the can—the one who has to clear up after all your crass mistakes, remember?'

'But there's no clearing up to do now. Günther can keep his mouth shut, you can depend on that.'

'Leave it to me. I'll take care of it.'

'But what about the solicitors?'

Cave-Browne was making for the door.

'Call them off. God knows, they've done enough damage already. I'm afraid you'll just have to kiss your twenty million marks goodbye.'

The door slammed behind him and within a minute or so Peter heard a car engine revving up and then the noise of tyres scrunching on the gravelled drive.

CHAPTER SIX

As soon as Cave-Browne had departed, Peter decided to go in search of a drink. He badly needed one. As he got to his feet he happened to see a torn envelope, lying on the ground by the door. Picking it up he saw it was addressed to Lieutenant Colonel B.A. Cave-Browne O.B.E., at a house in a small village some twelve miles distant. It must have fallen out of his pocket on his way out. The envelope was empty and Peter was about to throw it away when he thought better of it and put it in a drawer of his desk. He had had no contact with Cave-Browne except through his local P.O. Box number, which amounted to no more than a "poste restante". Cave-Browne had given no clues as to the whereabouts of his base. Until now.

At approximately the same time that Peter and Ilse sat down to their midday meal, a young woman was enjoying her lunch break in the company of her boyfriend in a cafe in Frankfurt. They had picked a table close to the serving bar and after they had given their order they sat holding hands, talking. The hard-faced, ageing blonde barmaid had her eye on them and was listening in on their conversation, but soon dismissed it as idle chit-chat—it was everyday gossip such as any young couple might exchange. Their talk bubbled along in the background, until the name 'Tahlmann' suddenly made the barmaid prick up her ears. She leaned closer over the bar behind them on the pretext of retrieving a couple of empty glasses and strained to catch what was being said.

Magda Ziegler, once an orderly at Dachau concentration camp, had been only a very minor cog in the wheels of the Nazi death machine. But after the surrender of Germany in 1945 she had paid the price and had been tried, convicted and sentenced to a period of five years in prison for her crimes. On her release in the summer of 1950 she had spent months looking for work before finally securing a frugal living in the small cafe where she now worked. Since the money she was paid barely covered the essentials of life, she had taken to occasional prostitution as a means of supplementing her wages. But the collapse of her country and the ruin of her ambitions had filled her with rage and disgust.

Magda had taken her revenge by turning informer to the East Germans. It was a task she performed eagerly and with all her characteristic thoroughness and efficiency. Her masters had come to trust her.

The couple by the bar were quite oblivious of the fact that they had been overheard, and continued to chatter away gaily.

'I don't believe it,' the young man was saying.

'It's true—I tell you, I saw the papers in my boss's office.'

'Tahlmann? The Luftwaffe ace? Rubbish.'

'Listen, I typed out an entire report about it only this morning,'

Magda's pulse was suddenly racing, her excitement growing with every word. She had a frantic fear that she might already have missed the gist of the conversation and stood rock still behind the bar, terrified that any movement on her part might give her away.

'But the man was a war hero—'

'I *know*, stupid, that's what makes it so unbelievable.'

'But how could he be?'

The girl shrugged helplessly.

'I don't know, but the report's quite definite about it. You know what lawyers are like, they have to have everything in black and white.'

The boy scoffed. 'Yes, but it's absurd—'

'Listen,' the girl took his hand, 'just take it from me: Johannes von Tahlmann isn't German at all—he's English.'

Neither the young girl nor her companion noticed the sudden exit of the woman behind the bar. Magda had hurried off to the nearest phone. As soon as she was connected, she announced breathlessly: 'Meet me tonight at 21.00 hours, usual place. I've something that might interest you.' Then she returned hastily to the bar. The couple had finished their coffee and were about to leave; Magda gave them their bill, they paid and made for the door.

The young man smiled at her briefly. 'Keep the change.'

Magda sank down on a stool with a sigh of relief as the couple disappeared and mopped at her brow with the corner of her apron. She had tried once before to settle her score with the Baron—one time, long ago during the war. Things had been very different then: she had been a mere housekeeper, a woman whose words had counted for nothing, and her adversary had been a man with connections, an aristocrat with powerful allies. It had angered her when her suspicions had not been acted upon, but she had expected little else. But this time she had more than suspicions to go on—she had facts. This time, there would be no mistake.

Within twenty-four hours the K.G.B. knew that they

had been double-crossed by the man they believed to be Johannes von Tahlmann. They realised now that the mysterious loss of five of their agents—and a sixth, a clerk in the British Embassy in Bonn—had been no stroke of fate. All had at one time or another, directly or indirectly, been involved with the career of the former Luftwaffe ace. Colonel Cave-Browne's swift intervention had given Peter a brief stay of execution: the Embassy spy had been removed before he had a chance to report back. But now time was running out. Shortly after Magda's story had been received, a simple directive was issued concerning the future of Johannes von Tahlmann—simple, and final. The tightrope he had been walking throughout those long months since his release from captivity had been frayed to breaking point. Now it had snapped.

'The Strauchs are very late. It's not like them.'

Peter and Ilse were sitting in their drawing-room one evening a few days later, waiting for Günther and Hildegard, who were due to come to dinner. Peter walked over to the telephone and dialled their friends' number. There was no reply.

'What'll we do now?' Ilse asked.

Peter replaced the telephone receiver.

'I suppose I'd better get the car out and go and see if they've broken down or something on the way.'

'Good idea, darling. But don't be long or the dinner will be ruined.'

'I'll be back as soon as possible.'

Peter walked out to the garage and climbed into the seat of his blue Mercedes 300. He put the key in the ignition. The car started immediately and he drove off down the drive, gravel spurting from beneath the tyres. He turned out of the gate in the direction of Schwandorf. As he rounded the first bend he noticed a dim orange glow in the sky, the strange light throwing the trees ahead of him into sinister relief.

As he negotiated another bend he saw a number of cars, vans and a fire engine. At their centre were the still-smoking remains of another vehicle. Already the area seemed to be teeming with policemen and other officials, some uniformed, others in plain clothes. Peter slowed the Mercedes to a crawl, a hundred yards short of the throng. A policeman approached with his hand up to bar further progress. He leaned over and Peter wound down the window.

'I'm sorry, Sir. There's been an accident. The road will be blocked for some hours yet. Where were you heading?'

'Nowhere in particular, officer. I was looking for some friends of mine.'

'I see, Sir. Well, I'm afraid you'll have to back track and make a detour.

'That's some accident,' Peter said, trying to hide the tremor in his voice. 'Whatever happened?'

'I can't say exactly, Sir. It looks like the car had a bomb in it. It's still too hot to get close enough to make a detailed examination.'

'You don't happen to know what make of car it was?'

'A Porche, Sir.'

Peter took a breath before replying.

'I think I'd better leave my car here and have a word with your Inspector.'

Peter turned off his engine. With a heavy heart he trudged along behind the policeman. Surely, it couldn't have been a bomb. Damn petrol tank must have blown up—it must have been an accident. Nobody could want to kill Günther or Hildegard. They didn't have an enemy in the world.

Peter introduced himself to the Inspector and the pair of them talked for a few minutes before they both approached the wreck. Inside were two people, or what was left of them, both charred beyond the point of recognition, smashed bodies twisted grotesquely in their seats. Peter felt the vomit welling up from the depths of his stomach, and broke out in a sweat. One glance was enough. The blackened horror in the driving seat was missing part of a leg, beneath which lay an obscene mound of what had only recently been metal, all that remained of an artificial limb. Peter turned away and staggered a few paces towards the ditch by the roadside.

'Günther,' he cried out. 'Not Günther and Hildegard. It can't be true.'

'It was an explosive device, I'm afraid, Sir. That much we know for certain.'

Peter, a sickly green even under the police arclights, said nothing. He turned his back on the Inspector and retched again, but nothing came. His mind was in a turmoil. Of course, of course; Colonel cursed Cave-Browne. Christ Almighty, he'd taken care of Günther alright. Peter felt the bile rise again, and with it guilt. He knew he was responsible for his friends' death. In an instant he decided to confide to the policemen no more than the bare essentials. He swore to God and to the corpses before him that he would have vengeance. An eye for an eye, a tooth for a tooth. In his own way, in his own time, he would exact retribution from that slayer of the innocent.

The very venom of his hatred for Cave-Browne sent the adrenalin pumping through his system and made for a rapid recovery of composure.

'Sorry about that, Inspector. I've seen much worse. But somehow one only expects such things of war.'

'I take it you knew the people well, then?'

'Yes, Inspector, very well. Günther and Hildegard were our best friends. We were very close indeed.'

'I'm very sorry, Sir. You'll understand, I'm sure, that I have to ask you a few questions. No doubt you're as keen as I am to catch whoever's responsible.'

'Of course.'

'Do you know any reason why anyone would want to kill them?'

'I haven't the slightest idea, Inspector.' Peter lied. 'They didn't have any enemies—I just can't think of any possible motive.'

'Somebody must have had one.'

'Obviously, but I honestly can't help you there.'

'Did Herr Strauch ever mention any trouble that he was in? Business, emotional, anything like that?'

'Never—and believe me I'm sure I'd have been the first person he would have turned to if he had been in trouble. I'm sorry Inspector. I really can't help you, I only wish I could.'

The two men continued to exchange questions and answers for another half hour or so. Finally the Inspector said: 'You can go home now, Herr Baron. But will you please make yourself available should we want to ask you any more questions? Doubtless we will.'

'If there's anything I can do, I'll be there.'

'Thank you. Are you all right to drive yourself home?'

'Yes, Inspector, thank you. I'm shattered, I admit, but I'm quite capable of driving my car—it's less than a mile.'

'I'll say goodnight to you then.'

'Goodnight, Inspector.' Peter walked slowly back to his car.

Ilse was worried sick that Peter hadn't returned. When she finally heard the car approaching she rushed out to meet her husband.

'Where have you been, darling? I was going crazy.'

'I'm afraid I was delayed.'

'Did you find Günther and Hildegard?'

'Yes, I did.'

'Then where are they? Why didn't you bring them back with you?'

'Let's go inside, darling. I need a drink. I'll tell you about it indoors.'

Peter put the car away in the garage whilse Ilse returned to the house. Peter followed at a distance. He still hadn't worked out how to break the news to her. She was very fond of Günther and Hildegard was more than a childhood friend—they had been more like sisters. Peter walked into the drawing-room with two large whiskies. Ilse looked in amazement at the brimming glasses.

'I want a drink not an anaesthetic, Peter,' she said. 'I've had my share for tonight already.'

'You take it, my love. I think you might need it.'

She took the glass, worried anew by his gravity.

'They've had an accident?'

'Yes, I'm afraid so.'

'Are they hurt?'

'Yes,' Peter took a swig of his whisky.

'Badly?'

'Yes,' Peter took another slug. Then he put his glass down and settled down on the sofa beside her. Looking her straight in the eyes and holding her hand, he tried to begin, but Ilse knew already. 'They're dead, aren't they, both of them?'

Peter leaned across and kissed Ilse on her forehead.

'My poor love, I am so sorry.'

To his surprise, Ilse remained perfectly calm.

'How did it happen?' she asked softly.

'A bomb, Ilse. They were murdered.'

'Who by?'

'Cave-Browne. I'm absolutely certain of it.'

Ilse bit her lip, trying to swallow back the pain.

'If it helps at all, Ilse, I promise you that there was no suffering. They must have died instantly.'

'But why? Why would Cave-Browne want to kill them?'

'It's my fault.' Peter paused. He shot a glance at Ilse and saw the expression of incredulity on her face. He averted his gaze, unable to look her straight in the eyes. He rose from the sofa and started to pace round the room. Ilse didn't press for an answer but Peter knew she was waiting.

'I just didn't think. Poor Günther, poor Hildegard. Damn my bloody crass stupidity.' Peter stopped for a moment. He took another long slug from his whisky glass and emptied it. He was on the verge of tears now, realizing the hopelessness of his position and fearing for Ilse and Ernst as well. He had to face the fact now that Cave-Browne would deal with them all as he had with the ill-fated Strauchs if he refused to play along.

'Günther was such a good friend of mine, Ilse. We had no secrets—he knew the truth about me and accepted it completely. I'm afraid that's why he and Hildegard are dead now.'

'But Peter, it was I who told him—I thought it was safe; Günther could keep a secret, anyway—'

'I know, I know.' Peter took her hand to reassure her. 'You weren't to blame. It was my fault. I told Cave-Browne.'

'Told him what?'

'That Günther knew my real identity. I had to. Cave-Browne demanded to know who else knew besides the solicitors in Frankfurt.'

'What solicitors?'

Peter turned and faced her. He knew he must tell her everything. 'A firm of solicitors in Frankfurt. You see, I was left—or rather, Peter Hutley was left, a large fortune—nearly 20 million marks. Since Peter was officially dead the money was supposed to be mine. Do you remember that I went to Frankfurt last December?'

'Yes.'

'That was when I went to see about it. Like an idiot, I thought that the privacy of our conversation was sacrosanct. But the solicitors found an anomaly in the records of Peter's death and had to make enquiries through the British Embassy—for all I know they're still at it. That's how Cave-Browne found out.'

'Who left us all that money?'

'A distant cousin, Otto-Ulrich Borchers. Don't you remember, I searched through all the family records to see if we could find any mention of him?'

'Of course, I remember—early in December. You said

you'd met someone who claimed he was a cousin.'

'That's right—well now you know the real story.'

'Why didn't you tell me the truth at the time?'

'Because I didn't want to raise your hopes until the money was a certainty.'

'But I don't want the money now, not any more. Anyway, we don't need it.'

'Refusing it won't bring Günther and Hildegard back.'

'It's blood money now.'

'No, you're right. It might have made things easier for us, but now we'll just have to get out without it.'

'Out? Out where?'

'Out of here, out of Germany, out of Europe, Ilse. Out of the whole bloody mess. We must get away from here—away to the other side of the world. My mind's made up. Will you come with me?'

'Of course. You know that Ernst and I will follow wherever you go.'

'I'll make the arrangements as soon as I can work something out.'

The dinner was long since ruined. Peter didn't feel like eating and nor did Ilse. They retired to bed around midnight. Unable to sleep, Ilse clung to Peter, knowing the burden of guilt he carried. Somehow she drew strength from his weakness, from the knowledge that she alone could prevent the hopelessness from engulfing them.

CHAPTER SEVEN

The day following the death of Günther and Hildegard, Peter went to his office as usual, but his mind was not on his work. Instead, he thought of all that needed to be arranged for a successful flight for his family out of the country. Every eventuality, every possibility, had to be allowed for. Nothing must go wrong. He had thought of

Mexico but discarded it as being too close to the U.S.A. He finally settled on Argentina, where there was already a small German community. With a bit of luck he could get a job there and start anew. His knowledge of French, German and English and some Spanish must have some commercial value. Perhaps he could return to flying. At least they would be safe, as safe as anywhere that Peter could think of.

On Saturday Peter received two callers at Tahlmann. The first was the Police Inspector in charge of the enquiries concerning the death of Günther and Hildegard. His questions were mostly routine, but Peter was unable to help him. He could not afford to get too closely involved for fear of interrupting his plans of escape.

In the afternoon Peter was sitting at his desk, writing off for visas and travel documents when Ilse walked in to the study. Peter looked up and smiled at his wife, but she looked troubled.

'What's the matter?'

'You have a visitor—she insists on seeing you personally.'

'Who is it this time?'

'You'll never believe it, after all these years.'

'Try me.'

'It's Magda Ziegler.'

'Magda? What the hell does she want?'

'She wouldn't say anything except that she has a confession to make. Apparently she wants to return something she stole when you turned her out.'

'Can't you get rid of her?'

'I've tried, darling, but she insists on seeing you. I wouldn't be surprised if she wants a reward for her honesty.'

'I suppose that you'd better show her in.'

Magda Ziegler, eyes downcast, walked into the room holding a small package in her hand.

'Herr Baron,' she began, 'it's so kind of you to see

me—if only you knew how I dreaded facing you. My priest would not give me absolution until I had returned this to you.' Magda held out her hand with the package in it. Peter was suspicious. Why had she chosen this moment to return? Where had she suddenly sprung from?

'Magda, how good to see you.'

'It is good to see you too, Sir, but please . . .' Magda waved the package at Peter.

'What is it?'

'Something I stole from his house.'

Peter was embarrassed but still wary.

'Why don't you open it, Magda?'

'No Baron. You open it, please.'

'Why, Magda?'

'You're very suspicious, Sir. But if you insist, very well.' Magda tugged at the paper and removed a small gold and enamel brooch with the Tahlmann crest on it.

'Here you are,' she said. 'I've brought it back now—and please, Herr Baron, may I ask your forgiveness, if not for the way I behaved, then at least for my theft?' She handed the brooch to Peter. It meant nothing to him. He'd never seen it before, though he recognized the tiny facsimile of the family crest immediately. He handed it to Ilse. She knew at once it was genuine. It had belonged to her mother-in-law, and she had never even missed it. It had had unpleasant associations for her.

'Of course I forgive you,' said Peter. 'Life's too short to harbour grievances. It's all in the past now.'

'And Madam?'

'Yes, Magda, of course,' Ilse replied. 'It must have taken a great deal of courage for you to come here.'

'It did.'

Ilse walked towards Magda. She held out the brooch. 'You've given it back. Now I can return it to you. Keep it, it's yours. Thank you, Magda.'

'Thank you, Baroness. You are too kind.' Magda

started to cry, gently, the tears rolled down the hard lines of her face, the sight somehow outrageously incongrous.

'You will stay and have some tea with us, won't you Magda?' Ilse asked. The tears ceased abruptly.

'Thank you, Baroness, but I must be going. I don't want to be any more of a nuisance.' Magda wiped her eyes.

'Don't be silly, Magda. Of course you must stay. We want to hear all your news, don't we Peter?'

'Absolutely,' Peter winced.

'Very well then, thank you.'

Ilse went off the order tea to be served and Peter led the former housekeeper to the drawing-room.

Eventually the time came to go. Magda looked at her watch.

'Goodness, just look at the time. I'll never make it.'

'Make what?' Peter asked.

'I have a date with a friend in Regensburg in just over an hour.'

'Of course, you'll make it. I'll drive you there.'

Magda tried to conceal her excitement, but her plan was working out to perfection.

'I don't want to be any trouble.'

'Nonsense, Magda, it's no trouble at all.'

'Well, thank you, Herr Baron. That is most kind.'

Magda shook hands with Ilse and thanked her again for the gift of the brooch, the tea, and for all her kindness.

On the journey, Peter found Magda surprisingly easy to talk to. She asked no questions, whilst answering Peter's questions about herself quite frankly. Or so Peter thought. As the Mercedes approached the spot at which Magda had asked to be dropped, she opened the handbag which matched her smart black dress. From it she took an elegant pair of gloves which buttoned at the wrist. Peter halted the car beside the pavement. Before he could move to open the door for his passenger, Magda pressed the handle herself and got out. She shut the door behind her, leaving Peter sitting in his seat. She walked round to the driver's side. The window was down.

'Thank you again, Herr Baron. I am so glad to have been able to meet you just once more.'

'Oh you never know, we may come across each other again. It's a small world,' Peter replied, sticking out his hand to say goodbye. 'Good luck.'

'And good luck go with you too.'

Magda's gloved hand closed on Peters. He was at once struck by the firmness of the clasp and of a sudden sharp pain that spread to his wrist.

He went pale, and Magda immediately released her hold.

'What's the matter?' she asked.

'Nothing, Magda. A slight pain.'

'Oh, I'm so sorry. I hope it will not last very long.'

'Don't worry, it's nothing.'

Peter grinned at her. Then with a final wave he put the car into gear and was gone.

Magda smiled briefly to herself, then turned and walked to a telephone box. After a minute or so, the call over, she walked to the station to await the train that would take her back to Frankfurt.

The next day was Sunday. After lunch Ilse went riding. In the mid-afternoon there was a telephone call for the Baron. It was Magda Ziegler.

'Herr Baron?'

'Yes, Magda.' Peter was puzzled. He had never imagined that he would hear from her again, certainly not so soon.

'Herr Baron, do you remember the pain you felt when you shook hands with me yesterday?'

'No? Oh yes, now you mention it. It was nothing. I'd quite forgotten about it.'

'I'm afraid you will find it will return.' Magda paused, relishing the moment of triumph. 'In fact, Herr Baron, it was your sentence of death.'

'What the hell—?'

'I don't know exactly when, but quite soon you will be dead. There is no antidote to the poison, no chance of a reprieve. In a matter of weeks a case of heart failure will be entered on your death certificate.'

'Magda, are you mad?' Peter said hoarsely.

'Don't believe me if you don't want to, it will make no difference. You will be dead in two weeks, three at the most. You betrayed the just aspirations of the oppressed people of our beloved Fatherland to British Intelligence, and for that you have been killed. Goodbye, Herr Baron; I will no doubt see you in Hell.'

The telephone clicked.

The receiver fell from Peter's hand as he sat in his chair, shocked and scared into total immobility. His body shivered and he felt the talons of terror clawing at his soul. He had no alternative but to accept the woman's sentence. Had he not been warned that Soviet agents could reach out to any point on earth to avenge themselves against those who crossed them?

Peter experienced the worst fears of his life in those minutes after Magda's call. Not even the threats of Heydrich at Gestapo headquarters, or the long years of misery as a prisoner of the Russians could equal the pain and despair he felt now. Now there was no prospect of release, no future, no hope to cling to. Nothing this side of the grave. The desperate plans for escape melted away like a mirage.

Slowly Peter pulled himself together. He had no idea how the poison would take its course, how long he would retain his faculties, in what manner he would die. He could only guess that at the most he might have a week in which to do what he could to protect Ilse and Ernst.

By the time that Ilse returned from her ride, Peter was calm again, icily cool in his determination that Ilse should never discover his fate.

He had one more meeting with Cave-Browne on the

following Tuesday. He did not mention the death of Gunther and Hildegard. Cave-Browne was surprised and brought the subject up himself, taunting Peter with his condolences. Peter, to all outward appearances, kept his temper and thanked the Colonel for his kind thoughts, though the words made him seethe with a raging desire to tear the assassin to pieces right there and then.

On the Wednesday morning the mail brought Peter a letter from Luftwaffe Headquarters informing him finally of his appointment as Major in the fighter arm, and ordering him to report for duty two weeks hence. Peter laughed to himself and threw the missive into the waste-paper basket.

As the day passed Peter discovered, to his surprise, that far from becoming increasingly overwhelmed by panic, his resolve was hardening, his mind clear. His powers to plan, to think of every eventuality, to see and understand his next move, became sharper almost by the hour. He was saddened by the fact that he could never say goodbye to Ilse and Ernst, but tried to stifle the sorrow by taking every possible step to ensure that his wife and child would be adequately provided for after his death.

On Friday morning, Peter awoke and noticed a slight stiffening in his right hand. He flexed his fingers but the movement had no effect. He looked at the back of his hand and saw that a small reddening surrounded the spot where he had felt the pain from Magda's glove. So she had spoken the truth. His death sentence was in the process of being carried out.

All week Peter had gone about his employment as usual. All week that is, until that Friday. Instead of driving to work as usual, he drove as far as Regensburg and parked the car at a local motor cycle dealer's showroom. There he purchased a BMW and black leathers, crash helmet, gauntlets, and boots. 'Just a whim,' he explained to the surprised salesman who had seen the smart limousine arrive on the forecourt. Peter asked if he might leave his car with them while he tried out the bike. The salesman was only too pleased to be of assistance, especially as the customer paid in cash.

Peter hadn't ridden a motor-bike since those far off days at Netheravon before the war, but this was an altogether more sophisticated machine than the dear old B.S.A. of which he retained such happy memories. He set off, gingerly at first, threading his way through the mid-morning traffic, heading towards the village where he knew Cave-Browne was based. He had intended to ask at the local post office where the house might be situated, but instead he decided to reconnoitre first. It was well that he did. Today luck was with him.

About five kilometres short of his destination he negotiated a bend and there, in front of him, was the familiar green Opel. Peter accelerated and as he drew level he looked into the car. In it were two men. The driver was Cave-Browne. Their eyes met, but in Cave-Browne's expression there was no spark of recognition. It would have been too easy to draw a pistol and kill him there and then, but Peter had other ideas. He swept past the Opel and roared off ahead until he came to a crossroads. There he stopped, pretending to be fiddling with the bike, and in seconds the Opel passed him. Peter remounted and followed at a discreet distance. Cave-Browne drove straight to his home. Peter kept well back and watched through field glasses as the two men got out of the car and disappeared into the house.

The place was situated a little outside the village by an isolated group of trees. There were no other buildings within 500 metres. Peter studied the area for a full hour, making rough sketches and noting various landmarks. Satisfied with his efforts he started the motor-bike and returned to Regensburg. There he left the machine, promising to collect it next week. He had lunch in the town, before driving to the U.S. Air Force Base at Erding. His was a familiar face at the huge sprawling complex with its maze of buildings, concrete runways and large numbers of aircraft. Armed with the necessary passes and special warrants, Peter was permitted to move freely wherever his duties might take him. With the excuse that he had lately fallen behind with his flying hours, he made arrangements to fly a T.33 trainer the following morning and specially requested full fuel tanks for maximum endurance.

When the Lieutenant, the duty flight officer to whom he made the request, jokingly asked if he was intending to defect to the East, Peter assured him that seven years as a Russian prisoner were sufficient insurance against any such notion.

Peter arrived back in Tahlmann late that evening. Ilse as usual was worried by his non-appearance. Peter apologised for forgetting to mention that he had had business that day. They dined alone that night, and during the meal Peter announced that he would have to go back to work the following day.

'A Saturday? Can't it wait till Monday, darling?'

'No, Ilse, I'm sorry.'

'What's so special that it won't keep?'

'Look, if it wasn't absolutely essential to work tomorrow, I wouldn't bloody well go,' he snapped.

Peter groaned inwardly that he should have shown even a small measure of petulance on this of all nights. He saw the pain in her face.

'I'm sorry, darling, please forgive me. If you really want to know, there are some things that have to be done before I . . . before we get out of it all. We can't just walk away, not quite yet.'

'When will it be, then?'

'In a day or two, perhaps.'

Ilse wanted to go to bed early that night. Peter said he'd be up as soon as he could, but delayed as long as prudence would permit. When they were in bed he turned away from Ilse, his heart heavy.

Ilse was puzzled and hurt for a while. Peter had repulsed her every advance for more than a week now. She had to make allowances for her husband and the tremendous pressure he was so obviously under, but wondered how long it would last. She propped herself up on her elbow and gently kissed Peter on his forehead.

'My poor darling, I do love you,' she said.

Peter felt his wife's breasts brush his shoulder, he smelt the heady, scent of her hair and skin, and longed to reciprocate. He was forced to draw on every ounce of self-control. Ilse assumed he was already asleep and fell back on her pillow. She lay awake for some time yet. She whispered aloud: 'Please, God, help us. I beg that it may all be different for us very soon now.'

CHAPTER EIGHT

Peter rose early on ths Saturday morning and had dressed even before Ilse was awake. Although not visibly swollen, his hand hurt like hell and the pain had now extended up to and beyond his elbow. He stood by the bed for a long time looking at Ilse, more beautiful than ever, as she lay asleep.

He crept out of the bedroom and along the corridor to take a final look at Ernst. The boy was not only wide awake but out of bed already and putting the finishing touches to a model aeroplane. Peter had walked straight into the very situation that he had sought to avoid at all costs. For a few minutes father and son played together. Peter straightened out odd bits and pieces that had been incorrectly assembled and showed Ernst where to stick the insignia transfers. Drawing once again on his rapidly dwindling reserves of self-control, he told his son that he must leave and go to work.

'But it's Saturday, daddy,' Ernst protested.

'See you later,' Peter replied, already on his way out of the room. 'Tell your mother I've gone to work early because I couldn't sleep. And tell her I love her, won't you?'

'Yes, daddy. Hurry home, I want you to help me finish my plane.'

'I'll try, but I can't promise.'

Peter gathered his son in his arms and hugged him. Then he left his room and closing the door quietly he walked slowly away, down the stairs and out of the front door.

He arrived at the Air Force Base at Erding before 8 a.m. and booked in at the flight office. The duty officer looked at the flying roster, surprised to see a visitor at such an early hour.

'You booked for a flight in a T.33 at 11.00 hours, Herr Baron. You're a bit early aren't you?'

'Something came up. I hope that you can get me clearance now?'

'Impossible, Sir. You may be entitled to free rides on Uncle Sam, but this is an operational unit, not a civilian flying club.'

'I'm well aware of the status of this base, Lieutenant.'

'And I have my orders to follow, Herr Baron.'

'Of course you do. All I'm asking is that you try to bring my flight forward. Surely that's not contrary to regulations?'

'All right, Herr Baron. I'll see what I can do.'

The American lifted the telephone and talked briefly into the mouthpiece. Then he replaced the receiver and looked at Peter.

'Sorry Sir. Your aircraft isn't even ready yet. We can stretch a point and try to bring the flight forward, but I doubt you'll be able to get away before 10 o'clock.'

Peter swore under his breath.

'Why not have some breakfast while you're waiting?'

'Thanks. I'll see you later.'

The last thing Peter wanted was breakfast. Nevertheless, he found he had a surprisingly sharp appetite and tucked into waffles and maple syrup, followed by ham, eggs and coffee. Just as he was finishing his meal and wondering what to do to fill in time, the public address came to his rescue: 'Baron von Tahlmann, please report to the flight office immediately.' Peter took a final gulp of coffee and then returned to see the Lieutenant. He had gone off duty and his place had been taken by another young officer.

'I'm Von Tahlmann,' Peter announced as he walked into the room.

'Good morning, Sir,' The officer saluted.

'Good morning, Lieutenant.'

'It seems you carry one heck of a lot of weight in these parts, Sir,' the man laughed. 'Your T.33 has gone U/S but we have arranged for you to take up an F.86. Is that O.K?'

'Suits me fine. When?'

'Now, Baron. It's waiting for you at dispersal. You know the way?'

I should by now.'

'Right, Sir. Then go ahead.' The Lieutenant smiled at Peter. He never quite knew whether to salute these odd Krauts in mufti or not. He gave Peter the benefit of the doubt. Peter raised his hand nonchanlantly as he left the office.

Peter walked briskly towards where he knew his aircraft would be waiting.

'She's got full tanks, Sir, as you requested,' the chief of the groundcrew told him as he swung his legs into the cockpit. He strapped himself in and then went through the usual drill before starting the jet engine. Peter closed the cockpit canopy and called the control tower for clearance take off. The formalities over, he taxied to the runway before making his final checks. Cleared to take off, he gunned the throttle and started to move along the concrete. The Sabre gathered speed before lifting off and climbed away at a steep angle. With his landing gear safely stowed, Peter set course for Tahlmann. It was but a few moments flying time away. Peter couldn't resist one last look at his home and the estate. It was a familiar sight from the air, but he had never before flown past it so low. Throttled right back, the F.86 streaked over the house, then Peter accelerated again and under full power the jet rose rapidly to 3,000 feet. Peter eased back on the throttle and glanced at the sketches he had made of the area surrounding Cave-Browne's house. There was no mistaking the building and the green Opel parked outside – Cave-Browne was home. He made three tight turns, checking and rechecking again before turning away in a wide sweep. With his target five miles dead ahead now, he increased speed to the maximum and came down in a dive. Faster and faster the Sabre plummeted. Peter felt quite calm during those last split seconds. He knew he was doing the right thing. At the sacrifice of his own remaining few days of life, he would avenge the murder of Gunther and Hildegard and release Ilse from the clutches of Cave-Browne and his files.

The Sabre plunged into the house on the outskirts of the village at a velocity approaching 900 m.p.h. The whole structure erupted in a fountain of blazing kerosene. The explosion was heard fifteen miles away. Five people died on that Saturday morning. Peter, two other men, a secretary and Cave-Browne's wife.

Colonel Cave-Browne had planned to be home all weekend. But he had chosen that morning to walk down to the local shop to buy some pipe tobacco. He had been standing in the shop waiting to be served when he heard the scream of the jet, followed by the ear splitting bang. The windows of the shop rattled and the very ground beneath his feet shook with the impact. Cave-Browne rushed out of the door. He knew at once that the crash had come from the direction of his home. Now he saw the black, oily cloud of smoke billowing skywards, uncomfortably near. He half walked, half ran in the direction of the inferno.

When the disaster area came fully into view, Cave-Browne felt sure his eyes and ears must have deceived him. It couldn't be real. The house had been all but demolished. Nobody, nothing, could have survived such a conflagration. Only a section of the tail plane of the aircraft, itself burning furiously, assured Cave-Browne that he was not experiencing some macabre hallucination. He had heard and now he had seen. There was no room for doubt. His wife and his associates were surely dead. All his work, his records, everything that he had devoted his life to during the last decade, must also have crumbled to ashes, swallowed by the all-consuming flames. Cave-Browne was left with nothing but the clothes he stood up in and his car, which by some miracle had survived the crash unscathed. He approached as close as he dared, but the intense heat burned his face from a distance of fifty feet or more. Then there was another explosion and a fresh geyser of angry orange flames burst forth from the ruptured central heating oil tank.

Cave-Browne could do nothing. He watched, temporarily speechless, unaware of the crowd already gathering. A fire tender arrived within ten minutes, but the firemen had only to take one look at the situation to realize there was no point in even trying to run out the hoses. All they could do was to let the blazing rubble burn itself out.

On the face of it, Peter had not entirely failed on this, his last, mission. The hated files, symbols of Cave-Browne's deadly hold over him were no more.

News of the disaster was broadcast on German radio that night, but already both Ilse and Cave-Browne knew that Peter had died in the accident. Ilse had seen Peter die a thousand times before. She knew as well as anybody alive the desperately thin tightrope upon which he had been forced to walk for the last sixteen years. If his death was no real shock to her, she was surprised and puzzled by its manner. Suicide? He had been so full of plans. Accident? It couldn't be, not crashing smack into Cave-Browne's house. Peter must have known something more which he either couldn't or wouldn't tell her.

Cave-Browne stayed the night with friends. He heard on the wireless that the U.S. Air Force F.86 had been flown by a senior official of the Federal German Defence Ministry, a former veteran ace of World War II, Baron Johannes von Tahlmann. Cave-Browne showed no sign of emotion. His host apologized and got up to turn off the bulletin.

'No, no, leave it on, it's all right,' Cave-Browne said. His host sat down again without a word, marvelling at Cave-Browne's self-control. Cave-Browne's surprise and shock at the mention of the pilot's name was entirely invisible from the outside. Years of training had taught him to remain inscrutable at just such moments as this. Already his mind was elsewhere.

Ilse ate sparingly at the next few meals, uncertain what to do now. After tea, the day after the accident, she walked down to the little bothy by the lake at which she had spent so many happy moments with Peter. Here she knew she would not be disturbed and felt she could give way to her grief in private and release the enormous burden of her sorrow. She sat on the old oak seat, staring out across the water as tears coursed down her cheeks. All she had now was her own loneliness and sense of loss, a sense of the utter pointlessness of life without Peter. The waters of the lake beckoned welcomingly. From their depths, trout recovering from their winter spawning in the feeder streams, splashed and plopped, dimpling the surface with their rings as they snapped at insects, or the small fry, sputtering along the surface in frantic effort to escape.

Wood pigeons cooed and flapped in their characteristic rising and dipping courtship flight. From all around the air was resonant with the sound of spring bird song.

Ilse had slowly risen to her feet and taken a few steps towards the water's edge. It would be so easy; the water there was deep—at least twelve feet. She knew that God would forgive her for ending a life of torment, a life that without the man she adored would only be one long hell. Standing on the very edge of eternity, she hesitated. She was thinking only of herself; for that she could not expect forgiveness. What would Peter want her to do? There was Ernst to think about.

Ilse slowly walked back to the oak bench and sat down again. Now she experienced a strange, unreal calm. She was quite certain that Peter was with her. She could feel his aura.

On the opposite side of the lake a man had moved stealthily through the rhododendrons. He had watched the woman through a pair of field glasses from about 75 metres. He saw her get up from the seat and walk to the edge of the water, hesitate for a full minute, and then return to the seat. He waited for perhaps five more minutes, checking and readjusting the telescopic sight on his rifle. From his pocket he extracted a single .30-06 calibre cartridge. Then he opened the breech. Noiselessly he closed the bolt. The man lay prone and, supporting his weight on both elbows, slowly raised the muzzle of the rifle, fixing Ilse in this sights.

As the seconds ticked by, Ilse became more and more convinced that she could even hear Peter's voice, beckoning, calling. She got to her feet and stared towards the lake. Then she knew that her imagination was not playing tricks. There was the voice again. Peter's voice.

Ilse never felt a thing. She never heard the echoing bark of the rifle as the bullet hit her squarely in the brain, blasting a section of her skull from the back, splattering the lovely hair with a mess of blood and brain tissue. Her body tottered for a split-second and then crashed back over the oak seat.

Cave-Browne didn't bother to check the accuracy of his shooting. He had always been superb with a rifle.

EPILOGUE

More than twenty years later the Baron Ernst von Tahlmann, who, like his uncle before him was raised an orphan, is a Captain in the Luftwaffe in the fighter branch of the service – the third generation of fliers. He is married with two sons. Peter is the eldest and Rudolf the youngest. He also has a daughter whom his wife suggested they should call Ilse, after his mother.

Two of Ernst's proudest possessions are The 'Blue Max', awarded to his grandfather Rudolf, and the Knight's Cross with Oakleaves that his father had won in the last war in Europe.

Ernst and his wife Erika no longer live at Tahlmann. The estate was sold off piecemeal when he was still a minor by the family solicitors in Nuremburg, and the proceeds invested. The 20 million marks that his father should have inherited from his cousin eventually came to him, and these funds were also invested.

Ernst and Erika are an exceedingly wealthy couple and have no need to work. Ernst flies because he loves it and because he feels it is his duty to serve the country of his birth. Only occasionally is he haunted by the image of his father that he never really knew, promising to return.

ICEQUAKE

Crawford Kilian

Antarctica, 1985. Buckling under unimaginable pressures, the earth heaves and settles – and thirteen million cubic kilometres of icecap glissade inexorably into the sea. The entire world climate changes overnight, a new Ice Age begins. Famine follows swiftly, with disease, flooding and the breakdown of civil order.

In the remote New Shackleton Station, at the heart of the Antarctic icecap, the survivors of Icequake battle the elements and themselves, to cling to a life more precarious than they had ever known. No rescue was possible, but to stay was to die.

ICEQUAKE – the super-chiller of the decade.